THUNDER STATION

A NOVEL BY
DONALD N. NORMAN

D0033738

WARNER BOOKS

A Warner Communications Company

America's mightiest supercarrier... a trio of the most hellwhipped seadogs to ever steal a Navy payroll... the Soviet mole working patiently toward his hour of total revenge... the top-gun pilot outmaneuvering both the enemy and his own superiors—the Kremlin coup masters poised to re-ignite the Cold War to blistering critical mass—all are set to collide in the floating warzone destined to earn its name...

THUNDER STATION

"*Thunder Station* is an intricate tale that smacks of an insider's bridge-to-bilge knowledge of Fleet operations and supercarriers, and is driven by equally authentic insights into the men who serve on them."
—Greg Dinallo, author of *Rockets' Red Glare*

"Complex, imaginative, exciting... the technical aspects are well researched... and the unusual nature of the climax, which has older, rudimentary aviation meeting up with today's high-tech Navy, brings things to a feverish pitch. ...*Thunder Station* is a real smash."
—Maj. Gen. John P. Condon, USMC (Ret.)

"One of the best depictions of carrier life I've ever read.... Norman writes about Tomcats as well as Stephen Coonts writes about the *Intruder*."
—Charles D. Taylor
author of *Choke Point, Silent Hunter,* and *Boomer*

"Highly imaginative... the what-if scenario is just plausible enough to be scary.... An entertaining read."
—Col. Jim Lemon, USAF (Ret.)
F-15 Squadron Commander

"The adept handling of high-tech and hijinks makes for high drama and adventure.... Those who've experienced, or simply imagined, armed conflict will be captured by the story—not to be freed until the tale is finally told."
—Lt. Col. Richard Alger, USMC (Ret.)

Donald N. Norman has combined outstanding careers in writing, filmmaking, and advertising. *Thunder Station* draws on his experience in the U.S. Navy as a surface warfare officer and his broad expertise as a writer of nonfiction books and films on military subjects. He has been an Emmy Award-winner, a prize-winning creative director, and an internationally published author. He splits his time between rural New Jersey and the South Shore of Long Island.

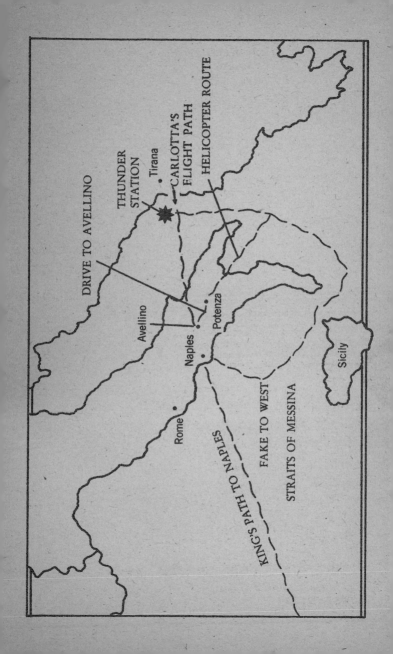

DRIVE TO AVELLINO

THUNDER STATION

Tirana

CARLOTTA'S FLIGHT PATH

HELICOPTER ROUTE

Avellino

Potenza

Naples

Rome

Sicily

KING'S PATH TO NAPLES

FAKE TO WEST

STRAITS OF MESSINA

Tyuratam, U.S.S.R.—May 15

The unreported events in Tyuratam had the simplicity that marks the beginning of all great complications.

Cyprien Gavenko enjoyed—thoroughly enjoyed—a front row seat. Indeed, he was so close that at day's end he found some of the General Secretary's blood in the creases of his crepe soles.

Tyuratam was a more or less regular stop in the purgatory the General Secretary had been putting him through the past two years. The Missile and Space Center was forever honoring groups of weary cosmonauts just arrived from some bungalow that had been whirling about the earth for a number of months. The fact that the General Secretary often came along himself bought no forgiveness from Gavenko. The chief had an avid fondness for science that was incomprehensible to other members of the Secretariat whom he dragged along.

Doubtless the ceremonies would have been less onerous if things had turned out as he'd hoped those few short years ago. Then he, Cyprien Gavenko, would have been the General Secretary, free to tug about whomever he wished. It certainly would have been less onerous for the Soviet

Union, he'd been thinking as the General Secretary talked to them in the base's "clean room."

The welcoming business had ended the day before. Except for a bout of foul weather, they would have been long gone. Another leader would have let himself and his accompanying party of five sulk in what comfortable rooms there were in this southern hell near the Aral Sea. But the General Secretary had not been nicknamed The Broom for nothing. *All* the old ways were to be swept out the door, which meant the top leadership was to be available to the people. For Gavenko and his ruling brethren it was down off the Kremlin wall and into the workshops and mess halls of Tyuratam. "How many times do you have cabbage soup, comrade? . . . Is your hearing properly protected against the engine blasts?"

Not that the General Secretary could be blamed for dragging along this particular entourage. Gavenko knew that if the political situation had been reversed, he himself would have been loath to let the two men who represented his bitterest opposition far from his sight in such a time of ferment.

Ferment. A process in which bubbling change is harnessed until it gradually subsides into a subservient brew waiting to be swallowed. A glum but accurate analogy to the future of Cyprien Gavenko and Tolstoy Lubachevsky. Here they were, inspecting latrines while they waited for a storm to abate, when they should have been raising a storm of their own in Moscow to blow away this sanctimonious fake of a General Secretary. Gavenko guessed that his sullen traveling companion, Lubachevsky, did not so deeply lament his frozen political position. Lubachevsky was a good man, but clearly not up to leading the Soviet Union. The old fighter's greatest virtue was his unswerving belief in the same iron doctrines championed by Cyprien Gavenko.

The so-called clean room at the Missile and Space Center was a place where the returning cosmonauts and their equipment and experiments were processed through to prevent contamination of various sorts, as Gavenko understood it. It reminded him of nothing so much as a morgue—a similarity that was later to amuse him. It was a perfect sea of white tile. Floor, ceiling, walls, tables, benches glared in the light of the biggest fluorescent fixtures he had ever seen. They had only been trapped in the place because lunchtime had arrived during their inspection.

The base's supervisory staff was prepared to whisk three of the highest officers in the state to a rather sumptuous meal in the dignitaries' special dining room, but The Broom was having none of it. The new leadership did not expend the time and treasure of the nation. The General Secretary had ordered that the same meal being fed the base's workers be brought to them right where they were.

As if that were not bad enough, while they waited he had decided to regale them with one of his inspirational addresses about the new course of the Soviet Union. He took a position on some sort of tile podium at the head of the room and spoke as if he were addressing a crowd in Red Square. Never mind that the entire audience—thanks to his determination to keep his traveling circle spartanly small—comprised Gavenko, Lubachevsky, a colonel, a major, and a captain.

"Comrades, the battles that will win the future for us will not be fought in the Fulda Gap and in missile silos, but in a hundred thousand rooms like this, where individual citizens working at small tasks advance the flag—"

Notwithstanding that Gavenko loathed completely what he stood for, the General Secretary wove a small spell. Damn it, there was no doubt that he was good, and that he believed in all this crap. No wonder he was able to take down the drawers of a nation and bugger it so completely. Unfortunately it was his own nation.

Gavenko's glance at Lubachevsky showed a man in terminal discomfort. At sixty-five years of age, Lubachevsky was not the direct link to the old revolutionaries he longed to be. His huge washboiler of a head, with hair uncut for years, and his pince-nez glasses looked vaguely ludicrous in the new era. The badly cut suits he purposely affected belonged in a museum. Everything did compared with The Broom. He would soon replace all the old-liners.

Now in his fifties, the General Secretary showed a vigor that suggested a soccer coach who'd been a great star. He was stocky, trim, and graceful. He would have been movie-star handsome if he had not been starkly bald and the possessor of a heavy and discolored scar that ran from the right center of his forehead well back onto his scalp. But what would have been a distinct disfigurement in a lesser man had simply become his signature. The Western press, totally taken with him, treated his mark lovingly in their caricatures.

As the General Secretary continued his peroration, Gavenko stifled a sigh and shifted on his metal chair. The Broom had segued to a particularly orotund passage. It was at this moment that Gavenko wondered whether there had been a gradual flaring of the room lights. The General Secretary seemed to have been growing paler over the last minutes.

"—the passage from an economy blinded by a need to look back over its shoulder for a war that might be approaching, to one that looks forward to a likelihood—no, a *certainty*—of peace will—will—will . . ."

The General Secretary's face seemed to blossom in a whiteness greater than that of the glaring tiles all around him. The hole of his mouth seemed to fade from pink to blue. He looked about with starting, widening eyes for something to support him, but found nothing on the stark podium. An immaculately tailored sleeve shot skyward and a hand grasped the shiny edge of the shade of a hanging light.

The small audience gave a collective gasp at the sight of the leader of the Union of Soviet Socialist Republics beginning to sag at the waist and knees, turning slowly around his own axis from the end of a stretching electric wire.

The colonel was on his feet first, overturning his chair with a ringing clatter as he raced to catch his leader. But he was quickly driven back by a shocking explosion of blood.

A red fountain fired in a straight line from the General Secretary's mouth, his spin from the tightly clutched light shade sweeping the gush in an arc toward his ashen audience. The crimson arced to the floor and spread calamitously. An eye calmer than any in the room would have counted three full turns on the wire before the twisting death grip pulled it loose from the ceiling. Then there was a popping shower of sparks and a great blinding electric flash, as though a mighty soul had broken through a barrier.

By the time the General Secretary corkscrewed to the floor, he appeared half the size he had been a moment before. It was as though he were dissolving in his own blood, which continued to pour out of him, although it had lost its earlier propulsion.

An unnoticed declivity in the floor sluiced the red pool toward the paralyzed spectators with such speed that the youngish captain raised his feet for a moment, as though to preserve his boots from defilement.

They were swarming over the fallen man in another instant. All but Cyprien Gavenko. It was not that he was a man without feeling. Even detesting all the things that the General Secretary stood for had not protected him from his leader's charm, openness, and admirable character. But he knew a man beyond help when he saw one. And once that had registered, the enormous stakes on the table became far more important than the fallen player.

It is the hallmark of natural leaders that their minds never fully stop churning on all the possible ways to power. So it was not as though Cyprien Gavenko exactly formulated a great scheme on the spot. Rather, he was able to instantly call forth all the pertinent pieces of his bottomless musing and translate them into an action that was a thousand miles from his mind but moments ago.

The first thing was to stop the officer who was rushing for the telephone. "I'll make that call, Major," Gavenko said sharply. And the way he spoke told everyone in the room, including Lubachevsky, that the Soviet Union was about to come under new management.

He reached the commanding general. "Comrade General, I want you to compose yourself so that whoever is with you can determine nothing from your face. If you behave in any other way than the way I am about to instruct you, you will have greatly damaged the security of your country. You will then bear the gravest consequences. Now listen closely. Tell no one—*no one*—anything, now or later. Call the doctor you trust most and tell him to rush a resuscitation team to the clean room at once. We'll need blood. All you've got. The team must be instructed as I've instructed you. Security is everything. Then drive here by yourself. Get it done."

The commanding general arrived first and was held outside without explanation by the captain. When the medical team screeched up in an ambulance, Gavenko allowed only the lead physician into the room.

"What in the world—"

"No time to be astounded, Doctor. Tell us quickly whether there's any point at all in letting those others in here."

The ashen doctor went to the sodden, bluish heap that had now been raised onto a tiled table. The men who had lifted him looked as though they had finished a day of hog butchering.

A scissor quickly cut away the upper clothing of the still figure, which commenced to emit deep internal heaves and gurgles. The doctor looked into the glassed, wide-open eyes and listened along the torso. He was not a young man, and had doubtless in his army career seen other cases that looked like this. Gavenko suspected that he had been half looking for bullet holes.

"He's dead, of course," the doctor said shakily. "You don't see an abdominal hemorrhage like that very often. He couldn't have lasted more than ten minutes, losing all that blood." It had taken a bit more than that to alert and assemble the team and drive to this location.

"Then there's no reason whatsoever to let anyone else in here?"

"None."

"What was the cause of this, do you suppose?"

The doctor, for all his attempt at professional poise, found himself sagging against Gavenko, who supported him beneath the arms until equilibrium returned. "Almost certainly the result of a gastric ulcer," he said finally. "We have the General Secretary's medical records on hand. They were sent ahead on previous visits. Standard procedure. He'd been advised to have an operation—"

"Thank you very much, Doctor," Gavenko interrupted. "Can you do an autopsy yourself?"

"Of course."

"The country must have assurance that this was a natural death. That is, when it becomes time to announce that there has been a death."

"We must begin to attend to that," the colonel said.

"We will attend to no such thing," Gavenko snapped. "Listen to me. All of you. A most dangerous gap in the leadership of the Soviet Union has occurred. For reasons of state unknown to all but the topmost level, it would be disastrous for this misfortune to become known at once."

Lubachevsky looked startled, but only for a moment. Gavenko had the right ally. He spun on the commanding general. "You and the doctor will show deep concern but no alarm. The General Secretary has been taken ill with a gastric hemorrhage. He has been treated here for the moment, but will be flown to a clinic outside of Moscow for extensive emergency surgery. Prepare him for transportation not as a dead man, but a man in critical condition. I hold you and the doctor responsible for the discretion of your men. I direct that all who must know the actual events here be confined to this base under tightest security until I announce otherwise. Please proceed quickly now. There is much to be done. Too damned much."

Moscow, U.S.S.R.—May 21

The KGB were not fools. Coming in separately, as the system allowed, a small, elite team reconstructed the events at Tyuratam infallibly in all the physical details.

If the General Secretary had been able to decree from beyond the grave, his new policies of openness would have described to the world the tragic moment with as much accuracy as dignity allowed. But other things in the Soviet system—some as permanent as the General Secretary's death—contrived a different scenario. Things that Cyprien Gavenko built on.

For one thing, the KGB's findings, disseminated at Gavenko's insistence only to the tightest and most wary of the top leadership, were not fully taken at face value. Could there not be clever and corrosive poisons made to mimic the work of an existing serious ailment? Was Stalin really entirely wrong in his long-ago purge of doctors? Didn't the greatest leaders have the greatest enemies? So having silently accepted the possibility of assassination, the factions within the Kremlin confronted the nerve-racking assessment of its possible engineers. First on the list was the faction led by Cyprien Gavenko, which viewed with the greatest alarm the General Secretary's lessening of the ages-old grip. But since this faction, despite its losses, was still the strongest in sight, all who were sensible submitted to its apparent will.

After an excruciating two days, with the site of the event smothered under the tightest blanket, the report to the world went out:

The General Secretary had suffered a severe gastric accident while visiting the Missile and Space Center at Tyuratam. Exemplary emergency work by the staff there had saved his life, but there had been need of extensive further surgery at a better equipped facility. The General Secretary had been flown to a clinic in the countryside outside Moscow, where the best men had operated successfully. But there had been various misfortunes of blood pressure and anesthesia that had deprived the brain of oxygen at a critical juncture. It might be a considerable time until its full effect on the intellectual capacities of the General Secretary would be fully known. Meanwhile, there would clearly be need for prolonged observation, treatment, rehabilitation, and, above all, long rest.

In Washington, London, Paris, Tokyo, and Beijing the lights burned bright and long, and political temperatures soared. Had the world marched so far toward peace under the banner of this stricken innovator only to fall backward into the hands of the conservatives?

Reassurance was not long in coming. Recovery would be long and arduous, but full. The caretakers would carry his programs forward. Especially comforting to both the people of the Soviet Union and the world were the messages from the General Secretary's family. Although he had no siblings or surviving parents, his handsome wife and vigorous children appeared on Soviet television and on the world's news networks to thank all the nations for their concern. They assured everyone that, for all his weakness and the extensive rehabilitation he was having to endure, his spirits were good and he was confident of a full return.

Cyprien Gavenko was especially proud of the way he'd handled the General Secretary's family while they were still reeling from their awful loss.

Artfully he'd parried their questions and in the most affecting terms communicated his own sense of bereavement. Once he gained their confidence he convinced them to do their duty like the true lovers of their country they were.

The Cruiser *Kirov*, the Black Sea—May 24

A nuclear-powered missile cruiser is not put to sea lightly. The captain of the *Kirov* was the only regular crewman aboard who could guess the magnitude of the meeting being held in his quarters—quite out of his own sight and earshot. Whatever it was, it required an 814-foot, 28,000-ton meeting room that could have stood off the best part of a fleet or an army. The meeting, as the captain understood it from Comrade Gavenko, was called on behalf of the Commander in Chief of the Soviet Armed Forces, the temporarily fallen General Secretary. Why aboard a ship cruising aimlessly off Yalta instead of one of the thousand meeting rooms in the Kremlin? The captain grinned wryly to himself and thought no further than the obvious: because this meeting would be extremely hard for unfriendly intruders to interrupt.

The calm of the Black Sea and the smoothness of the *Kirov*'s humming turbines almost let the men in the captain's cabin forget where they were.

Cyprien Gavenko had chosen the participants of this meeting with the greatest care. He never doubted for a moment that he had chosen correctly. In orchestrating power he was a Mozart, sure of the perfection of every note.

The old Russian habit of conducting a meeting across a wide space instead of face to face across a table was in effect. The five men ranged about the bulkheads in chairs were all in civilian clothes. But three of them could have filled a room with the military plumage they'd put aside for this trip. They had more the bearing of politicians than soldiers, which at this level reflected reality.

Silver-haired, but with black bushy brows, was Genrikh Batev, Minister of Defense. He couldn't have been in this room, Gavenko had decided, without the soft, sleek, big-nosed man who faced him from the other bulkhead. This was Zhores Arkadin, Chief of the Main Political Directorate. Gavenko could think of no way to safely break the military component away from the political. The last man, short, wiry, and restless, was Izaak Dimitriyev, Chief of the General Staff.

In any war these men would have been, with the General Secretary, at the top of the Stavka—the military Supreme High Command. They were tough, self-assured survivors. They had seen everything. They could not be surprised.

"Dead, you say," said Batev carefully.

"And only we know," said Dimitriyev.

Arkadin, of the Main Political Directorate, thought for a moment. "I must tell you, with the greatest respect, Comrade Secretaries, that my whereabouts are known. If I do not return—''

"Please don't be slow about this, Arkadin," Gavenko said. "We all know what this is about, and we also know we won't get three feet ahead without all of us being in it together. Nobody is going to muscle anyone."

"As you know, I am responsible for the political health of our nation, and the leadership succession according to its laws is part of that. I will listen to anything that might be said here as a matter of state interest. If I believe that there is nothing more than ordinary self-interest—nothing seditious—I will be tempted to forget all I've heard that might be of an irregular nature."

"Now that you've covered your behind in the matter of any recording devices, Comrade Arkadin," said Batev, "let me hang mine out." He turned to Gavenko. "If you get the military support you're so obviously angling for, Comrade Secretary, what will you do with it?"

"Go slow, Genrikh Ivanovich," cautioned Dimitriyev.

"No time for that. It's all in or all out right now. Speak to us, Gavenko."

"I hope you appreciate my directness as much as I appreciate yours, Comrade Marshal. Here it is: If there were a God, I would feel that he has created this moment to save our nation. If there is a man among the leadership who does not feel that our last General Secretary has been a disaster, that is a man who has been appointed in place of a patriot. Already there are almost as many of The Broom's men at the top as there are ours. Counting people who don't declare themselves clearly, there may be more. There is no guarantee that a disciple—a man every bit as weak—would not replace him in the normal procedure."

Batev frowned deeply. "I will not help my country into another Red and White war—"

"Neither the people nor the world are going to let us replace the policies of this man—"

"Let him finish," Lubachevsky interrupted.

"I'm aware of the attractiveness of what the General

Secretary has sold the people, my friends. Given a perfect world, I would like to try it myself. But it's a world full of snakes, and he's turned them loose all around us. The arms supremacy that's cost us such treasure and genius is thrown away at conference tables. The economic system that was the only hope of the world is being thrown to the money grabbers everywhere, including inside our borders. The peoples who looked to us for freedom are facing arms supplied to counterrevolutions everywhere.''

"What happens if the world finds out the General Secretary is dead?''

"A lot of things. All bad. At home we take our chances of getting another just like him. Around the world we get pressure for exactly that. Worst of all, we let the world wake up.''

"What does that mean, Gavenko?'' asked Arkadin.

"The General Secretary has established his advantages, if someone is strong enough to use them. He has everyone asleep. A Russian Neville Chamberlain. Peace in our time . . . until the roof falls in. Well, we can decide right here whether that roof is going to fall on us . . . or on them.''

Batev and Dimitriyev stood up as one.

"Pearl Harbors were for an age without nuclear weapons, Comrade Secretary,'' snapped Dimitriyev.

"I think we should leave now,'' said Batev.

Though Lubachevsky rose to restrain them, Gavenko stayed where he was.

"It's not inspiring to see marshals of the Soviet Union soiling their laundry,'' Gavenko said. "Now I'm going to insist that you hear me out. I promise that at the end of this I won't press you further. You can go and do as you wish.''

"Finish then,'' Arkadin said after a moment.

"This may be the last moment when the Soviet Union will be supreme as a military force. I've seen the next economic plan. It can in no way support the armed forces necessary to secure our borders, much less move our doctrines outward. There will be vast reductions. The cuts will be heavy at the top. People in this room will be living a far different life very soon."

"My God, are you hoping to frighten us with the loss of our posts?" asked Batev contemptuously.

"No, just pointing out the inevitable loss of the best military leadership. And also that this is our opportunity to make the military move that will guarantee the country's future."

"And what move is that, Comrade Secretary?"

"I haven't the faintest notion."

"I beg your pardon, sir."

Now Gavenko was on his feet, belly to belly with the Minister of Defense. "I want one of the old thrusts. One that follows the doctrine that's got us where we are. Sudden, surprising, ruthless. With the lowest possible price for the highest possible gain."

"You do remember Afghanistan?"

"Too well, Marshal. But it's only a disaster if we let it paralyze us. I tell you I applauded Reagan when he shook off Vietnam and rooted us out of Grenada. For a handful of lives he reestablished the United States as a world force."

The Chief of the Main Political Directorate saw the point first. "You want to undo everything the General Secretary has worked for in a single action," said Arkadin.

"There you have it," said Gavenko softly. "A surge of pride in the fighting forces means more to the man in the street than all the scrapped missiles on earth. And the people will know—and the people who appoint the leadership will know—that only the strongest will do at the top. There'll be no turning back anymore."

"And the other countries?" asked Batev.

"Stunned. How could the gentle General Secretary do that to them? But then he'll die. The next man will shrug and point to the grave accusingly."

"Will they act on that rage? Will they fight us?"

"Not if we surprise them. Not if we stay away from their strength until it's too late to act."

Lubachevsky had positioned himself near the door, as

though he expected the military men to rush for it. Gavenko lit a cigarette and began to smoke it with a smile that betrayed no uncertainty.

The three guests went off into a corner and spoke too softly to be overheard. Lubachevsky went slowly to Gavenko. "Do you suppose we're headed for a cell?"

"I don't give a damn whether we are or not," replied Gavenko. "This country won't be worth living in anyway if they don't come in. All I care about is Russia, Tolstoy Ivanovich. Do you believe that?"

"Not for a moment, my friend. Why are you so sure they'll do this?"

"Because they're afraid that if they say no someone else will do it without them."

The others came to them.

"This would depend entirely on the particular operation, of course," said the Minister of Defense.

"Of course," said Gavenko.

"You understand that even a small, controlled, surprise action involves weeks of staff work and field preparation," said the Chief of the General Staff.

"Naturally. But I'm certain that you fellows have a shelf full of interesting things for which you've already prepared all the basics. Am I wrong?"

"Not entirely."

"Well, pick one then, on the chance that you'll want to go along with us. The General Secretary can't live forever, can he?"

"That's understood . . . if we wanted to go along, that is."

"Are the first deputy ministers of defense reliable in this?" asked Lubachevsky. "Are the deputy ministers?"

"Not all of them. Lurakin and Rhonev were forced in on us. They're quite liberal, Comrade Secretary."

"If you were to pick a man who thought the way we did for a theater commander, who would that be?"

The military men thought for a time.

"It would be a bit outside the expected, I think," said the Chief of the Main Political Directorate.

"It would be Sarkissian," said the Chief of the General Staff. "He's Navy, but he has the right heart and the right head. And our opposition would come from the sea."

"And the objective?" asked Gavenko.

"Albania. Our western port."

Gavenko nodded. "What could stop us?"

"A carrier," said the minister.

"We're lucky the General Secretary smiled them out of the Mediterranean."

"But they'll have the *King* on exercises in the North Atlantic over the next weeks. She could get there if they suspected. And if they lost faith in the General Secretary."

"That's not good."

"What is good, Gavenko, is that we've planted a capable man aboard. We could add a better one if we have to."

"Could they stop a nuclear carrier?"

The minister made a rocking motion with his palm to indicate a shaky outcome. "They're like all Americans. They promise you they can do anything."

U.S.S. *Ernest J. King*, the East Atlantic—May 26

Most of the seamen deep within the numberless steel tons of CVN-76 knew no more about the sea than the farmers, clerks, and confused idlers that many of them had been short months before. The crew of the *Ernest J. King* were often people of quite ordinary intelligence who had been made terribly good at a job they had no possibility of completely understanding. Perhaps alone among United States institutions, the Navy and its roughshod offshoot, the Marine Corps, did not coddle the country's youth. In a brutal routine perfected and administered by generations of iron-eyed bosun's mates and career officers who did it one way only, a superb killing machine was crafted out of soft and unlikely material.

Still, the Navy's children came to know the moods of the impossibly complex supercarrier deep in their bones, and felt viscerally the power of the ocean ranged against it. So here, on a nastily chopping sea in the eastern Atlantic, work parties near the bottom of the twenty-five-story building that was the *King* felt its wound.

In compartments along the centerline, the soles, the ears, even the skin sensed a subtle, abnormal twisting of the miles of steel, a disturbingly long and complicated rhythm that ended in a shudder just below anything a landsman might have noticed.

Of the four 22-foot, five-bladed bronze propellers that converted the 280,000 shaft horsepower sent by the *King*'s twin nuclear reactors into forward thrust, only two were turning. Number three was inoperable, an object not much larger than a man's thumb having somehow been introduced into its boxcar-sized interlacing of reduction gears. The object had worked its way through the maze of hairbreadth tolerances, converting several million dollars of precision machinery into a junkyard.

The separate gearbox of number-four shaft had also ingested a metallic foreign object. Although it had kicked clear before it had done more than begin to eviscerate the various splines and pinions, the engineering officer, Commander Ramsey, had found it prudent to disengage the shaft and apply the jacking gear before vibration and unbalanced strain caused a massive, perhaps dangerous, failure.

So the uneven pull of the two portside shafts, as they dragged the frozen starboard propellers through the sea at twenty knots, twisted the hull along its gigantic beam and 1,100-foot length, and caused it to breathe low, painful moans.

The appearance of such damage—engine casualties, in the language of the Navy—to two key, separated propulsion units was so far beyond the likelihood of accident that eight of CVN-76's contingent of sixty-five Marines now guarded the engine spaces at all times. These spaces were designated an exclusion area, and the M-16s in the Marines' hands were loaded.

On the bridge, the damage was not so apparent, except in the much-reduced speed of the *King* and its four scattered escorts. These escorts, the *Oliver Hazard Perry*–class frigates *Randall*, *Blackston*, *Quinty*, and *James*, wallowed far ahead, astern, and abeam like leashed whippets, their red and white yardarm blinkers sullenly, repeatedly affirming the sluggish speed of the wounded group.

U.S.S. *Ernest J. King*, the East Atlantic—May 29

In the moonless darkness of the midwatch, the boiling, dirty-white Niagara that was the wake of the colossal carrier seemed a half-mile below.

"I'm crapping out," said Floater, mopping his brow with his crumpled Dixie-cup hat. The pimples in his pasty face showed as dark spots below wide, shiny eyes.

His companion, resplendent in baggy, flowered shorts running to red and green, placed his hands reassuringly on the fueler's purple-shirted shoulders. "A deal is a deal, Floater," said young petty officer third class Hink Lydecker, his sweet California vowels not at all devoid of menace. "Especially when it cost me a month's pay in advance, and when you've already spent it. Now if I dropped you off this stern, you'd get sucked through the screws and pureed and I'd just go find somebody else."

"No you wouldn't, Hink. 'Cause there's nobody as stupid as me on this whole ship, except you."

"That's true, Floater," Lydecker said softly. "And you're also the only one in the fleet who could possibly understand what this means to me. We are of the brotherhood of the California wave."

"I been on a surfboard maybe ten times."

"It's like circumcision. Once is enough to bring you into the true faith forever." Lydecker's goose-bumped flesh covered a boy's body that could have served as a lesson in muscle anatomy. His face would have been freckled, wide-eyed, and juvenile handsome if it had ever been held still long enough to examine. Lydecker was one of those right-brainers with a body meant to fly rather than ambulate. He was always twisting off into some spectacular handstand or planche. Sliding down railings, swinging through overhead piping, muscling up ladders with arms alone, he seemed to be subject to separate laws of balance and gravity.

He sprang to the top of the three-inch-wide railing fronting the dark sea and paced back and forth along it, staring accusingly at Floater.

"Water skis are a long way from a surfboard, man," Floater said lamely. "A helluva long way."

"Don't you see what I have here in front of me, numb nuts?" Lydecker pleaded. "The ultimate everything for everybody who ever put a wet plank under his foot, board or ski. The ultimate tow—ninety-one thousand mother-humping tons—and the ultimate tingle. I lose the handle and I either swim to Gibraltar or get a propeller massage from either us or one of them frigates out back."

"What makes you think the life-buoy watch isn't goin' to see you down there and think you're some wacko Libyan sand commando? They'll fire a Stinger right up your ass."

Lydecker smiled. "Ah, they're trained to see seagulls at eight thousand yards. Their eyes can't focus on anything under a half mile."

Floater still seemed unconvinced. "I don't know if I can do all this shit you want me to do, Hink."

"A fish could do it if he had arms, legs, and balls. Look, there's the block already strung off the rail. There's the line all rove through it. That's your end and that's mine. You just let me down with the skis. My weight'll do it. Just keep an even strain. You'll know from the rope when I'm in the water. Keep paying out till you reach that knot near the end."

"I can't believe I'm listening to this crap," Floater said.

Lydecker gathered up a pair of water skis, freshly painted black, and mounted the rail. "'Bye," he called as he snatched up the handle end of the rope and jackknifed into the void.

"*Ohmygodmotherbitchinsonofan*—" squealed Floater as he scrambled to seize the departing line close enough to the block so that the shock of arrest wouldn't jolt loose the free-falling Lydecker. He almost sobbed in relief as he felt the weight kick against his hands and remain there.

As he braced himself to begin hauling his addled friend back to the rail, knowing there was at least an even chance that the skis had been jounced loose, he abruptly decided against it. "Let the crazy son of a bitch drown for putting me through this." Besides, Lydecker would just take the dive again when he was back on his feet—maybe take a bench with him for a board this time.

Minutes later Floater could tell from the angle of the rope that Hink was in the water and beginning to trail backward. Never mind that it was impossible he'd found the strength and agility to make the transition to the maelstrom that was the wake of a supercarrier traveling at twenty-one knots—he was doing it.

Floater stifled a whoop of elation and relief and tended to his work. He made no attempt to try to spot the deranged skier below him. For one thing, he couldn't have found the speck in the night and the exploding foam. And for another he was afraid to look. He would count off the fifteen minutes he had promised and then reel in his berserk mackerel.

Far below, his elated yodeling swallowed by the propellers' churning and the passage of the giant through the sea, Hink Lydecker saw a sight and felt a surge heretofore denied to every other man in the universe. The unimaginable bulk of the *King*, all its power, all its majesty, all its billions of cost, were there now just for him. Racing, swerving, swooping in amazing feats of balance, Hink Lydecker released one hand and snapped a salute to the glorious gray slab looming against the menacing sky. The moment demanded an incredible coda.

He spun backward, somehow let down his Hawaiian baggies, and mooned the mightiest warship ever.

And this was the lesser of his plans. "You ain't seen nothin' yet, Navy," he shouted to the roaring, cascading sea.

U.S.S. *Ernest J. King*, the Western Mediterranean—May 30

In midmorning on payday, the division chief for S-4, the Disbursing Division, was not at his post. Lieutenant-Commander Wade McGregor had money problems of his own, and the unexpectedly extended deployment of the *King* was amplifying them.

He had the look of a man tired from a lifetime of always expecting better than he found. The light behind his eyes had dimmed. The hectic crisscross of wrinkles that crowded his pale eyes had not yet been able to undo the effect of his good nose, lips, and chin.

Even the fresh Navy haircut couldn't keep the curl out of the gray-peppered locks that showed under his pushed-back khaki garrison cap. His forty-six-year-old body was the same straight, hard blade it had been when he played basketball twenty-four years ago at Boston College, but there was rust beginning to form. Sitting jackknifed behind a fifty-five-gallon drum of solvent, he felt twinges of age in both knees. The caressing Mediterranean sunshine and crisp breeze that poured sweetly through the open cargo hatch abaft the hangar bays had no restorative powers. The bright sea that gushed by a dozen stories beneath his elbow might have been blacktop in a supermarket parking lot for all it stirred him. He was not attentive to the noticeable improvement in the weather since last night's passage from the open Atlantic.

As McGregor flicked his cigarette out into the sea, he heard the rumble of one of the ubiquitous electric tractors used to move equipment across the wide expanses of the ship. Leaning inboard, he peered around the solvent drum and found himself behind a "grape," a purple-helmeted, purple-shirted fueler from the flight deck. He recognized the man, a short, red-faced youngster in his second hitch, rumbling continuous streams of profanity as he worked. The tractor contained four large fire extinguishers, their thick hoses and wide nozzles making a tangle at which the man tore with both hands. As he worked each extinguisher loose, he carried it to the open cargo hatch, peered once down the passageway from where he had come, once up, down, and sideways out the port, and dropped the heavy cylinder into the sea. After the fourth extinguisher disappeared, McGregor's accountant's mind estimated that something above two thousand of the taxpayers' dollars had just disappeared into the Med. McGregor stood up and spoke. "I presume we're sinking, Floater, and this is some desperate attempt to lighten the ship."

"Oh, shit, sir," the man said, going dead pale under his flight-deck windburn. He'd spotted the gold leaf of a lieutenant commander, and he knew well that the Navy's ability to punish had not declined appreciably since the days of the cat-o'-nine-tails. He came out of his salute just in time to keep the tractor from creeping out the port.

"Wow, am I glad it's you, Mr. McGregor. One of those boat schoolers would've stuck my ass in the turbines." He referred to Naval Academy officers.

Even the coolies know I'm just a seagoing bookkeeper, McGregor thought. "More likely a special court, six months making pebbles at Portsmouth and a dishonorable. And if I catch anything like this crap going on again, you'll be seeing me on more than the payroll line."

"Aye, aye, sir." The relief on his face was quickly replaced by the anger McGregor had first observed. "But, sir, I been haulin' them things up and down ten decks for service for nine months now, and it ain't even my job, 'cause they don't get enough people to ship over. Now we're s'posed to get back stateside and we're goin' the wrong way. For *months* is the gouge I'm hearin'. I'm sick of haulin', this crap that the firebugs are s'posed to haul. And the shop is tired of workin' on it. We're all tired of the forty pounds of papers to shuffle on the deal, so I decided to deep-six the friggin'—"

"It's not up to you to make those decisions," McGregor interrupted. "Now get back on the roof."

"Aye, aye. Thanks, Commander. See ya on the pay line." He sped off in the tractor.

McGregor knew he should have destroyed the man. Besides the broken discipline, a carrier was a floating firebomb of JP-5 jet fuel, where everything that could pour foam might be needed to save the ship and crew. But he couldn't bring himself to single the man out for something so common and, he was afraid, so understandable.

The brutal demands of running this jungle of technology overworked the best men without mercy, and when you took away their rest, you took away their heart.

No civilian would have put up with the work load and hours. Because men could not be retained, the ship was sailing shorthanded by upwards of 350 men. Everybody handled extra jobs.

Beyond that, the Navy's disastrous supply and requisition system produced paperwork in tons, and equipment in trickles. So the crew had learned to bypass and circumvent the system. The disbursing division was under the huge and infamous Supply Department, and McGregor knew its workings all too well.

The computerized supply system was mostly useful in covering up sloppy accounting and outright theft. The paperwork, when done at all, was often pure fiction, understating or overstating inventories in carloads.

Considering that one enterprising unknown had ordered up thirty-one silver bars out of the computer and made them dematerialize into his pocket, it was a wonder the men weren't selling whole F-14s to Iran instead of just parts, as had once been discovered.

McGregor ruminated on the inefficiency of the modern Navy: billions of dollars' worth of the world's most brilliant technology, not to mention the moment-to-moment running of the hugely complex ship, was entrusted to the hands of people who were little more than children.

An attacking gnat couldn't get at the *King* as long as the bug followed expected gnat protocol. But anyone with more than a gnat's brain could find holes in the system that would accommodate a division of Soviet Naval Infantry aboard, and the theft of the carrier's engines.

Now a pipe squealed and a voice bawled, *"Attention, all hands. Crew now being paid."*

Nowhere on the ship was there a refuge from the never-ending drumfire of bells, whistles, gongs, and bugles that accompanied announcements piped over the squawk boxes. A flight surgeon had told him that continuous cruising, even away from the earsplitting roar of the flight deck and catapult spaces, would result in permanent hearing loss.

The payroll job could go forward without him. The dozen men in his division could handle the disbursing without him—despite the presence of Ledges and Lydecker. But then again, some Academy ring-knocker just might come by and begin to notice that he was spending less and less time where his job was. He began to drift back to the division office. There he would check the division's numbers one more unnecessary time before he showed up to supervise the converting of three and a half million dollars into cash.

McGregor reflected that in addition to being low on everything else, the *King* was running out of money. The crew was paid by check, but cashed them instantly. Even with most of the crew participating in the Navy's direct-deposit program, there were still *thousands* of paychecks and personal checks to be cashed each month. One of the things they were going to have to take aboard in Naples was enough cash to make payroll for at least three months, maybe more. Thirty-five million might do it.

Thirty-five million. McGregor compared that hulking sum with the $5,500 shortfall in his own affairs that was about to wreck his family's life. The Navy's family benefits weren't bad, but a seventeen-year-old daughter with an emotional breakdown created financial demands that far outstripped any medical plan.

As a mustang—a staff officer up from the enlisted ranks—he was allowed to remain as perhaps the oldest lieutenant commander in the fleet. And he wasn't going any farther.

For the hundredth time in the day, he went over his finances. As an 0-4 with twenty-two years service, he had basic pay above $35,000 a year. On top of that he got his BAQ, the basic allowance for quarters, his FSA, family separation allowance, his sea pay, and his Foreign Duty Pay. A lot of civilians his age wouldn't mind making over $40,000 plus meals, medical, and thirty days leave. But day care, sitters, therapists, rents, and his wife's inability to leave Kiki long enough to hold a full-time job made it all inadequate. And now he was tapped out at the Navy Credit Union, and there were big dental bills for some back teeth Kiki had broken in one of her tantrums. He wasn't going to let some Navy butcher get at her.

He could get out on a hardship request, but had no faith that at the age of forty-six and with no real-world experience he could duplicate what he was getting here. He wasn't sure that the joy of being with Tess again and being there to help with Kiki would outweigh watching them starve to death.

His mind kept returning to the thirty-five million.

U.S.S. *Ernest J. King*, the Western Mediterranean— May 30

Feet are never the same after 56,000 pounds of loaded F-14 have rolled across the instep. So Senior Chief Petty Officer

Rocky Ledges appeared to the new men to be at a disadvantage in the fight.

Ledges had one of those bodies that looked as though it should be towed by Clydesdales. Thick as a beer wagon, it masked his above-average height as he turned awkwardly on crookedly healed metatarsals.

"Knock his nuts off, Wide Load," someone called from the back of the crowded compartment in the ordnance spaces. He was encouraging a huge blond sailor who huffed and growled his way around Ledges, showing evidence of having been trained in the ring arts. He unloaded a good hook that caught the senior chief explosively below the ribs.

Grunting, Ledges cursed himself again for having brought this one on. There was nothing more of a pain in the ass than senior noncoms who offered to take off the badges and duke it out. If he beat this dopy parachute rigger second class, he was a bully on the prod, an intimidator. And if he lost, as seemed increasingly likely, he would be slowly and humiliatingly run off the ship.

The man called Wide Load drilled two fast jabs into Ledges's forehead, a purposefully sculptured ring opening two red holes there.

"Want us to take his arm off along with the ring, Chief?" snarled someone behind Ledges.

"Naw. Keeps me awake," said Ledges in his growly basso. He had the eyes of a hater, gray, dead, and fixed on the very soul of his opponent. Forty-six years of time and heavy weather had damaged the square, honest-looking face beyond what the other man's fists might do.

"Show 'em what you done to that Limy marine in Trincomalee, Chief."

The old hands, Ledges thought as he parried a steaming right with a meaty forearm. Not many of the old guys left. And they were remembering a body fifteen years younger with two good feet in its shoes. He was devoutly grateful that the blond slab before him wasn't one of those flashy Puerto Rican kids who could hit you twenty times between the eyes before you could twitch. This mountain was going for the knockout rocket, which was a lot easier on an old man's stamina.

The twenty or so red-shirted ordnance men crowding around were almost whispering their yells. Officers were never very far from the ordies in their dangerous, restricted domain near the keel, and they didn't want any interference in the possible crowning of a new, unofficial ship's champion.

"What the hell you waiting for, Wide Load? You been heftin' fifty-pound chutes while this dipshit ain't been liftin' anythin' heavier'n a ten-dollar bill."

An ominous purple-red flush crept out from the neck and arms of the chief's skivvy shirt.

"I think the magic words have been said," muttered an old hand, taking a step backward.

This fight had begun many decks above because Ledges had again been rubbing his ego raw against the never-ending thought of his enormous loss of manhood. Just as he had always considered the churning uproar of the "roof"—the flight deck—the only place for a real man to drag his balls, he had been always equally vehement about places like the Disbursing Division. They were the befouled lairs of the emasculated and misbegotten. The misery and humiliation of parking his bulk behind a small metal desk—a thousand sheets of steel away from the storms, friends, noise, and dangers that were the fresh air of life—was just about all he could bear.

Wade McGregor's gruff, patient kindness only made him wilder because he knew he was that worst of Navy designations, a "weight." Somebody who wouldn't or couldn't keep up with his job. Not only should he not have been the leading petty officer for the division, he shouldn't have been permitted into it at all. He always felt that the thousands of sailors on the pay line had been assembled primarily to contemplate his pukey, enfeebled downfall. Never mind that he had almost fallen on his knees weeping as he begged the Navy to find him some spot where he would not be invalided out.

All this had been cooking in Ledges when this hulk of a parachute rigger had trampled on two exposed nerves in one surly sentence. In the course of a squabble over temporary assignments, he had turned and whispered to a friend, "Hey, how does Clarkie count that money when his thumb is always up his ass?" The overheard references, quite trivial and typical of the standard salty barrages of the Navy, reminded Ledges that he had both a first name he hated— Gable, courtesy of his movie-loving mother—and a job he hated, courtesy of an improperly towed F-14. He had called the lower rank a string of words that might have sunk a smaller ship. The parachute rigger had been entirely justified in asking Ledges to set aside his rank in an invitation to the present dance.

"Way to go, Wide."

Wide Load executed a near-professional sequence of footwork and feints, all of which baffled the lurching Ledges as he tried to turn with the much younger man.

Now the rigger unleashed a brutal uppercut with each hand against Ledges's middle. The fists sank through some flesh and encountered boilerplate beneath. He had just learned that the chief heaved two hundred sit-ups every morning with a twenty-five-pound grating held behind his neck.

Shaken, Wide Load turned his skills up another notch. "Try these, Clarkie." He banged Ledges almost at will, every punch encountering another part of the chief's merciless exercise program. Ledges's head, bobbing and hidden between the logs of his forearms, was elusive.

Made bold by his opponent's awkwardness, Wide Load tried a slightly off-balance dart to the chief's left. The hand that should have been helping guard his chin lowered a hair for a pile driver to an outflanked jaw.

If the rigger had been longer in the Navy, he would have known that all men who survived decades of enlisted men's shore dives came to settle on one or another devastating tactic that never failed them. It might be a kick or a choke or a gouge or a throw. The fighter would preserve his body with whatever stopgap tactics he could, waiting with infinite patience for the chance to deliver his haymaker.

In Ledges's case, he was waiting for just the sort of overbalanced veer that Wide Load was now executing. The chief had been holding his six-pound fist like a C-13 catapult ready to hurl an A-6. Ledges let loose as Wide Load's face appeared around a forearm.

Several people said, "Oh, shit," almost simultaneously as the sound of the punch faded.

The men who had been standing behind Wide Load worked late that night to wash their shirts clean of blood before the stains set in the fabric.

Senior Chief Ledges remained unmollified. His watch told him that he'd better get back to the most hated day of his life—payday.

Black Sea Fleet Headquarters, Sevastopol, U.S.S.R. —May 28

Viktor Sarkissian, Admiral of the Fleet of the Soviet Union, stood at the center of the War Games Room. His agitation showed itself plainly to the stolid ranks of chief marshals and upper-echelon admirals circled about the sprawl of the games table.

The thick sweat that gathered beneath the stiff, medal-heavy tunics did not flow entirely from the failures of a primitive air-conditioning system trying to deal with hot lights and packed bodies beneath the mountain. Fear also formed the fetid droplets. An American MX warhead careening into their redoubt would have frightened them less than the explosion of their squat commander. He was known to be something of a performer, not a bit above noisy, shameless melodrama when there was a point to be made. But you never knew when the act had ended.

Admiral Sarkissian bent his thick waist and reached far

across the games table to a point just east of Gibraltar. There his square fingers closed on the object of his yearning.

The exquisitely done miniature he held in his palm was crafted perfectly, right down to the shades of gray and black favored by the United States Navy. Precisely to scale and the largest on the table, the little ship symbolized the mountain of force that was CVN-76, the U.S.S. *Ernest J. King*.

"Would you like to compare this superb thing with one of our own magnificent carriers? Make it our beloved *Kiev*. Would anyone like to compare *Kiev*'s air group of thirteen ponderous, vertical-takeoff bathtubs with what the *King* can throw against us? Ah, those expressions tell me you'd rather not. Let me do it for you."

Inwardly, the staff members boiled. The ascendancy of the Navy, whose power had suddenly grown to the point where the upstart Sarkissian commanded this critical operation, sat badly.

"This is unseemly, Admiral," said the Chief Marshal of Armored Forces, who had himself hoped to give the orders for the upcoming engagement.

"Unseemly is not enough of a word for it," Sarkissian said. "This *King* can throw ninety planes into the air against us. Not our limited Yak 38s and Ka-25s, hardly capable of controlling a lake in Moscow, but an aerial armada that can blanket the Mediterranean. There are F-14s to control the air, A6Es to strike in all weather, E-2Cs for radar surveillance, EA6Bs for electronic jamming, SH3-Ds against submarines. Everything but a sightseeing balloon for their President to watch us as we go up in a mushroom cloud. All the while steaming three years between refuelings. Eight hundred thousand miles."

"But, Admiral," said a Chief Marshal of the Air Force, "our land-based aircraft are prepared to stand off the carrier planes if they intervene."

"Let me make clear *again* that we don't intend to begin something that will touch off nuclear exchanges. Our units will in no way openly engage those of the United States.

Our Mediterranean Squadron will not reappear in that sea to openly violate our agreements with the Americans and NATO.''

''Then if that carrier leaves Naples to go on station off Albania, our naval base on the Mediterranean remains an Albanian fishing port.''

''The *King* could be held back,'' said another admiral. ''There are political considerations in their Congress. They won't endanger the glasnost gains.''

''If it was their congressmen instead of their admirals who were sitting aboard that ship on top of nearly a hundred warplanes, I would say you had a point.''

''But if we have the new government in place in a few hours—''

A mirthless laugh burst out of Sarkissian. ''A few hours? I see you've never bitten into an Albanian. They're filled with poison like one of those South American toads. For a thousand years they've sat in their dark castles in the crags, making bones of anyone deranged enough to want that miserable rock pile.''

But, of course, it was not the rock pile they wanted, he thought. It was the seas it touched. What a cruelty. His great country owned a sixth of the land surface of the world. But the accidents of geography kept the extension of its might inside three bottles with small necks. In the north, NATO and the ice kept them stoppered in the Barents Sea and the Baltic. In the south, the Black Sea Fleet had to kiss the Turkish ass to pass the Bosporus. In the east, they were stuck in Vladivostok, halfway to the Arctic Circle, so a child could cut their supply lines to the south with a penknife. Adding to their predicament was the great reliance they placed on friends in Syria, Libya, and Vietnam—countries where political allegiances could change overnight. The memory of Egypt lingered.

''Albania is the right size and the right place,'' Sarkissian went on. ''It will give us one port of our own—beyond ice, beyond Turks—right under the Italian boot. And so we flank NATO neatly and for good. Then one day we can move into those fine facilities at Naples ourselves. And later, maybe Plymouth.''

Sarkissian stomped around the table to the papier-mâché mountains that represented the deeply folded hills of Albania. He stopped at the location where the Soviet Airborne troops would land, if needed. ''Landing zones like these are meat grinders without full control of the air. The leadership has given us eighteen hours to make this 'popular uprising' succeed on its own. Then, if the *King* isn't on station, we are supposed to go in with airborne units to support it. As you can see, this is not military planning, it's political planning. We may pay a heavy price.''

The political officer, a general wearing civilian clothes, was the only man in the room who could speak to Sarkissian as he pleased. Loyalty and socialist dedication, not the arts of war, were his business. ''This is defeatist, Admiral, and disrespectful of the leadership that has placed its faith in you for this great step forward in our security.''

''Is it the same faith they placed in the intelligence imbeciles who promised us the *King* had been given problems so severe that she'd have to leave the North Atlantic group and return to Norfolk for repairs? We assumed the only carrier that could be here in time, without it seeming to be an unfriendly act, would be sitting disemboweled in some drydock.''

A second man in civilian clothes stepped forward. He wore a pin indicating service in Afghanistan. He'd been scorched about the chin and lips, and his hoarse voice hinted that he had breathed the fire. The tone of Valentin Zyshnikov was one common to high officers of the KGB: it said that whatever position of inferiority they found themselves in was temporary. The neck of any tormentor would sooner or later come under their ax for review. ''The word 'imbecile' is very harsh when you are directing it at brave men risking life and freedom to bring us our information and do our work,'' he rasped. All his sentences always seemed clipped out of some phrase book left behind a regime or two ago.

Sarkissian never flinched. "Did I say imbeciles? I meant geniuses, of course."

"Are you drunk, Admiral?" the political officer asked quietly.

"This mess of yours sometimes makes me wish I were."

"Our information was good. The damage was extensive. Our surveillance trawlers show an eleven-knot reduction in fleet speed. Two screws dead. Ordinarily it would demand a return for major repairs."

"Why didn't it, comrade expert?"

"Because United States Naval Intelligence is beginning to sniff things. But they can't believe that our dead General Secretary, the man they have waited for since Czar Nicholas, will let down the high hopes and agreements. They won't jump to a distressing conclusion while they have their trust in our late General Secretary. But they do sense something big is coming. The *King* is currently deployed in desperation. She's crippled. She's been at sea nine months and the crew is fatigued and inefficient. They want to be home screwing their sweethearts, not serving more weeks at sea. Knowing they can keep only four of their fourteen carriers deployed, and that the other three were in the Pacific, we had every right to believe we'd be free to work in a short time period."

"We're not many days from the moment our people in Albania shoot their first generals and politicians. Is there no way to postpone this mess, since we can't hasten it?"

"None, Admiral. Some distrustful people in our government are demanding access to the General Secretary. Actually, you've done wonders as it is, considering the standing start."

"So, then, our *Ernest J. King* will proceed to Naples. We'll have no reason to complain about our feelings being hurt by her presence, since she needs emergency repairs. She'll rotate her crew ashore for a few days to quiet their grumbling, and meanwhile take on enough stores to stay on station forever. So let's say she'll be two days reaching Naples, six to make temporary repairs and replenish. After that she'll be—even at reduced speed—only a day's steaming around Italy to station off Albania. Still no sign of other carriers rushing here?''

''No. The others at sea are staying in the Pacific. The President respects the feelings of the General Secretary, apparently. Only the *King* is a factor in our schedule.''

''Only the *King*, eh? Only the *King*.'' The Admiral of the Fleet circled the games table until he was close enough to Zyshnikov to see where skin had been grafted to his lips. ''I will go forward with a plan never formulated to deal with any United States aircraft carrier. It will all have been done on your assurance that their *Ernest J. King* could not be present. So we may have a Dunkirk without boats.'' He handed the receiver of a red telephone to Zyshnikov. ''Let me see you stop ninety thousand tons, and, say, one thousand megatons, with one of your clever calls. Please. Do your part.''

Sarkissian was gratified to see the hand that took the receiver sent forth just the slightest tremor. But the rasp into the phone, asking for a number on Dzerzhinsky Square, was firm and confident.

The Admiral of the Fleet waved the others out of the room and leaned over the game board on his elbows at a position above the heel of Italy in the Adriatic—where the *King* would arrive if this call did not achieve anything. He had retrieved the elegant model of the *Ernest King* and added it to the others entering the Mediterranean.

''Thunder Station, we hear they've named it,'' he said to the agent who waited for his call to go through. ''But is it their thunder or ours?''

U.S.S. *Ernest J. King*, the Western Mediterranean— May 30

Above the signal bridge, the pigstick flew the flag of a vice admiral. Jack Irons, alone on the open ''goofer's gallery'' on the flight-deck side of the island, glanced up at the flapping pennant and felt the new third star weighing heavily on his collar. Not as firmly attached as one would like, he thought.

As a flag officer Irons was badly miscast. He was filled with New York City ideas and accents, with a face and body like a badly carved potato. It sometimes took weeks for others to realize he was at least twice as smart as anybody else in the room.

There'd be one hell of an investigation when they got back to Norfolk, he was thinking. Carelessness or sabotage, it came to the same thing in the Navy. When something went wrong in a big way, the man at the top was never quite the same afterward.

A surge of helpless rage ran up his spine at the thought of a United States Navy sailor deliberately damaging his ship in a potential combat situation. What *was* an American anymore, anyway? He had heard flight-deck men yelling instructions at one another in *Spanish*, for God's sake. They might salute the flag of Puerto Rico or Mexico before the Stars and Stripes. He managed to bring his cranky intolerance up short, knowing full well that his crew, however nontraditional, contained some of the greatest young men in the world.

He let his eyes drift across the awesome four and a half acres of the flight deck and knew the same disbelieving wonder that had swept him upon seeing it for the first time. Irons had always agreed that handling the *Ernest J. King* was like steering Central Park from the top of the Empire State Building.

One of the four 150-ton outboard elevators was just rising from the port side with a gray pack of F-14s for the deck park. The stubby wings were folded back, sleek and mean.

The nerve-shattering thunder and stink rising up from the flight deck below made the confusion of scurrying deck crewmen seem even more chaotic. The dozens of men made a riot of wild colors, each shirt and helmet color-coded to a different specialty—ordnance handlers in red, fuelers in purple, plane parkers in blue, and the rest of the rainbow distributed over the uncountable jobs that launched, recovered, and protected the air group that was the *King*'s only reason for being. There was as much death on the deck as there was in the sky, but better hidden. The jet blast could blow a man overboard so quickly that no one would see him go. Or he could be sucked up an intake and blown through an engine as soup. A snapping arresting wire could take off a lucky man's legs or an unlucky man's head.

All the disorder disappeared in the crisp operation of the four 312-foot catapults, two on the angled deck that pointed eight degrees off the port bow and permitted double-runway operation, and two at the head of the foredeck, well clear of recovery operations at the stern. The catapults were the mighty C-13s that did not have to depend on the forward motion of the ship into the wind to launch aircraft. From a carrier dead in the water, their steam-driven thunder could propel 78,000 pounds of man, machine, fuel, and ordnance into the air at 150 miles an hour. With these marvels the *King* could launch and land a plane every fifteen seconds.

Irons had learned in the hot crucible of Vietnam that without catapults a carrier is not a warship, but a hotel.

In the bulk of the *King* lived and worked a force of 500 officers and 5,500 men. They were served by two thousand phones, a shopping mall, barbershops, snack bars, gymnasiums, hobby shops, and all the amenities of a medium-sized city.

He thought it remarkable that all this could be run on a mere $40,000 an hour—about one million dollars a day.

The admiral was so filled with the mundane operational facts of his hulking charge—90,000 dozens of eggs, 120 tons of meat, an eighty-bed hospital with two operating rooms, a TV studio, a desalinization plant that made his hot-water showers almost as available as they were at the Waldorf—that he wondered if he would be able to sort out the parts he might soon need to fight a big-navy war.

Washington was worried. Otherwise CINCEUR—Commander in Chief Europe—would never have had this crippled, depleted force steaming for Naples instead of home. Only the niceties of international protocol were holding them short of Condition Three, a modified wartime cruising status. The inevitable Soviet AGI trawler trailed a mile back, missing nothing.

Nobody had identified the trouble for certain, but they suspected it was building. Something in the Balkans maybe. Intelligence was catching hell for not knowing more. But everybody knew that with the Sixth Fleet pulled out of the Med by the new President, matching the withdrawal of the Soviet Mediterranean Squadron, they had to reassemble some sort of credible trip-wire force. And without making it look like all the diplomatic breakthroughs of the past months were dissolving in a total, distrustful buildup. The *King*, steaming on her half-dead drive plant, carrying reduced stores and an exhausted crew that had been due back in CONUS—the continental United States—weeks ago, was evidence that the high commanders were desperate to maintain a predominance in this enormously strategic sea.

Number-one catapult boomed and a howling F-14 shot off forward in a billowing blast of steam. The plane sank out of sight for a moment as the lip of the angled deck lifted in the swell, and then the Tomcat rose into the sky, its engines two blazing white candles, its lethal load of Sparrows and Sidewinders distributed from hard points across its belly. Two F-14s were launching on an Alert Fifteen—an intermediate alert that had them in the air within fifteen minutes of a warning. They were off on a common occurrence. A Bear hunt.

Some minutes after the second Tomcat had thundered forward, the voice-activated phone boxed under the rail buzzed on the 22JS Air Search Radar circuit. Irons picked up.

"Bridge. Radar," the voice said in the unvarying Navy phone routine. "Bear still coming in. Position zero-one-zero relative. Range ten thousand yards."

"Bridge. Aye." Irons hung up and turned his eyes ahead.

Soon a dot became discernible. A Soviet Tu-95 Bear reconnaissance bomber, thick with cameras, was making a run a
thousand feet above the water.

The age of great kings had not passed, Lieutenant Commander Mudcat Walker thought, guiding his hurtling F-14
into a thundering, glittering arc that drew eyes for twenty
miles.

Walker, advancing the twin gray throttles in his left hand,
was in the grip of ecstasy that other twenty-nine-year-olds
were able to reach only with the heaviest recreational drugs.
He, in the vehicle that was the only thing on earth that he
loved more than himself, was contemplating his own glory.

So accomplished at this was he that he was able to run
through his majesty flawlessly even as he closed at Mach 0.8
with the Bear approaching the *King*.

In the towering hierarchy of the Navy, aviators appeared to
float to the top effortlessly. Carrier pilots floated much faster,
and fighter pilots more than any.

Ahhhhh, Walker thought, but then there were the fast-
track carrier fighter pilots. *They* burst upward like Trident
missiles from the hatches of a submerged boomer. He,
Mudcat Walker, was just such a missile.

Top of the hottest Annapolis class in twenty-three years.
Not just a lieutenant commander. A fighter squadron commander. Not just any squadron, but the legendary VF-36
Bloodbaths. The last commander had been an old Vietnam
mosshorn pushing forty who'd have gone out a lieutenant if
several MiGs hadn't skidded in front of his Sidewinders.
But now the *new* Navy was here.

Mudcat Walker knew how to build his own legend. The
officers who went up fastest were the ones that everybody
had a When-I-Flew-With-Old-Steel-Ass story about. He pushed
mercilessly at the already overstrained envelope of privilege
around a big-carrier air group. When he mouthed off against
certain procedures and tactics, he could be quieted only with
care, because he was Going High.

Which was not to say he wanted to get a reputation as a

double-domer, an intellectual, like Admiral Geinz, who—unfortunately a lot of old thirty-one-knot destroyer drivers thought—now headed the Joint Chiefs. Walker wouldn't have too much of that. He knew that flying was where it was at, and what had taken him here. He had sweated the blood, racked the muscle, and twisted the brain to make himself the shit-hottest fighter jock since . . . who? . . . Butch O'Hare.

He laughed out loud in his oxygen mask. Old Butch did well enough splashing five meatballs one day flying a $33,000 Wildcat that this multimillion-dollar Grumman could have almost carried in its weapons racks. And that stubby F-4F could be flown by any ninety-day wonder who could handle a Studebaker in a tight turn. It took a million beans and undetermined years to turn out a Mudcat Walker . . . if you could find one. Butchie, he chortled, the future Admiral Walker could wax your tail then as now.

His racing mind thrilled to think that this one bird of his could have cleared the air group of the old *Akagi* out of the sky in twenty seconds. It could do it so easily that he couldn't get a good-conduct out of it, much less O'Hare's Congressional.

But someday he'd get the Big One for a necktie. And he didn't care what or who were the baddies sent up against him.

Wound up, Walker rolled the streaking Tomcat onto its back and, from his spot two miles behind and four thousand feet above the Soviet Bear, poured more throttle into a long, inverted, parabolic dive.

Over the headset came the caterwauling of his backseat, Lieutenant Bad Apple Burns. *'Aw, c'mon, Mud, you pigporker.''* The radar intercept officer's Alabama twang turned all his words into a series of hog calls. ''Air boss is gonna see this shit.''

''That's right, Bad. And Ironhead, too.''

''You goddamn nipple. *Yow . . . Yowieeee*—''

While the prying Bear was loafing along at a comparatively stately four hundred knots, it added a more than

interesting demand to the tight-stretched reflexes of Mudcat
Walker in the maneuver he now began.

Knowing with what fervor the eyes and voices in the
afterbubbles of the Bear were calling his approach to the
cockpit, he committed.

Delightedly he felt the earsplitting power that he knew
had called aloft all the eyes of the surface fleet. *"It's that
crazy Walker"* he knew they were laughing.

"Amerikanski bastard," the officers on the trailing AGI
trawler would be screaming.

If the Bear pilot had any balls, Walker exulted, he'd make
a move—any move—to muck up the show-boat maneuver
that must be coming. Even if it splashed everybody. But he
must have kids back in Smolensk, Walker saw. He held his
course as if he were on tracks.

From behind the Bear, on their back in the rapidly
tightening arc of the dive, the Tomcat crewmen felt their
G-suits squeeze down and their lips drag away from their
teeth. Walker held his breath for four and a half minutes six
times a day to get his brain used to doing with less oxygen
on such pulls. Burns's eyes pulled up and kept going.

At the moment the Tomcat flashed downward past the
nose of the Bear, the big Soviet bomber's prop-driven four
hundred knots were headed at all of that speed for the diving
canopy of the American fighter. Since any jet pilot knows
from his first moment in the air that any object suddenly
appearing fifty feet before his windshield will be his last
sight on this world, the pilots of the Bear experienced the
most violently miserable moment it is possible for an airman
to survive. Men of cool courage and exceptional skill,
battling the mangled airstream, they dissolved into raging,
swearing animals, a reaction that drifted out onto half the
listening circuits in the Med. Mudcat Walker, when he had
made his huge triumphant wheel around the sky and returned
to tuck up against the long-nosed Bear's port quarter, could
still see the pilot's contorted, working face.

"So that's what they mean by the *Red* Air Force, huh,
Boris?" Walker cooed into the air-to-air.

A burning stream of Russian flowed back.

With his incredible visual acuity Walker had recognized the Soviet pilot. He prided himself on knowing them all, and had given them names. This one was Boris Badunov. He liked Boris because he got so mad. And because he could be intimidated.

Aware by now that Boris spoke some English and monitored the 333.3 air-to-air frequency, Walker unleashed a torrent of unintelligible nonsense in the tone of an urgent, dangerous warning: *"Bear! Crumbling on your boglush. . . . Repeat! Crumbling on your boglush! Goddammit! Adjust your rumblegork. . . . Hey! Learn to fly, Boris. . . . Watch that rumblegork—!"*

He accompanied this with the moves of a New York taxi driver, seeming to attempt to cut too sharply across the Bear's nose and then pulling back in seeming frustration because the Russian had blown the communication.

Close in on the other quarter of the Bear flew Walker's wingman, Lieutenant Mickey Maussman. Coordinating beautifully with Walker, he yawed and jerked his Tomcat with elaborate panic and imprecision each time Walker forced the Bear in his direction. Maussman had trained his RIO, Greaser Escobar, to emit yelps of perfect panic.

The Russian must have known that this sort of thing was not done since the Sixth had left. Previously, games of "Mediterranean chicken" had sometimes gotten close to out of hand when both sides were out of sight of their leaders. But not now. And not here. They were right over the United States battle group. The Soviet flyer must have been listening hard for a sharp reprimand from the *King*. Walker was half expecting it himself. But it didn't come.

For nearly twenty minutes the powerful gray terriers herded the propeller-driven giant where they would. Walker imagined the turmoil in Boris's heart as he finally decided to turn back with his camera packs unspent. There would be hell to pay, and Boris would be the one with his hand in his pocket.

* * *

Back down on the goofers' gallery, Admiral Irons had been joined by Red Bedford. The faded "Air Boss" stencil on his yellow shirt was sweated to a full black. The mini-boss was minding the store back up in PRI-FLY. They watched the end of the show above with a difficult mixture of delighted awe and terminal annoyance.

"Respectfully, Admiral, we should hook up his balls to the number-four catapult, set 'er for eighty thousand pounds, and blow the little fucker back home." The difficult work of air bosses made them endlessly florid. Bedford was called Red not because of his hair, of which there was none, but because of the color of all his visible skin.

Irons grunted. "I'm not sure that wouldn't wreck the catapult. Anyway, we've got to be careful. We might all be working for that twerp one day."

"Not if we drown him right now."

"Trouble is, we need two thousand more just like him, and maybe there aren't three hundred in the whole country. And he knows it."

"What about my young birdmen, sir? What're they gonna think about what they can get away with?"

"Red, they're just going to think that things have changed again. I wouldn't have picked this way to let everybody know it, but here it is. I'll use it if the Pentagon lets me. Maybe we'll find out whether 'eighty-six meant a shit."

Irons referred to the Goldwater-Nichols Department of Defense Reorganization Act of 1986, in which the structure of military command from the Joint Chiefs down underwent radical surgery. It went back to the Lebanon Marine disaster, when the chains of responsibility for men in the southern deserts had to be cleared backward through platoons of generals and admirals scattered from London to Rome to Washington D.C. Now, in theory, the services were no longer four squabbling turf protectors. The head of the Joint Chiefs of Staff, now Admiral Geinz, was supreme above his fellow chiefs. In effect, the "Cincs," commanders in chief of all theaters, reported straight to him. And, most importantly, the senior officers on the scene had sweeping powers to act on their own initiative. Of course one risked one's own testicles, not to say those of one's forces.

Bedford appeared to be dwelling on what the scene below might be if that Bear had hosed some twin 20-millimeter on his tightly packed deck park of thirty-one fully fueled warplanes. "You think it's time to keep 'em away, then?"

"Time to show them in Washington that we have to commit to something damn soon. This stop at Naples while they try to find out who's in charge at the Kremlin isn't going to hold us for long."

"Somebody must know more than we do, sir, or they wouldn't be shoving us in here with a half-dead crew and a one-lung power plant. We never should've pulled the Sixth Fleet out of the Med. Our beanhole President gave this puddle to the Ivans."

"They got a new man on top, we got a new man on top. They want to kiss and climb into bed."

"Yeah. And it's us who'll get the clap."

"I'll have Admiral Geinz pass your thoughts straight up to the Joint Chiefs."

"And Walker, sir?"

"Use the asshole drill. But we need him in the air. Preferably in a bad mood."

The *King* maneuvered to recover aircraft. The air boss in PRI-FLY gave the orders and the returning F-14s made their swoop and round-down effortlessly, slamming the deck at full throttle. The power was needed for a go-around if they missed the arresting cable and boltered. But not a man planted his hook beyond the second wire.

Irons wondered just how ready he was for a war or anything like it.

McGregor arrived at the division office and found it looking as though it had taken a hit from a five-inch shell. He was certain he had assembled the sloppiest and most clerically incompetent men in the fleet to make up his Disbursing Division. But they were loyal, a lot harder-working than he had been lately, and he looked after them like the stray dogs they were.

He could not be certain whether it was Ledges or Lydecker who had done the most to screw up the division. If he had shipped them away, acknowledging a major mistake, or been ordered to do so by Commander Hatten, the blithe head of the vast Supply Department in which they all labored, things would have improved hugely. Even the outrageously slack and timid Lieutenant Bluehoffer, with the addition of two bodies devoted to the world of numbers and efficiency, might have been able to function as an acceptable number two. But hell, anybody with the good sense to blow out Ledges and Lydecker would long ago have done the same with Bluehoffer and most of the rest.

McGregor had always found it appalling how the Navy spared nothing to attract its recruits, then casually chewed them up, broke their hearts, and spit them out when they failed to live up to Navy standards. Time and again he had seen the terrible bewilderment in the departing faces of men and boys who had looked to the Navy as the last golden chance they would ever have at a few decent things in life.

At some unknown moment right after the days he had served off Nam, McGregor had decided he couldn't be part of it. His division had become a legion of the lost. Although none were lost as thoroughly as Ledges and Lydecker.

He guessed that the only reason the other men didn't rebel against the special slack he cut for these two was that they were as fond of them as he was. Also, he did not completely rule out their not fooling with his weakness for keeping the marginal alive.

Bluehoffer answered his phone call to the disbursing line. "Did Rocky and Hink get there?" asked McGregor.

"The chief got here just now, sir. His forehead looks like steak tartare and one hand is twice as big as the other. But he's kind of cheerful. I'm expecting Hink any minute. It would be . . . nice if you were here, Commander."

"Soon, Bluehoffer. Soon." He hung up, heartened that

Ledges and Lydecker might both appear at an observed naval function.

His devotion to Ledges was easy enough to understand. They had been through it all together in the awful months on Yankee Station off Vietnam. McGregor had come across the burly giant in tears at a far corner of the roof one night. There the iron chief had broken down and shared a soul bleeding over the boys and old friends who were not returning from the flak-filled skies. He had been almost instantly ashamed he had spoken. But after they had seen each other and two bottles of Jim Beam through the night, the unlikely pair had bonded as only old sailors can. For long months they had leaned upon one another for a kindred ear and heart. And, years later, when the crushing tire had done its work on Ledges, McGregor had not hesitated to call in the dozens of favors accruing to the man who gave out the money.

Hink Lydecker was as much Ledges's fault as his own. Simply, stupidly put, he had become their lost, hopeless son.

In every unruly pack of infuriating young men there is one in whom a man, however soured, apathetic, and uncontemplative, sees the fire, the joy, the exuberance that he imagines would spring from his own genes.

For McGregor, ever trying to overcome the grief and disappointment that lived alongside the love he felt for his own flawed child, the association was as easy as it was irresistible.

For Chief Ledges it was not so simple to see. He had been left by two wives who had not been able to live with the boredom of fleet-town life. The loss of the women had not haunted him for long. There were always plenty more for a big, strong sailor who knew how to laugh and buy drinks. He never spoke for a moment of any desire for the lost joys of children or a sense of immortality. But when Hink Lydecker had shown up aboard Ledges's last ship, the *Forrestal*, arrogant, bewildered, uncontainable, and already earmarked for elimination, Rocky Ledges became a grumpy, bewildered parent.

It was Ledges who tried to tame him for his deck force, protecting him with all his brawn and power. When the metatarsals broke, the boy was left behind and began to sink rapidly. Now it was Ledges, himself hanging on by his fingernails, who used every friend he had to bring Hink to his own savior, McGregor.

Both the chief and the officer never ceased being alert for signs that the boy had seen their weakness and was playing them for fools. But such duplicity was clearly beyond the openhearted boy. As for the other men, nobody seemed able to resent Hink Lydecker.

They all did their best for one another. In the case of this division, that was not much.

If his assistants had been born to introduce chaos into a situation, McGregor had been born to achieve order. His mind was ten thousand neat, numbered, instantly accessible compartments that without visible effort subdued and made sense of the Navy's jumble. He swept over the desks and through file cabinets like a sorting machine, attracting papers, files, books, and tapes into the proper piles like some swirling magnet.

An envelope from Commander Hatten was under a pile of manila folders on Ledges's desk. It might have been there for days. He tucked it into a pocket and kept working. In minutes the office looked like a page out of a recruiting manual.

McGregor's deadly eye for the square and true caught at something against the rear bulkhead.

"Oh, for the sweet love of Jesus," he groaned. The five-foot circle of the vault door was not quite flush. Those idiots had left it open when they'd rushed off to the pay line. As keeper of the division's keys, he again affirmed his insanity for ever letting them into the hands of anyone else.

He ducked into the ten-foot-square vault and was relieved to see the stacks of currency sitting crisp and new in their bands. After months of paying out, the money no longer needed the hand truck upon which it sat, but there were still, according to his rapid calculation, $2,443,000 on hand. The distrustful bookkeeper in him checked the little irregular-stacking tricks he used to make sure nobody was moving the currency around. Lydecker had once goaded Ledges, the magisterial SCPO, into the equivalent of a snowball fight using bundles of twenties, and nothing like that was ever going to happen again.

Everything looked fine. Only the currency he had set aside for the cashing of checks was taken out. He shook his head in bemused relief. Here the Navy, with its customary structural overkill, had built a vault with walls of chrome steel two feet thick. But one of his airheads had forgotten to slam the door and spin the locking wheel. They were up there doing the pay line with armed men making sure they wouldn't get ripped off, and any swabbie who had come nosing around the office to check his travel allowance could have walked in and stuffed a duffel bag. Hiding it wouldn't have been a great problem. There were over two thousand compartments on the ship, and no man living, including the builder, knew where more than a third of them were located without consulting deck plans.

He was about to leave the vault when he saw Hink Lydecker's beloved ghetto blaster on a shelf. The enormous, multispeakered radio and tape deck was the only thing in the world the boy cared to protect. He would come for it as soon as he returned and fill the office with the earsplitting thump of taped heavy metal. But a small punishment was in order, as well as a rest for the ears.

McGregor stepped out of the vault, but did not stop with spinning the tumblers closed. He took out his pin keys and set the time lock. Now the Secretary of the Navy himself couldn't get Hink his beloved songs in anything under twelve hours.

Laughing, chattering men stood on endless lines before the disbursement windows, turning their checks into cash.

At a table behind the D-Ks manning the windows, McGregor sat with his two chief miscreants.

Ledges looked up sheepishly, the purple around his eyes looking vaguely like a party mask. "Your face looks worse than mine, Commander. Troubles?"

"Yeah, Chief. We'll talk later."

Again McGregor saw the misery of Ledges at a desk. The chief had only Lydecker and a handful of contemptible ratings to bark at, although he sometimes forgetfully included the shrinking Lieutenant Bluehoffer. It had always galled Ledges to deal with anything smaller and less important than an A-6, and here he was dealing with a wispy sea of flabbergasting paper, numbers, and computer hieroglyphics. It was fortunate that McGregor had the last word writing the fitness reports.

Lydecker didn't look up from sorting checks as he spoke. "Sir, if it's that damned deviled crab I forgot in the bottom of that file cabinet—"

"My nose found that snack a couple of days ago."

Lydecker's charm and attractiveness lay in the fact that he had no idea he possessed so much of these useful items. The endless surprise with which his clear hazel eyes looked out upon the world showed only boundless innocence. The gold hair, the dancer's grace, and the neatly chiseled surfer's body he regarded as standard issue and not worth attention.

Perhaps if he had heard the word "no" in the first eighteen years of his life, he would not have remained so inclined to satisfy any wild and vagrant whim without an idea of what it might cost him or anyone else. Back in Norfolk he had taken on two giant swabbies off the *Peoria* when they had referred to Ledges as "Gimpy." The results might have been fatal if Ledges had not arrived from a far corner in time.

Like Ledges, the boy looked pathetic thrashing a calculator. Born into the sweet California sunshine in the universal forgiveness of the late sixties, he had grown into a world where sand, surfboards, and beach-blanket kisses appeared to have turned a fine head into an unfurnished room.

"Hey, sir," Lydecker called, an infrequently used frown visiting his smooth forehead. "Am I doing this right?"

McGregor looked over his shoulder. "You aren't. But if you stop right there, I might be able to straighten it out inside of a week." He no longer got mad at them. He now realized that he covered their uncaring incompetence in a job they hated because he cared so little for it himself. And by saving their tails, he made himself feel able to protect at least some of the people he cared about. He sure wasn't doing much for his real family, he thought.

The Pentagon, Washington, D.C.—May 31

Admiral Theodore Roosevelt Geinz was not only the most powerful military man who had ever lived, he was also the most despised by the forces he commanded.

As head of the newly rearranged Joint Chiefs of Staff, he was vilified not just by his sister services, but also by his own. And he relished the opprobrium. It was why he had been appointed.

The Pentagon rounded into view through the window of his swiftly cruising limousine.

He had heard that the huge five-ringed building had been considered as a hospital to receive the expected hundreds of thousands of casualties earned in the contemplated 1945 invasion of Japan. Nobody ever thought to question the endless ramps inside, spared, perhaps, by two cruel atomic bombs from fifty years of wheelchairs and gurneys. The Japanese got all those instead, while he got office space.

Always he laughed at the reaction of first-time visitors to the Pentagon. Rather than a bristling, impregnable, immaculate bastion of United States military glory, they found a place into whose lower reaches any street person could stagger. The bottom level resembled nothing so much as the hideous Port Authority Bus Terminal in New York City, a glaring fluorescence of ugly shops and drumming confusion.

It was a bit harder to make one's way upstairs, but no more impressive.

In a maze of small, drab offices of the sort to be found in any marginal firm in New York, sat an incredible profusion of military officers. Far from being shirkers of effort, as they were often portrayed, they were almost pathetically eager to find something to do.

The car sped through the river entrance and dropped him off. He headed at top walking speed for the Chiefs' Room.

There was nothing military in Geinz's bearing. He was the picture of a big, portly, jowly Midwest banker anxious to get some ugly farm foreclosures behind him before lunch. His walk and bearing was much parodied.

"He even walks like a politician" was a favorite growl behind his back.

Politician. The deadliest word that could be leveled at him by his military brothers. He had at the midpoint of a fine career in the fleet abandoned the sacred nuclear submarine program to go for a Navy-sponsored Ph.D. program in international relations at Yale. Rickover had stopped just short of ordering him to return to the nukes, and his stubborn refusal to do so had seemed to sink his career deeper than the twisted *Arizona*.

The politician always wins, was the certainty he had depended upon all along. And now he had, after many miserable years, been proven right. The new structure of the Joint Chiefs needed a man who understood diplomacy and international geopolitical tensions better than he did the handling of a destroyer in a beam sea.

His fellow chiefs sprang to their feet as he brought his bounding slouch into the Situation Room. That was new. In the old system of co-equals they never stood for one another. They hated doing it, especially the other services. These were represented by General Uddely of the Army, Griffith of the Air Force, and Brown of the Marines. Not one bit less hostile was Admiral Cross. Their aides were there in profusion, in seating far less comfortable than that at the Joint Chiefs' table.

Whatever the aides wanted to show on their faces, they wisely did not. Their professional lives were in the Chairman's hands. As part of the reorganization, he had power over the promotion of many of them.

That was by no means all. Geinz could not only overrule any military advice from any service, he could *steal their people*. He had not just stepped across the old set-in-iron division lines of the services; he had bent them, broken them, and cut them up for scrap.

Army helicopter pilots were practicing landing on Navy ships and getting mine-sweeping training against emergency need. Navy gunnery officers were studying infantry tactics and field-artillery principles to make naval gunfire more effective in support operations.

The Navy saw utter apostasy. He was letting money escape the fleet. The Holy Grail twenty-carrier goal was leaking away in such fripperies as artillery shells, machine-gun bullets, fuel depots, and small-arms ammunition to insure supplies for a war that might go more than five weeks.

"Be seated, gentlemen, and good morning," Geinz said as he took his place at the center of the table.

"Why are we here?" he said. It was the way he opened every meeting. He kept his eyes on the table mostly, dividing by services the voices he heard.

"The birds don't give us any kind of solid answer yet, Admiral," said Air Force, referring to the photo satellites and SR-71s crisscrossing Russia at heights well beyond the naked eye. "They're still moving those airborne units a lot in the south. Plenty of big airlifters on hand. Helicopters, too. And there's armor moving inside the Soviet Union and stacked around the southwestern Bulgarian border."

"Got anything on aerial tankers for refueling fighters?"

"Nothing much, sir."

Geinz felt the exasperation growing. "Assuming they're

up to trouble, that would mean they're planning an armored attack without air cover in place. Comment?''

"Ambiguous, sir."

Geinz tapped a ballpoint loudly against an ashtray. "Didn't somebody once write something like, 'Being prepared to respond only to warning indicators that are unambiguous means being prepared for the kind of warning we are least likely to get'?''

"That was Mr. Weinberger, sir."

"Anyway," said Geinz, "you can't photograph what's going on in people's heads. What do we have on their sick chief?"

"If he's sicker than they say, they're doing a great job of hiding it," Naval Intelligence said. "Plenty of bulletins."

"Too damned many if you ask me," grumped Marines.

"I don't think so," sniffed Naval. "We issued more stuff than that when Eisenhower and Reagan went down. And we've had some possible live spottings reported. From too much distance to be sure it's him, but he was in the expected place. He was being helped, but he was on his feet.''

"How are the conservatives behaving?"

"Sweethearts. They could get elected here on the Republican ticket."

"Worry me some more," said Geinz.

"The Albanians shot twenty-six people in a prison in Korce last Thursday," NI said.

"In Albania that could be because they overstayed their parking meters."

"Our man there got handed their records to burn. Five of the best operators Ivan had. The rest not far behind. They weren't there counting the sugar-beet crop."

"Are the Albanians talking to us?"

"They don't talk to their mothers, sir."

"The Russians wouldn't want another Afghanistan after all this reforming business."

"Not the General Secretary, anyway, sir."

"If they went into Albania—ignoring national policy and

Congress for a moment—what could we do?'' The answering voice had an odd smugness to it.

"With a carrier like the *King* on close station, we could do plenty. Sitting at Naples when something pops? Not much. If the Soviets have just been pulling our chain—if they have airborne ready to go or if they're willing to chance a quick flight through Yugoslavian airspace, and if it's Albania they're after, they might have it wrapped.''

"Keep going,'' said Geinz.

"They'd try to make it look like an internal grab. The Albanians' only chance would be to ask us for help fast enough. One second after the first IL-76 heading west lugs its paratroops over the Yugoslav border.''

"What are the chances of that?''

"Well, the Albanians might be hating our guts a little less than the Russians'.''

"Tell me the picture if we go in time.''

"We could put in precision air support. Standing right off the coast, we're there first. Our planes would have plenty of loitering time. Nobody on the ground could stand up to what we could lay in. Shoulder antiair we could handle. And if we had what were supposed to be rebel air units come up against us, they wouldn't reach a thousand feet before we killed them, Admiral.''

"Recommendations, please.''

The answer came a little too quickly. "Do the Albanians a favor. Respond to a request for security a bit before they ask for it themselves. Get to Thunder Station fast, sir.''

"And if Albania screamed because we'd just parked a carrier force off its coast?''

"Better to mill in diplomatic shoving matches ten miles off the Albanian coast than sitting in the Bay at Naples. Without us there from git-go as a trip wire to more trouble than the Soviets would tolerate, it's over. Remember, if the Russians don't succeed in the first day or so with infiltrated people, they'd order up one of their own famous requests for intervention from revolutionaries. By the time we got there from Naples we couldn't help out the government without hitting Soviet units. End of game."

"Would they meet our air with theirs?"

"More likely it would be like Korea. The Reds kept the international lid on by holding the MiGs pretty much on their side of the border."

"So we'd have control of the air if we had to beat up ground targets. Their airborne couldn't come in."

Others jumped in.

"But we're helpless the way we are."

"There's no meaningful projectable power."

"We're spectators."

"Without the Sixth we have no teeth in the Med—"

"Okay, okay," said Geinz, working hard to keep his mind open. "What else do you want to say?"

As expected, Brown, the bristly Marine general, spoke first. "Summing up, stopping at Naples for mechanical Band-Aids and beauty rest out of concern for the General Secretary's feelings is just so much bull. Screw pretending we're just there for repairs. I'd bring the *King* straight into the Adriatic, damage and all."

The deputy chief followed the blocking. "Right. I'd get the *King* and what Pacific carriers we can muster headed full steam for Thunder Station. Even if the others couldn't get there in time, it'd tell Red Square that we've got our eye on them here and they'd better watch themselves." At this point the general sensed that he had said too much, and amended, "Of course, we just execute the policies, and the rest doesn't concern us." Even with care he was only a half inch from naked sarcasm.

"You're damned right that's all we do, and all we'll keep doing," said Geinz coldly. "This isn't Argentina yet. Whether or not you voted for this particular President and Congress, they've got the best shot at peace since some ass let Hitler out of the clink. And if it puts every man in this room out of business someday, I'm going to cheer myself silly while I'm headed for the unemployment line."

This produced the longest silence yet.

"'The President could handle this on the phone right through to the top," Air Force said at last.

"There have been several short conversations," Geinz admitted. "With Gavenko, mostly. Nothing to get our teeth into."

"What's the thinking, sir?"

"Our medical people suspect that the complication they described will have caused some serious . . . intellectual problems."

"'That's wonderful, Admiral," sighed Army. "We're afraid to offend a man who may be mentally incompetent, while his armed forces might be getting ready to eat the Med on us. What about the Foreign Minister?"

"He assures us that the General Secretary remains in full command of his country. And that it would look extremely bad to the Soviet people if we took the occasion of his illness to move our forces in an unusual and truculent manner. He was far from happy that even the *King* was in the sea we had worked so hard to demilitarize. And he pointed out how carefully they were keeping their own forces out of that pond. We had to make him see that our visit had to do with the emergency repairs and rest for the crew, although he probably knows better. And now you know as much as I do."

Marines forgot manners and slapped two shrapnel-scarred fists down loudly onto the polished table. "Suppose that poor son of a bitch dies?"

"We'd need the strongest confirm, sir," said NI, miffed at the amateur postulations of General Brown.

"Well, General Brown, then I think we'd be heading for Thunder Station," said Geinz.

Plesetsk, U.S.S.R.—May 31

Major Fyodor Leshko's ears were so unused to noise that the clatter of the four sentries leaping to attention grated on him. It seemed ludicrous that such splendid-looking soldiers had to snap up like that for the likes of him.

He was a stooped little man, although still young, whose posture and expression always seemed to be that of someone peering into an oven at a burned roast.

"You should have chairs," he told the sentries for probably the hundredth time.

"It is forbidden, Comrade Major," came the standard answer.

KGB stiffbacks, Leshko thought.

The soldier in the sealed box in the rocks above rolled back the vast, blast-proof doors. Leshko smiled inwardly at the conceit that doors could contain what lay in this long cave. The doors protected only against a mishap with the triggers. And there never would be anything wrong there, because he was in charge of those.

As the steel rolled shut behind him, he began his long daily walk, the only exercise he ever took, down the length of the man-made cavern.

Even though it was late spring, the temperature outside still fell below freezing at night. Uncomfortable, but a long way from the seventy-two degrees below zero recorded outside during the last winter.

Not that Leshko had an interest in the weather in the upper world, or anything else out there. He had never taken the twenty-five-mile flight or personnel-carrier trip to the missile test center at Plesetsk, even though it held the only women between here and the Arctic Circle. And not since his first months had he cared to watch the few lumbering cargo planes as they bumped down in the eerily colorless northern sunlight onto the long metal runway floating on the permafrost.

Leshko had no need for sex, no need for friends or family, no need for television, nature, music, or books beyond his beloved technical manuals.

He had his weapons. Nuclear weapons. Of every sort. A quarter mile of them lining both sides of his cave, and many of the galleries that led off it. Every ship of the Northern

Fleet, every plane of the Northern Command had at one time or another carried some of his precious children.

He wasn't in charge, to be sure. The general lived in a fine house on a scenic bend of the ice-choked Dvina at a distance well beyond the danger of most small accidents. But Fyodor Leshko was the man who truly commanded. He had no politics, no patriotism, no knowledge of world affairs, no military training that he still remembered. By keeping so many things out of his life, he was able to husband all his concentration for all things nuclear.

Leshko walked between the lines of railway tracks that ran the cavern's length. They were a standard gauge. Nothing huge and intercontinental went through here. His children were the stuff that men delivered from cockpits, howitzers, and torpedo tubes. But that they were even weapons was not important.

What counted was the crisp, beautiful physics of the atom, and how its slumbering furies could be first wakened with a series of simplicities an intelligent blacksmith might contrive with a little instruction. He foresaw a world where simplifiers like himself would supply all the power needs of all the nations with safely harnessed nuclear forces.

Major Leshko would study the designs of the Soviet civilian reactors and groan. Chernobyl was the indictment not of nuclear energy but of a system that put loving innovators like himself into the weapons complex, and idiots like the civilian engineers into the peaceful generation of power. He was certain they would blow up more people with their ponderous designs than he ever would with his efficient beauties.

It amazed him that so few people chose to wander about his dimly lighted netherworld. And those who did were smothered in sweltering white anticontamination suits, no matter how safe the location.

His uniform was always stained, always shabby. To him it might as well have been coveralls. He was not ungrateful to the military for having given him what opportunities he had to develop his gifts of physics. But he always let the high officers see that their relationship with him was of the most accidental sort. They were a rich uncle upon whom a talented orphan had been thrust. They fed him and promoted him in return for services about the house.

He turned off into a chamber where triggers were worked upon. It was his favorite place. It was where the keys were put into locks beyond which lay the elemental fire. As usual he had to force himself to zip into an anticontamination suit. There was no question that the room was too hot to stay in unprotected for long. While there was nothing individually dangerous lying about and everything was sensibly shielded with his own sensible designs, the accumulated years of polonium and the like passing through had built up an ugly little background. If it had not been for a device sewn into the breast of the protective suit to show sensors that protection was being worn, there certainly would be alarms ringing and flashing.

But the truth was that emotionally he didn't fear these forces at all. He didn't think of them as passing through flesh and slicing into his cells with a billion tiny knives. Instead, as he sat down to some new designs, he felt mystically that the pulverizing rays might be just a way of becoming one with a greater universe.

Major Leshko deplored inflicting pain upon flesh. But mixing flesh with a sublime higher energy? That was much different.

What possibly could be wrong with that?

He fiddled happily with one of his triggers.

U.S.S. *Ernest J. King*, the Eastern Mediterranean— May 31

As head of S-4, McGregor might well have been the only man on the ship who, sooner or later, got to see every man, and learned to associate a face with a name. He was able to greet by name an enormous number of the men who filed by the disbursement slots. Even the pale, seldom-seen druids who spent their lives in "the crypt," the sacrosanct confinements where the volcanic forces of the nuclear reactors were tended, got his accurate greeting.

When McGregor spotted the jolly gray eminence of Commander Ralph Hatten making his way through the lines from the far side of the area, he remembered the forgotten envelope. It wouldn't do to have his boss catch him with his communications down.

Although Hatten wouldn't have known a strategic sortie from a wastebasket, he was the most important man on the ship after the admiral and the air boss. As head of the *King*'s Supply Department, he supervised the procurement, stowage, and issue of virtually all the stores and equipment of the gigantic ship. Every egg, chop, bandage, shackle, spoon, engine, or dollar that came aboard came through him. His department paid the bills, paid the crew through McGregor's division, ran the messes and ran what alone would have been one of the thousand or so largest corporations in the United States.

The message that McGregor read caused him to give a little involuntary whistle. It was damned lucky he had found it. Otherwise there would have been the little matter of thirty-five million dollars falling through the cracks.

Meanwhile, there wasn't a man in line who knew Ralph Hatten who didn't know why he was rushing down for his money.

The last hours after a long cruise were an interminable agony for the sailors. Channel fever, they called it. All their pent-up desire for comfort, mobility, and privacy burst free and nerves frayed. Not the least of the frustrations on a ship so huge was the certain knowledge of delay in getting off. The vicissitudes of rotating liberties in an uncertain environment meant hesitations and revisions. And the slow shuttling of the contracted liberty boats, coupled with the arcana of the quarterdeck, meant precious hours lost from a time off already certain to be short.

And then there would be the crush of thousands ashore, from the *King* and its escorts, battling for the best places in the restaurants, the best women, the best accommodations.

It was in avoiding all this that Commander Hatten had attained a certain legendary status. He easily outshone the flood of fellow officers who had given all their genius to jumping ship early. Hatten's arrangements were so artfully done, his guile so seamlessly hidden, that no power could keep him aboard once the ship came within three hundred miles of a liberty port. Like a chess master setting up a final assault a dozen moves ahead, he was unstoppable.

Hatten cut behind the barrier of disbursing windows and punched McGregor's shoulder playfully. He was in dress blues and fine humor, his several chins and fine gut wobbling in anticipation of magnificent pasta-heaped platters at a table overlooking the bay. "Hi, Wade. Stealing much?" he said with a twinkle. "Sorry to jump in, but would you believe that the Wops have lost four whole boxcars in the rail yards? Might have let it go, but one of them's got fresh barrier nets. You know, Wade, when you have a hundred twenty tons of energy to soak up, you've got to be sure. People could get hurt. And those boxcars could be anywhere between here and Milan. I've gotta take care of finding 'em myself."

"You don't mean you're leaving early?" McGregor said, trying, with difficulty, to keep his face straight.

"Yeah," Hatten said, every bit as serious, as though he didn't know the exact rails upon which the cars sat. "Damned lucky I had a C-2 come on board with a load of boiler chemicals. I can catch the hop back to Naples if I hurry."

"So you want to grab your money now, right, Ralph?"

"That would be great, Wade."

Ledges had overheard and got a clerk to handle it. "Sounds like you're going to be lucky to spend any of this, with all you've got to do."

"Guess you're right. Maddening. And after I sent them a

new computerized system to work the train routings. Maybe I should've put it in Italian.''

"Yeah. Maybe then you wouldn't have had to be rushing away," said McGregor. "Hurry it up, Chief."

While Ledges worked, Hatten pulled McGregor out of earshot of the men at the table. "You're on top of the group payroll thing, aren't you, Wade?"

As though he had not read the message in his pocket only two minutes ago, McGregor grinned with assurance. "C'mon, Commander. Thirty-five million bucks is something that doesn't slip your mind. It's bad enough having our own six thousand swabbies looking for their bucks like hungry hyenas. But having the whole battle group coming after me with empty pockets is something I don't like to think about."

"It's a pain in the ass, I know. What a crappy deal they've pulled off here. Having one ship take on cash for a whole group is ten miles outside of procedure and they know it. We get all the responsibility, paperwork, and shuttling, and all they have to do is show up with their hands out."

"Well, a potential Condition Three makes for a lot of changes."

"Sure. But they're hiding behind the alert. They love it. This is the last time they get away with something like this. Count on that."

Ledges brought the money from the cashed check, and Hatten took it with a grin. "Okay, Wade. With this in my pocket you'll have room for that thirty-five million in the vault. Wish I could be more help, but I've got to keep after the Wops. I left a bunch of signatures for you to put under what you want. You'll handle it okay."

"I'll try not to drop the money overboard, sir."

"Sure appreciate all the extra effort, Wade. Follow me up on the roof. I've got a couple bottles of Rémy in the C-2 that I'd like you and your main guys to have to make the day go fast. Do you good to get a little air after being caught down here all morning."

Hatten had missed the fine ruddiness McGregor had picked up sitting in the open. "Yes, sir. It would be nice to take a breather."

Ledges heard this and rolled his eyes at McGregor as his boss followed Hatten topside.

When they stepped onto the flight deck, McGregor remembered that this was the last place on earth anyone wanted to come for air. Even with only the C-2 and a couple of F-14s spooling up, the air reeked with kerosene. His nose twitched and his eyes watered as they made their way across the scarred and oily nonskid coating of the deck. A line of sailors making an FOD walkdown—the never-ending sweeps for foreign objects that might be sucked devastatingly into the engine intakes of a jet—had eyes the color of automobile taillights.

The C-2A Greyhound, a blocky, prop-powered workhorse, was a twin-engine high-wing transport that could be handled off carriers, and so did much of the drudge work of the fleet.

This one had landed less than an hour ago on the angled deck, unloaded, refueled, and was now being pushed into the number-four catapult for launch.

Number four was the outboard waist cat. While the plane would shoot over the lip of the angled deck rather than the main, the slot aligned with the ship's centerline to take the most advantage of the speed into the wind. That wind continued dead on the bow, meaning no change of heading was necessary.

An SH-3 Sea King helicopter rose from somewhere at the bow for plane guard rescue duty. This copter was always the first aircraft off and the last back aboard in any air operation. The Navy kept these and "Texacos," KA-6 tankers, in the air at great expense during flight operations to protect its pilots to the utmost.

The green helmets and jerseys of the catapult crew swarmed about hooking up the C-2. The catapult officer, identifiable by a yellow jersey, drove them hard.

McGregor knew only the rudiments of a launch, but could appreciate the miraculous technical ballet that shot huge airplanes into the sky in seconds from impossibly constricted spaces.

A green shirt standing to the left of the C-2 held up a board with the number 46,000 on it. This told the pilot that the takeoff weight for this short flight was 46,000 pounds with crew, fuel, cargo, and passenger. The blast of steam that would be set into the launch valve to hammer this airplane forward at 150 miles an hour would be predicated on this critical number.

A hookup man waddled under the plane and hooked the launching bar on the plane's nose gear into the catapult shuttle. The shuttle's visibility above the deck was confined to the catapult hook rising out of the 312-foot catapult slot. McGregor knew vaguely that beneath the flight deck, as part of a dizzyingly complicated and powerful mechanism, ran an eight-wheeled trolley on a track. The plane, attached to that trolley, rode a giant double-barrel piston driven by a shattering blast of high-pressure steam. For all the brutishness of the operation of blasting tons of warplane into the sky, it was also a matter of extreme delicacy.

If all the power available was thrown into the hurtling of the trolley, a small building might be thrown a good part of a mile. Or an airframe might be torn to bits like a rag. And if insufficient steam powered the shot, the plane's racing engines could not possibly build takeoff momentum on the three hundred feet of deck before the lip. A "cold cat" meant an airplane in the water.

The hookup man now checked the hold-back bar. This led from the nose gear to a slot in the cat track. A mighty dumbbell-shaped bolt held the plane back until the cat hook exerted a precisely preset pull. This would break the bolt, sending the plane rocketing.

McGregor wondered how many men had gone into the drink while the technicians were working out these mind-boggling complexities. Hatten scrambled up the ladder into the plane, motioning for McGregor to follow along.

Inside, McGregor found Hatten gathering up fine pieces of soft luggage that had been loaded aboard for him. The co-pilot, entering the cockpit, pointed the commander to a seat up forward. Seeing that the portly officer was having trouble dragging his bags up the narrow passageway between tied-down cargo, McGregor crouched down and moved through to give him a hand. As he squeezed along, tugging at the luggage, he thought to himself that the C-2 was an awfully tough airplane to get in and out of.

"I can smell the tortellini already, Wade," Hatten chortled as he strapped in. Before he pressed the last bag into a stowage net, he zipped open a compartment and pulled out a boxed bottle of Rémy Martin. "This search is going to chew up a lot of travel money. You'll be able to grease my slip through real fast, won't you?"

"You bet, sir. Thanks for the drinks."

Grinning, they snapped unnecessary salutes.

Back on the deck, McGregor retreated to a safe distance at the edge to watch the launch.

The cat officer waved a green wand in his right hand horizontally, telling the pilot to advance throttles. McGregor could see the hallowed Father, Son, Holy Ghost testing of the controls—moving the stick left, right, forward, backward. The left and right rudder pedals made the amen.

The green wand moved up and down. The throttles went all the way forward. The plane strained against the hold-back.

The hookup man slid underneath for a last check and gave a thumbs-up as he scrambled out. The air boss knew the plane was ready to be flung. The men inside would be tensing their necks against the coming jolt.

A light on the island went from yellow to green.

Facing the bow, the cat officer knelt and touched the deck with the green wand. On a catwalk at the deck edge, a green-shirt pushed the red rectangle of the "fire" button on his instrument panel.

The blast of steam from Cat-4 seemed a full-fledged thunderclap to McGregor, but the V Division, veterans of ten thousand takeoffs, instantly heard an untrue note in the symphony of force.

"*Cold shot*," somebody next to McGregor bellowed.

The C-2 shot for the lip, and now even McGregor could tell that the crisp final hammer of the catapult had not come.

Deck men were already signaling to the plane guard copter when the C-2 cleared the lip.

In the slow motion of all terrible events, the crew saw and heard the evidences of the pilot applying all the reflexive perfection of his superb training.

The gear snapped up. With no more than sixty feet between the uncaring sea and his mushing, careening air-craft, he went against every nerve and instinct to push the wheel forward to gain the critical knot of speed that might keep him aloft. He didn't get it.

Ground effect, the small, whirling cushion of air between the descending aircraft and the water, held the nose out of the reaching sea for a few ragged seconds. Then the right wing dropped and caught a wave far ahead. The C-2 lurched, buried its cockpit in a flight-deck-high plume of spray and cartwheeled.

"Plane in the water! Plane in the water!"

The *King*'s giant horn thundered five short blasts while the helmsman threw hard starboard rudder to try to avoid the fallen bird.

The Sea King tilted on its rotor and wheeled to come in over the wreck.

Frozen at the edge of the flight deck, McGregor watched. He had seen birds in the water before. Everybody who served on a carrier had. What chilled him most was the cold capriciousness of the ocean.

At times a shattering impact resulted in nothing more than a plane floating upright and a dry, embarrassed pilot stand-ing in an open cockpit waiting for the sling. But at other times the plane slid beneath the swells without ever again showing so much as a rudder tip to the sky.

Once he had seen such a sinker reemerge for a second after a full minute. There had been just time enough for the pilot to flop out from under the canopy, an unwanted morsel spit back by a thoughtless universe.

But these souls, McGregor could see, the sea would

keep. The C-2 had no ejection mechanism to save the pilots, and the doors would be buckled.

The plane floated on its back, beginning to sink by the nose as it fell back into the carrier's churning wash.

Beautifully flown, the Sea King seemed to screech to a stop above the hulk. A crewman crouched in the door ready to jump, his yellow life vest a small splash of hope in the awful scene. In the best position to scan the water for emerging swimmers, he would remain in place until he spotted something. The copter could move to a survivor a lot faster than he could swim there.

Nothing appeared.

Astern of the carrier now in the broad, milky band kicked up by the screws, the C-2 stood on its nose and slid under.

McGregor had a vision of Hatten, an unflappable and single-minded man, sitting in his immaculate blues in the cold, dark water and cursing the ruin of his neat liberty scheme and the lack of a good restaurant at the bottom of the sea.

The Trawler *Vinza*, the Western Mediterranean— May 31

Since the North Atlantic there had been another ship that had been a constant part of the *King*'s battle group. But it was not in the service of the United States.

The Soviet AGI trawler *Vinza* was a trawler only in the sense that it followed the hull design of the commercial workhorse in order to obtain its good sea-keeping qualities. Such qualities were of premium importance because the ships were often on assigned stations for many months, refueling and reprovisioning at sea from various mother ships. At well under two hundred feet and displacing only 720 tons, the battle with ocean swells and storms was as unending as the tedious duty.

The crash of Commander Hatten's C-2 was only one of several thousand separate events noted and photographed by the *Vinza* since she had sailed from Severomorsk in the far north four months earlier. Her AGI rating identified her as an auxiliary vessel dedicated to the gathering of intelligence, for which she was extremely well suited.

No harvester of fish would ever have been found at sea with the massive overload of electronic gear that shot up and draped down from every part of her. At the stern there was a disc-cone omnidirectional receiving antenna. Above it was a radar receiver of remarkable power, and just above that a massive direction-finding loop. Strung between the masts was a folded dipole for high-frequency reception. Up from the pilothouse grew vertical-rod antennas. On the forward mast hung a directional-finding loop with an earth plane.

As captain of the *Vinza*, Yuri Tiomkin enjoyed no great career in the Soviet Navy. But he sailed closer to the bristling United States warships than any of the grander units of the Red fleet and had a chance to show his skill, courage, and bravado a dozen times a week.

During the launching and recovery of aircraft, as well as in other complex operations, he would interpose his tiny craft in ways that often put it in mortal danger of being ridden under or sliced to bits by some American behemoth. His mission was not so much to interfere with the operations—although that had been frequently his assignment—as to record it. The Soviet Navy had estimated that the efforts of trawlers like his in photographing United States carrier operations had cut as much as six years off the learning curve for their own budding big-deck carriers.

The work of these little beavers had proved so important that there were now much longer and heavier craft, built for intelligence from the keel up. When this mission had become as important as it had, there had been a thought to replace the *Vinza* with one of these bigger ships midway through. But that was the sort of indication that something had changed that no one wanted. So Captain Lieutenant

Tiomkin had continued his business. He and his tiny ship were well up to it.

The Americans had certainly noticed the more or less regular appearance of a Bear-D passing overhead, a sure sign of a radio link for passing information that couldn't wait for processing upon the trawler's return to port. What they didn't know for sure was that the appendage to the *Vinza*'s deckhouse contained a satellite communications antenna that tied the ship to a whirling messenger in space that could carry any truly important information home in an instant.

It was by means of this device that the fall of Commander Hatten's bird was relayed to Soviet Naval Intelligence and from there to Admiral Sarkissian. Captain Lieutenant Tiomkin had found it hard not to maneuver for a better photographic angle of the impending crash, but that would have been very bad if noticed.

The *Vinza* was following close enough to have become involved in the rescue efforts. For a moment Tiomkin found himself better positioned to help than the Americans themselves. He wondered what he would have done if some of the American crew had popped free of the sunken plane within his reach. It would have been the worst manners to run them down. And machine-gunning them would have been absolutely out. Perhaps the men in a rescuing rubber raft could have reached them before the men from the helicopter and discreetly held their heads under.

When he was sure there were no survivors, he retired below. The standing orders were clear. Stay glued to the *King* as though on a towline. Clock her speed, notice her handling, even though he had given up hope of these deteriorating any more. Somebody had not done his job quite well enough. But he certainly wasn't going to fail in his.

The Rémy Martin worked its way through McGregor, Ledges, and Lydecker, unable to drive away thoughts of a lost shipmate.

The three men were sitting in McGregor's compartment.

The presence of enlisted men in an officer's quarters was something not done in the spit-and-polish Navy, but McGregor had abandoned that sector long ago. At 2000 hours the squawk box popped and a bugle played taps. The disembodied voice, more somber than usual, spoke the words that the whole battle group was hearing from other voices at the same moment. *"Taps, taps. Lights out. All hands turn in to your bunks and keep silence about the decks. Smoking lamp is out in all living spaces."* A bosun's pipe shrilled and the crackling stopped.

The S-4s didn't ordinarily stand the same kind of house-keeping watches as the men who ran and fought the ship. Hidden away, the day's work done, they weren't much different from any nine-to-fivers ashore. They sipped their glasses—a violation of a serious sort—burned their lights, smoked their cigars, and kept the last day of Ralph Hatten's life going for a while longer.

Ledges, sprawled on his bunk in skivvies, waved his glass.

"Bon voyage, Ralph. Hope you saved a bottle for yourself."

"At least he wasn't married," McGregor said, oscillating slowly in a swivel chair.

"Think he was a fag?" Lydecker asked.

"Naw," Ledges said. "Or he would've requisitioned a gay bar for the ship. He liked his conveniences."

Lydecker stretched out on the deck. "Guess he won't even have a tombstone."

"What would you put on it?" said McGregor. "'Here lies a man who wasted his life spending a billion dollars running a three-billion-dollar warship that never shot at anybody'?"

"That reads a lot better than ours would," Ledges said.

"What would that be?" asked Lydecker.

"'They spent their lives paying out money for the spread of clap over five continents.'"

"You old guys got no reason to knock on the Navy. You're getting a good buck, and you've got damn good pensions coming."

Ledges and McGregor stared at the boy to make sure he wasn't kidding before they groaned together.

"Kids three days out of Stanford Business School make an admiral's pension these days, knothead," said McGregor. "What the chief and I are going to get wouldn't put us in a good trailer park. I hope my wife's been lining up a boyfriend with a good job. She's going to need him."

Ledges knew of McGregor's troubles and let it drop. Lydecker pressed on.

"I'm getting a bit over six hundred a month, Commander. And I'm never gonna stay in long enough to get much more. I can't sit still long enough to do a real job anywhere. Even if I want to stay in, they'll finally eight-ball me out and I won't have enough to buy a chick a pizza. Shit, I might need the pizza myself."

"Twenty-one years old ain't the time to worry about your pension, kid."

"Can't help it. Way down deep I'm a worrier. Maybe that's what makes the rest of me so wacky. Trying not to care about anything. I remember when I was ten and I was shooting the greatest wave you ever saw. Beautiful sunshine, sparkly water, dynamite ride. And I'm thinking, what if Mom's gone when I get home? For good. And I'm walking through the streets barefoot in the winter, with nothing but my wet suit and my Hobie board."

"Lighten up, Hink," Ledges laughed. "Winter was never that bad in Malibu."

McGregor was frowning now. "Looks like we're going to have to break in a new department head."

"Yeah," Ledges said. "I was thinking about that. Hatten was a damned good boss. He put up with a lot of shit from this operation and still left us alone, as long as we did the job."

McGregor nodded. "He was smart enough to treat us like what we are—civilians."

"Hey, hey, hey," said Lydecker. "Where's all the Navy blue?"

"The only thing blue in this part of the Navy is the ink. Think it'll be somebody off the ship, Commander?"

"No. Too big a job. A plum. You run a supply department on a flattop for a couple years and you've got a senior vice-presidency waiting for you somewhere on the outside."

"Got any guesses?"

"Royce off the *Long Beach*? Holcomb, the number two in the department on the *Nimitz*? But they're up for pension. I think it'll be some young hotshot who they want to keep inside for a while."

"Bet they've got those personnel tapes spinning."

"It won't be a big search," McGregor said. "There's probably not more than one guy with just the right mix. And Navy ambition being what it is, I bet that guy knows exactly where he's going already—right here onto Big Ernie."

"This has been an almighty shitty day," said Ledges.

"But probably twice as good as tomorrow," said McGregor.

Outside Tirana, Albania—June 1

A parachute caught in the trees, especially trees far back into a large apple orchard and well back from the only appreciable road, would not have been a matter of deadly concern in most countries. But Albania was not most countries. Here the wasps of the government were the ultimate terror. In a nation whose achievements otherwise placed it in the Stone Age of national accomplishment, the police and spy apparatus were the equal of any other in the world.

It was for this reason that the sweating, swearing crew of men in farm clothes who had jolted out to the chute in a clattering truck slashed away so eagerly at the shrouds. Most of them used the saw-toothed boot knives issued to certain units of the Soviet *Spetsnaz* special service forces.

Ali Mahmoud drove his government Zaporozhet straight

through a gap in the fence rails and headed down the tree rows to lend a hand. His old and tiny automobile was desperately ill-suited to the terrain. Its chancy suspension would almost certainly be ruined. But in his clutching anxiety he was not inclined to treasure his special privileges as he usually did. Droplets of sweat gathered on his bald head and found gaps in the tattered sweatband of his hat, running all the way down into his big brush of a mustache. He could feel his heart pumping where his broad gut was wedged against the bottom of the sawing steering wheel.

As was his lifelong habit as a member of Albania's volatile Turkish minority, Ali Mahmoud roared at people who couldn't possibly hear him: "Idiots . . . imbeciles . . . asses—"

Through the windshield ahead he could see among the working men the blunt figure of Colonel Bartsev. He would have much to say to the colonel.

It only now occurred to Mahmoud that his impulsive swerve might have fatal consequences. With the heightened senses of the suddenly terrified, his vision shot into focus on a man behind the truckbed. He saw enough of the stubby little RPG-7 rocket launcher to be sure that it was now leveled at his jouncing radiator. He was seconds from extinction.

Bartsev turned around at the sound of the car and seemed to grin his recognition. But he neglected to inform the aiming man that it was time to desist.

The raging spirit that had enabled Mahmoud as a fifteen-year-old to kill fierce German SS troops by the dozen surged up in him. He tramped on the gas and tried to get more acceleration out of the gears. He would lay tire tracks right up their red-painted asses.

The spinning of the rear wheels and the further softening of the ground ahead just slowed the car further. The grenadier stepped aside with a mock bow as the car slewed sideways and stalled near the truck.

By the time the gasping Mahmoud unwedged himself from behind the wheel, the men had a half-dozen large aluminum canisters loaded onto the truckbed. Other men were in the trees cutting free the last of the chute.

"You're a bastard, Colonel Bartsev," shouted Mahmoud, slow to retrieve his sense of humor. His volume indicated that he was among friends for a considerable distance.

The colonel, a jolly blond man with the physique of a scaled-down sumo wrestler, hopped onto the truck. Inspecting the interior of a canister that had broken open in the landing, he said, "The sergeant was playing. Do you think we're so blind and deaf that we can't recognize that broken-down car of yours from three miles off?"

"You were blind enough to leave a parachute hanging in the trees with the sun well up. And deaf enough not to hear the plane that dropped it."

"If we hadn't made the mistake of putting some Albanian cretin in charge of our communications, we'd have known it was coming, wouldn't we?"

"You squealed like a stuck pig to have this shipment delivered fast. We got the word through. Your people botched the details."

Bartsev was reassured by what he found in the big, black corrugated cylinder. "All right, Mahmoud. You did well enough. This thing could live or die on a big mine in the right place. Knowing these beauties are around can slow up a column of tanks better than a whole platoon of men with rocket launchers."

The last of the chute joined the canisters in the truck. Bartsev extended a hand and strained to drag the portly Albanian into the truck with him. The others scrambled up in back, only one remaining behind to bring along the car.

Both the colonel and the Albanian liked dangerous, demanding work. In the brutal requirements of this operation they had found a happiness that had been missing from their lives for years.

Mahmoud had never rediscovered until now the joy he had known ambushing retreating German columns in the closing days of the Hitler war. Bartsev had been fuming for three years while the surgeons tried to satisfactorily restore the femur of his left leg. It would never be what it had been before a special *muahedin* bullet, rubbed with poisons gathered from the rebel's own infected wounds, had splintered it. But there were enough surgical pins and tubing to keep him functioning if he could manage to sleep through the pain.

The truck pulled straight into the barn. The mines were rapidly uncased and the canisters added to the several dozen that had been dropped over the previous nights. A wide interior door, ordinarily concealed by bales of hay, stood open and showed that the stack of weaponry had grown considerably since Mahmoud had visited two weeks before.

"Still no heavy stuff?" Mahmoud asked the colonel.

"Some pretty good sized mortars and bigger antitank rockets. The mines that just came in, when we put them in the right places, will be good enough for the best tanks they have. They're basically wood, and they're not ready to sweep those. But this is not going to be a matter of outmuscling anyone. It's all surprise. All preparation. All ruthlessness. If you haven't done your job as well as we've done ours, that government of yours is liable to resurrect the old national art of impaling, just for us."

"It's good for constipation, I hear."

"But terrible for hemorrhoids. What have you done for us?"

"As I told you from the first, all the main people of the government oppose us. They have all the power and privileges in this sad place. They believe in their leadership to the death. They'll never help, or even pretend to. They'll be of no use as figureheads. Make sure they die on the spot. No prisoners."

"You set them up the way we've planned and you can order the shovels now."

Mahmoud grunted his satisfaction. "At my level, I have good success. Many idealists. Many people longing to have their own day. And, of course, many who are just tired of waiting a half day to buy a rotten cabbage."

74 • Donald N. Norman

"Which of those are you, comrade?" asked Bartsev, with just a hint of mockery.

"I am the most reliable of them all. First, because I am about to smell some powder and kill some vicious and unpleasant bores—something I have missed since 1945. And next because I actually believe that you have deposited those one million beautiful, stable Japanese yen in the FOCO Bank in Zurich as you promised. And I do so want to take my poor arthritic wife and sit in the Algarve sun eating fresh fruit for the next thirty years."

Bartsev laughed. "If you can't trust such a man, you can't trust anybody. Any more luck with the army?"

"Still only one dependable unit. But it's well placed and well led. Don't worry, when the time comes you'll be well supported."

Naples, Italy—June 5

Centuries of unthinking building and sulfurous pollution had been powerless to diminish the beauty of the stunning blue sweep that was the Bay of Naples.

Commander Richard Manning hugged his thick briefcase to his chest and peered down at the bright bay and his new ship through the tilting window of the Sea King.

His generally handsome face had been pulled perhaps an inch too long by the sculptor, making his eyes appear just a bit too wide and startled, his teeth a touch too intrusive, and his mouth unable to quite completely close.

The four-block-long carrier looked like a huge armored beetle under attack by an endless swarm of shuttling ants. The combined commotions of arming, provisioning, repairs, and liberties had the sea around the *Ernest J. King* alive with the curving wakes of small craft heading to or away from the floating island of gray and black.

Manning's was a face devoid of any of the lines that

might have been caused by laughter. For a man who was not an air, submarine, or nuclear officer, his rank of full commander at the age of thirty-six showed that this was someone who had impressed the Navy greatly.

Soon the pilots were chatting with the approach controllers and the Sea King quickly bled off altitude and dropped neatly onto the flight deck near the bow. Manning stepped out while the rotors were still unwinding. A JG in rumpled khakis was there to salute him, looking intimidated by the imposing figure in spotless blues, the commander's three gold stripes new and shiny on the sleeves.

"Lieutenant Junior Grade Sammler, Commander. Welcome aboard. The captain says to come right up. We'll get your stuff later."

"Thanks, Lieutenant. Let's go."

They walked briskly for the island, the lieutenant leading the commander by several steps.

"First carrier duty, sir?" Sammler asked.

"Yes. I've been operating ashore mostly. On the other side of the counter, you might say. I think there won't be many mysteries, though."

"Getting around will be a mystery, sir. A lot of new men draw maps to get to their station. And then that's the only way they know to get there."

"Good tip." Actually, Manning had been busily studying deck plans of the King. He probably knew the ship's layout as well as the skipper did.

A tech rep fell into step a few paces from the commander. He was one of the forty or so outcast civilian technicians who roamed the ship in the employ of various military contractors. "Welcome to the Ernie, sir," he said not quite pleasantly.

Sammler turned to glare at this upstart chiphead, but saw that Manning didn't yet understand that these arrogant, overpaid princes were to be kept at arm's length by real sailormen. The tech-rep quarters were luxurious by Navy standards and the occupants stayed together in a revolting brotherhood founded on wealth, privilege, and comfort while the military fraternity did the heavy lifting. The lieutenant bit his lip and marched on. The commander, showing a mentality more that of a storekeeper than a naval officer, spoke to the civilian cheerfully. "Thanks. Chilly out here, though. When does it really warm up?"

"Pretty soon, Commander. Pretty soon. Listen, I understand you're our new head of supply. I'd sure like to talk to you about equipment availability."

"That can be arranged, I think. What's your name?"

"Tree. Theron Tree."

"Okay. Carry on."

Tree peeled off and young Sammler, fuming at the breakdown of the walls between the sailors and chipheads, ushered Manning into the island and up the ladderwell to the captain's sea cabin. They announced themselves to a Marine, who disappeared for a moment and then returned to admit them.

Captain Arlen Ash was not the highest-ranking officer on the *King*. But he, not Vice-Admiral Irons, commanded the ship.

The captain had a face as sharp as a destroyer's bow and the blood of four generations of seamen pumping through his heart. Quickly he waved Sammler out and Manning to a chair. He was hardly aware of the perfunctory greetings they exchanged before he began. Manning's papers were in his hands, and he ruffled through them as he spoke.

"You're the most important man on this ship for the next few days, Manning. She's exhausted in every way. From fuel to chow to condoms, she's running on dead low. That wouldn't be so bad with the crew in high gear, but they're used up, too. Tired, sloppy, slow. This is a dull tool we have here. I can flog the part that makes knots and makes war. Only you can do the rest. And my part can't run right without your part to ride on."

"Are my division officers competent, sir?"

"I always thought most of them weren't Navy enough, but during what seemed like two hundred and forty straight days of gales off Iceland, they did pretty good. It was Hatten's way to be loose, and I don't know if that helped them or hurt them."

"I'll be looking at it right away, sir."

"There's one other thing, Manning. Something I don't want to get around until you're sure who you're talking to."

Manning edged forward on his chair. "I already know something's on the stove, Captain. But I'd sure like to know more."

Ash started to stiffen, not knowing whether this naked prying into fleet objectives was insolence or the kind of involvement he was looking for in this key officer. He looked into the strong, solemn face, remembered he was second-generation Navy, and decided to let the annoyance go by. "We've got a three-star admiral aboard ready to run an awfully big show. We're cleared for thirty-second weapons release from the Pentagon. But we don't know for sure what the hell it is we might be shooting at, and we don't want to appear belligerent by going Condition Three. Intelligence suspects two things I can tell you. It could be serious and it could be soon. NI's getting closer to an answer."

"I'd sure like to know when we hear, sir."

Again Ash fought back his irritation. Damned grocery store clerks would never learn the difference between their business and Navy business. But he supposed he couldn't expect all the help he needed without Manning's knowing what they were operating against. "If we can get back to the point now, Commander," he growled.

"Excuse me, sir."

"The other thing I started to talk about was, we've been having some . . . I won't use the word. It sticks in my throat. We've been having some damned odd operational accidents."

"Like the one that brought me here?"

"Yes. I've had half the Air Department and the whole Deck and Engineering Department standing on this carpet over the last couple of days. Know what a launch valve is?"

"No, sir."

"You could say it's the most important piece of equipment on the ship. It's what adjusts the charge of steam pressure that blows the planes off the catapults. When it fouls up you've got fifteen million dollars and a lot of dead men in the water. Well, not one of my squadron of experts could tell me exactly what went wrong with that valve for sure. It worked fine the next time they tested it.''

"Maybe somebody set it wrong.''

"The officer on that cat has been doing the job four years. Flawlessly. That kind of experience doesn't make mistakes, Manning.''

"You think it wasn't a mistake, sir?''

"Lieutenant Woodhart had the right numbers to wind in. We know that. The launch valve didn't deliver them, just that one time. Machinery can break. But it doesn't fix itself, as a rule.''

"You're certain it was the valve, Captain?''

"We take pictures of every launch. Play them back after every accident. There was no fault in the hookup and release.''

"You suspect Woodhart?''

"And the six thousand others aboard. Everybody but you, Commander Manning.''

"I'm sure you've taken steps, sir.''

"Not very impressive ones. You see, this ship, which can deal with a couple of dozen planes and missiles coming in at two thousand miles an hour, can't deal with one man who lobs a handful of titanium bolts into the turbine blades. It doesn't do any good to have Marines watch a launch valve because somebody a hundred yards away with a screwdriver can change the internal calibration on a readout so the setting is something cockeyed. And he could switch it back just as easy afterward. The chief master-at-arms and his men are trying hard, but they're trained to take care of race riots and stolen radios, not this.''

"I can help you, sir.''

"How's that?''

"Supply is the only department that gets pretty much all over the ship. My people can spot patterns of activity, groups acting not quite right, people where they shouldn't be. I'll have my men looking sharp, sir. And you can bet I'll get around plenty myself."

"It's a good thought. But what I want you to watch— now hear me—is what comes on this ship. It all comes through you. Thousands of tons. Your imagination is the only limit of what could be hidden. Guns for a mutiny, communications equipment to help an enemy track us, jamming equipment, explosives, poison gas, incendiary material—you name it. The stuff could come on packed in everything from grapefruits to A-7s. I want every package, every crate, every piece of machinery that's been sitting on Italian soil for longer than three minutes taken apart and fine-combed. I've got sixty-five Marines looking for things to do. Have a square painted somewhere in the hangar bay and see that the whole works gets set down there for checking before it gets stowed. If anybody sets foot on the square before the check, have the jarheads shoot him right in the ass."

"Aye, aye, sir. But you don't think anything they could bring aboard in a toilet-paper box could stop a ship like the *King*."

"No, they'd have to sink us for that," said Ash. "But they could still screw us up pretty bad. And they could make us look like asses in front of the dozen countries around this lake who don't think very much of us. We don't have any guns that shoot down public opinion. They let us stay because we keep people they like even less from dropping nasty things on them. If they see we can't do that, we're gone."

"Nobody could afford that, sir. I'll get to work."

"Glad to have you aboard, Commander."

"Glad to be here, sir."

Naples, Italy—June 6

The ability to provide dispensation from the long, slow cash line was a negotiable currency on an aircraft carrier. So Lydecker and Ledges were in the first liberty boat off the ship. The *King* had been stopping in Naples for years before the Sixth left, meaning the sailors knew precisely the moves that would make their four liberty days most productive.

No men in the boat were faster to the waiting line of rickety cabs or more certain of the Italian phrases that ordered their destination.

The cab moved through the cacophonous city at a pace well above what it would be when the liberty parties of the carrier and four frigates hit the beach. The assaultive smells of overspiced cooking and ill-handled wastes filled air torn by car horns, roaring trucks, and conversations carried on in screams.

Both sailors loved Naples for its blast to the senses and spirit that made even its relentless larceny seem a cheerful art of the Mediterranean.

In little more than an hour the cab had moved through the northern suburbs, noisome with utilities flaring off gases, and turned far toward the east into a countryside of farms set between lush volcanic hills. It was to such a farm, larger than the others and more closed off from the long views of the terrain, that the cab finally brought them. Overflowing with accumulated sea pay, they tipped the driver lavishly and told him when they expected him to return, four days hence. As the man waved a happy good-bye, a dusty, toothless figure, bent but undefeated by age, came out of a large barn in a rapid hobble. He cackled laughter until he reached them and embraced their shoulders with crushing strength.

"God bless America and the good captains," he bawled.

Ledges, having foreseen the romantic possibilities of Italian during his younger days in the Med, had invested heavy time in Navy courses and learned a clumsy version of the language. His command of the tongue ignored all grammar and niceties, but he navigated fearlessly in an impeccable Iowa accent. With Ledges's shaky tutoring, Lydecker was only half as good.

"Vincenzo, you miserable old ravioli," Ledges cried, planting a loud kiss on the leathery forehead. "You better tell me our yellow *bambino* is holding up as beautifully as Sophia Loren's tits, or we'll have a load of napalm dumped on this desert of a farm."

The old man tapped the side of his head and crossed his eyes. "I am at an age, Mr. Captain Rocky, where I cannot think without something in my hand."

The sailors plunged into their pockets and brought out $260. "The United States Navy pays the rent, Vincenzo," said Lydecker.

"That's almost a year's worth," said Ledges. "In America you'd be a rich man. Everything ready?"

"Hey, Mr. Captain. You call one hour ago. A man whose arms and legs are as stiff as his cock used to be only moves so fast. But I have poured the petrol."

"You check for water in it?"

"It is fine. And the magnetos. Also I have dusted, removed the supports, and put air in the tires. One leaks a bit. Take the pump."

They began to follow his sprightly shuffle into the barn. "What about the strip?" asked Ledges.

"Rolled for eight hundred feet by my own tractor."

"Yeah? How long ago?"

Vincenzo, a man never terribly concerned about time, shrugged. "A month ago. Or maybe three. But there has been little rain. Crops are bad."

Inside the barn their eyes were shut down after the bright sunlight. All around them were the dark hulks of cars and tractors, scavenged for parts to repair several vehicles whose condition seemed not much better than the others.

"The only crop you raise is these junkers, Vincenzo," Ledges said, wedging his way through the derelicts.

"The gentle Lord saw fit to make me a masterful mechanic."

"As long as it doesn't take more than a hammer."

Lydecker reached the back of the barn and unlatched the

big doors. As he rolled back one, Ledges handled the other. Sunlight flooded in, and they turned to look upon the object that would advance the fortunes of their leave.

The airplane they viewed was one of the loveliest, most useful, and most durable ever to fall from the hand of man. It was designated J-3. In the thirties the Piper Aircraft Company had acquired some designs and tools for a low, slow, two-place trainer and knockabout. They scribbled in some inspired changes and began to build a great classic of the air.

If anybody had seen a Piper Cub in any color but yellow during the fifty or so years it had been in the air, he was as rare a bird as the Cub had become. With main production petering out in the forties, the fabric-covered little plane, all 680 pounds of it, had resolutely resisted all the souping up made available through the golden age of the piston engine.

Stronger power plants than the original 65-horsepower Continentals, Lycomings, and Franklins had been tried, but none greatly improved its agonizingly stately performance. Wild-eyed liars wandered into hangars now and then swearing they had seen one with its wooden propeller shredding the air at 90 miles an hour in a windless condition, but they were rightfully laughed to scorn. Those who had known and loved its gentle, forgiving ways for years knew that an old one liked to ease its creaking bones along at 65 or so, and doing it at an altitude much beyond two thousand feet made it tired and cranky.

"Rocky, my man," Lydecker purred, "I wouldn't swap her for anything, even for an F-14."

The young man could not tell the exact vintage of the Cub, which had the name *Carlotta* painted in red on the nose. The plate holding the serial number and other data of interest had dropped off into the maw of time. But from her general state of droop, he guessed her to date from 1940. She had ridden from Newport, Rhode Island, on a stock-broker's yacht in 1948, intended to be fitted with floats and used as a toy for a teenage son while the broker romanced away the summer with an expensive mistress. But the son had found a mistress of his own—the Carlotta whose name was now immortalized in paint. The plane was meanwhile judged too underpowered for floats, and it was left behind as payment to a farmer who had supplied the yacht with fresh vegetables. That farmer was this selfsame Vincenzo, then a young man with a mechanical inclination who thought he might succumb to the call of the sky one day.

In fact, Vincenzo had gotten no farther than buying a flying helmet, rolling a strip down a field behind his barn, and taxiing happily around his property for a couple of hours a month. Although this added precious few hours to the engine time, he maintained the power plant as rigorously as that of a Pan American clipper. The stage was set for the appearance of Petty Officer Third Class Hink Lydecker and Senior Chief Petty Officer Gable Ledges.

On liberty in Naples three years before, the sailors had met old Vincenzo when they had engaged him to repair an ancient Fiat that they had purchased. They had stored it for their idea of beating the liberty crush in the city with forays to the earthier beauties of the outlying towns. As he worked, Vincenzo had confided in them that he was not actually a lowly mechanic, but a man of property whose farm included an American airplane and an airstrip.

The Americans recognized the call of fate. Lydecker's astonishing genius with all forms of locomotion, helped somewhat by an old manual left with the plane, had them lurching into the air in comparatively short order. While he would have destroyed an F-14, he was utterly competent in an ancient Cub. The need to apply for the licenses and learn the rules of the tightly regulated Italian airspaces never seriously concerned him as things that needed doing, and a deal was struck with Vincenzo. They sold the dying Fiat and entered into a long-term lease and storage arrangement for twenty-five dollars per month, arrears payable when the men got liberty.

For this consideration they were free to break Earth's rude bonds and head for the fabled pastoral sirens of Abruzzi, just seventy-five miles to the north. Their aerial canvasses of romantic opportunities during the golden days of the Sixth Fleet in the Med, free of the competition of shipmates and fueled heavily by sea pay, had met outstanding successes. They were off to visit their latest finds.

Lydecker checked the bobbing stick that stood upright in front of *Carlotta*'s windshield. Its bottom was a cork floating in the gasoline tank, the only one-hundred-percent reliable fuel gauge in the history of aviation.

The strip stretching straight out the door and running markedly downhill gave Lydecker the luxury of flying directly out of the barn without regard to the gently prevailing crosswind. He unlatched and let down the long entrance flap on the right side, exposing both tiny tandem seats. The Cub, with its low speeds, could be flown with the flap open, creating the closest thing to the joys of open cockpit flying that could be had in a high-wing monoplane.

Ledges slung their duffels into the enlarged baggage space behind the rear seat. The chief thumped Lydecker's bulky bag with his fist. "Jesus, Hink, don't tell me you got that twenty-pound radio stuffed in that bag. We're gonna end up needing a C-5A to carry our shit."

Lydecker made a rude noise with his lips and climbed into the backseat, which was the pilot's slot in a Cub. "Get in and play stewardess." He pumped the throttle and yelled to Vincenzo, "Okay, you crazy spaghetti burner, earn that fortune we pay you."

Vincenzo pulled the prop through a few times to prime the engine. "Ready, *Signor* Captain."

Lydecker flipped the switch. *"Contacto!"*

The magneto hit perfectly and the engine caught on the Italian's first spin of the prop. In ten seconds the old power plant was running as though it were ready to cross the Atlantic.

Lydecker moved to full throttle, and the old Cub with its marvelous high-lift wing was off the ground in 250 feet, as if it, too, were heading for a long neglected mistress.

It would have been nice to fly the entire trip at housetop height, but since neither Lydecker nor the airplane owned a single official document that might have allowed either of them into the sky in any known nation, the pilot thought it prudent to take the ancient yellow Cub up to two thousand feet. Not that a reading of the fading numbers on the fuselage and high wing would have corresponded to any record left in the world, and not that the low-keyed Italian police in the localities kept much of an eye on the sky, or anything else. It was just that Hink felt that not tempting fate with small things would make it more forgiving in larger matters.

A climb to two thousand feet in a 1940 Cub was not lightly undertaken. The wheezing Continental made altitude at a stately 400 feet per minute. This climb was slower than usual, and somewhat more dubiously trimmed. The considerable weight of Ledges in the front seat was now more than offset by the weight of the package in Lydecker's duffel bag. He had chopped away at the tiny baggage area behind the backseat to allow what they carried to intrude into the fuselage. Not good policy for the loading envelope, he knew, and an invitation to snag a control cable fatally. But it was either that or tow the stuff behind on a rope.

The difficulties with weight and balance were such that Lydecker found the underpowered little plane mushing perilously. Yet he viscerally trusted the J-3 more than any 747. From her spars and frames to her fabric and propeller, she consisted of material made by God. She was all wood, fabric, and iron. He found it in his heart to forgive her for the miserable plexiglass windshield and tiny skylight, the only plastic in her.

Lydecker was devoutly happy that the day was cloudless and that the winds were light and mostly from behind. Also he was glad that Ledges had put on another fifteen pounds during the long Atlantic winter, or no pilot alive would have been able to keep the Cub from tilting backward into a stall and then a spin.

"Is this altimeter busted?" Ledges called backward over the little engine's full-power clattering.

"We're still blowing out the carbon. She'll go up faster," Lydecker lied.

"It's all that crap you got in that bag. I leave behind an extra set of clothes I need so you can bring an anvil."

"Please refer any complaints to the airline office."

When they were at last at altitude, they found themselves looking down at a Giotto landscape. The hills beneath began rapidly to branch and rise as they headed for the opposite coast. The ugly modern buildings became fewer and the roads went from the wide, straight highways around Naples to the meanders of a much older Italy. Smaller, more widely spaced towns began to appear. Time was winding backward beneath them as the light of Italy created its magic.

Lydecker had fastened to his thigh with a rubber band a motorist's map of the area, and he kept his thumb moving along the streams and towns to mark his progress. He had no knowledge of navigation, nor did he have a radio of any sort. It was as though he were embarked on a Sunday drive. It was that casual.

The bobber stick jiggling on the other side of the crackling, yellowing windshield told Lydecker that Vincenzo had filled the tank to the top, and they were operating comfortably off the Cub's tiny twelve-gallon reservoir of fuel. In a no-wind condition they might actually make two hundred miles without gassing up. Not that refueling was any great problem. The forgiving little engine, although designed to burn 80-octane aviation gas, had been adjusted by the canny Vincenzo to function acceptably on the premium product available at any filling station. Some sag in power and an occasional cough were small prices to pay for the convenience.

Well into Abruzzi, the high ridges fell away and they saw a sight that never failed to move them. Far in the distance the midday sun turned the River Pescara into a sinuous silver ribbon. To the east they made out the sprawl of red roofs that was Sulmona. They whooped together, and Lydecker made the small eastward correction that would bring them to the long-sought embraces that would be waiting.

At length a landmark bell tower was spotted and the Cub

dove happily. Lydecker brought his fragile yellow bird around a steeply rising hill, clipped the top of a grove of olive trees, and chopped power. The Cub, with a stalling speed of just 38 miles per hour, even though it did not have a flap of any sort to add lift to the wings when landing, slipped neatly onto a broad cobbled driveway. The plane rolled out 190 feet from touchdown without need of brakes, which did not function in any case. Lydecker had to add power to bring the plane close to the elaborately paneled front door of the large house.

That door quickly banged open and two women rushed forth squealing. It was as true as ever—everybody loves a sailor.

"Hey-y-y, Rocky, you white-a like a cheese from a goats," shouted Rosalia, her schoolgirl English showing much decay.

"Hinky-y-y, *bambino*," purred Concetta. "You come quick to you old mama, huh?"

They were pretty by any measure, already as dark as espresso from spring sunbathing and as cheerful as unending comfort could make them. The sailors knew there was much to be thankful for.

Rosalia pressed a button on the doorjamb and an enormous garage door rose at the end of the house. The Ferrari and the Porsche that it ordinarily sheltered were on the lawn so, as always, there would be a place for the Cub.

Ledges grabbed the tail wheel as soon as he could disengage himself from Rosalia's hug, chatter, and kisses. He heaved the plane around and started to haul it into the garage.

"Hey, Rock, c'mon. Leave it there," said Lydecker. "We didn't come all this way to be valet parkers."

"Concetta likes us to put it out of sight in case the cops or neighbors come poking."

"Is okay, Rocky," said Concetta. "*Molto* rain up here. Nobody open other houses yet. People in town don't give no shit. Crazy Romans, they think. Screw, screw, screw." She laughed loudly enough to confirm that she and Rosalia were already well into the wine, and pulled Lydecker's sweatshirt up over his head with a sudden swoop. As he struggled blindly, she steered and shoved him through the front door and motioned for Ledges and Rosalia to follow. "But they no like us-a do it on-a drive-a-way."

And so the holiday began.

Much later Rocky Ledges didn't have the strength even to force his eyes open. The gallon of red wine that Rosalia had poured into him had metamorphosed into a seething cosmic glue that oozed into every part of him.

The wet spot felt by his hip on the mattress, and Rosalia's coolly damp skin against his shoulder, told him that the evening's main work had been accomplished some time ago. The sweet musk of her brought gently wonderful stirrings.

Tree frogs rioting outside a wide-flung window gave assurances that it was still deep night. He had a brief, shimmering sense that another rhythm had come in behind the frog chorus. It pulsed, became quicker and higher pitched until it achieved the sound of a small airplane, its power unevenly applied. Ledges had just begun to ruminate on this when snoring oblivion overtook him.

Monaco—June 7

A certain Monsieur d'Alembert, an estimable French mathematician who last drew breath in the eighteenth century, would surely have been shocked at the number of people who had been bankrupted in his name over the years since his death. Indeed, he had tried to prevent such ruin by being the first to point out the fallacy in what was once called the "Law of Equilibrium." In a paper called the *"Traité de Dynamique,"* he wrote to the effect that all doubling-up systems in gambling—even ignoring the casinos' freedom to arbitrarily limit the size of bets—were doomed to failure in "a brief array of events limited by the mind and time of man." It seems obvious that this would include a dozen spins of a roulette wheel. Yet, perversely, the good man has been charged with responsibility for the various "d'Alembert systems" that have served their users so poorly.

Now, in the casino at Monte Carlo, one of those users had recently abandoned the slow, steady losses of one of these systems in an attempt to reestablish himself, although the damage was already irreversible. Not that so much as a line of concern creased his brow or diminished his blissful smile as an endless succession of *en plein, cheval, transversale, carré, sixaine, colonne,* and *douzaine* bets went cruelly against him. His day had been too marvelous in every other way.

From the moment he had strolled through the sublime Monaco twilight, his rented evening clothes frayed, shiny, and impossibly ill-fitting, accompanied by a beautiful woman, he had known this would be the day of his life. Tripping lightly up the shallow steps of the fabled building, he had been certain it was beyond the powers of anything that happened at the roulette wheel to spoil this golden moment. The graceful twin towers of the old Winter Casino stood above the soaring palms like two guardian angels of his happiness.

He had never thought for one moment to play in the large room for tourists, contemptuously called the Kitchen, as he knew from his reading. Instead he had gone through to the *Salles Privées,* the suites where roulette, chemin de fer, trente et quarante, craps, and baccarat were played, and where the big square chips called plaques were bet in denominations of two thousand dollars and up.

On the way in, he had gone through the other rooms. In the *Salle Blanche* he had marveled at the huge Gervais panel of the Florentine Graces. In the *Salle Vert,* now a bar but once a smoking room, he had chuckled at the cigars in the fingers of the nude women on the ceiling painted by Galleli. Surely, he had thought, nothing unhappy could ever occur in such a paradise.

It was shortly afterward that the theories of Monsieur d'Alembert had begun to assert themselves.

The two croupiers at the table were unable to place the joyful gambler. By his face and speech they had originally suspected that he was some junior stockbroker from Chicago who had come to lose his modest bonus in a single heady day. But his bets were far too large for that, and the insouciant manner with which he treated his considerable losses indicated that the young man was well able to lose. Cocaine money, perhaps?

"Faites vos jeux," the operating croupier said, and the bets went down from the dozen people around the table. The stakes being set out by the American player had drawn a tense circle of watchers. *"Rien ne va plus,"* and a practiced hand sent the little ivory ball counterclockwise into the colorful clockwise-turning wheel.

The American was not unskilled. He had played the d'Alembert system as well as it could be done, and was now competently playing the Biarritz. He did not understand that the system was one to undertake when your stake was in good repair, since it was made for players who found even-chance systems too slow and tame.

He was trying for the big payoff on *en plein* wins, and had now reached the stage in the system where he made up to thirty-four successive bets on a single number. He obviously thought that number, having been counted fewer than ten times in more than a hundred previous spins, was likely to occur during the next thirty-four attempts. If it had been achieved on the first spin, the payoff would have been large. Even now, on the last, money might be made. A win coming later than last was a loser overall. It was an interesting play that even some jaded croupiers enjoyed tracking. But, ineluctably, the dead hand of d'Alembert was making itself felt. Paying no attention to the alleged probabilities, far too many zeroes had come up to pay off the house, and not a single 19 to pay off the American on his choice.

On this, the thirty-fourth turn of the series, the young

man, ignoring the frightened and fascinated squeals of his girl, pushed a fearsome pile of yellow and green plaques onto the backed number—the sweatily anticipated 19.

The ivory ball bounced over the thirty-seven spinning slots, hovered tauntingly above two or three, then caught and held.

"*Dix-sept, rouge, impair et manqué,*" the croupier intoned, and it was over. A wipeout.

The American grinned, tipped the croupier a handful of lower-denomination orange and pink plaques, and waved good-bye to the players and watchers. Several of the less sophisticated applauded him commiseratingly. He took his saddened companion on his arm and led her out of the hallowed rooms into the soft Mediterranean night.

They walked through the glorious air to where the Hôtel de Paris glowed around its magnificent marble and stained glass. Here they would have champagne, a last wonderful dinner on the terrace, and a room for the evening.

Petty Officer Third Class Hinkley Lydecker knew that he was going to have difficulty replacing from his Navy pay the $785,000 he had taken with him from the vault of the *Ernest J. King*. It was now all quite gone.

He was, of course, stunned. He had enough currency in his shoe to buy gas for the Cub, pay off the owner of the closed auto racing track for use as an unauthorized airfield, and otherwise complete his delightful three-hundred-mile sojourn to the Riviera with the deeply impressed Concetta. But naval prison? An unpleasant tingling ran all through him.

Lydecker didn't have the bleak comfort of knowing that thousands of other men who intended to become million-aires with the same system—most of them a hundred times more intelligent than he—had come to the same sad end with their borrowed stakes.

Of course, most of them would have been smart enough to try to disappear.

Naples, Italy—June 7

For perhaps the twentieth time over the past day and a half, McGregor called Norfolk from the post office. Like all long-voyage sailors, he was beginning to fear that he had only dreamed his life ashore. But this time Tess was on the wire, his wife's husky wake-up voice as heavy with gentle, sensual invitation as he'd always remembered it. He imagined the thick honey of her hair spread on the pillow, her heavy breasts and good hips showing through her nightdress in the thin light of the East Coast dawn.

"Hey, Olive, it's Popeye," he said, all of his relief and longing in the silly words. "Hearing you makes me want to shuck out of my sailor suit right here. Trouble is, this phone booth is all glass and half of Naples would get to me before you did."

"Maybe I'd like you all covered in salad oil," she said, the joy he heard seeming overlaid with a terrible weariness. "I've missed you."

"I've been trying like hell to reach you."

"Kiki got away again."

"Oh, my God, Tess. Did you call the police?"

"I find her faster myself. She's back."

"Where was she this time?"

"A gin mill a couple of miles down the road. I guess we were lucky. The guy she was staying with upstairs was almost human, and tough enough to keep the others off her. But I had to talk to him with a big two-prong fork from the free lunch before he was ready to let her go."

"Goddammit," he shouted hopelessly, "there's got to be some kind of law—"

"There isn't," his wife said evenly. "She's not retarded. She's not been judged officially incompetent, mostly because we wouldn't let the judgment be made. Officially she's just an unusually beautiful young girl who attracts men she's not emotionally equipped to send away."

"You should let the Navy do more."

"She doesn't need the Navy. She needs you."

He didn't want to face that. "How did she slip away from you?" he said, knowing it sounded accusatory and knowing he could never cope with the problem half as well as she did.

There was no defensiveness in the answer. "I've been trying to take a word-processing course so I could go into hock for some equipment and work from home. I had the landlord's wife trying to keep an eye on her in the apartment, but the guy came to fix the wiring in the corridor and she sneaked out through the utilities room with him."

"Get her to the doctor. Have her checked."

"I know the drill by now, Wade. It's all done. I should know pretty fast whether she's got some disease, or if she's really been swallowing the birth control pills I give her."

"Can . . . should I speak to her, Tess?"

"I don't think so. I'm holding back on the tranquilizers, and she's been in bed twenty straight hours with the covers over her head. Maybe by the end of the week. She'll be asking for you by then. Anyway, you'll be home real soon, won't you?"

He waited as long as he could to answer. "No," he finally said. "There's been a change in orders. I can't talk about it much. I don't know how long it'll be, anyway."

Tess was, by this time, a master at keeping her hurts and disappointments from being heard over the phone. But there was a new kind of desperation now, bred out of bone-shattering exhaustion, that all her spirit couldn't hide. "What are we going to do, Wade? Just tell me. I'll be able to go on as long as you tell me that you know where we're going. I don't care how hard it is for me, so long as I know we're not just adrift."

"I figure it would take thirty thousand a year just to get Kiki the help she needs. Not only to keep her out of the institutions, but to get her well. Enough people have told us that's possible.''

"The Navy can't do that.''

"They can do it better than I can outside. Swabbies in their middle forties don't step out into fifty-thousand-dollar jobs, Tess. And Kiki can't do without my benefits.''

"I guess I know that. But lately I think I wouldn't mind us all going to hell if it could happen with you in my arms every night.''

The happiness he had felt at hearing her voice was drowned in a rising tide of misery. "God, how I've screwed us up with this Navy.''

"Wade, promise me one thing so I'll have the strength to hang up this phone.''

"Anything.''

"Look for an answer. Anywhere. Anything. I've got to have some shred of hope that something might turn up.''

He swallowed hard. "Something will turn up. I promise you.'' He wondered what it could possibly be.

U.S.S. *Ernest J. King*, Naples, Italy—June 7

Richard Manning had learned from his father that in the old Navy the officers had various nonofficial codes that they wrote into corners of promotion jackets to subtly damn the subject. One of those codes, he had heard, was SIHR. It meant, nominally, Stays In His Room. But, certainly, it meant much more. It said that this was an officer who did not mingle. He kept out of other sailors' lives and expected that they would stay out of his. He did not swap scuttlebutt, go to the officers' club, or run whoring with his peers. If he was married he accepted and offered invitations at a minimum. In short, he refused to accept the Navy as an exclusive Club of Great Guys, where backs were scratched, shit was ingested and served, and career goals achieved.

Up until he was a bookish thirteen-year-old, young Richard had lived only to join that wonderful Navy club one day. He had watched the god that was his father, Lieutenant Peter Manning, thrive and revel in it. That is, for a while.

Richard had been unaware when his father had begun to have his first frightening doubts, doubts that had been finally validated when the crushing tons of sea at 1,500 feet had pinched flat with all in it the pressure hull of SSN-590, the nuclear attack submarine *Sawfish*.

In his neat room deep in the *King*, Manning opened a fresh tube of plastic model cement. The sweet, sharp smell brought him back to a time of immense happiness. If he closed his eyes, he was again at the elbow of his father, tall and laughing. Home from the torturously long nuclear submarine patrols, Peter Manning had always thrown himself joyously into making up the lost time with his son.

The models had been the very symbol of his love. The building of the intricate plastic replicas of Navy ships allowed them to share their joy in anything to do with the fleet. And it kept them side by side for hours, chattering excitedly about the new ships coming on line, the wonder that was *Sawfish*, and the coming glory of Annapolis for young Richard.

If his mother had ever felt left out of their days, she had never shown it. A laughing and beautiful redhead, she had enjoyed the sight of them hunched together over the work table, almost one mind and body.

And when Peter had risen to join her for a cocktail toward the end of the evening, Richard had understood and accepted that it was now his mother's turn to bask in his father's love. Although it was early enough to stay up longer, Richard would go unbidden to his room. There he would work alone on the models for a while and study his Navy books. Later he would hear their bedroom door click closed, and he would turn his radio up so that he would hear no more.

Manning's long fingers now moved magically in the assembly of the model. He worked with tweezers and a special pair of magnifying eyeglasses that flipped up or down from a strap about his forehead. Seldom did he glance at the plans, intuition and encyclopedic knowledge of the subject guiding him onward.

Manning's room would have struck an observer somewhat oddly. If its occupant had not been known, he would have been thought to be not a man at all, but a precocious boy. It wasn't just the models he had brought from ashore to line the shelves and desktops; many sailors filled the hours with such hobbies. There was a preoccupation with a family life left behind, as seen most often in the dwellings of very young college freshmen.

There were four different photographs of his father, ranging from his Annapolis graduation portrait to the grinning studio production taken when he had first been assigned to the *Sawfish*. There were also three fine pictures of his mother, including the wonderful one with her proud new husband at the Academy wedding. The frame that included their growing son was of the variety that permitted a dozen or so assorted snaps in a single mat. Manning probably would not have realized that he accumulated as much as an hour a day staring at these.

Then there was the leather box. Red. Hand-tooled in gold leaf. And locked. It stood on the shelf between the pictures. In it were the letters.

A few from Mom. Cheerful ones written to him at summer camp. Heartbreaking ones from the last days.

The rest were from Dad. Almost a hundred of them. From every station he had ever been at, from every ship he ever been on. Some were to Richard. Some were to Mom, retrieved after she had shot herself with the small .25-caliber Colt Dad had given her for her protection. The most special letters were from the last months on the *Sawfish*.

Manning didn't ever have to read Dad's letters anymore. He knew every word.

. . . I tell you, Audrey, I find it unbelievable. A boat built with so many basic design flaws I might have been able to understand. The nuclear program was new. The concepts

were daring, not fully proved in operation. And it was accepted that the boats would be operated under limitations while improvements were evaluated. It made sense to cover shortcomings when the program had so many enemies in Congress who could have broken our back. I admit I was part of glossing over some things. In fact, I mostly went along when they started to push us past the performance envelope we agreed on. They wanted evidence that we could match the new Russian designs, and I hardly blamed them. But if I didn't know that major refittings were coming up soon, they might have had to go along without me.

I should have figured something wasn't just right when they made it tough for us to visit Sawfish in the Hydralectric yards. Hydralectric does some great work for us sometimes, but this wasn't one of them. Maybe it was a money squeeze, maybe it was a time squeeze. But things haven't gotten better, they've gotten worse. The fixes look good on paper, maybe, but paper isn't what keeps the water out way down there.

But I'm pretty sure they'll wake up before the sea trials—

Young as he was, he had been able to detect the rising state of alarm, the disbelief that something was not being done as more and more of the *Sawfish*'s crew saw what had been returned to them. And then Richard had felt in the written words the battle of conscience—his father's devotion to the Navy put against his duty to his family and crew. There were hints of increasingly difficult confrontations with brass outside the ship. Rickover must not become involved, he'd been told, for the old man's own good.

The worst was yet to come. Letters in a slurred hand, the deepening depression evident in the downsloping lines. Stark ramblings of the submariner's never absent fear of the icy, strangling sea waiting to claw through the pressure hull and steal the breath of the intruders into its alien world.

Where had the flesh-and-blood Lieutenant Peter Manning been—the arms that had so gently cradled his beloved infant son, the lips that had so often brushed his cheek? Where had the warm, handsome form been when the ocean's vengeful squeeze had overcome the inept fittings and torn to bits the helplessly backsliding *Sawfish*? Asleep in his bunk, merely exchanging one deep sleep for another? In the control room, desperately running through the Navy "book" on what one must do when a through-the-hull fitting failed below a thousand feet and the pressure of incoming water might tear a man's head off as it shot in the fatal tons?

A deep-diving Navy DSRV, not built until many years later, had finally gotten down to the *Sawfish*. The pressure had imploded the boat with such force that the debris field was tangled over hundreds of yards.

Much debris was secretly brought up, none of it human, just classified parts and papers. They were even pretty certain that they had found the fitting that had failed, and the scandalous reasons why. Breasts were quietly beaten. The culpable heads in the Navy were made to roll unobtrusively. The guilty at the shipbuilding yard had been decimated earlier in a separate scandal.

Richard Manning turned on a radio so that there might be something else to occupy at least a few of the screaming cells in his head. But then the scrawled drafts of his mother's letters came crowding in:

. . . Don't try to tell me that it wasn't government people who broke into our home.

Her handwriting, always small, became more crabbed as she became angrier.

Perhaps if you had told me what you were looking for I might have given it to you. Or perhaps not. Perhaps I was foolish to give you the letters from my husband without making photographic copies. Am I wrong, or are you treating someone who has only the Navy's interest at heart as some sort of enemy? I should think you would badly want these deficiencies looked into. . . .

Poor naive, trusting, heartbroken Mom. She might have thought being slowly frozen out of her Navy friendships was because of defects in her personality that had been previously hidden by her husband's brilliant likability. But even young Richard could see that the chill had been unspokenly decreed from high up. And if Audrey Manning had believed that her hard-won job as a substitute history teacher in the Norfolk school system had vanished of its own accord, she was sillier than Richard knew her to be.

She kept what Peter Manning had shared with her tightly to herself. He had made clear to the end that this was his wish.

So Audrey wrote ever fewer of her disappearing letters to the Navy Department and sent them no more of her husband's writings. She moved down to housekeeping jobs, always drifting toward the Midwest. This gave her lodgings for her increasingly more disturbed son, and moved her ever farther from the ocean she had come to loathe.

For a moment Manning stopped his sanding of the plastic piece in his hand and looked at one of the snapshots in a multiple frame hanging on the bulkhead over his desk. Audrey was standing on a magnificent stone patio on a house he remembered, outside of Cincinnati. She was wearing a ridiculously cute maid's uniform, but was beautiful despite it. She had her arm around her son, the sparks of madness now growing in his eyes.

His breakdown had brought out the last of what was left in her. As he fell apart, screaming for his father through the night and increasingly terrified of cold water, she found the place best for treatment with discretion and put him there. Richard had shared his doctors with the scions of Denver mining families who wanted their children's records unblemished for later life.

Her moderate trust fund, so carefully set up to provide a comfortable supplement for a lifetime, was violated unwaveringly. As the last of it disappeared, Richard, thinner, quieter, grimmer, emerged again into the world. To all eyes he was cured. He always managed to choke back any cries when cold water hit him. After a time he didn't even flinch.

On the morning that she shot herself behind the ear in a Leadville hotel, Audrey Manning had pawned what good jewelry she had remaining, cashed in her insurance policy, since it would pay nothing on such a death, and left the proceeds on a nightstand for Richard. She also left tickets to Washington, a short list of names of well-placed Navy people who had not deserted her, and a terse note. This note urged him not to mourn her worthless life and assured him that she would be with his father, together loving their son for eternity. The next to last lines said, *'Annapolis. They owe you that.'*

The final line, scrawled with a different pen, apparently some minutes later as an afterthought, was written much larger and pressed in so hard that the ballpoint had broken through the paper on the last words: *"You owe them, too."*

Her idea had been good.

In Washington and Baltimore Richard found top Navy people furiously determined to make up for outrageously hidden wrongs to the Manning family. Even among the former culprits there were always muted mutterings from Commander So-and-so and Admiral Such-and-such that he— almost alone—had stood against certain unfair, unspoken proceedings.

Young Richard Manning found himself adopted into the Navy family, now that his own had been wiped out. The Navy family is a wonderful one to have looking after you.

He found himself eased into the finest preparatory school in Washington. Money materialized from various Navy benevolent society funds and the pockets of many high officers in the submarine program. The school was as eager as Richard to smooth out the ground in front of him, and he made remarkable educational strides. When he'd graduated two years later, only one previous student—who became a noted astrophysicist—finished above him.

The pull to get into Annapolis took two years longer. During the wait, while a stubborn wedge of congressmen and naval personnel were helping him forward, he had free living quarters in the homes of three different officers. For what little spare time he had away from studies and to satisfy his small monetary needs, he always had the pick of low-level jobs from the great federal cornucopia.

By the time he had come through Annapolis, the Navy

family felt it had handsomely washed away any stain in the matter of the late Lieutenant Peter Manning.

It was time to stop for the evening. He carefully packed the parts of his model into its box along with his tools and paints and stored it in a drawer.

Then he reached up and took a model of the very ship in which he sat, the *Ernest J. King*, and held it close to his face, taking in the thousand details.

The smallest smile crossed his lips. He imagined that he could hear, scaled down in size like the model itself, the sound of seawater rushing into its breached compartments.

The smile twisted and broke.

"Daddy," he sobbed once before his icy composure returned.

Abruzzi, Italy—June 8

The cloudless sky of Abruzzi burned with light from a white noonday sun. Lydecker and Ledges, their total nakedness hidden from the few nearby field-workers by the waist-high parapet of the balcony, contemplated the sprawling land beneath them.

The town, mostly simple houses of white, yellow, and blue, all under blazing red roofs, was slowly losing its rural character. The prosperous upper classes of the cities had discovered the charming homes and the bright river winding through a narrow valley. The gently rising purple hills surrounding the town changed shades at every hour of the day, and gave balm to weary accountants, attorneys, and physicians. It was a place to buy, to build magnificently in, to rest. *If* the time could be found.

Indeed, the bare, sleeping bodies of Concetta and Rosalia belonged in marriage to two such weary, overworked men. As was so tragically often the case, their husbands had been unable to break away to accommodate the springtime sunshine and ardors in midweek, and the sailors had been able to reestablish delightful old friendships in congenial surroundings.

"How could you blow two days of this?" asked Ledges, probing.

"You wouldn't understand," said Lydecker.

"Okay, then. How could you just fly off and leave a shipmate without a word?"

"I think I tried to tell you about it. You were making a lot of noise throwing up. Ask Concetta."

"Tell me again. Concetta is a clam."

"It might break the spell."

"Hink—"

"It might also get my ass broken."

"Think of me as a caring father."

"When I start thinking of Concetta as a loving mother."

"Okay. I'm not curious. I can wait till we're on the ship. Unless you wanna tell me now."

Lydecker ignored him.

"It ain't natural the way we live, Rock," he finally said.

"Gee, I never noticed that."

They sighed in unison.

If sailors on the old tea clippers clawing around the Horn lived an icy, exhausting, perilous hell high in the shrouds, the modern big-navy sailor had an existence that sometimes sapped the soul even worse. It was something they seldom dared to contemplate, except when poignant glimpses of other, happier worlds made the thoughts unavoidable.

"How many hours a week you reckon you spent outside the tin in the last six months?" asked Ledges.

"Maybe an hour and a half, because I made it a point to jog around the flight deck every other day when the weather wouldn't blow me overboard and they weren't screwing with the airplanes."

"Less than that for me," Ledges said, "because I can't run with this caved-in foot. Not that working the deck was much better than in the tin. Shit, when I cross the street now

I'm afraid to go behind or in front of the cars, expecting either to get sucked up or fried in the jet blast.''

They looked out across the beautiful, sunny valley, realizing sickeningly that this would be their last day of freedom.

The peaceful fields of green and golden brown became sullen, lead-gray seas, heavy and spitting. The bright blue sky became the sheeted steel of an overhead, its sweating, cold skin pressing down just inches above them. And the warm, glistening bodies of the sleeping Concetta and Rosalia were the sodden, sour-smelling bodies of snoring men.

In Lydecker's mind, the contemplation was a lot grimmer than that.

"Ever count the little things we'll be missing?" asked Ledges.

"Nooners."

"Matinees."

"Ball games."

"Down to the corner for pizza."

"Tanking in dirty saloons."

"Long drives."

"Fireplaces."

"Privacy."

"Yeah. Crapping alone."

"Good restaurants."

"Bad restaurants."

"Plaid shirts."

"Calllng in sick in June."

They went on for a very long time, then lapsed into a morose silence as they pulled on shorts and went to get the Cub ready for the flight back to Naples in the morning.

"Maybe there's something else we can do," Lydecker said as he poured gasoline into the funnel Ledges held in the opening of the gas tank.

"Sure, Hink. I can find some big corporation that needs a guy who knows how to shackle a five hundred-pound AP bomb to the belly of a desk, and you can join up with some hot film company that's looking for an extra in Frankie Avalon's comeback surfer movie."

"Wanna jump off the roof?"

"Not until I jump off Rosalia. C'mon. Last one in has to knot the condoms."

U.S.S. *Ernest J. King*, Naples, Italy—June 10

Commander Manning found the middle part of the morning watch—from 0500 to 0700—the best time to do his prowling about the *King*. The activity at these hours of the cold-iron watches was not so thin as to call attention to his movements, nor so heavy as to overly inhabit the areas of his investigations. Besides which, there was a certain generalized lassitude in the routine before morning colors. The testing of the general alarm, the droning announcement of uniform of the day, and the pipe to breakfast were as close to a family routine as life ever got on a ship so huge. Comfortable ritual was beloved by sailors. It made them friendly and talkative, and that was very useful to Commander Manning.

Without the "water wings" of a surface warfare officer on his breast, he found the crew was relaxed with him, treating him as something of a visiting executive clerk despite his precocious rank.

Since the powerful Supply Department reached everywhere and he was a new man orienting himself to the ship, neither his presence nor his absence was ever questioned.

He marveled at the efficiency of the apparatus that had brought him here on such a critical mission. But that was something far short of telling him how to do a job beyond the present abilities of the entire Soviet military machine.

Me and Tree, he thought, letting the rhyme bounce around in his head. Tree, the tech rep, had already done more than well enough with the gearboxes. And he had done magnificently for Hatten. Perhaps he would be useful again. Perhaps other people could be found.

Manning was not discouraged. It was like building an exceptionally complicated model kit. Laying out the parts, sanding off the edges, assembling in just the right order. And patience. More patience than the world ever allowed for. And steadiness of hand. This was no place for nerves.

He had broken down the areas of opportunity into two: what he could accomplish from the inside, and what he could discover to make easier intervention from the outside.

In many ways the vulnerability of the carrier worked against him. All that fuel, all that ordnance, all that precision equipment packed into such tight spaces meant that a small action could create a great catastrophe. Witness the bolts in the gears. But this was as known to the Navy as it was known to him. The systems were protected by careful layers of men and prevention systems. Especially now that there were suspicions.

He was completely familiar with many of the installations he visited, having studied carefully the manuals supplied by his contacts in San Diego. But manuals were poor substitutes for close-up examination and in-depth questioning of operating personnel.

A chief fire control technician he had approached near the stern at one of the *King*'s four Vulcan Phalanx Close-In Weapons Systems proudly lectured him. He circled a six-ton, fifteen-foot-high installation that encased itself in an egg-shaped, fast-swiveling turret. From this turret protruded a multiple-barrel weapon that any veteran of the Spanish-American War could have identified as a Gatling gun. But what a Gatling gun.

Manning made no attempt to impede the informational avalanche as the techie went on as though he had built the formidable machines himself.

"Sir, the Phalanx can defeat any antiship missile there is. It's fully integrated with a weapons system that includes the VPS-2 search and track radar, the gun, the magazine, the weapon control unit, and the electronics. That gun is a six-barrel General Electric M-168 twenty-millimeter Vulcan. It's got a selectable firing rate of three thousand rounds per minute, with fifteen hundred rounds in a magazine. And she fires a depleted-uranium bullet. A penetrator, we call it. It's two and a half times heavier than steel and steps out at one thousand feet per second. No airborne armor can stop it."

"Tell me more about that radar," said Manning, letting unabashed awe show.

"There's a built-in J-band, pulse-Doppler radar that follows the bullets in flight. It's what we call Closed-Loop Fire Control. You see, the shells fly out about two miles in a cone. Then, get this. The radar tracks not just the incoming target, but the gun's own shells. Computers do a split-second bearing computation to converge the two and swivel the barrels, and *whoomp*, you've got aluminum and meat splattering all over the sky."

"How fast can it start spitting?"

"Within two seconds of threat identification."

"But we've only got four of them."

"Sir, that's all it takes."

Manning was familiar with all this, but pressed on. You never knew what you might overlook in the familiar. "The Vulcans are for close in. What have we got for longer range?"

"Three eight-cell Sea Sparrow launchers. They'll reach way out. Twenty-eight miles at three times the speed of sound for head-on targets. Radar inside the missile picks out the directional bearing of targets. The bird adjusts its flight to climb or dive with movable wings."

"Wow," said Manning. "And that's not counting the escorts' firepower. Devastating stuff."

The techie allowed himself a dubious moment. "Trouble is, sir, it's all so high-tech that there's always ten million things that can go wrong. And nobody can react fast enough to do anything about it. Everything you stuff in the front, something falls out the back. I get a feeling that somebody's gonna come up with a fleet of rowboats and board us with cutlasses, and we won't know what to do about it." He pointed behind Manning. "I tell you the truth, sir, those babies over there are the things that'll make me feel warm all over if the Ivans get close with missiles.''

The sailor pointed to a group of installations that looked like four clusters of large-diameter sewer pipe gone schizophrenic. The six tubes in each cluster were paired, each pair facing the sky at a different elevation angle.

''Is that supposed to sink us or them?'' laughed Manning, knowing very well what the things were.

''Neither one. It's a Mark 33 RBOC. That means a Rapid Bloom Off-Board Chaff system. We've had 'em on escorts, but they're new on carriers. The Falklands taught us how important these things are. We fire 'em when we've got something like an Exocet or a SCUD antiship missile homing in under radar guidance. The chaff is strips of metal foil, like the old stuff they dropped in World War Two. Window is what they called it then.''

''That was to confuse defensive radar?''

''Right, sir. But this is to screw up what the offensive missiles' onboard gear is seeking. We try to get the bird to lock on to a false signal, or even to break a lock that it already has.''

''Doesn't it also screw up our own radar?''

''The theory is that we have the strips cut to lengths that confuse their frequencies but leave ours alone. But it ain't all that exact a science. Especially when we figure we can't break the bogeys off and we just fire big clouds around ourselves to give them a lock that's way off center.''

''I don't know whether I feel better or not. Thanks for the fill-in, sailor. Carry on.''

Manning continued his prowling.

Any place of sensitivity had become an EA, an exclusion area. Wherever he looked he saw Marines and rough-looking seamen wearing master-at-arms brassards. He could talk past almost any one of them with his credentials, but a pattern of doing so would be quickly noticed.

Although he was almost certain that the *King* would stay in port until intelligence and the politicians released her, Manning was tense. When she left Naples he would be cut off from any help he might want from ashore. Then it would be just himself and Tree.

He found himself hypersensitive to signs of getting under way.

They had already adjusted the trim tanks in the forepeak and the aftertank for fast sailing with the newly distributed tons of stores. The bailing turbine, used to go astern, was all tuned and tested.

Every hour Manning found himself going over the timing of the various parts of the procedure for getting under way. Once they started the gyros and energized and calibrated all the radar repeaters, he would have only hours until sailing. When they verified a schedule for lighting off boilers—an anachronistic term with nuclear fires—he would know that he had virtually no more time.

He yearned to get down into the Crypt, where the nuclear fires raged behind the reactor shielding. He would be able to accomplish something very quickly there.

Alert as he was to the awesome force that drove the ship, he was preternaturally aware of what no unschooled visitor would have noticed.

The vessel was eerily clean because no stacks gases or soot were present to contaminate the air and decks. Down below, the internal spaces of the *King* were vastly more cavernous than would have been possible with a huge volume of tanks for bunker oil. The space gained translated into extra warplanes, their fuel, and their ordnance. The combination of this and the improved catapults that reduced a takeoff run from a mile to two hundred feet meant the vessel could carry forty percent more warplanes, and heavier ones, than conventional carriers. This was a staggering advantage in consideration of the crushing offensive power of each aircraft. No other class of ships ever known could present this force in a single package. *That* was the entire problem.

Manning kept a special eye on the men who worked near the reactors. They were easy to spot, no matter where he met them. Each wore a dosimeter, a small glass cylinder worn on the belt that warned of the exposure to radiation that was the overriding fear aboard any nuclear-propelled ship. All day long there were teams wiping down random spots with paper disks that would spot any perilous build-ups. He badly needed to reach just one of this clannish lot of nukies. But a clandestine perusal of snivel sheets—various written complaints bucked up through the system via the command master chief—had not turned up any hint of serious disaffection.

A shame, because those who felt caught, betrayed, or endangered by the system often could be made to perform more heroically against it than the best professionals.

U.S.S. *Ernest J. King*, Naples, Italy—June 10

Although it was not especially hot in McGregor's compartment, sweat formed on his forehead and fell onto the carefully studied pages of the Uniform Code of Military Justice. ·

"No chance of holding it down to a summary?" the weary-eyed Ledges asked without hope.

McGregor wearily shook his head. "You don't have to be a sea lawyer to know $785,000 is worth a bit more than forty-five days in a stockade at hard labor."

"What about a special?" asked Ledges, his ruddy countryside color having vanished in the past two hours. "You can request one-third enlisted men on the court then. They'd understand better. The top sentence'd be six months in the slam and a dishonorable. No fun, but—"

McGregor slammed the code shut. "Let's get it in our heads, guys. This isn't going to be a summary court. It isn't going to be a special court. It's going to be a pipe-the-admiral, five-star, man-the-side, twenty-one-gun, thirty-years-in-Portsmouth general court-martial."

Ledges nodded reluctantly. "If Hink hangs around here, he's going to miss your golden wedding anniversary party."

"Not necessarily," McGregor said heavily. "I'm liable to be his roomie."

"Oh, Jesus," Lydecker said, his eyes widening. "Have I pushed you overboard, too, sir?"

"What the hell do you think?" said Ledges, pounding the boy's shoulder with a big fist. "Do you think the Navy's gonna believe that a total dumb-ass eight-ball like you could get into that vault without top-level help?"

"Don't be crazy," Lydecker said, frightened for the first time. "I'll tell them the way it was. That's why I didn't just disappear. They've got to know that Wade trusted us so much that even a dummy like me could pull it off without any help. Just watching his habits and using cut-up paper and phonied stacks of money—"

Ledges groaned loudly. "I got a better idea. Tell 'em you did it while he was busy opening the sea valves, or throwing the ship's bowling trophies into the gearboxes. Maybe they'd go easier on him."

"Hink," McGregor said, half mad with exasperation, "what in the hell were you smoking when you decided to do it? Maybe there's some kind of incompetency plea."

Lydecker gave a weak grin. "This is going to sound wackier than the rest of it. I really did it for you guys. No shit."

More groans.

"It's better in the Army," muttered Ledges. "They only throw grenades at their superiors."

The boy was not put off. "Hey, I wouldn't have a place in the whole world without you guys. You think I don't know all you put up with from me, and how much covering you do when I screw up? And I don't see how Wade's in all that family trouble, and Rocky's dying by inches behind that tin desk and turning into something as useless as me? So while I was soaking up a bottle of Jim Beam with one of the signalmen, I got to thinking how great it would be if none of us had to worry about retirement and wives and kids. Then we could just enjoy being in together. Get some neat furnishings and liberties going. And I wouldn't have to worry about you just disappearing on me forever someday.''

The sincerity in his face was so fierce that the others lapsed into an embarrassed quiet for a moment.

"Tell us everything," McGregor finally sighed. "We hate to wait for the newspapers."

"Well," Lydecker went on, "I had this uncle who was a mathematician out of MIT, and he used to work with these roulette systems to demonstrate things to students. He was always showing them to me, and they stuck in my head."

"Surprising, considering when we do payrolls you can't get as far as your pinky when you count on your fingers. Your uncle was a billionaire from those systems, of course."

"Hell, no. He was just a little rabbit of a guy. He never bet a nickel in his life. So I figured with his brains and my balls—"

"*Our* balls. We're all going to lose them, Hinkley."

More subdued now, Lydecker went on. "I knew we wouldn't be back into that vault money until after we left Naples. I just rigged things inside, being careful to use all of Wade's tricks, and brought most of the money ashore. It took half my sea bag and almost didn't fit in *Carlotta*. I knew the masters-at-arms could've got me with a spot check at the ladder, but I wasn't even nervous, except about sneaking what was missing back into the vault after I won."

"What about the chick you said you were with? Was she part of the omen?" asked McGregor.

"Yeah," Ledges said. "An omen of getting laid."

Lydecker looked stricken. "I was so sure we'd clean up. Besides, I always wanted the kick of betting my whole ass on one throw. I'm glad about that part. Even if I never see free blue sky again."

The others felt their hearts cracking at that thought.

"Sir," the boy said, his color now drained, "who do I turn myself over to? The skipper? The chief master-at-arms? I hope it can be you."

"That'd be best for you, Wade," Ledges said leadenly. "It would look better."

"Nothing's going to make any difference for you and me. They'll nail us too for something. The stockade and a dishonorable are probably the best we can hope for. This is too big for even an undesirable or a bad conduct."

"At least the rest of us don't have families to worry about," Ledges said. "God, Wade, what's going to happen to yours?"

The strength seemed gone from McGregor. "None of it amounts to anything compared to what's going to happen to Hink."

Their eyes turned to the boy, who now seemed half the size he had been. His glowing youthfulness had suddenly faded, like that of some beautifully tinted fish dying out of the water.

Ledges couldn't seem to lift his eyes off the deck. "Should we check out what's missing, while he's here to help us?"

McGregor shook his head. "Why should we help them adjust the noose?"

Now Lydecker donned his shirt. "Let me go find some clothes and my hat," he mumbled. "Then you can take me."

As he opened the door and stepped through into the passageway, a tall Marine sergeant, rocklike in his taut khakis, came striding past. He kept his heavy shoulder down and knocked the preoccupied Lydecker to his knees.

"Watch your candy ass, swabbie," the Marine said, not looking back.

Waiting for Lydecker to return, McGregor's mind whirled in an agony of thoughts and feelings. "If Hink lands in the brig aboard, dicks like that jarhead will be in charge."

"Yeah. . . ." said Ledges. "Hey, Wade. I wonder—We're really in the shit now. . . ."

McGregor cautiously pondered the thought that they both shared. "It's incredibly dumb. But if they're going to tie us to a grate anyway—" There was a new glint in the iron blue of his eyes. "Are we thinking about this? On top of whatever anchor they're already getting ready to drop on our heads, we're going to add the weight of aiding in the escape of a military felon."

"Shit, Wade," said Ledges, "this tub's so big we can slip him over the side a hundred different ways. Maybe even get a life raft away. We just got paid. We could throw together what we got for a start for him. Throw in some of what's left in the vault. In Naples he could get all the clothes and documents he needed. Hell, he could've kept on going if it wasn't going to leave us holding the whore's tit."

"Hey," McGregor interrupted. "Remember who you're talking about. A kid who speaks nothing but English and a little bedroom Italian, knows zero about hiding out, and in general just doesn't know shit, period."

"Yeah. Yeah, by himself they'd snag him in a week . . . but suppose he wasn't alone?" asked Ledges, almost under his breath.

"Go with him? It wouldn't work. We'd need money. Lots and lots of it. More than we can imagine. That would be the only way to buy clear of the net the Navy would throw out for us."

At this moment, sweating but smartly turned out, Lydecker returned. "I'm ready."

Ledges, McGregor's words not yet settled in his head, turned on the boy with a venomous mixture of fury, sorrow, and despair. "Why in hell couldn't you have just *stolen* the frigging money without the casino crap. Then we could do something for you because you'd still have it. Shit, we could do something for all of us."

There was a harsh chuckle from McGregor. "Funny thing is, we wouldn't have been much worse off if the whole bunch of us had just cleaned out that vault."

"And the thirty-five million coming in behind it."

And suddenly there it was.

An unthinkable thought brought pulsing to life by the even more unthinkable alternative. As certainly as if they had discussed the possibility for days before deciding, McGregor and Ledges knew what they would do.

Hink Lydecker sensed the change in his fortunes so completely that a grin escaped him before he realized what it was for.

"Take off your lid, kid," McGregor said. "You aren't going anywhere." The billion precise compartments in his bookkeeper's mind began to break down the problem of stealing a fortune. And of how to get it—along with themselves—off a U.S. nuclear carrier that might soon be steaming into a war zone.

McGregor cleared his throat and set his cap. "We've got a lot of talking to do," he said evenly. "But meanwhile, life has to go on as before. There's plenty to do for our employer. Including checking in with the new boss."

Ledges sighed. "Commander Manning is going to be straight up our ass for days while he's taking hold. He could be in the way. He could be in the way real bad."

"Let's pray he's finding a lot to keep him interested," McGregor said as he buttoned his uniform jacket for his interview with Manning. "So he won't get too interested in us."

Naples, Italy—June 11–13

Wade McGregor observed the surprises and challenges of the new profession they had entered so unexpectedly.

Even the gentlest, most honest soul undergoes an awesome metamorphosis once circumstance has decreed the commission of a great crime. All the powerful attributes of goodness—patience, care, bravery, devotion—even righteousness—become tools with thrilling new uses.

The most exciting of these tools was in this case the most obvious. Trust. The trust built up over a lifetime, the plotters instinctively knew, would be the key to getting what they needed.

Then there was guilt—and fear—and confusion. Every hour brought long, dark thoughts of one more unforeseen difficulty or consequence of their impending action. Slowly they realized that the virtuoso criminal—and they could be nothing less if they were to succeed—did not spring up full-blown to genius like some larcenous Mozart. They didn't have the years of trial and error, tutoring by brilliant mentors in dark alleys, backrooms, and jail cells. They didn't have the instinctive, ever-probing eye and ear that never stopped looking for weaknesses in the system. They had no running start.

On the other hand, they had something no career criminals could hope to have—innocence. They would not recognize problems that would send the professional scurrying.

So, over the hours, they let the intellectual eroticism that is part of all important criminal planning pull them forward.

The broad strokes were easy. Rank never seemed to relax itself in the Navy, so McGregor made himself appear to be in charge. But, as any old swabbie knows, it is the chiefs who make the gears move and the wheels turn.

So Senior Chief Rocky Ledges was, it was tacitly known, to be a full partner in the planning.

McGregor formed the broad picture. Since Hink shared an eight-man compartment and Ledges a four-man in CPO country, they did their plotting in McGregor's tiny but private spaces.

"We're like embezzlers where the bank president is in on it. We can do a lot of covering up on the books before the auditors catch up. Bluehoffer is a problem, but I can keep him off us for a while. With luck nobody'll know what we've done until somebody doesn't get paid down the line. But plainly, the sooner we move the better.

"Somehow we've got to get several cubic yards of currency weighing hundreds of pounds off the ship. And we have to get ourselves out of here with it."

"Desert, that is," said Ledges, grimly determined not to understate what they were about.

"The penalties for desertion won't be a patch on the penalties for the rest of it, Rocky."

"Yeah, especially for me," agreed Hink.

"I know," said Ledges. "But I can't get over the old feeling that deserters are people who eat horseshit and bay at the moon. Go on."

"We've got to figure out a place where they'll never find us. Or where they can't get at us if they do."

"You've got a problem we don't, Commander," said Lydecker. "What about Tess and Kiki?"

McGregor's face failed to hide his consternation at his wife and daughter's fate. "I'll get word to Tess that I'm going to need all her guts. That I'm going to disappear for a while and get them over with me when I can."

"Wrong way," said Ledges with vehemence. "Once they start watching her, screwing the McGregor family will be a new Navy tradition. You won't be able to get a nickel or a word to her. Her getaway has to be done first. And done just the right way. She doesn't come to you when it's done. You go to her."

McGregor flushed. "I guess I would have seen that if I had a brain, Chief," he muttered.

"So where do we go, sir?" asked Lydecker.

"Make it Wade, kid," said McGregor. "They didn't call Dillinger sir."

"Where, Wade?"

"Rocky?" passed McGregor.

"Eastern Europe at first. One of the more primitive spots. Romania, Bulgaria, Yugoslavia. They don't play much footsie with the West. Hard currency can buy anything. Hiding and changing identities are national sports. Payoffs at the top aren't too expensive and set-up time is short. We could live like admirals for fifty years."

"Or slip out when the heat goes down," tried Lydecker hopefully.

"It'll never be off," said McGregor. "But they have great water skiing off Dubrovnik."

"Maybe," Ledges said, "it'd be easier not to bring the money on the *King* at all. Snatch it ashore and leave out a step."

"Negative," said McGregor. "All the security goes into protecting the money from hits ashore. A panzer division couldn't get at it there. The system is made to protect from the outside, not the inside."

"Right," agreed Ledges. "We get the hardest part for free. The bells would go off if we *didn't* pick up the bread when we were supposed to."

"Neat," chirped Lydecker. "Then all we've got to do is get the money and us off this tub later."

"Think we can do that before we sail?" McGregor asked Ledges.

"Maybe, but I don't think we should plan that way. Naval Intelligence is going to slip that one little piece into place, and this ship is going to lock down and go out of here like a barracuda with a hotfoot. It could happen tomorrow. And we don't have one damned thing set up ashore anyway."

"Couldn't we just hide it somewhere ashore on the base?"

"Hink, the SPs fine-comb that real estate like they were looking for Naples pussy."

Ledges said, "Yeah. Even if we did it, how do we get into the base to pick up the scratch later on? Then how do we get out?"

"Exactly," said McGregor. "The Navy won't accommodate our schedule. And if we turn up missing, they check the cookie jar right away. I don't think the sentries will welcome in a gang of deserters looking to retrieve thirty-five million bucks they stole from the Navy."

"You may be right," said Lydecker.

"Okay, we've all decided that it's impossible to do in port," said Ledges. "Do we care that it's even more impossible to pull off at sea?"

"What do you mean impossible, Rock?" said Lydecker.

"You're a real sailor, aren't you? We get us and the money off in a boat. Right on?"

"No, right off. You two are bank tellers, and I'm a former airplane parking lot attendant. None of us is up to date on sailing anything bigger than a Sunfish. We sure aren't about to shove off from this floating Chrysler Building of a ship while it's making twenty-two knots in an open sea. Besides which there are no boats ready for launching except the one the lifeboat watch is on. Also there are enough lookouts in the group to replace the population of Naples."

"What if we went at night?" Lydecker persisted.

"We trade the problem of being visible for the problem of being blind."

"Any more ideas?" murmured McGregor.

"I feel like we're pissing up Niagara Falls," said Lydecker.

Naples, Italy—June 14

Tess McGregor had to take her husband's phone call in the bedroom. Kiki, as she sometimes did when something bad was building, had taken possession of a piece of the apartment. This time it was a square of the living room that included one end of the couch, the floor before it, and an end table that held a lamp and the other telephone.

She was not in any standard state of catatonia that would again necessitate psychiatric or pharmaceutical intervention. She would have answered politely, with the minimum words necessary, any question put to her.

Except that she had been sitting there in bikini briefs and a light bra for two days and two nights, she might have been any pretty sixteen-year-old taking a moment's breather from a hectic schedule.

Each time she left for the bathroom, no more than once a day, Tess would remove the romance magazines and stuffed animals to try to break some of the unknowable rhythms of her periodic self-imprisonments. But then Kiki would return, patiently discover the missing articles, and replace them exactly.

"There doesn't seem to be much depression," Tess said, just managing to keep the misery out of the voice that was crossing the Atlantic to Naples. "And she's been washing herself beautifully up to now. Even doing her hair. I think she'll be out of it by tomorrow."

Through the open bedroom door Tess looked directly at her daughter. The old guilts and self-doubts had long ago died of exhaustion. There remained only the fact of a charming, loving girl who had been fighting bravely, with all her might, to remain part of the world.

Kiki sat now, legs crossed, her sometimes bright and eager mind again smothered. Luckily she had the genes of her father's lean, hard body to go with the wonderful face that might have been Tess's own. The girl had no more than five extra pounds on a stunning body despite disastrous habits of diet and exercise.

Tess waved to her from where she sat. The round face and wide hazel eyes turned away from her.

The cost of the overseas call was climbing and her husband had not yet been able to get to the pressing point that lay so obviously under his every word.

"All right, Wade," she finally said. "Whatever it is, I can take it."

He sounded profoundly grateful for the opening. "Tess, I'm going to ask you to tear up your whole world. And I'm not going to tell you why. Not for a while."

"If this world I have here was worth the faintest damn, I'd be worried."

"I'm going to wire you some money. Enough for some tickets and temporary living expenses. A letter is on the way. Follow the instructions in it no matter how crazy they sound."

She tensed. "Wade. What kind of trouble is this?"

"No worse than what we're in now. If it works out, we

might be able to get Kiki everything she needs. Maybe we can even get her completely straightened out.''

''Oh, God. If we could do that—''

''I can tell you . . . you're going to leave the country with Kiki. For good. Don't do anything with the stuff in the apartment. Leave it there. Pay the rent for a couple of months and walk away. Tell people that there's a new treatment for Kiki I heard about. In Switzerland, say. You have to live there for a long while maybe. I'll back it up with some calls.''

''Wade, you've got to—''

He rushed right over her, as though he might not be able to go on if he stopped. ''You'll be flying into Genoa. You know where the passports are?''

''Sure, but I don't know anything about Genoa.''

''Rocky is arranging to have some people from Naples meet you there. Italians. You'll have to give them some money. The letter will explain that. Then they'll take you somewhere.''

She was beginning to feel dizzy. ''Where? Please. *Where?*''

''Another country, sweetheart. That's all I can say now. Don't fail me. You two are all I have.''

Her ordinarily slow-speaking husband's words were tumbling one over the other. She wondered if she would believe this had happened after McGregor's voice had faded. ''I don't know, darling. If I could have a little time to—''

''We have no time. None, for God's sake—''

''Wade—''

At the vehement sound of her father's name, Kiki stood up. She began to tremble lightly. Tears started into the corners of her eyes and she crossed her arms across her chest, hugging herself as though freezing.

Tess sensed a weakening of the dreadful spell. She covered the mouthpiece of the phone and spoke to her quickly, softly. ''Go get washed, honey. And dressed. We'll eat in the kitchen, okay?''

The girl nodded slowly and shuffled away from her invisible prison. She almost smiled.

Now Tess broke. She pushed the sobs back into her throat and went back to the phone. "All right. Anything. Whatever you say. I want to be with you. We both do. What else is there to care about?"

U.S.S. *Ernest J. King*, Naples, Italy—June 15

The *King*, in the eyes of the new criminals, had become a twenty-five-story, thousand-foot-long department store. From somewhere in its two thousand compartments and twenty-odd decks, from somewhere among the thousands of tons of steel, cloth, explosives, fuel, paper, wire, engines, food, wood, and living flesh they had to quickly shop for the solution to their terrible need. Without any real idea of what they were looking for, they began to search out the means by which they might remove three cubic yards of currency off a moving warship in a way that would permit them to later retrieve it.

McGregor and Ledges held their minds obstinately away from the thought that if they failed the two of them might suffer lightly after all. Hink would cheerfully give himself up to any lie they might concoct about his genius in bamboozling them. As head of the division, McGregor bore the responsibility and would surely be through in the Navy. But responsibility might not be the same as proving guilt. There was a bare possibility that his discharge might after all be a general. Ledges? He might even stay in the fleet with a reduced rank if they could find another place. He had a thousand friends and a flawless record. Everybody knew the job was a shitstorm to him. He didn't know enough to be responsible, much less steal.

All of this had to be kept out of their heads as they fought fear and despair. They had to keep it so only Hink counted.

McGregor was glad of every day that passed, because each one would make it more definite to any future investigation that he had known the money was gone. The deeper he sank in, the easier it was to stay as committed as he was.

Rocky Ledges had less doubt about the solidity of his own involvement. He had spent a lifetime exercising his loyalties as hard as he did his body. As with his thousands of sit-ups, he traded pain for strength gladly. Naval prison was a perfectly acceptable pain, he insisted to himself, if it was the price of standing by a friend.

"We split the ship among us," McGregor had told them. "I'll get us all the deck plans we need. We'll check the ship, compartment by compartment. We don't have time for duplications."

"Great," said Ledges. "Now if we only knew what it was we're looking for."

"Knowing what we have to do is the best we can manage for now. I'll make sure we have a reason to be wherever we want to go, within reason."

"What about Bluehoffer and the rest of the division?"

"No trouble so far. I'm keeping them busy. Out of the way and certainly out of the vault. Now let's get on it."

And so they began.

Since there was almost always some supply foul-up in any given area, the group found reasons to go almost anywhere, including areas marked limited and controlled. Trust was a formidable lever.

When there were no reasons to gain access, McGregor deftly created them with a few keystrokes of the division's computers.

The three worked on nothing else. Bluehoffer ran the division as instructed by McGregor. McGregor's secondary division assignment—personnel—was left in the care of a leading petty officer, who by this time did not expect to see his nominal boss above once a week.

Their stalking turned up brilliantly hidden whiskey stills, lost compartments converted to fine sauna baths by clever steamfitters, and a dedicated pornographic film theater.

But after 514 separate compartments, including hangar

bays, mess decks, and other spaces larger than Carlsbad Caverns, they had found nothing of use.

Ledges made the first and only promising discovery.

The compartment, deep down in the bowels of the ship on the port side, had a final designation letter of *V*. The chief had not come across that in his assigned search and momentarily forgot that this was the indicator for "Void."

Although it had a hatch and walls, it had no use. It was merely an accidental, weirdly shaped swoop of the hull where it made a sharp bend to accommodate the beginning of the bilge keel. Most voids were sealed by bolted manholes.

Ledges could see that he had momentarily blundered, and he had started to back away when the dim passageway bulb showed an oddly tumbled bulk at the pinched rear of the compartment.

Perhaps sensing something, perhaps just desperate, he stepped inside and eased the hatch closed. He unclipped the flashlight from his belt and played the beam.

Bombs. Hundreds of yards from the insanely secure and orderly ordnance spaces along the keel, here was a shocking, heedlessly distributed stack of bombs.

No matter how disinterested a sailor is in the ship's intricacies outside his own duties, there is a sixth sense of what things are and how they are done aboard.

What he was seeing here was not done.

There were none of the shapes and fittings of the new rocket ordnance that cluttered the bellies of departing birds. Plain old iron bombs were what these were. The old "fat" design. Their granddaddies had fallen over Schweinfurt and Tokyo. He knew that these were five hundred-pounders.

Something else was wrong here. Color. The bombs he had seen loaded on the roof were a menacing shade of gray. Even by the dim flashlight he could see that these were a pale blue. And that the color was faded, white streaked, rusty in places.

He found a bomb where the stenciled words on the case were upright and readable. The gods of circumstance, perhaps tired of the muddling, had at last presented him with something he could not mistake. The words read, *"Practice Bomb."*

Setting himself to gain leverage, Ledges grabbed one of the mock weapons by the fin assembly and hefted it upright. With more effort he was able to swing it clear of the deck. Empty. Yet it had to weigh five hundred pounds in use, or it would be useless in a practice drill for bombs of that size.

"It's fillable," Ledges breathed into the darkness. "It's fillable."

More grunting and pulling showed him that the fin assembly, though frozen in place from rust and disuse, was manifestly detachable. So the casing could be filled with sand or water to make the weight.

It could also be filled with money, he surmised.

U.S.S. *Ernest J. King*, Naples, Italy—June 16

His face creased with feigned concern, Ledges played his light into the compartment for the benefit of Aviation Ordnanceman First Class Cary Thumble.

"Nahhh, no sweat, Rock," Thumble said. He was one of the few ordies who occasionally fraternized above his home on the main keel. Ledges had speeded allowances for him a couple of times.

"Well, that's good," the chief said guilelessly. "When I saw those things right in the middle of where I was going to dump a couple of old desks to get 'em outa the way, I said, uh-oh, the ordies are going to be in terminal shit for this. I know the egghats are madmen about keeping the boom-boom stuff in the secure places."

"You're right on about that. But these things are orphans. They ain't real ordnance. The Air Department is maybe who they belong to. I don't know offhand, and I'd guess nobody else does. That's how they got here, you can bet. Somebody got tired of always being sent someplace else with 'em and spilled the things the first place he could hide 'em."

"How come nobody missed them?"

"Probably just wrote 'em off. Hell, they must've been losing 'em all the time anyway. You drop a hundred bombs in the drink, you lose some even when the water's shallow."

"I never saw them practice with dummies on any carrier I've been on, Thumbs."

"That's 'cause it's more fun with live stuff. These days the skippers love to use up their bomb allowances tearing up the water with big noises and fountains."

"How would they have retrieved these things in the water?"

"Any jerkoff with a magnetic anomaly detector could pinpoint 'em where they settled on the bottom. Then they just grapple 'em up."

"Think anybody'd mind if I sneaked out one or two? You could cut them in half and have a helluva nice souvenir trash can."

"No shit would be given, I guarantee," said Thumble. "Help yourself."

"My plan exactly," said Rocky Ledges.

U.S.S. *Ernest J. King*, Naples, Italy—June 16

Theron Tree, although earning above $70,000 per year as a technical representative of Haddison-Dizzard aboard the *King*, lived in a ghetto. They wryly called it St. Moritz. It housed forty-two men, all civilians. It would have been safe to say that the multibillion-dollar ship could not have functioned without its denizens. Indeed, there had been hints that locked file cabinets in the Pentagon held completed plans to induct these men into the armed services on the first day of any national emergency.

As technical representatives of the dozens of defense

contractors that had their equipment crowded into the ship, they represented an expertise beyond the powers of the Navy to supply.

Supposedly they were here on the *King* to work the glitches out of newly installed equipment and manage the training of the first generation of users. But anybody who knew a male from a female socket accepted that they were in effect members of the crew. Their numbers never lessened no matter how long the ships were in commission, although the faces might change.

The tech reps were for the most part aboard under duress no less direct than if they had been actual Navy enlistees. Their employers had made it known that their continuing prosperity in the company was dependent on their agreeing to give up shoreside comforts for long cruises on warships.

Even the knowledge that the citizens of St. Moritz were in a bondage of their own did not lessen the distaste of the regular crew for the interlopers. It rankled that the regulars were thought not to have the brainpower to handle their own ship, and that the Navy men standing with the techies on the check-cashing line saw stacks of currency that could not be contained comfortably in two hands.

Even if all that were put aside, the techies were simply not members of the Navy Club. They had no loyalties, no traditions, no friendships that would last fifty years. They spoke of lunches at restaurants in New York and Washington that sailors would never know. And of the conquest of women where money and position counted for more than balls like brass gongs.

Theron Tree was a novelty. He had not only volunteered for sea assignment on nuclear carriers, he had made it clear that he preferred to be left in place. The delight of the Navy and Haddison-Dizzard knew no bounds.

H.D. made several small components of the Raytheon SPS-49 2D radars that directed the *King*'s search for incoming antiship missiles. But those parts and their role necessitated such wide knowledge of the entire system that Raytheon was happy to have Tree oversee much of their own responsibility. For considerable extra pay, of course. This made Theron Tree a rare bird.

Theron Wilkes Tree of Jacksonville, Florida, was, however, a bird of an even rarer kind. He was a third-generation agent.

His grandfather had worked in the desert under Oppenheimer in the first nuclear weapons program. He had escaped the Red hunt that scooped up so many of his colleagues because he had foreseen what would happen and kept his announced political leanings broadly Republican even in the most trustworthy company. So camouflaged, he expatriated much useful information.

Grandfather Tree had passed his real political views on to his only son when that boy was mature enough to understand that the salvation of this world was in the hands of a power hated and feared by the United States. The model of the boy's indoctrination into the intelligence community was so perfect that its passage down to Theron required no modification.

Theron's father had long smarted under the knowledge that he had wasted his life as a military projects engineer on programs that became such long-winded and embarrassing failures that his prying produced no useful result. So he was especially severe in his expectations for his son. And especially successful in his teaching.

Until a pancreatic cancer had killed him a year ago, he was glowingly proud of Theron.

The last Tree was costing the Soviet Union exactly $52,000 a year. He could have asked for more, as valuable as he was, but he was idealistic. A thousand dollars a week struck a nice balance between need and nobility. It also paid for his rather considerable cocaine habit.

He liked to think that he could already see the results of information he had passed on. There was a new, distinctly American flair to the profile of the radar arrays on the new Soviet fleet units.

It might have been argued that all of the Trees could trace basic alienation from standard loyalties to their shared ugliness.

Each of the male Trees had faces excessively broad, excessively squat, and with chins and foreheads that sloped backward with startling pronouncement. Their eye sockets were of markedly different sizes and not quite at the same level. A body good enough to have made Tree a starting linebacker at the University of Miami was quite overshadowed by all above his collarbone.

In any event, the face of Theron Tree made it easy to remain separate, as did his dry and humorless technical fixation.

"Tree, do you ever get a hard-on?" he had been asked by a fellow resident of St. Moritz, searching for some sign of humanity in his roommate.

"Sure. When I saw how they hooked up those four UYK-7 digital computers to the PY-1 Aegis AAW system," had been his answer.

The others in the ghetto didn't rag him much because he tended to be short-tempered and, unusual for a chiphead, quick-fisted.

He didn't like Manning.

The commander, about his own age in the middle thirties, looked like all the clean-cut pretty boys who had spirited away the few decent-looking women he had found willing to spend time with a bright but ugly man. And Manning had assumed command of the operation on the *King*. That coming so soon after Tree had been able to cripple this Goliath—at great risk and only days after his activation—was impossibly bitter. Especially considering that Manning would not even be aboard except for Tree's neat and timely disposal of Hatten.

He felt an utter fool for the years he had volunteered his readiness in the floating prison. Well, he would show Moscow. But first he would show Manning.

Who was it who had killed three men, although "wet affairs" were presumed outside his technical specialty? Who was it who had subtracted eleven knots from the ship's top speed? Why should he be unspokenly reprimanded for not stopping it entirely?

Tree had considered limiting his help to Manning. He could easily do this, because it was he who had all the means of communication with their controllers. No one could ever say what he did or didn't receive. Anyway, if there was credit to be given here, it was Theron Tree who was going to have it.

It was easy for him to meet with Manning. The tech reps were always needing long consultations, special tools, special parts, special accesses. Much of what they dealt in was deeply classified. They were cleared to visit the highest officers on the ship without much hindrance. It was part of the reason why the swabbies despised them.

Tree liked being despised, especially by Manning. It was a rare pleasure to put the cold, uppity commander in his place. "Am I supposed to be impressed by the difference between your little palazzo here and St. Moritz?"

St. Moritz had been a cramped berthing space inhabited by junior officers, two or four to a tiny compartment, before the techies moved in.

Manning had the privileges of a major department head on a big ship, including a generous, well-furnished private cabin. "I just thought you might like a special private meal on my mess bill. And whether you appreciate that or not, it's a chance to talk without having to grab odd minutes in passageways."

It is an article of faith that outsiders are notoriously intolerant of other outsiders.

As hungry for it as he was, Tree ignored the excellent food. Manning ate steadily, showing he was not in the least put off.

The tones of business improved the atmosphere somewhat.

"First, what do you hear from the outside?" Manning asked.

"Not a great deal. You know we don't work this from a phone booth. You'll learn what you must when there's need."

"Look, Tree," Manning said, "I'm here because they decided that a little guy working alone couldn't handle it. So they went the other way. We go in from the top, maybe. Sure, it's too bad I'm not the XO instead of the head storekeeper, but I have an opening to anywhere and anyone. And I can get things moved and I can get things stymied, with nobody double-checking me."

"I'm not saying I can't use you, Manning," said Tree, letting his disdain show.

"It's going to take more to stop this ship than driving a nail into the odd electrical cable."

"It could take less than that. I have some ideas."

"If they concern ordnance, fire, or anything in the Crypt, forget them. I've talked to the skipper and taken a closer look than you ever could, and it's all locked down hard. You'd get a .223 in the bridge of the nose."

Tree's misaligned eyes burned into Manning. "Don't you think I'd be willing to die for what I believe in, Commander? Our cause has gone on because men have held their lives as cheap as a snap of their fingers in the world's service."

"I'm sure you're very devoted."

"Don't sneer at me. You know who the greatest American was?"

"Certainly not Richard Nixon," said Manning, needling.

"It was John Reed. A man who turned his back on one country to help an entire world. He lived in poverty. He never held an office. And that man is buried in the Kremlin wall with the titans. Remembered. Venerated. That's something a man could give his life for."

"Yes. That's also the history of Jesus, except for the Kremlin Wall. It was typhus that got Reed, wasn't it? Fleas. Even the greatest revolutionaries should wash now and then. Are you sure you won't try that steak?"

Tree picked up a cruet of vinegar and poured it over his plate. "No, thank you."

"I interrupted your ideas, Tree. Where will you look for martyrdom?"

The tech rep couldn't come up empty. "The catapults," he finally said. "Chop the catapults and this is just a used-airplane showroom. They can't launch and can't fight. They can't get off to a base ashore."

"You won't get at the launch valves again any more than you'd get at the gears."

"Of course not. But on a machine as complicated as the *King*, one thing bears on the other in very funny ways. Break what they're watching by breaking what they're not watching."

"We can't depend on that."

"We'll see."

"You'll keep me informed."

"If you can be useful," said Tree, not relinquishing control.

Manning finally lost his appetite. "Did you bring what we talked about?"

"Yes. Now lock us in and keep everybody away until we're done."

While Manning rose and tended to that, Tree took from beneath his chair a cloth toolbag of the sort he carried about all day.

Working aboard in high-level electronics was something of a wonderful dream for an agent like Tree. All his equipment was a hopeless cipher to the eyes of the uninitiated. And those items he wished to disguise were easily transformed by the addition of concealing layers of extraneous hardware. What techie was to say what another company's test devices were supposed to look like?

So, as the representative of Haddison-Dizzard, he had been able to bring aboard any number of subversive devices, although he hadn't pushed his luck. Reticence was probably silly. The couple of times that the Navy had inspected the black boxes the tech reps had dragged aboard, the poor officers had been entirely dependent on the inspected to understand what was being shown.

He laid out two items for Manning. "Either of these will do well enough. But they represent some risk, and I still don't see how much they can help us."

Manning was finding his patience again. "It's important

to know what this battle group is doing. If we can't get anything done ourselves, then it may become necessary, politics permitting, to do something from the outside.''

"Something military? Something that will leave you and me sitting on the bottom of the Med?''

"I thought that didn't matter. Maybe they'll bury a fish in the Kremlin wall to represent you.''

"Tell me how you want to use this stuff,'' snapped Tree.

"I want to be able to listen in to key places on the ship.''

"Where?''

"The admiral's cabin. The skipper's cabin. The XO's office?''

"Hold it, pal, we've got to cut back. I have a limited amount of hardware. You're looking at it, essentially. Also, because you can't stay around listening all day, I'll have to rig up a little tape recorder to the receiver. I've got one receiver other than my main one.'' His main device communicated to their people off the ship. "Pick *one* spot and make your plant. I'll set up the receiving end of it here when you're ready.''

"How does this stuff work?''

"This ballpoint pen is a transmitter and mike. The battery's good for five weeks. Lose it under a sofa, behind some chair cushions, on a shelf. Easiest plant in the world.''

"Drawbacks?''

"It's not very powerful when you don't have major equipment to do the listening. All the steel and electrical garbage on a barge like this could play hell with it over any distance. And where you hide it could muffle it completely.''

"Chance of discovery?''

"Of the device? Pretty good. People are always scrounging for pens and cleaning up. Discovery of what it is? Almost zero. It's an empty ballpoint. They scratch away and they find it's out of ink, out it goes. Keeps working in the wastebasket until they dump it.''

"Sounds kind of chancy.'' Manning picked up a black plastic wafer about the size of a quarter, maybe a quarter-inch thick. "How about this?''

Tree took it from him and snapped apart the two halves. There was a track obviously meant for an insulated wire, with sharp press-in prongs at the bottom of the track. The rest of the wafer was a colorful mass of near-microscopic electronics.

"It works best on a floor lamp because it hides nicely under the base. But any plug-in electrical device you can be alone with for a couple of seconds will do. Just lay the wire in the groove and snap the halves together. The prongs will penetrate and turn the room's wiring circuit into a wonderful broadcasting station. Put the thing where it won't be seen and I guarantee you'll hear every word inside those walls as plainly as if you were inside the room yourself."

"Okay, that's the one."

"Try it someplace safe first."

"What for?"

"Because a warship isn't a house or an office building, Commander. We don't know if the ship's wiring will behave exactly the same. And you should get used to handling it."

"Can you adjust it if it doesn't work right?"

"Sure. No problem. Anyway, what you want to do is hook it up someplace where you can be anytime you want, and where they're not too careful. Then I'll fix up the receiver and recorder so they'll look like a transistor radio with an earplug. Record for a while. I'll adjust it so it's perfect. Then all you've got to do is decide where you want to listen and how to get this there."

Manning dropped the wafer into his pocket.

Tree returned his ballpoint to his bag and closed it. "Thanks for a wonderful evening, Commander."

He studied the shelves on the way out. "Nice models. Hmmm. Your father looks like a bit of a stiff. Your mother though . . . I like her in that maid's uniform. I bet she beat a mean rug."

U.S.S. *Ernest J. King*, Naples, Italy—June 18

There had been nothing in the least elegant about getting a 500-pound practice bomb out of the lost compartment. Thumble had one of the dozens of carts with which the ordnance spaces were awash brought up from over the keel and left at a spot convenient to Ledges's use.

Ledges's tools of deception were nothing more complicated than two standard Navy blankets stripped off his berth. When he'd wrestled a bomb onto the cart, he simply threw the blankets over the hulking five-foot cylinder and trundled it off to McGregor's compartment.

The imposing object leaned against a bulkhead, uncovered. Penetrating oil having worked the rust loose from the threads near the tail fins, Ledges was at last able to unscrew and open the loading port. He peered inside uncertainly. "You're the accountant, Wade. What does your geometry tell you about how many of these things we're going to need?"

"For the whole thirty-five million, in the usual smallish denominations, we'll need eight of these."

"No problem with that," said Ledges. "There are forty-four practice bombs down there."

"Are we sure they're waterproof?" McGregor wondered.

"Reasonably," said Ledges. "No sign of saltwater inside. In any case, we could wrap the money in plastic bags or get it into some kind of waterproof containers."

"Maybe the damned things won't sink," said Lydecker. "That'd be interesting. We slip them over the side, and when we come back a year later all we find is a bunch of happy Sicilian fishermen sailing yachts with helicopters and starlets on the fantails."

McGregor checked some calculations. "My displacement numbers tell me they'll go down. Now we need a report from the dumping committee. What's the best place to get these over the side, Rock?"

"Okay, here's how it figures. Since we decided it didn't matter whether we took our land bearing on the same side of the ship that we dumped the bombs out of, I had a lot of latitude." He spread several varieties of deck plan out on a berth. "There were a lot of things to look out for."

"Better tick 'em off," said McGregor. "We wouldn't want to miss anything."

"It had to be someplace where there'd be no traffic for at least fifteen minutes at a time."

"More'd be better, but okay."

"It had to be accessible to a tractor."

"We could do it with Thumble's cart if we had to. See if you can get away with forgetting to bring it back. Keep it in with the bombs."

Ledges kept going. "There had to be a place where we could hide eight of these big attention-grabbing mothers for at least twenty-four hours."

"Add to that having to stay clear of snoopers while we sneak the bombs below."

"Also it has to be far enough back along the hull so the bow sweep doesn't make contact and scatter the drop. And not so far back that the propeller wash doesn't do the same."

"Good point, Rock," McGregor said.

"I figured it's best if we drop them as close to the water as we could. Even at night there are people hanging over the catwalks grabbing a smoke. They might not be able to make out what's going on, but why give some ring-knocker the chance to decide we're poisoning the whales."

"Great. And now the envelope, please."

Ledges ran a red marker pen through the deck plans to illustrate his choice. "The door in the hull is way down here on the starboard side, O-8 level. It's only used for ordnance loading off a pier. The passageway behind it is practically a straight run to the ordnance hoists over the centerline. Which is great for us."

"Why's that?"

"Well, the passageway doesn't take you anywhere important on the beam unless you're a Sidewinder coming aboard.

The bow-to-stern passageways that intersect aren't very many.''

"But somebody could see a long, straight distance if he looked our way.''

"Not if we close the first door inboard.''

Lydecker, who had mostly remained bemused, thumped Ledges on the back. "I get it. Nobody checks a closed door in an integrity check, only an open one. Especially one that doesn't go anywhere when the ship's at sea.''

"Bull's-eye. So we don't have to find a compartment to store the stuff on the night we move. We line it up right in the passageway that dead-ends against our door to the Med.''

McGregor grinned his wonder at the thoroughness of this amateur. "If we can do our part half as good as you did yours, we might actually have a shot at this inside straight.''

Ledges nodded, but his brow was still furrowed. "We've got to coordinate the drop perfectly with the land bearing, or we'll have half the Med to search.''

"That's the simplest thing we have to do," McGregor said. "I've boned up on the piloting books. I'll be up at one of the azimuth circles, and we'll do it just by hacking watches. Rocky, you be sure you can get all the bombs pushed over the side in under thirty seconds. I'll be marking my bearing out over half a minute.''

"Commander, why do I still have trouble believing you're going to be able to get a shore bearing at night?''

"God wouldn't have invented night glasses if he didn't want night bearings.''

"He also invented featureless topography. You might not find anything to sight on. And if you do, you might not recognize it in the sunshine a year later,'' said Ledges.

"Maybe I'll do a star shoot. I wasn't bad at that. We'll have to get some luck from the weather, in any case, or wait on it as much as we can. Or there could be a way to tap into the main navigation system and use the radar bearings.''

"How come we worry about the little things when we have such marvelous big things to sweat out? Like suppose we steam out on a course and schedule where we're out of sight of land when night falls? Or we miscalculate depth somehow, and deposit thirty-five million bucks where we can't get it back with available locating equipment and some scuba gear. Even if we're going to have enough ready scratch in our pockets to keep us going until the pickup, we're not going to be in any position to engage Jacques Cousteau to help us get a mile down.''

"How can we cut the odds, Chief?''

Ledges placed copies of *Coast Pilot* and *Sailing Directions* at the center of the table. "I don't have to tell you that the distance between an easy retrieval and one that's impossible can be ten feet. Some of those drop-offs are sheer cliffs. All we can do is try to make our drop over a broadly shallow area with a land bearing. The bottom depths and bearings to them from shore points are charted in these pages. If we had the slightest idea of what our course and sailing time might be, we could pinpoint a good place right now. As it is, we'll have to pick a lot of spots and hope one fills the bill.''

Gloom passed over Lydecker's sunny face. "The odds on this ain't nearly as good as the ones I had in Monte Carlo, are they?''

"Hink," said McGregor, "the last thing we need now is a realistic assessment of our chances. What did you find in the medical books, Rock?''

"Not the right thing yet. The way I see it, it's got to be something with food, so it would be plausible that we all came down with it together, and something so life-threatening that they'd fly us to a hospital ashore and not try to fix it here on the ship. Botulism is close, but I'm not sure we can fake up the symptoms with the medicines we can get hold of.''

"Don't forget, we can't make ourselves so sick that we can't truck out of a naval hospital once we're ashore.''

"Got you. I'm buttering up a pharmacist's mate. Maybe he'll have some ideas. Nobody can think of more ways to fake symptoms for goofers than a pharmacist's mate. They should write a book.''

As periodically happened, they subsided and gave way to thoughts of the utter bleakness of their prospects.

U.S.S. *Ernest J. King*, Naples, Italy—June 18

Richard Manning, to all appearances, was sound asleep in his berth, apparently having neglected to remove the featherweight headset that led to a small Walkman radio on the deck beside him. This was far from the case.

Manning's mind was racing.

For the third time he was playing through a tape that had been recorded that afternoon by Tree's device during its test.

Despite Tree's doubts, the wafer fastened into place by Manning had functioned well if you didn't count an occasional crackle as something elsewhere in the ship had surged through the electrical circuit.

From the first moments of listening, the commander had known that the sound quality would be just fine for a more serious application.

Then, with the urge to eavesdrop bred into even the most sober creatures, Manning had let his ears linger on the conversation in McGregor's compartment. He had chosen that spot to test his device because it was safely accessible and on the same circuit as the island above with all its choice listening locations.

It had taken awhile for his half-dozing mind to begin to tumble to what he was hearing. Even an attentive second hearing had not quite dropped the pieces into place. Now, however, it had become clear, and his closed eyes no longer signaled rest but a concentration so fierce that he wanted no outside glimmer to intrude.

What he had heard could have disastrous effects on his position.

While the plan had a certain élan and was not devoid of inspiration, its chances of success, its immense likelihood of a misstep, told him that they would be found out. And at the most inopportune moment, if fate hadn't changed her ways.

If the egghats were to uncover a major scandal in one of his key divisions, it wouldn't matter whether or not he was implicated. The swarm of investigators would put him under a scrutiny that would make any further action all but impossible.

There were a couple of obvious ways to go:

He could use his own powers to make it easier for them to succeed. By neutralizing the inept Bluehoffer even further and building a bureaucratic wall around the division, he could substantially reduce their chances of discovery. But then, if that discovery came anyway, he would have made himself more culpable. Then he'd really be finished.

On the other hand, he could thwart the plan before it got going. Knowing their plans, he could throw a series of stumbling blocks into their path, apparently by chance, that would cause them to abandon their plot.

He distrusted this last notion. They had already shown themselves desperate and resourceful. If they changed their intentions because of obstacles, next time they might not be so accommodating as to discuss it in front of a lamp with ears.

Now Manning remembered something his father would frequently say to his mother when he thought his son was out of hearing. "Audrey, the world will belong to the man who finds some use for assholes, because those people are in inexhaustible supply."

For the next two hours he lay, moving hardly a muscle, while his mind sought, raced, nibbled, and turned.

By and by he had the beginnings of a way to use the plotters. He thanked his dead father silently.

U.S.S. *Ernest J. King*, Naples, Italy—June 19–22

Manning would have liked to exclude Tree completely. But he would settle for incompletely. As Tree would share information with him only selectively, Manning felt no compunction about doing the same. And he would not be foolish enough to announce his resolution as Tree had.

What Tree hadn't stopped to think about was that each of them had their own off-line code—a standard precaution against the capture and compromise of a member of the team. Ordinarily Manning might pass information to Tree for relay in plain English, leaving it to the technician to send and to read as he did so. An on-line encrypter would then take care of the coding as the message was sent. But with Manning also having the option of a personal off-line code, he could keep Tree ignorant of what was being sent. And with a request that all transmissions be kept in his own cipher, he could fix it so the techie would learn nothing from receptions either. Manning imagined the ugly man's fury and savored the thought.

The plotters didn't take long to accommodate Manning with their first mistake.

So often a well-conceived plan will begin to come unglued when the designers add casual elaborations. It was not surprising that the boy, Lydecker, would be the one to go wrong.

Lydecker was unable to wait until the ship was at sea to begin the transfer of the bombs to the dead-end passageway. He had decided, apparently without consulting the others, that ordnance loading was complete and the transfer spot was secure. Possibly he felt that moving the bombs was a more secure thing in the greatly reduced traffic of the cold-iron watches in port. He didn't consider that the bustle of a ship at sea would be the best camouflage for any kind of clandestine moving.

Whichever point of view would have proven right became moot at once, because the very night that Lydecker had moved the first bombs on Thumble's cart, Manning made his daily check of the blind passageway.

Alone, he gave one of his rare smiles.

Naples, Italy—June 19-22

Suddenly Manning was in their life. Sometimes it seemed every hour. They were baffled, as well as appalled.

Everything they had heard about Manning through the eerily efficient fleet grapevine told them that their new commander was the coldest of all the cold fish in the sea. He would show no mercy where he perceived failure. But if your unit functioned efficiently, he would stay out of your way. You were not to be downcast if he didn't talk to you, because he talked to no one. Until now.

To be sure, he didn't get to the Disbursing Division right away. He did full inspections and reviews in the other parts of his immense domain, working his way through them one by one. Through General Supply Support he went, then General Mess, Clothing, Small Stores, Ship's Stores and Services, Officers' Mess, Aviation Stores, and all the rest.

Wherever he passed, tails were reamed, stripes shrank, transfers abounded, and a smartness unknown under the late Commander Hatten arrived.

The men in the Disbursing Division had every reason to be terrified, including those who had not the faintest idea that $785,000 was missing from the vault.

The plotters, not yet professionals despite all the strides they had made, were frozen like deer in the glare of a jacklight. They never thought to make a desperate run off the ship although they realized that any careful scrutiny would destroy their plan and them together. Like good losers in a gentlemanly chess game, they were prepared for a checkmate that appeared inevitable.

In fact, the day that Manning had first arrived in the

Disbursing Division office they all put on their cleanest uniforms, perhaps to look their best in any arrest ceremonies. Also, they had done as much to put their affairs in order as men might who were waiting execution. They saw no way to extract themselves from their tangle.

Manning had disposed of an hour's worth of formalities in the office with most of the staff drawn up, and then indicated that he wanted to be alone with McGregor and his LPO, Ledges.

This was the point when he would begin the examination of the records and initiate the audits that would effectively end their lives as free men.

Instead Manning had smiled and asked that the young man at the desk outside the door, Petty Officer Third Class Lydecker, be sent for some coffee and buns. Then the commander placed his feet up on McGregor's desk and threw his cap onto a chair.

In the unspoken ritual of the Navy, an officer's cover is the annunciator of his mood and approachability. That and his uprightness of posture, or lack of it, was a bellow indicating what was to follow.

And now there was a smile. Commander Hatten himself could hardly have approached its radiance.

"I guess the word in the fleet is that I'm a pretty stiff dick," Manning said.

"Every new man gets that treatment, Commander," said McGregor. It was a bit unfriendly of McGregor to keep his familiarity so far beneath Manning's. "We haven't been sweating." He was glad he wasn't hooked to a lie detector.

"Good. Believe me, I don't try to unscramble a good omelet. I've been going back through Hatten's papers, such as they were, and this division shines out."

"Thank you, sir," said McGregor in utter surprise.

"My dad was a submarine man, and he said that the boats that ran the best were the ones where veteran crews rewrote the rule books."

McGregor caught Ledges's eyebrows going up sharply. "You do sort of get a system."

"The long leash that Hatten used didn't work in all his divisions, but I see it's working here. So if you've been pulling books and folders for a combing or an audit, you can put 'em back. The men on this ship are stretched out too far as it is."

"We appreciate that, sir," said McGregor as one might who had just postponed an excursion to Portsmouth.

Manning showed no inclination to leave. He reached inside his jacket and brought out a deck of cards. "Anybody here got a gambling gene hiding inside him?"

"No more than most, sir," said McGregor with care.

"Well, I do. My DNA is divided up into four suits, I swear. Poker is the only way I've ever found to relax." He shuffled the deck not much better than might an old lady from Mason City. He had made plain what he wanted to be asked.

"I guess we could get up a little game here now and then if you wanted, Commander. We've been a little tight ourselves."

"I'd appreciate that. Let's keep it small. Say you, the chief here, and maybe one other. Make it an enlisted. Give me a chance to get to know what those guys are thinking. And to show them I can bend a little."

"It's not exactly according to the *Division Officers' Guide*, Commander, but it sounds like a good time to me."

The best freedom in the Navy is that which permits sailors to pick the friends they want and leave the rest to the duty hours. Manning's overtures were anything but welcome. Especially now.

The commander rambled on for another fifteen minutes, touching on the backgrounds of the men, the increasing bleakness of a career in the Navy with the ever-growing specter of cutbacks. He even touched on sports, of which he obviously knew next to nothing.

When he finally left, he might have heard from halfway down the passageway the sighs of those he had left behind.

"I don't know whether to scream or giggle," Ledges said. "I suppose he knows about as much about the real Navy as the guy who runs Sears Roebuck, but I've been in too long to do anything but piss on an asshole like that."

"Something's off center here. You don't move up in the fleet the way he has when you operate like that. He knows what he's doing."

"Well, Wade, if you can drag up from the bilges some reason why he'd want to butter up this deadass division, put it on the speaker."

"Cards are cheaper than Hatten's Rémy for squeezing little favors out of us. Especially if the guy wins."

"I never saw a ring-knocker who could round up three deuces yet."

"He's given us the time we need."

"But suppose he's all over us when we have to be operating?"

"Hey, Chief, nobody ever said we weren't going to be spending a lot of hours with the laws of chance."

Ledges said, "That's fine, Wade. If chance is what this is."

The games began with a vengeance. Manning called late the next afternoon and asked for one to be organized in McGregor's compartment for that evening. His voice on the phone belonged much more to the stone-faced commander they had heard about than the one they had been with.

He arrived carrying a large envelope which turned out to have in it a great deal of money in small bills.

As he piled it before them, the discomfort grew. Financial transactions of any sort between officers and subordinates were frowned on in every manual that the Navy wrote. The writings didn't dwell much on gambling between the castes, assuming that common sense would take care of avoiding that.

"I could get us a lot of change," Ledges ventured.

"Any game worth playing is worth risking something," Manning came back. "Isn't that right, Lydecker?"

He said that before Lydecker had been introduced, showing that he was ahead of them in ways they didn't expect.

"I don't mind a little risk, sir."

"Then we'll get along."

Manning played badly. It was not the bad play of a stupid plunger or one ignorant of odds and subtleties. He was setting a tone.

He bet every hand aggressively, showing early that he would not be backed off until everyone had showed. Early on, he forced uncomfortably large pots on bluffs, taking several before the others could catch his rhythm. And then several more when he backed the bluffs.

If the plotters had hoped to forget their early distaste of Manning in the heat of the game, they were disappointed. Sailors, whose long, forced community made them grand masters of poker, were completely put off by such an unreasoned element in his play.

Nor was Manning's poker technique the only source of tension. There could be none of the horseplay and brutal bantering that made Navy play so often a roughhouse joy.

Manning became the parent who had permitted the children a night of tenting in the backyard, only to insist on sleeping with them.

When the others finally broke through the commander's wild play and began to nail him with substantial losses, there was little of the usual gloating and catcalling that could be expected as the reward of incompetence. Even though he made no sign of discomfort, there was something so alien in the taking of such sums from an officer that they found themselves squirming.

When the first evening ended, the players left behind felt as though they'd been wrestling a bear. There were circles of sweat under their arms, and their neck muscles ached from tension.

"Do you think he had as much fun as we did?" asked the drained Ledges.

"Let's hope so," McGregor said. "Then we won't be seeing him until the next century."

But Manning was back the next night. He called McGregor at almost the same moment of the afternoon to set up the game.

McGregor tried to beg off. "We've got a lot of things to catch up on in the division, Commander."

"That's fine," Manning said. "While we're playing we'll talk about what kind of help you need. In fact, you could walk me through the details before it gets too late and I could stay around and advise you some myself. I've packed away a lot of courses in accounting and finance since I've been in. See you about 1930 hours, then."

This being the last thing McGregor wanted, he never brought up the issue during the game. Manning didn't either.

When Manning called again for a session on the following evening, McGregor made no attempt to dissuade the commander. The plotters now understood that they were part of a game more complex than poker.

If the man's intention was to let them stew before he pounced, what was the point? He didn't seem emotional or imaginative enough for cruelty.

Were they just seeing a bogeyman under the pressure of their guilt?

It was accepted in the Navy that two or three times during a career you would find yourself in the hands of a certifiable madman. Perhaps he was one of those.

After Manning had called for the fourth straight afternoon, Lydecker leaped up in exasperation and stepped into the open vault. "I'm setting the time lock for next November. If you want me in the game, you'll have to wait till then."

"If we're not nice to this guy," Ledges warned him, "you're going to be in a vault a lot longer than that."

"God, I wish he'd make some new friends. There must be someone else on the ship he could tie up with."

"Matter of fact, he has another buddy. Just what you'd expect. That techie with a face that looks like somebody tried to squeeze it under a door. Name's Tree. One of the messies told me Manning had him in for a big feed."

"That must have been more laughs than root canal with a hot ice pick. You think we can teach the techie to play cards?"

"Maybe he already knows, Hink. McGregor says our commander is bringing along another body tonight."

"I never thought I'd be looking back fondly to the days when all they could do was flog and hang you."

The unknown guest was not the civilian tech rep.

A petty officer first class arrived early. As soon as he stepped through the door, the plotters could see on his face the same brand of confusion they wore upon their own.

"Name's Williger," he said, his face as flat and devoid of distinguishing features as the Midwest farmland in his voice. "Commander Manning, he . . . uh . . . said there was gonna be a poker game here." He had left his body half turned toward the door, apparently hoping that all this was a silly mistake.

"You heard right, sailor," Ledges said. "C'mon in and relax."

McGregor made the introductions, noticing that Williger was no more likely to relax than they were. "Pretty hot with a deck, are you, Williger?"

"Me, sir? I haven't won a hand since I played spit in the ocean with my eight-year-old sister. I watch the other guys go at it and I know I wouldn't last three minutes with 'em. I can't afford this." He felt a need to explain what he was clearly unable to. "This isn't even my ship. I'm on the *James* in the escort. A chiphead name Tree got me detached for a couple days."

"What the hell does he want with you?" asked Ledges.

"Something about sonar electronics," he said. "I ain't had a chance to work it out with him yet."

Lydecker now saw that Williger's sleeve badge showed the headphones crossed by an arrow that marked him as a sonar technician. "What's a carrier got to do with sonar?"

"How the hell should I know? This guy says his company, which is Haddison-Dizzard, might want to find a way to coordinate sea-search units with a carrier's airborne-search equipment. Might be totally fulla shit, too, but these chipheads have the same weight as admirals these days. You never know when they might dream up a new piece of junk for the Navy to get another ten billion bucks in appropriations for.''

"We still don't get what this has to do with cards," said McGregor.

"Hey, sir, when a full commander says play cards, you play cards. He came in while I was talking to Tree in the mess. If it wasn't me, it would have been somebody else with bad luck.''

Ledges doubted that.

Manning arrived shortly afterward, and for the fourth straight night the joyless game began.

If the commander was no more likable, he was a good deal more relaxed. His eyes sometimes joined in his chilly smile now. It was the look often seen on officers who had successfully sweated out a doubtful promotion.

He took extensive pains to bring Williger into the flow of conversation. More words were said in the opening half hour of play than in all the previous games combined. This was largely the contribution of Williger. He was eager—as the plotters had already seen—to parade his knowledge and worldliness.

The commander led him through the midwestern viewpoint on farm politics, and the heartland as the manufacturer of great college football players. The others, pleased to have the ponderous burden of conversation removed from them, goaded the sonarman along when he seemed to be losing momentum.

After losing a substantial bet, Manning flicked at the badge on Williger's sleeve. "You know, Williger, people like me mostly don't know that there are still guys like you in the Navy. Isn't this listening crap straight out of World War Two?'' He pursed his lips and made a reasonable imitation of an echo ranger's pinging. "The Russians have got to be able to mask that out. It's just one of those traditions that they won't let die.''

The sonarman grew red. "No, sir. We just have to get the best men and the best equipment in the Navy. The Ruskies have subs that make ours look like something from Toys 'R

Us. If we didn't pick 'em out wherever they were, and damn fast, we'd be going down to join 'em.''

"What've we got? This group, for instance. If we had to get on station somewhere, what'd we have going to defend ourselves under way?"

The cards were now forgotten.

"At any given moment, while we're steaming on anything from Condition Three on down, we've got a mix going that a scuba-diving flea couldn't get through. Dunking sonar, towed arrays, sonobuoys, SOSUS listeners on the bottom—"

Manning wouldn't let up. "That's passive listening, isn't it? I mean what's the use of having good underwater ears if your target isn't making any noise?"

"If somebody belches aboard one of those subs, we'll hear 'im, sir. And anyway, we've got plenty of active sonar. We've got more transducers pinging sound into the water than the Marines have crewcuts. Doesn't make any difference how quiet a thing is down there. If it's bigger than a football, we've got a good shot at making it."

"You mean to say if I dumped a perfectly noiseless item of any decent size off this ship the group sonar would nail it?"

"How big are you thinking, Commander?"

"Ah, let's see," Manning said. "Let's say I dumped . . . what? . . . half a dozen filled fifty-five-gallon drums off the end of this carrier in the middle of the battle group. More or less together."

"Wouldn't make any difference if you dumped 'em together or separate. We'd be looking so hard for things like mines that we'd make our challenge on every one of 'em."

Williger was working up a head of steam and Manning kept at him. "What would we have doing the pinging?"

"A lot of our gear can go active as well as passive. We've got the SQS-53s bow mounted on the frigates. Those've got a digital interface with the Mark 16 ASW Weapons Control System. It can track multiple targets real easy."

Manning raised a palm to slow the headlong flight of the

sonarman. "Suppose we're not pinging at all because an enemy can home back in on those transducer beams?"

"The newest equipment uses what you call spread-spectrum transmission. You spread the signal energy over a whole range of frequencies. It's in a definite, useful pattern, but only your own equipment knows the pattern. The pinging, spread in all those little pieces, gets lost in the sea noise."

"I think I just got lost in the sea noise myself," said Ledges.

"Okay, okay," pursued Manning. "So you pick up those drums drifting down. You have no idea what the hell they are. Maybe it's a bunch of Italian auto heiresses riding dolphins. What do you do about it?"

Williger puffed up. He was ready for this. "First thing we'd probably trigger an RDSS. That's a Rapidly Deployed Surveillance System. It's a sonobuoy about the size of a Mark 46 torpedo that has the equivalent of a whole shoreside intelligence department in it. It anchors to the ocean bed under the target and pinpoints everything about it from location to the size of the captain's dick, begging your pardon, sir."

"I guess the carrier's antisub planes would figure in."

"Before you could blink, Commander. An S-3A would stick that MAD probe out of its ass and overfly the alert area. The Magnetic Anomaly Detector's not much good over a whole ocean, but inside a thousand yards it can find things not much bigger than a sardine can. It detects the difference between the electrical conductivity of water and metal materials passing through. And don't forget the sub has MIDAS, which is a Mine Detection and Avoidance Sonar that would—"

The commander interrupted. "There'd be an awful lot going down in an awfully few minutes. Who makes the decisions about what's to be done? Who's smart enough?"

The plotters had by now deduced that Manning had crammed himself as full of this arcana as Williger, but that made the cascading information no less horrifying to them.

They had by now stopped trying to keep their despair from showing.

"Computers do most of the deciding, sir. They've got enough info in the data banks, where they can come up with the exact location of the Russian sub as well as its name, number, and officers. If they buck the data processing up high enough, it gets into the Illiac system—that's sixty-four supercomputers working in parallel to coordinate defenses and tell you what the bogey is and where. Then you get whatever defense it takes. Anything from ASROC to homing torpedoes to nuclear depth charges." Williger finally stopped for breath.

"Seems like an awful lot of fuss for a few little chunks of metal dropped overboard."

"Just responding to the commander's example," said Williger, thoroughly pleased with the defense of his specialty.

"Moderation in all things, Williger," Manning said. "You've taken us away from the game with all your gabbing. Who was dealing?"

They played for another hour until it was close to 2200 hours and lights out. Then Manning sent Williger back to his berth.

The commander, studying the plotters, made no move to leave. "You seem sort of down," he said.

"Any idea what it might be, sir?" grated Ledges.

"Yes," said Manning. "I've been meaning to talk to you about that."

"I guess there'll be no more cards," McGregor said.

"Right. We'll get to do some good talking. I'll be busy a day or two before that, though. And listen. Department heads have been asked for a list of sensitive personnel to be restricted to the ship while the present tension is going on. I'm going to put you all on that list."

"In case we run out of ammo in a tussle and have to load the guns with dimes, I guess."

"I hope it makes you feel important to me, because you are. I'll say good night now."

U.S.S. *Ernest J. King*, Naples, Italy—June 23

Boiling inside, Tree carried Manning's stopwatch high into the forest of radar arrays above the *King*'s island. The weather was gray and dirty, and a rainsquall drove sheets of water against the technician dressed in yellow rain gear. A flannel shirt was already coldly plastered to his chest. Below, the ends of the flight deck stretching fore and aft were invisible in the blowing rain.

Even as he had been goading Manning, he had known that it was not prudent. People in his dangerous profession lived or died on the possession of the smallest bits of knowledge. By shutting him out of what was contained in this transmission to the controllers, Manning had made it less likely that Tree could anticipate and survive a major mistake. Or perhaps something that was not a mistake.

Tree considered that there might be nothing of real import in the last several communications. The insistence that he turn out on this miserable afternoon to send this one could just be Manning punishing him for insolence.

The technician had run down the possibilities. He might play sheepish and apologize to Manning, hoping to regain full partnership by simple ass-licking. He could simply insist on knowing what was in the transmissions. But that would just give Manning a chance to laugh at him. Tree saw how he had caught himself and could only shrug his soaking shoulders and go forward.

From the canvas toolbags, which were suspended from his shoulders by straps, he withdrew a light, stiff plastic sheet and swept it up over his head. When he squatted beneath it against the house of the SPS-48B radar he was supposedly adjusting, he was hidden from the view of any watchers, however unlikely, and reasonably dry. The sheet was just translucent enough for him to work without a flashlight.

After he had squirmed out of his equipment straps, Tree set up the unit that was to transmit his message. While the item could actually be made to twitch its dials in some elementary testing operations, its main circuits lent themselves to a unique and powerful radio signal.

The technical side of Tree greatly admired the genius that had gone into turning Manning's stopwatch into a coding machine. The operator's job was simplicity itself. To encipher, Manning had to use nothing more complicated than his memory and small manipulative variations of the standard stopwatch controls.

Each second marked on the watch's face corresponded to a letter, number, or randomized scrambler. By turning the hand down to the proper second and pressing the winding stem in a special sequence, he was able to program his message into the internal circuit in plain English. Then one of the scrambler settings jumbled the information ingeniously and stored it in Manning's own code—all on the power of a battery not much larger than one needed to power a good photoflash.

The rest of the intricate system lay in Tree's device.

Tree withdrew from a bag a cable with a thin single prong at each end. One prong he fitted into a nearly invisible socket at the bottom of the watch's case, and the other into his "tester." He worked a knob in the back of the tester and saw a green diode glow for almost five seconds.

The message had not yet been sent, but had now been drastically altered in the volume it occupied in space and time. All extraneous and repetitive space had been squeezed out. It was a technology beginning to come into important use in civilian applications from telephone systems to credit-card-sized dictionaries. But the other systems had not been brought to anything approaching the art of the one Tree held in his hand.

He checked his own watch and saw that he had come into the narrow time envelope where the electronics on the Soviet AGI trawler *Vinza* off the coast would be fine-tuned to the frequency of his transmitter. He estimated the effect of the passing squall on clarity and decided that the power of the listening devices and the short distance of broadcast alleviated any problem.

After checking the power of the nickel-cadmium battery, he held down a white transmission button with his forefinger. Even above the percussive drumming of the rain on the plastic sheet he could hear the single split-second electronic burp.

To all the sophisticated NATO listening devices employed from the shore and from ships and planes, his message had been just a small chatter of static in the squall, lost among the thousands just like it. But on the AGI trawler, a delicate, computer-tuned receiver taped it, rewound it, and replayed it at reduced speed, allowing the operator to identify it by its code flag as a first-priority message. No one on the ship would ever know the exact content of the message. It was sent on a larger, more powerful version of the equipment used by Tree, and in the same sort of burp.

"There you are, Commander Manning, you prissy bastard," murmured Tree beneath his rain-beaten sheet.

Remaining uncomfortably situated for an extra five minutes, he reconnected the other end of the cable that ran from Manning's stopwatch and put the gibberish down on a tiny, battery-powered tape recorder. This time, though, he made the adjustment necessary to bring the scrambled information back to its original volume and speed.

Commander Manning would be made to wait a bit for the return of his watch. Tree knew that cryptography was not one of his own skills, but he also knew that he was a richly gifted electronics technician. And that he had quite a lot of time and all the resources that could be scrounged out of a vessel four blocks long.

Before he had finished climbing down out of the spinning radar arrays, he thought that he might already have found the answer to decrypting the message.

Tree looked forward to the work. Every serious man needs a hobby.

* * *

McGregor's compartment had, by now, taken on the aspect of a much-used torture chamber.

"Is he late?" asked Lydecker, although he'd just looked at his watch.

"When he comes, he comes," said McGregor, not bothering to glance at his own timepiece.

"Blackmail," Ledges muttered. "It's going to be blackmail. It can't be anything else. He's been softening us up to say yes to anything."

McGregor shook his head. "It doesn't make enough sense. If you put all our savings and yearly pay together on that table, you could hide it under the ashtray."

"But this division is where the money is, Wade. He might make us set up a deal to funnel him something out of the vault."

"That'd be wacky, too, Rocky. Then we'd have something on him as fatal as what he might have on us."

"You think it's just some kind of low-grade sadism?"

"I don't even know if this is about anything more than a guy who doesn't know how to conduct himself in a game of cards."

The door opened and Manning stepped in.

"Good evening, Commander," Ledges said. "We're ready for you."

With a pocketknife, Manning dug the wafer off the cord of the desk lamp. "Since the Walker spy case, the Navy's been a lot more careful about espionage rings on the inside. As part of a super-hush op, they've been giving some department heads the independent authority to bug. Just an experiment for now, you understand. Nobody went for it much, but they're hot for us to get our feet wet. Reports due every month. I stuck this thing in here because I couldn't think of any place else to try it. Well . . . wait a minute. That's not true, either. I just couldn't figure out why Lydecker was stashing those practice bombs in the passageway. I'd seen guys stealing just about everything in this Navy you could think of. This one baffled me. And I have to tell you, I underestimated you. You knocked my skivvies off. But after what I heard the first time, I kept on listening. Believe me, I have it all."

"We could just deny it," McGregor said.

"I have it on tape. That's the way the item works. I'll play it for you if you want to be sure."

"We might ask you to do that," Ledges said, stonily composed.

"And I might just tell you to screw yourself. Look, if I was going to have you arrested, it would already be done. And if I was going to wait for you to commit yourselves so as to catch you with the money in your hands, I wouldn't be here now."

"Why'd you wait this long? Why all the playing around?" Lydecker asked him.

"I have to be honest. I wanted to check out some things. Make sure I could handle some arrangements. Just to be certain it wouldn't be better for me to call in the master-at-arms after all and have you shipped out."

Lydecker cut short something McGregor had been about to say. "Look, Commander Manning, we can all get something good out of this. We'll make it up so you look like some kind of hero, with a full confession from me about how you were too smart for me. No defense. It can look like I did it alone, which I really did. These guys were just trying to get me away. If they thought I could handle it by myself, it would have gone down that way. Let them stay clean."

"Sonny," said Manning, "I'm not all that interested in the sentimental attachments in the Disbursing Division. But you're definitely right that we can all get something out of it— Meet your new partner."

If Manning had expected to surprise them, he passed all expectation. Of the hundred awful things they had imagined, this simple resolution had remained unthought.

"Welcome aboard, Commander," was all McGregor could finally think to say.

* * *

"I have to thank you men," Manning said. "One minute I was sitting there ready to scream myself to death with boredom for the goddamned Navy, and the next I was listening to the answer I might've been praying for. At first all I felt was envy that somebody else had the guts to break away, not just from the fleet, but from their whole awful lives. Then it just struck. Why not me, too? Why not just break in on them?"

"What was all this business with Williger?" Ledges asked.

"When you work as hard on a plan as you guys did, it's tough to admit it isn't worth a damn. I wanted you to hear it from somebody who didn't have anything in the pot. If you'd gone ahead, you'd have blown us all away."

"I have a feeling," said Ledges, "that we're about to hear some things you've been thinking about for most of a week."

"Bingo," said Manning, removing his cap for the first time since their first meeting. "It turns out, like it or not, that we're the answer to one another's prayers. I can make things happen further up the system than you ever could. And you can cover up the details down below in a way I couldn't manage if I'd been recruiting helpers for a year."

Desperation makes strange affiliations. The plotters now turned to Manning as though they had been planning together for a lifetime.

"We're almost out of time, Commander," Ledges said. "Give us the top line."

"Okay," said Manning. "Here it is in shorthand. Aside from all the problems of sonar picking up the bombs, your ideas about getting off the ship and picking them up had too many moving parts. I intend for us to get the money and ourselves off the ship at the same time. Your botulism routine to get you off depended too much on putting yourself in the Navy's hands. It's a lot safer to work a straight smuggling operation. I go and you and the cash go with me. It's all done in a single day."

"Details, please," said Ledges softly. His eyes had not widened the way the others' had.

"Working that out will take a bit more doing. We're going to need some help from ashore."

"We couldn't figure out any good way to do that."

"Because you couldn't go up the chain as far as I can," said Manning.

"Do we have to split more ways?" asked McGregor.

"Negative. If anybody found out how big this was, we'd have half of NATO and half the Italian government as partners. No participation. Buy-outs."

"How can we help with that when you've got us stuck on the ship?" Lydecker asked.

"I'll handle it alone. You don't even have to know what I'm doing. In fact, it's best that way."

"If you say so, Commander," said Ledges.

"Let's make this an early evening, men," said Manning. "I've got a lot of thinking left to do," he said, turning toward the door. "Don't talk in your sleep."

The cold-iron watch found the passageways and their turns empty. Manning started when the hulking chief came up alongside in his rapid limp.

"Did I forget something, Chief?"

"I don't think you ever forget anything, Commander. I know that I don't. My friends are a lot nicer than I am. They don't have my nasty, distrustful mind. They haven't asked themselves what happens if we do our work and then you disappear alone with the money. And we're back here shaking hands with the master-at-arms."

"Aren't you neglecting to address an officer properly, Ledges?"

"This deal was rough enough with people who trusted one another."

"Oh, I trust you all right."

"I guess there's still no way for all of us to back out of this."

"No way." Manning did not take the moment he should

have to make sure that they were under some sort of observation.

The chief's big hands spun him powerfully. In an eyeblink Manning's left arm, its wrist and elbow joint taken to the breaking point, was up between his shoulder blades. Thus surprised, he was borne quickly into a compartment housing contamination garments. Its lack of use was apparent from the deep layer of dust on the floor. It was one of the least visited compartments on the ship.

Any thought that Manning might have entertained about crying out was cut short by a hard paw that clamped shut both his mouth and nostrils. The grip told Manning that he could not expect its relaxation during his lifetime.

Ledges held Manning's back tightly against his own chest. "How long does it take the brain to die without oxygen? Five minutes probably. Less with a heart beating like yours, Commander."

Surprisingly, Manning was not making any mortal, instinctive struggle. He was conserving his air. Thinking to the end, Ledges thought with grudging admiration.

Now Manning's free hand appeared with a felt-tip pen. His thumb flipped off the top.

Ledges ducked his head to avoid any backward thrust at his eyes, but Manning, incredibly, was writing.

On the bulkhead he just had time to whip off the scripted word "*Tree*" before Ledges jerked him away.

"Is it Tree who has the tape?"

The smothering officer nodded desperately beneath Ledges's unrelenting clutch.

"Is Tree in on this?"

The imprisoned head twitched a weakening no.

"He's just holding the tapes?"

The head attempted yes.

"He won't know what's on them unless . . . you fall overboard?"

Yes. Just barely moving now.

"Have you got an idea what might happen to you if you don't play this straight?"

Manning started to sag. Ledges took his hand off his face and caught him under the arms. "We've got a better understanding now, Commander."

It was minutes before Manning could disengage himself from Ledges's paws and retrieve his fallen hat. "Yes, Chief. I now understand that you're someone who runs a pretty fair bluff." Gazing resolutely into Ledges's eyes, he left his erstwhile execution chamber without haste.

The chief was gratified to see that there was a small pool of wetness on the deck near the toes of his shoes.

Moscow, U.S.S.R.—June 24

Gavenko had not slept for forty-eight hours. The crackling currents of power that he'd been manipulating bled off into him and provided an unnatural sustenance that blended day into night unnoticed. Nearing the end of the early critical days, he found himself staggering through Red Square well after midnight.

The much older Lubachevsky, weaving by his side, had been falling asleep wherever he had been seated and so might have been in marginally better condition.

"We're vulnerable here," Lubachevsky said.

"We're not vulnerable anywhere anymore," Gavenko said. "I told the Chief of the Main Political Directorate that our everyday security wouldn't be reliable enough anymore. They've been replaced by his own men. They're out there in the dark."

"They'd better be. Our friends Lurakin and Rhonev might not be as civilized as we take them to be."

"Believe me, they're more afraid of a bullet than we are. They know they've all but lost. They prefer to meet here alone and in the dark because they're already afraid they'd be hooted down in an open meeting. They want to make a private deal. Grant us their support so they'll have some sort of control, some sort of word in what happens next.''

Lubachevsky cleared his throat. "I must say, Gavenko, that I'd like to have some say about what happens next myself. I'm giving considerable support to you—indispensable support with the members I influence. I've bowed to your greater youth and energy. Yes, and to your strength and ambition. But if I wanted to be a waiter on the mighty I'd apply to one of the new hotels, wouldn't I?''

Gavenko waved his arms over his head to a group of men who had appeared in a streetlight far across the vast square. "Tell me then what it is you're after, old friend.''

Lubachevsky removed his pince-nez and placed his face three inches away from that of the bigger, taller man. "I have lived at a very bad time. I saw Russia move from the fallen beggar of Europe to a giant that was big enough, powerful enough, ready enough to bring the struggling people of this earth to a great victory. That the other countries formed an iron belt around us and denied us the international predominance that should have been ours was just an irksome postponement to me. It was just going to make the breakthrough sweeter. Then came The Broom. In two years he undid the moral force of a quarter century. We who shed and sweated the blood have been swept aside. Fakes like those men walking toward us came into power. What do I want? I want our destiny back. I want, before I die, to sit on the Atlantic coast of France and know that every national capital stretching behind me back to Moscow has no more to say against our will than Bucharest or Sofia has now.''

The men across the square were soon upon them. There were five of them. Three were uniformed officers of middle rank, obviously bodyguards and obviously tense. Gavenko was pleased to see that he was right about their insecurity and surprised how the unending Russian paranoia could make even full members of the Politburo tremble.

None of them offered their hands.

"Ah, Lurakin. Ah, Rhonev. Your love of the open air is giving us a cold. Please be brief."

"Gavenko," said Rhonev, "you know it's within our rights and our power to insist that these illegal . . . proposals of yours be postponed until we have direct contact with the General Secretary. It's monstrous enough that you have denied most of us the most basic knowledge and contact with him. The cheapest sort of power play, I'd say. And we wouldn't be the slightest bit surprised if you were taking advantage of a man not fully in control of his faculties."

"Those are miserable and incorrect charges. We who were at the scene of the General Secretary's misfortune naturally took the responsibility for his continuing recovery. The physicians in attendance are the best, and they have demanded that contact be held to the minimum. You have our word as fellow secretaries of the leadership that the General Secretary is intermittently able to function in his role as Commander in Chief of the Armed Forces. As you can well imagine, Marshal Arkadin, in his role as Chief of the Main Political Directorate, has seen the General Secretary and made certain of his will and competence."

"You expect us to believe that a man so dedicated to disarming the world would conceive a miserable scheme like the one that you're hatching?" Lurakin said.

"Please don't tempt those of us who are loyal to the General Secretary to launch an investigation of security leaks."

Lubachevsky jumped in. "It's serious enough among ourselves. If it spreads outside these borders, it would be the highest sort of treason."

"We are very aware of treason these days," said Rhonev without emotion. He let them see he knew both the power and the danger of the knowledge he held.

"We are going to propose through formal channels that the General Secretary be examined by physicians acceptable to the entire leadership and a report be prepared. If that report contains what we expect it might, we will suggest that we get about the business of choosing a new General Secretary.''

"What do you demand?" asked Gavenko. "What's the price of doing the right thing for your country?"

Rhonev spoke. "This is very simple. Most important is that we do nothing to disgrace the Soviet Union in the eyes of the world and its own people. Stability is everything. Civil war, even a small one, is out of the question. So our terms are more generous than they would be outside that consideration. First, of course, you drop this military adventure and cover every trace of it. Then you agree with us on a date when the General Secretary is to be returned in full health or replaced. We'll permit you—both of you—to remain in your positions until after the selection, if that becomes necessary. The matter of that selection will be very close. So we'll expect your support in it. To show our gratitude, any of the unfortunate things you might have done will be forgotten. You'll have an honored and prosperous retirement.''

It was only with the mightiest control that Gavenko could keep the glee off his face. He had to manage to appear dubious and disadvantaged as he contemplated his rivals' stupidity.

"Done," said Gavenko, after his apparent deliberations had grown uncomfortably long. "That's fair enough."

He named a date not far ahead for the consideration of a new General Secretary.

The date was one day after that set for the explosion in the Albanian capital of Tirana.

Plesetsk, U.S.S.R.—June 25

The huge Ilyushin IL-76 was the largest plane that had ever let down on the metal runway near Major Leshko's cavern. Leshko had been returning on a bicycle from the base pharmacy when the giant bird thundered above his head, a lumbering junkyard of lowered wheels and flaps. Squinting against the seldom-seen sunshine of midday and the blowing dust of a newly dried road of springtime mud, he half guessed that the plane would be bringing important visitors.

One of the things he had observed about the Soviet military system was its obsession with using equipment of maximum size as the paraphernalia accompanying enormous decisions. As long as this was the nation of the biggest submarines, tanks, artillery pieces, and missiles, how could they bring a huge task from anything less than a flying hotel?

As it was to turn out, a hotel was more or less what the Ilyushin was.

Leshko could hardly contain his laughter at this typically Soviet operation. On the one hand they were dealing with the wild-eyed passion for logistical perfection that they had carried over from World War Two. And on the other hand they were consumed with the need for secrecy bred into their bones since they had fought the White armies. So the men who knew Operation Borodin, but nothing of nuclear expertise, had gone to the men with nuclear expertise, but no knowledge of the operation, and asked them to assemble equipment and staff able to fulfill any contingency of an unknown nuclear project.

Leshko had come to know this only after the superior officials on the flight had come to see him in his tunnel quarters. They had not wanted an eye, electronic or otherwise, to see them at this site with a man of Leshko's specialty. Not at this time of edgy international maneuvering.

He had gotten no more than a phone call from a guard at the cavern's entrance to warn him of the visitors' approach. The knock on his door came as he was shrugging into the best of his tunics—the one that had most of the stains on the sleeve rather than on the breast.

The room they stepped into would have accommodated even the sternest monk. Leshko's bed was two piled mattresses. The lower, its mildew advancing, kept him from the worst dampness of the concrete floor. Whatever sins of soil the red comforter might have hidden were offset by its own griminess. The only furniture was a wooden straight-back kitchen chair facing a metal table, and a long wooden bench. The table, like the bench, was drowned under jumbled books and manuals. All the surrounding windowless walls were hidden to waist height by the same scientific litter. Somewhat more neatly stacked about the floor were piles of pencil-written sheets covered with equations and diagrams.

The one picture on the wall was that of Leonid Brezhnev. Leshko had fallen several General Secretaries behind.

Leshko blinked at his three visitors. He was amused to see that one of these was his own commanding general. Terrified always at the thought of radioactive ingestion, he alone had gotten into a contamination suit. Since he had not been able to convince the others to do likewise after he had confessed there was no strict necessity where they would be, he could not bring himself to don the sealing hood that he now carried under his arm. Sweat ran down his bald head into his thick brows, and he might have been trying to limit the number of breaths he was drawing. The odors of mustiness and personal neglect may have also been a motivator.

"Major Leshko," the commanding general gasped, "aren't there personnel responsible for maintaining this place?"

"Oh, yes, sir," Leshko said placidly. "Good conscientious men. I have to be on my guard about locking them out of here or they would have my work in neat files where I would never find it."

The general stiffly presented the two people with him.

The one called Zyshnikov struck an instant spark with the soiled little major. An awful smile squirmed on the scarred lips. "I hear that you do fascinating work," Zyshnikov said.

"It's nice someone remembers," Leshko said. "I publish so little anymore."

Zyshnikov dropped in the kitchen chair that represented the only place to sit. KGB men were used to ignoring rank in groups other than their own. He smiled again at Leshko, the physical oddity recognizing the affinity of the intellectual oddity. Each understood how easy it was, amid their handicaps, to deal with a world that would have liked to have excluded them. Cut off from the exchange of human feeling for so long, they saw the results of their actions as nothing more than the results of an equation in engineering. Human consequences were as remote to them as was color to a blind man.

"We have a challenge for you," said Zyshnikov. "And it has the shortest imaginable time schedule. This is not at all fair to you, really."

Leshko tilted the wooden bench backward to spill its mountains of publications onto the floor behind it. "I believe there is no such thing as unfair, Colonel. Decay of comfort and happiness is as physically inevitable and necessary as the decay of a radioactive particle. The atom teaches us all the lessons that there are to be learned." He indicated that his commanding general and the third man—a colonel general of the Rocket Forces Command introduced as Yenyev—were to be seated on the cleared bench. Leshko remained on his feet, prowling slowly.

"I will finally speak for all of us, Major, because I can come to the point fastest. But your commander and General Yenyev have something to say first." He nodded to them.

The commanding general, sweating in his unhooded contamination suit, spoke with obvious relief, happy to be taking himself out of a situation that he had no desire to touch further. "Major Leshko, I herewith release you from all regular duties with this command. I relieve you of all responsibility to me including the need for reports of any kind. I make available to your needs all the facilities and personnel of this base. You are free to place yourself anywhere you find convenient. No authorization of funds or material from this command are necessary. You may proceed as you wish. All our communications facilities are open to you on a basis of highest priority. We only ask your forbearance in the enforcement of maximum security procedures. Is that understood and satisfactory?"

Considering that the commanding general would only yesterday have stepped over Leshko if he had found him bleeding in the street, the major found his new status satisfactory indeed. "Everything is accepted, sir. I would hope, though, that I could obtain a much higher quality of food. As you can see, I am losing weight, and I imagine you will need more strength from me." He had no use for fancy food, actually, but he knew that it would have to be subtracted from the commanding general's own table.

Now the colonel general of Rocket Forces spoke his piece. "I am authorized to grant you the discretion to formulate and detonate a nuclear device. You are permitted to know that this is not for another test, but for use against an enemy menacing the Soviet Union. Any loss of life will be an unavoidable price to be paid for the security of our country and future peace."

Between Zyshnikov and Leshko there passed a wan smile of wonder at what this last could possibly have to do with anything.

For almost the first time in his life, Leshko felt playful. "But the colonel general disposes nuclear weapons to remove anything from the state of New York to an armored division. He has targeting devices that can hit the tip of Lenin's nose in his tomb. I fail to see how my modest talents—"

"Your talents, as you well know, are not modest," the colonel general snapped. "Given all the time in the world, we might work around you very well. But given our horrendous time difficulties and other limitations, you're indispensable."

"Ah, I'm about to hear the problem."

"That's my job, Major," Zyshnikov said. "Do you wish to make notes?" he asked, seeing that Leshko had nothing in his hands but a cigarette.

"My memory is not bad," said Leshko, who as an eleven-year-old had memorized all the logarithm tables in his books over a single day.

"All right. Even you, living these years in the worm hole,

know that there's been an unending war beneath what seemed to be peace. Odd that what peace there was has been enforced by the presence of nuclear forces. Nobody wished to take the step that would push us to uncontrollable exchanges.''

''What astounding things these weapons are, to have forced that much wisdom on us.''

''That might have been so as long as we made no mistakes. But of late the Soviet Union has made a large one. We stumbled to a leadership that made unwise concessions to sworn enemies.''

''Are you telling me that his illness has knocked some of those ideas out of his head?''

''Apparently that's so, Major.''

''What's my time?''

''Twelve days. We're timing this very delicately. A few hours after our main operation begins. It gives the target time to move, but no time to arrive on station. So the event will occur at a relatively benign location for civilian populations.''

''What's my target?''

''Very large. But we must have the smallest device for the job. And the cleanest.''

Zyshnikov rummaged in his commodious briefcase and brought forth a heavy sheet of paper folded many times. Taking his cue from Leshko in the matter of the bench, he abruptly tilted the paper-swamped table. ''By your leave.'' A billow of dust rose from the ensuing avalanche. The KGB man rapidly unfolded his paper until it had covered the newly revealed surface like a tablecloth.

What Leshko looked down upon was a huge blueprint profiling CVN-76. The plan of the *Ernest J. King* bore all the English markings of the United States Navy document from which it had been copied. Where there were details and figures likely to be of use to Leshko, the English had been inked out in red and handwritten much larger in Russian.

Leshko was resolved to give them no satisfaction from

any showing of shock or awe. He examined the massive objective as though it were the blueprint of an outhouse. "I took a ride on a large ferry on the Volga once. That's all I know about boats."

"We have naval architects waiting at the airstrip if you need them."

"I won't need them if you require me to turn all these tons into something that can be gathered up into a vacuum cleaner."

"Major," said the colonel general, whose technical grasp far exceeded Zyshnikov's, "we would like to closely approximate the detonation of a United States AR-71 warhead."

"Why that?"

"Because it represents the lowest-yielding weapon likely to be in the ordnance inventory of the *King*. We want to keep drifting contaminants as low as we can."

Leshko almost lost his facial control. "Do I anticipate a nonstandard delivery system?"

"Yes. You must have a look at that, of course." Zyshnikov motioned for the phone, and when it was handed to him he dialed the switchboard and relayed a short string of orders. He waited for confirmation before he said to Leshko, "We'll be holding up some critical calculations until we see your solutions. Radius of destruction, contamination, shock waves beneath and above the ocean, and so forth."

"I can do those," said Leshko, becoming possessive of the project quickly.

"That's just paper shuffling. Triggers are going to be the problem here, Major Leshko. At those you are the irreplaceable best."

Leshko was poring over the naval blueprint. "You'll want it as deep in the hull as you can get it, won't you? As far beneath the waterline as possible, I would think. All the blast that the sea can absorb will mean that much less contamination to blow in the wind. Of course, you'll then be to some degree exchanging radioactive steam for a debris cloud of drifting steel and meat. But I'm inclined to favor the steam. It's so much more easily dispersed."

"Choice of location is a luxury we don't have," Zyshnikov said. He tapped the blueprint at a place far astern and just below the flight deck. "Here's our spot. If it will ease your mind, a friendly trawler will happen to witness the terrible thing and will be radioing evacuation warnings to the surrounding territories immediately. And the prevailing winds should keep most of the drifting material over open water. Tangier, Gibraltar, a bit of Spain and Portugal might get a whiff. Really not all that much to worry about."

"Then it will absolutely happen at sea."

"Almost absolutely."

The commanding general and the colonel general looked uneasily at one another. Silence lay heavy until there came a knock at the door.

"Come," Zyshnikov snapped.

Two sergeants in KGB uniforms eased through the door. They carried between them a wooden packing crate crossed both vertically and horizontally by sealed metal straps. The top was hinged and further secured by a massive padlock through a heavy hasp.

In size the crate could have served an elementary science class as a full-size model of a cubic yard.

Zyshnikov waved for them to set it upon the table and then to leave. "Your delivery system, Major Leshko."

The major instantly perceived the challenge, and his pulse quickened to it. But like any expert worth his salt he screwed up his face and rubbed his eyes like a man unable to believe the foolishness of the uninitiated. "I'm surely not to understand that you expect me to create a nuclear device and trigger that will fit into that shoe box."

"A device, a trigger, and timer," Zyshnikov said.

"Do you imagine that a nuclear weapon is the sort of bowling ball with a sputtering fuse that you see in old cartoon books? There are irreducible lengths and masses."

"Are you saying it's not possible to fabricate what we need to fit into that crate?"

"It's quite possible. But not in twelve days or less. There's precise design and metallurgy. Dies. Fabrication."

"I'm confident you can make do by adapting currently available material. There are warheads in missiles, aerial bombs, naval torpedoes—"

"All designed with the delicious luxury of length. And with our kind permission to make as big a bang and as much dirt as they want, without having to impersonate the yield of somebody else's weapon, Comrade Zyshnikov."

"We certainly wouldn't suggest that it will be simple."

"The first device in the American desert was two percent bomb, ninety-eight percent trigger. Now perhaps you can tell me why we can't have a modestly bigger package than this one. Each wooden box looks pretty much like the other."

"Because," said Zyshnikov, "this is the precise package in which the United States Navy delivers its currency. When something has to do with a lot of money, people note the details with amazing thoroughness."

"I can't pretend that I understand, for the moment. But I do appreciate the idea of a capitalist society being undone by a crate of money."

Moscow, U.S.S.R.—June 26

The Glorious October Chess Club had existed for almost twenty years, and for almost all of that time was no more than it seemed—an outlet for the Russian passion for chess. Several future grand masters had come up through the ranks, but it played mostly at the upper middle level and was never a power in the interclub matches.

Then, perhaps three years before, there had been a break in the membership. The liberals, purely by chance, had become a great preponderance in the large, shabby room off Sadovaya Street. The conservatives, partly from conviction and partly from fear that they would be marked by their company, gradually withdrew.

That had been a mistake, the conservatives were to decide later. It was odd that men dedicated to a game that put such a premium on looking ahead did not see that they had lost their opportunity to observe what was to become an unofficial stronghold of the opposition. Not that anyone could have foreseen the sudden rise of the liberals with that of the General Secretary. But this was a city where men died of the unforeseen.

The present members had been wise in treating their hour in the sun as potentially fleeting. As the changes in the top had been rung in, they made sure to invite for membership a dour technician whose bad play was more than made up for by his high post in the intelligence apparatus. He kept the club rooms free of listening devices and quietly identified new applicants who had been put in place to observe. Both Lurakin and Rhonev expected that the technician would be posted away momentarily.

It was well known in the Glorious October that the games between Basil Lurakin and Nikodim Rhonev had been carefully rehearsed beforehand, so that they could be played through without thought. They and their small circle of watchers were playing a game that took all their thought. Suspect watchers were all but forcibly removed by confederates demanding a game.

The two liberal leaders played through a Ruy Lopez opening as they talked.

"They have been to Plesetsk. You could light up Red Square with the nuclear glow of the people on the plane, I hear," said Rhonev.

"The General Secretary is no longer a factor. We can begin to be certain of that, one way or the other," said Lurakin.

"We should have set that showdown sooner. They're racing to get something done. Something awful."

"Will they arrest us?"

"Not as long as we don't know anything."

"Can we get some of the military with us?"

"There's not enough time to figure out whom we can trust. Anyway, they'll wait to see how the operation goes."

"You know there's only one way to stop it," Lurakin said. "Find out and let it leak."

"We can't do that," one of the watchers whispered. "We're still Russians. Alerting the enemy, the West, means that our soldiers will die. It's treason of the worst sort. I want peace as badly as you do, but no part of that."

Rhonev moved his queen to the rehearsed spot. He was destined to win this game, he seemed to remember. "If we slip it out soon enough, the operation doesn't happen at all, Josip."

"I don't know, Rhonev. There couldn't be a move by the West until we had made our move. They'd be waiting for our soldiers. We can't let our own walk into ambush."

"If we can't make the government hold back, and we can't alert the other side to hold us back, we can't do a thing."

"Yes, we can," Lurakin said. "I'm going to join them."

The others almost physically recoiled from him.

"They wouldn't have you," Rhonev said.

"They might if they thought it was splitting us. And I may find out something from that side that I never could from this."

"What could you find out that would change our frozen position here?"

"That what we hear about Plesetsk has some substance. That there's going to be something nuclear about this operation."

"And if there is, Basil Gregorevich?"

"Then I think I have a duty to mankind that goes beyond duty to any nation, including the one I love. If someone has difficulty with that, I invite him to have me removed from the scene quickly."

The others seemed frozen in place. Josip broke away and took a slow turn around the room, the eyes of some of the players at the other tables following him about. Finally he returned to the game. "I despise the idea, and I fear it. But there's nothing else we can do. If we find out for certain that this is a nuclear adventure . . . Yes, I'm in. But only then. Only then.''

"Good," Lurakin said. "I'm very sorry to do what I'm about to do to Nikodim Ilyich. My regards to your home. We'll be in touch." With that, Lurakin called Rhonev an incredible string of words, and hit him in the eye socket with such strength that the other man's brow split wide open and poured blood down his face. A larger, stronger man, Rhonev rose reflexively and returned the blow, bringing an equally intense stream of red from Lurakin's nose.

The move had come so unexpectedly that there was not a bit of trouble faking the struggle of combatants and peacemakers. Even the two men they had positively identified as KGB joined in pulling them apart and were fully taken in.

Plesetsk, U.S.S.R.—June 27

Although he was entirely alone in his trigger room deep in his tunnel, Major Leshko was on center stage. On the airstrip sat the giant Ilyushin, its small army of technicians stopping up its lavatories and sweating because of its inadequate ground ventilation system. At the main officers' barracks Zyshnikov and the colonel general bit their fingernails waiting for the word to move all available forces as directed by the soiled little major. They never knew he was already well into his operation.

From the first he had determined that he would accomplish his task with the equipment right on hand in the cavern and, except for the heavy lifting and cutting, by himself.

The answer to the necessary device had turned out to be a nuclear artillery shell. To be precise, a shell developed for the 180-millimeter S-23 field gun. Not that the decision had been simple or automatic. There had also been the round developed for the 152-millimeter self-propelled gun, the

M-1973. Actually, that shell had solved his primary problem best. Its triggering mechanism fit more easily into the confines of the United States currency box. But the yield had been wrong. Its 0.2-kiloton warhead was likely to be noticeably below the performance of the American warhead whose discharge he was attempting to simulate. Which was a shame. The charge would have torn the ship to bits, but without the total pulverizing that he had been admonished to avoid for reasons of contamination.

However, the full kiloton in the 180-millimeter shell would send seismographs shimmying, and ships too close in could suffer greatly.

He contemplated for a moment the state of atomic weaponry. The bombs that had ended World War Two so decisively were now, relatively speaking, in the hand-grenade category. The very words "atomic bomb" denoted the crudity of the old fission devices. What were now true "nuclear weapons" were fusion-based devices of a size and sophistication that still eluded the scientific and economic capabilities of all but the strongest nations. The sort of device that fit into small battlefield weapons and measured their yields in kilotons instead of megatons were, relatively speaking, back in the realm of black powder. Indeed, it was their relatively low yield that made them usable on battlefields where armies had the problem of movement and occupation. It was these that held his interest at this moment.

Leshko had sent a few of his own men to a parallel tunnel for the device he needed—not the entire shell actually, which would have weighed 194 pounds in its entirety, but just the warhead and its unfortunately integrated detonating mechanism.

The integration was the problem. High-explosive shells of such sizes ordinarily had removable fuses to adapt the rounds to different missions. To some extent so did his present material. He could change settings for airburst, contact, or short delay. But he could not get into basics of the trigger without a total dismantling of the warhead. And to transform an atomic shell meant for artillery firing into a timed, hand-delivered system of destruction meant that such dismantling was not avoidable.

This was brain surgery of a sort, but with far greater possibility of complications. All the physics, all the metallurgy that had gone into making this projectile impervious to the shocks of transport and firing now worked against him. All the precise computations and juxtapositions of the equipment in the casing that he now had to cut away had to be reassembled in a new way in order to work.

The carpenters had quickly constructed a cradle to make the weapon easier to operate upon. His two most trusted technicians were on hand with their cutting equipment. The hot white work lights smoked in the humid air. All the men were shirtless, their military suspenders crossing their sweating bodies in the air made hot by blazing cutting torches.

When the last of the casing had been cut away, no regular artilleryman would have recognized what remained as ever having been part of anything to be fired from a gun barrel. After the plastic that had been injected upon fabrication to keep the delicate components from shifting had been pulled away, there was only what looked like the remains of half a dumbbell once used by an old-time strongman. There was a metal globe and a handle extending from it toward what would have been the nose of the shell. The removal of all the fusing equipment revealed that the handle of the dumbbell was hollow. Leshko moved the item around on the table without lifting it. The strongman who could heft this would have to have quite remarkable muscles. As cast iron of this size, the piece might have weighed twenty-five pounds. As it sat here it weighed closed to a hundred, because, inside the steel globe, really two hemispheres welded together, was pure uranium 235. There was another dollop of it in the handle.

The handle was actually a gun barrel of sorts twenty inches long. It was made to fire a plug of U-235 into a fist-sized ball of the stuff inside the sphere. There was a hole in the uranium to accommodate the plug.

Leshko mused aloud as he worked. "Odd things, atoms.

Some collections of them, like Muenster cheese, for example, lie there gently enough to grace our stomachs. Other collections, like uranium, are restless, prowling, eager to be gone. But they like to travel in a crowd of a certain size. And when they get enough of their pals together—just about the number in that ball of U-235 when we plug up that hole with the same stuff—they rush for the molecular exits.''

"It strikes me as simple physics, sir,'' one of the assistants said.

"Perhaps. But you'll still never appreciate it until you see it. The energy of that incredibly dense mass released in a hundred-millionth of a second. God, I wish they still tested in the air.''

Later, alone with his calculations, Leshko learned the best and worst of his situation. As he had suspected, length was to be his problem.

The thickness of the walls of the currency box was substantial. They subtracted three inches per side from the box's thirty-six-inch square. In the remaining thirty inches he had to include his cushioning material—he estimated this at a minimum of four inches per side—the basic detonating "gun" and sphere, and his timing device. With the present firing tube at twenty inches and its sphere at eight inches in diameter, he was already over by six inches. Even if he reduced the safety margin of the cushioning or improved it—unwise at best—there were going to have to be major modifications.

In ordinary times he would have allowed a month to make sure it all worked properly. He allowed himself three days.

He would require no time for the perfection of a timing device. He had, right on the bench before him, a device used to activate ocean-bottom listening devices for the fleet. It was too big, but by eliminating many of its components meant to thwart the sea he could bring it right down to where he wanted. The modification of the battery string was so simple that he impulsively went straight into the insides of the timer—its waterproof casing had already been opened—

and removed what he didn't need with a pair of wire cutters. For all practical purposes he could set the timer right now.

He worked on pulling the timer out of the naval device and soon had it sitting before him.

Major Leshko removed a ragged notebook from the breast pocket of his tunic. Written there was the precise moment chosen for the detonation.

He calculated the possible—and dire—consequences of a change in timing.

Carefully he placed his thumbs on two wheels at the bottom of the timer's casing. He moved the first, watching a digital readout spin through the months and days. He stopped at the designated day and moved to the next wheel. Now the hours and minutes were spinning through the clock.

He set the device to the moment requested.

U.S.S. *Ernest J. King*, Naples, Italy—June 30

The Navy was loaded with items that had just not worked out. They had been designed, fabricated, tried in small applications after short production runs, and discontinued. Of course it would not have done to just scrap the things. That would be embarrassing. So they went into installations and onto ships. For the same reasons that they had been discontinued, they were not used. They were dragged from building to building, compartment to compartment. And finally some remodeling of its lair gave someone the excuse to dump it or sell it as surplus to a baffled public.

Such an item was designated XU-231. The plotters had been able to trace it back through Manning's endless access to all the junk ever created by the Navy. The thing had arisen many years before. It began as a smallish commercial helicopter that had been adopted by the Coast Guard for search-and-rescue work. As the HH-52A Sea Guard, it was from the beginning doomed to be supplanted by larger, mission-specialized birds. Some enterprising supplier saw enlarging the capacities of the Sea Guard as a brilliant move. He thought that with an auxiliary carrying-pod slung beneath it the Navy might buy many of the off-the-shelf helicopters and earn everyone a neat penny.

The move didn't work out well except for the supplier of the several prototype pods.

Several things had eventually become obvious. The work in removing and replacing the sponsons more than offset the comparative ease with which the light plastic pods could be attached. Also, the pods created aerodynamic problems even when empty. Filled with any reasonable weight, they became close to dangerous in the handling of the chopper. Indeed, a late modification made them capable of detachment in the air when their weight became unmanageable.

So, naturally, several of the pods were delivered, and they languished at odd spots throughout the fleet.

It was the answer to the plotters' prayers.

Its discovery was a happy accident. The *King* had come into possession of a single old HH-52A during some shuttling operation with the Coast Guard, the pilot managing to make certain that the pod was attached when the chopper was transferred.

McGregor found it, the pod, still battered but serviceable, behind the hangar bays in a great warehouse of major spare parts. It was fifteen feet long, and as wide as it had to be to span the chopper's fuselage. Its aerodynamic modeling caused some space to be lost inside, but it would hold three men and a large volume of currency. The pod weighed 123 pounds empty. Loaded with the cargo he had in mind, there would be a total of just short of 700 pounds. Adding his own weight, that of two crewmen, fuel, and weight of the currency, he would be well within the craft's 3,100-pound carrying capacity.

"Is it going to work?" Lydecker asked his friends.

"Who knows," said McGregor. "But at least something is happening."

"If it flops," said Ledges, "we're going to have the

ugliest goddamn coffin anybody ever saw. And chances are good that Manning won't be at the funeral.''

Genoa, Italy—June 30

Tess had found the Hotel Primavera on her own. It was every bit as ugly as the flight and the trip from the airport. McGregor's letter to his wife had warned her that there might be slipups and to not be surprised if they did not meet her as they promised, so she was not more frightened and apprehensive than she usually was in her awful life.

She had taken perverse pleasure in discarding everything that could not be stuffed into the two suitcases she had taken. All the pathetic keepings of her bedeviled marriage had suddenly seemed a perverse collection of bad-luck charms. Although she had not the slightest idea of what they were getting into, she had been able for a while to fantasize a new beginning.

The flight had a connection in Hamburg, loading up an army of Turkish laborers returning from northern Germany. The trip destroyed what scant enthusiasm she had managed. The seating had been three and three, the winds perverse, the food bad, the way bumpy, and the companionship rude and smelly. Each time she had taken Kiki back for an interminable wait at the long lavatory lines, they had run a gauntlet of pinches and gropes, salted with rude words in an alien language.

She had finally, in some of the worst desperation she had ever known, overpaid for a penknife with which an old man was paring an apple. She had shown this open in her hand when she had to, and the look in her eyes had stopped the worst indignities.

The Primavera was close to the waterfront, but not on it. So the room received the worst of the noise and smells, but none of the views. She and Kiki lay exhausted on grimy beds for hours, still wearing their traveling clothes. Her daughter seemed to be heading back inside herself, and at this moment Tess was almost relieved. She might be easier to handle that way.

Tess checked the letter again to make sure that she had registered under the right name, *Signora* Naglieri. Whoever might come was supposed to look for her under that. There was no phone, so she was not even able to hope that Wade would call her here in the room. What could he tell her? He had let her understand that Rocky Ledges had actually made the arrangements, and that the chief himself was unsure of many things.

She had been asleep long enough for the sun to have vanished when there was a knock on the door. There was nothing timorous about it. The ancient blue-painted door leaped in the frame.

Tess found a switch that turned on a feeble bulb far overhead. As dim as it was, it seemed to magnify the dirt. "Who is it?" she asked.

"*Signora* Naglieri. We are friends of the sailor, Ledges."

She unbolted the door and two men entered. The one who knew English was not Italian. He might have been an old exhibit in a no-longer-elegant wax museum. Whatever his age, his skin had turned a dusty, lusterless beige, and he was hairless except for the sparse, lank strands of a drooping mustache and plucked, penciled eyebrows. Red-tinted hair spilled from under a once-white panama hat.. "I am Gavril," he said as he brushed past her and settled into the one chair in the room. "That is Guido behind me. He speaks only Italian. I don't speak much of that myself."

Guido was a boy no older than Kiki. He wore only shorts and sandals. He was cheaply good-looking with well-barbered hair. His teeth were bad and already badly stained by the kind of bad cigar he was smoking. A wallet rigged like a shoulder holster was draped across his muscular chest. "Ciao," he muttered to Tess. He flashed what he imagined to be a blinding smile at the impassive Kiki. He quickly sat on the bed near her. Tess went into her purse for a cigarette and kept the bag on her lap. She also eased the opened penknife into her palm.

"*Signora* Naglieri," said Gavril, "you must first put into my hand six hundred American dollars."

"I was told it was four hundred and fifty."

"I include the hundred and fifty for Guido."

"There is nothing for Guido, and four hundred and fifty for you. That's it."

Gavril didn't seem disappointed. He stuck out his hand. "That will be a beginning."

She took out a packet of precounted money and counted it again into his palm. "What now?"

"We wait. Two hours. Maybe a bit more, *signora*."

"Then?"

"Then the truck comes."

"Truck? We're not going to travel in any truck."

"For such a tiny price there is no other way. I must bring many people. I have expenses. I have risks."

"But surely a bus—"

"*Signora*, buses are noticed. Buses are inspected. You can see into buses. You can only carry so many people. I must carry many."

"Where are we going?"

"A long journey. You will see that it is a bargain."

"Where?"

"Across all of Italy. A couple of hundred miles. To Trieste. The other side of Italy."

"We're going into Yugoslavia."

"Exactly. Briefly. If my bribing is good. Then down to Rijeka, close by. You may know it as Fiume."

"Do we have a place to stay there?"

Gavril gave a great shrug. "I do not know, *Signora* Naglieri. There you are put into the hands of others."

Tess felt a sickness rising in her. "I wasn't told that."

"You cannot stay in Rijeka. The Yugo beasts make life too hard. They want too much. Perhaps a thousand dollars—"

"We had an agreement."

Guido used her distraction to run his hand along Kiki's

calf. Tess just caught the end of the movement. She elbowed Gavril out of the way and caught the boy by his thick hair. Jerking with all her strength, she sent him sailing off the bed and onto the floor. The boy came off the floor cursing, his fists balled. Gavril planted a pointed shoe into the pit of his stomach. He sat down again and looked sick.

"The Romanians come cheap. There is one who says he can get a government car. He will take you to Timisoara, in his country. It is a fine large city. Like Chicago, I think. Possibly it will cost you more money there."

"Chief Ledges won't like it if you fail him."

"The chief is a very hard man. But they take his Navy away from here. Maybe I don't see him again, eh?"

Guido remained glowering on the floor. Gavril settled back into his chair. Tess could only sit next to Kiki on the bed and wait. It was running out of control, she thought. Yet she had to believe that what these men did with them was what her husband wanted—their best chance for whatever it was he had in mind.

Guido heard the truck first. He sprang to his feet and shook the dozing Gavril awake. He was going for the bags when Tess jumped in front of him and took them herself. Before she could stop Gavril, he had lifted Kiki erect and pushed her in front of him out the door. Tess could only stumble along behind.

Gavril pushed some money at the man at the desk and they went out into the narrow street. There was a very old truck there, its motor idling noisily. The rear was enclosed by the sort of canvas framework seen on army trucks. The tailboard reached almost to the top of the framework, so when it was let down it reached to the ground. There were blocks of wood nailed to its inside to convert it into a steep ladder.

The moment it hit the ground an awful stench poured out of the truck body. By the distant glare of a streetlight Tess could see that the vehicle was packed. There were men on benches running along both sides, and the space between them was filled with others jammed in helter-skelter. A bucket of slops was splashed out, some of it running down the lowered tailboard. Other buckets rattled inside, but it was apparently not possible to work them free of the tangle of people and the sound quickly subsided.

Some of the passengers nearest the back tumbled out to stretch. Cursing men ran back from the cab and ordered them back inside in a language Tess didn't know. All of them, even those wearing ragged suits, were rough laboring types with dark, cruel-looking Middle Eastern features.

One of the men from the cab was huge and thick, obviously an enforcer of discipline. He cracked some of the men across the back of their heads with a stick and they quickly reentered the truck. The enforcer didn't let them settle. He came halfway up the tailboard ladder and kept swatting until they had cleared a place on the floor. He motioned Tess and Kiki inside.

There was ugly laughter and several hands reached out to them, clutching to help them up. Somebody struck a wooden match to a pipe and Tess saw for the first time that there was a woman inside. In the brief flare wide dark eyes showed their blurred terror. Her cheeks were bruised and she appeared to be trying to hold the top of her dress closed with a grip that might have been upon life itself.

Tess spun on Gavril. "We're not getting into there. Give me my money back. Give it back right now."

Gavril leaned over to bring his face an inch from hers. "This is not the United States, *signora*. Your word doesn't make the poor peasants tremble here. I have supplied my part. If you don't like my accommodations—"

Faster than he could have blinked, Tess had a hand behind his neck. Twisted into his hair, it prevented him from moving backward. Her other hand held the open penknife, its point pressing insistently into the corner of his eye. Her voice was a trembling hiss of desperation. "Mr. Gavril, I'm trading eyes for money, and the way I feel now, I don't really give a shit which way it goes." With a remarkably steady hand, she began a delicate slice along his eyelid.

Gavril, terrified of startling her and her advancing blade, could only squeal in a tiny voice. The enforcer from the cab started to take a step forward, then stopped and roared with laughter, slapping the stick against his own thigh with bruising abandon. Apparently Gavril wasn't popular.

"Give it," Tess kept hissing. "Give it . . . give it . . ."

The blade advanced along the lid, blood running down Gavril's cheek.

"Yes, yes, yes, yes, signora—"

He pawed into his pocket and produced the cash. "Push it down the front of my dress," she ordered. "And if you so much as brush my skin with yours I'll blind you."

She felt the transfer and shoved him away. He wailed and dropped to his knees, clutching his face. He still wasn't sure that he had his eye. The enforcer laughed harder and the men in the truck joined him. Guido, suddenly a confused child, was holding his mentor's hat under his chin, as though the dripping blood might be saved.

An enormous commotion was erupting from the rear of the truck now. A whistle sounded somewhere. Trying not to faint, Tess slung the bags onto her shoulders by their straps, seized Kiki's hand, and ran with her through a nightmare maze of streets.

"Wade . . . Wade . . ." Tess called, before she realized he was the last person on earth who might help her.

Naples, Italy—June 30

It's not wise to leave a United States Navy deuce-and-a-half truck unattended on the streets of Naples. The Navy trucks are known to be frequently loaded with readily resold treasures, and the thieves of the old city are consummate professionals. When they're faced with difficulty lifting a cargo, they simply take the truck itself. The Navy is accustomed to having a truck or so unaccounted for at any given moment, but doesn't upset itself. It'll turn up empty in due time with its more useful elements stripped away.

This made it surpassingly simple for the people in the city who were assisting Manning to get him his truck. Impeccably Italian in speech and appearance, they acquired just the vehicle they wanted from some reputable thieves who had stolen it in perfectly good faith. The new men changed the identification markings so that some alert shore patrolman would not stumble on it, and made sure it was in superb running order.

What they did not do was leave it in the streets unguarded during the night. That would not have been in order, because the solitary piece of cargo had enormous value. It had been rushed down from the northern reaches of the Soviet Union by plane, train, and van. It was three feet square and weighed 254 pounds. Beneath its wooden shell and its carefully replicated United States Navy stenciling, it was a fully armed and timed atomic bomb. The Soviet Union had brought it as close to its eventual target as it could. The rest was up to Richard Manning.

Naples, Italy—July 1

"Jesus, Hink, take it easy," yelled Ledges, snatching at the corner of the open jeep's windshield. "I almost lost my gun over the side."

"Hey, I ain't never seen thirty-five million bucks in one place before. Especially not when a lot of it might turn out to be mine."

"Seven boxes of cash," Manning said. "Better than one each."

The jeep was one of three in Navy gray that had peeled out of the checkpoint leading out of the base. The lead vehicle contained Lydecker, driving with all his customary flair and scattering even the wild drivers of Naples, Ledges alongside him in the front seat, and Manning and McGregor hanging on in the rear. All the men wore sidearm .45s.

Ledges was hanging on to a pair of M-16s and not liking the thought of Manning sitting behind him with a weapon. Behind them screeched two more jeeps, each loaded with four Marines from the *King*. Their M-16s were cradled comfortably between their knees.

"All the years we came in here we flew the payroll on board, Manning. Now we go to pick it up in the city. How do you explain that?" McGregor wanted to know.

Commander Manning was in fine spirits. "You only have to explain things like that if people ask. And people don't ask God anything. I am the god of supplies and nobody questions. If I rounded up fifty giant Nubians and had the stuff brought aboard in sedan chairs, nobody would question it. This job is so thankless and complicated that it's the only one in the fleet nobody ever messes in."

"I guess that goes for having the whole bunch of us along to pick it up."

"Sure. I doubt if anybody's ever picked up this much money in the history of the Navy. So the top dog goes along, with his financial guy and LPO and a driver he trusts. I thought it might help if nobody but us crooks were around to look after our interests."

"You might have a point. The truck park is right around that corner, Hink. Slow it up or we'll—"

The jeep lifted one set of wheels off the ground and made the swing. One of the Marine jeeps bounced over the sidewalk before it made its way back onto the road.

At the end of the street lay one of the many low-security military installations that stretched across the Naples waterfront. This one was a truck park and light repair facility. There was a sentry at a gate, but the installation was walled off only by a wire mesh fence through which aluminum slats had been inserted to block the view.

An alley ran from behind and alongside the area. A deuce-and-a-half in Navy colors was just rolling out of this, hidden by the fence from the gate sentry on the front street. To most of the approaching convoy, the truck seemed to have just issued from a side gate when they swung into view. Only Manning knew that the truck had nothing to do with the installation. He waved and the vehicle stopped where it was. A sailor with the crossed keys of a storekeeper on his sleeve got out of the cab and saluted. He had a clipboard filled with papers under the other arm.

"Couldn't give us a truck from the base. That would've been too efficient," said Ledges.

"Keep it in your face, Chief," said Manning. He hopped out and sped through a lot of signatures on the clipboard. "Okay," he motioned to Lydecker and Ledges. "Who's going to drive the truck?"

"Hey, me, sir," said Lydecker, always looking for another vehicle to abuse.

"Good. Both of you up front. I'll take point in the jeep."

As they climbed into the truck cab, Ledges's eyes followed the sailor with the clipboard as he strolled back down the street. "Good shit, what's this Navy coming to? Where the hell did that guy get those shoes? Brown, for chrissakes. There they go. U-turn. Make it quick."

The money had been flown down out of Frankfurt by an Army helicopter that was being ferried to Sicily. Ordinarily one of the ship's birds would have snatched it from the suburban copter base and whisked it straight to the flight deck, but that did not suit Manning's plan. So he had told his fellow plotters that he wanted to bring the stuff aboard in person with a top-security transfer so he didn't have to go through the ordeal of having everything inspected in Captain Ash's painted square in the hangar bays. That would invite unwanted attention.

Manning was out of his jeep before the truck stopped rolling. Ledges heard him drop the tailboard. "Hey, a commander who gets his hands dirty."

"Okay, Lydecker. Bring it back tight against the loading dock there."

Lydecker leaned out the window and put the truck into place perfectly. "There, sir. The money won't get sunburned."

"There's going to be a lot of paperwork. Get out and stretch for a while," said Manning. He waved to McGregor to stay back with Ledges and Lydecker. "I'll handle it." He disappeared inside.

"Shit," said Lydecker. "I wanted to pick out my money now."

"Yeah," Ledges said, "and maybe get over to the casino before it closes." He spat. "I wish to hell he'd let us in on what he's up to a little faster."

"Why does he keep looking nasty at you that way, Chief?" asked McGregor.

"Maybe I neglected my deodorant, Wade."

At length Manning returned. He was now carrying a hefty Navy envelope, well stuffed with what were undoubtedly the necessaries of the huge transfer. "Pull out, Lydecker. I'll lock her up."

Lydecker climbed back into the cab and moved the truck forward. Manning moved quickly to the tailboard. Ledges came up the other side to help him with the lifting. "They go up a lot harder than they come down, Commander."

As he brought up the board and snugged down the canvas over it, Ledges got to look inside. The seven big boxes stood unsecured in the middle of the truck just as they had come off the rollers. "If we get into a fender bender, we'll be able to settle out of court."

"I want to make sure that doesn't happen. Relieve Lydecker at the wheel for the trip back."

"Aye, aye, sir. And you won't forget I have an eye on you?"

"I'll never forget anything about you, Ledges."

As Manning turned toward the jeep and directed the Marine jeeps to fall into place ahead of and behind the truck, Ledges's eyes swept momentarily over the large envelope hanging from the commander's hand. Its back had a stamped sign-off space for each package. It tugged at the chief's consciousness that he'd counted just six stamps. But when he hoisted himself up on the tailboard to double-check, the count was just what Manning had said on the way there. Not six boxes. Seven.

* * *

The plotters went quickly up the brow and through the quarterdeck. Ledges remained behind on the quay to supervise the loading of the crates with one of the ship's booms.

Manning, McGregor, and Lydecker were there waiting when the last of the cargo came through the yawning elevator doors of the hangar bay. A Marine lieutenant watched the crates being scooped up by forklifts and piled onto tandem carts pulled by a tractor. Manning handed McGregor the paperwork for the Marine—actually a duplicate set of documents accommodating the extra case. McGregor made it plain that he expected to be gone without delay.

"They've got to go into the square, sir," the Marine said, pointing to painted yellow lines on the deck enclosing perhaps three hundred square feet.

"Perhaps you'll remember that I was the one who put that order into effect, Lieutenant Wagenheim," said Manning. "I ordered those lines painted."

"Aye, aye, sir. I know. The swabbies are pretty good at combing the stuff through by now. You'll be on your way pretty quick."

"You don't mean you're going to sort through seven crates of money that have come to me directly?" asked McGregor.

"I've got orders, sir."

Tarps had been hung about the square from the overhead to secure it from the eyes of the mobs of V Division people always rushing about the hangar bay, but the breezes shifted the canvas about, making the area seem less than secure.

"Lieutenant, you've read what's in those things. The money is in straps. Maybe ten pounds of straps. So are the crates."

"Sir, you'll want those outside straps off anyway. Then you could open those padlocks and we could just hinge up the tops."

"Wagenheim, there's such a thing as doing your duty. There's also such a thing as following it straight over the side."

"Only the skipper can rescind those orders, sir."

"Then he'll have to," McGregor said as he walked toward a bulkhead-mounted phone.

"Skipper's ashore, sir. Left at 1000 hours."

Manning had known that, of course. He had not known that he would come up against one of the most stubborn men in the Marine Corps.

"Okay, Lieutenant, have it the way you want," Manning said.

The commander reached under his jacket and brought out a broad leather wallet that had been clipped to his belt by a sturdy chain. When he flipped the wallet open, the Marine saw it was a keyboard with perhaps two dozen keys arrayed. Manning selected the key for the most distant and inaccessible crate and removed it from its clip. "Here you are. It's now your responsibility, Wagenheim. In fact, every nickel of this is your responsibility. I forbid anyone but your Marines to touch it. A man who grasps responsibility as well as you do will get my thrust."

The work party of six sailors was surprised but cheerfully stepped backward from the square, hands raised in the classic no-touch attitude.

Wagenheim looked uneasy. He had two lance corporals with him, but they were trained as killers, not stevedores.

"I can assure you, sir—"

"Just assure us that you're going to get on with it at this very instant," said McGregor.

"Aye, aye, sir."

McGregor made the lieutenant try each case in turn until he found the one whose padlock the key fitted. The sailors watched the Marines, superbly fit but in no way experienced in the ways of handling two-hundred-pound crates and twitchy forklifts, proceed to butcher the job. One of the lance corporals threw his back out immediately and became useless, so Wagenheim had to throw his slender physique and neatly starched uniform into the uneven battle. Splotches of sweat appeared across his back before the first crate had been wrestled into the square.

The incident, the lieutenant was only too well aware, had

degenerated into a battle between the services, and he was not about to show that the Marine Corps needed reinforcements.

He found a plier that could nibble through the straps on the first crate. Then he undid the padlock and raised the lid. Under a batting of foam he found a sea of money, fifty-dollar bills in this case. They were strapped, restrapped, and counterstrapped into solid, compressed stacks. The Marines hesitated.

"Well, get in there, Lieutenant Wagenheim," said McGregor. "Or is it Lieutenant Columbo? There might be a troupe of pygmy dancing girls down there in the middle."

"Sir—"

"Here, use this," McGregor offered, handing him a large clasp knife.

Wagenheim opened the knife and started to cut some of the straps off the money. As he tried to dig down, he repeatedly found some more binding he had to cut. Soon the top of the crate was awash with fresh, loose fifty-dollar bills that had sprung from their previous compression. Some of them slipped to the deck. The sweating Wagenheim was up to his elbows in money as he worked to the center of the crate.

Outside, the breeze shifted decisively offshore. A great warm gust swept in through the open hangar bay doors and blew the obscuring tarps sideways. Abruptly, the air was filled with swirling fifty-dollar bills.

A sweep of Manning's hand froze the sailors on duty in their tracks when they instinctively started for the money. The squeaking Wagenheim and his two lance corporals, one hardly able to move, were left to run down the blowing currency. As they scrambled at the perimeters of the tarps, more fifties blew off the top of the opened crate. Other bills scooted under the tarps into the hidden hangar bay.

On his knees, bills overflowing his hands, Wagenheim turned to Manning with imploring eyes.

"Every nickel, Lieutenant. You and your Marine Corps are responsible for every blowing nickel."

Blessed providence quieted the wind. The Marines stuffed

the last of the money back into place in the crate and gratefully closed the lid. "Next key, please, sir," said Wagenheim, as white as he had ever been.

"Haven't had enough, huh?" said Manning as he handed him the second key.

The lieutenant opened the second crate and lifted the batting. The bound currency looked up at him. He started to raise the knife to the top bands, hesitated, then closed the knife. He handed it back to McGregor. "Thank you, sir. I won't be needing that anymore."

"Well, thank God for that."

"Yes, sir, I can just peek inside each one. That'll be good enough."

Manning became aware of the gun belt used during the currency pickup. He held it dangling in his hand. The urge to pull out the holstered .45 and shoot this idiot dead was overpowering.

One by one Wagenheim worked through the crates, Manning handing him the keys.

Finally there was one crate left.

Manning was almost amused to see that McGregor and Lydecker, now having been joined by Chief Ledges, were utterly calm. Ignorance was as blissful as ever.

"Last key, please, sir," said Wagenheim.

The commander handed him a key to a cabinet in his room. It looked like the others. He couldn't hand him a real key because that would be back in Plesetsk.

The lieutenant fumbled at the padlock. Manning eased open the holster and loosed the .45 in it. Better to go out noisily right here than at the end of a leather-sleeved rope.

"Doesn't seem to work, Commander."

"Damn, Lieutenant, can't you just let this one go?" asked McGregor.

Wagenheim set his jaw. Where there was a shred of Marine honor to be saved, he would save it. "Sorry, sir. I'll need your permission to open that crate. Or the captain's orders not to."

"Okay. Open it." Behind his back Manning eased the safety off the big automatic.

The healthy lance corporal found a pinch bar. He inserted an end through the lock's hasp and twisted. Heavy screws pulled out of the wood and the top was free.

"You'll be done in a second, sir."

The Colt was now unholstered behind Manning's back.

Up came the lid and off came the batting. Tightly bound stacks of hundreds looked up at Wagenheim.

Manning had to step backward to catch his balance. He almost wiped his face with the back of the hand holding the gun. His heart pounded and he felt his blood pressure peak. He silently thanked the accountants of the Soviet Union for spending the few extra thousand on that one little extra layer of green camouflage. He wondered how deep the money layer went. He was pretty sure his knife blade pressing down between the stacks would have hit something solid.

Wagenheim handed Manning the ruined lock and started, with the other man, to wrestle the crate toward a tractor cart. "Seems like the last box is always heavier than the rest."

"Right, Lieutenant. Okay. The Navy can take it from here." The commander gestured to the sailors from the original loading team. Working expertly they quickly had the money loaded onto the carts behind the tractor.

At the division office they found that the vault hardly contained all of the boxes.

When the work party was getting ready to leave, one of them grinned and asked, "Can I take mine now, sir?"

"Not until we get ours," answered McGregor, spinning the vault door closed.

U.S.S. *Ernest J. King*, Naples, Italy—July 2

The head in his compartment was so small that McGregor couldn't get at the bowl properly to throw up. As he blotted at the mess with a ball of paper towels, he found bitter analogies to his own sad circumstances.

For the hundredth time in the last hour he gave heartfelt thanks for the great Navy network of friends. Tess had made it come alive for her in Genoa two days ago. Exhausted, at her wits' end, she had dragged Kiki into a post office and made the execrable Italian phone system serve her.

Like any Navy wife, she had in her purse a shattered address book held together by rubber bands. In it were penciled smudges representing a whole fleetful of Navy people left behind after brief, heartbreaking friendships. Promises to call or visit were so rarely acted upon that their occurrence was taken as some sort of wonder. But these phantom, fading names stood for the only friendships she had had a chance to make over her years as a Navy wife.

She knew some of the ways you could get in touch with a sailor in an emergency, even at sea, even in combat. But in the tone of her husband's voice and in his letter she had recognized that it was desperately important for the official part of the Navy not to know where she was.

So she had learned to use the phone and screamed her way past the language barrier. She called everyone. Everywhere. Back in the States, in France, England, and Italy. The clues were faint in her memory. Hadn't someone said that the Abels were at Holy Loch? Didn't Commander Edwards retire to that little town in the Algarve? Hadn't Chief Wilson been arrested by the Greeks for drunk driving in that place in Crete?

Mostly there had been no answers, disconnections, baffled, sleepy voices, and annoyance in several languages. But the word "Navy" had its effect.

Some of the people tried to remember things, asked questions of family members, went to lost address books. Somewhere around the thirtieth call the first connection had been made. A machinist's mate in Boston had served on McGregor's carrier off Nam.

Tess had been so near collapse that she had hardly known

what help to ask for. But the man had patiently worked the story out of her. He had gotten a number for the post office and told her to stay there until he could call back.

Within the hour he had located a discharged buddy working for a General Electric troubleshooting unit in Milan. He, in turn, had a supplier in Genoa who owed him a big favor.

Before the middle of the afternoon Tess and Kiki had been picked up and taken to a decent hotel. Most important, she had been able to make clear the delicacy of her situation in Europe.

McGregor had received a phone number and a sealed message that had been handed to a base sentry who knew him.

When he had been able to speak to Tess on a secure line, his flooding relief had been almost completely offset by the horror of what he had put her through.

He now saw the stupidity, the impossibility of his plan. For Lydecker, doomed to an eternity in naval prison, for Ledges, his Navy life having become agony and his young friend needing him so badly, there might be possibilities. They were adventurers, wanderers. They had no ties to a family and didn't want any. For them the theft and the escape were a real hope.

For Wade McGregor it was different. His little family, as bedeviled as it was, represented the only thing that had ever given him peace and satisfaction. All he had been expected to give them in turn was a normal, comfortable life, his love and support. And he had failed. If he'd been honest with himself he might have admitted earlier that the Navy had become a place to hide, where he could pretend sacrifice while sticking Tess with all the misery and difficulty of taking care of Kiki.

And now he was trying to tell himself that he could at last do right by them by becoming a thief. If the plan worked at all, it would be to drag them into a society that people risked mines, machine guns, and killer dogs in order to escape.

How could he go through with it?

But how could he get out of it now?

Before he could wrestle with any of that, Tess and Kiki had to be secure for the moment. To stay safely where they were they needed money. At least that would be no problem. There was still a lot of loose cash in the vault. And other than poor, dumb, honest Bluehoffer, the entire Disbursing Division at the top was as crooked as Pretty Boy Floyd.

For the first time in many days Richard Manning found himself with time on his hands. Until events showed him the next turn, his work was done. He recognized that this was the moment when a prudent man redoubled his care.

In his office he punched up a computer terminal and checked the results of some complicated work he had been doing. He first brought up the list of the fresh medical supplies he had ordered for the carrier. Ordinarily this would have been something handed up to him by the ship's Medical Department. But this particular list had been modified by Manning. The doctors were not to see it. While the supplies were all medical in nature, Manning had added one from a supply manual, based on bulk, weight, and applicability to his plans.

He ran a hard copy on a high-speed printer, then brought up a second screen. He used the access number of the ship's Medical Department for this. It was easily done because it was he who maintained the master list of such numbers. The new screen supplied what the doctors would get if they looked for an inventory of supplies. There would be nothing to bother them.

Now he cleared the screen and made a modem connection to a mainframe computer ashore at the NATO base. This was the tricky part. Here he had to depend on the honest, God-fearing personnel of the Navy and many civilian Europeans to do their jobs.

As he worked, he half wished that Tree could be here. It would provide a chance to show that incredible boor that a position as supply officer on a flagship made things possible that no hand worker like Tree could ever accomplish.

Manning accessed the mainframe of an immense NATO supply base in Frankfurt. There were some bases closer that would have served his purpose, but he wanted to work out of Germany. The Germans preferred trains to planes, and their railway system and routing procedures were impeccable. Even the Italians wouldn't be able to foul things up after the train crossed the border.

The screen told him things: Yes, the supplies had already been sent. As far as he could tell they were already nestled in place at a hospital near Potenza. The hospital had a working arrangement with NATO and had learned to pay little attention to the materials that came through so long as they received their payments and what was needed for themselves. The Western alliance had built a magnificent warehouse on their grounds, complete with helicopter pad. The Italians were free to use these almost as their own and found it a fine arrangement. It was certainly proving ideal for the purposes of Richard Manning.

He was not completely satisfied with the plan although he had crafted most of it. Communications through Tree being spotty and brief, he had not been able to press his way on some important points.

His inability to disarm the silently ticking weapon in the vault bothered him immensely. He understood the wisdom of their taking the great moral temptation out of the hands of the foot soldiers, but he didn't like it.

It could have been so much neater. If the ship remained in Naples until the job was irretrievably successful in Albania, the bomb could have been disarmed quietly. He could have discreetly gotten rid of it, as he had brought it aboard. Then he could have informed his fellow thieves that he was terribly sorry, but that it just wasn't going to work after all. He had left no concrete evidence that he had been involved with them. He would advise them to surrender themselves in the way they found best and offer to do what he could for them inside the system. The understanding would have been that he would come away clean.

But now there was to be an explosion at a time already decided.

It was unsettling to him that it could happen at this Naples dockside. His real war was no more with Italy than it was with NATO.

While it was almost inconceivable that the ship wouldn't make some desperate race for Albania when the shooting started, odder things had happened.

Manning was not entirely helpless in this matter. He could set a deadline of his own, perhaps. And if the *King* had not sailed by then, there would be the possibility of leaking just enough, just late enough, to get this hulking bomb out of port.

But there were enough problems without borrowing any.

He lay back on his berth and tried to figure the smallest bag into which he could fit all his family photographs.

Washington, D.C.—July 3

Admiral Geinz left the head of Naval Intelligence and his young aide standing in his living room at Bolling Air Force Base. He padded about his quarters long enough to find the special glasses he used to study intelligence photos. When he returned, the glasses perched on the end of his nose, he held a cup of coffee in each hand for the officers. The admiral's bathrobe had clearly been purchased when he'd been twenty pounds lighter.

"Captain Dumfries, Lieutenant Robbins, I'll trade you these for a look at what brought you here at two in the morning."

He led them to seats at the dining room table, where Dumfries spilled the pictures out of a metal briefcase with a combination lock and a special rib for a chain.

"We've just put these through a first look. But we think they're important enough for you to see right away," Dumfries said.

"What's the geography?"

"Outside Tirana."

The photographs had been snapped from an altitude of 81,000 feet by an aircraft so expensively specialized that even the United States thought it prudent to keep only a half dozen of them. The handmade Lockheed SR-71 Blackbird was a black-painted needle whose cluster of tiny wings and mighty engines at the rear made it look like a flying spoon. It flew mostly out of a base in the States, often Beale, and was refueled in the air off Spain.

The overflying of nations, especially ones with aggressively closed borders, was a question for international lawyers. But the SR-71 made a special case for itself. It flew at heights so great that it was perpetually invisible and inaudible to anyone on the ground. Such heights gave its awesome engines Mach 3 capability when needed, making the plane impervious to armed approach in terms of either altitude or speed. The plane also had immense loitering capabilities.

The craft was more a space station or satellite than it was an airplane. But it was in many ways more useful than either of those. Because it was not tied to an orbit, its appearance could not be timed to enable the hiding of embarrassing objects on the ground.

The particular bird that had given Admiral Geinz his photographs had recently been examining the Albanian capital and its environs with steadfast interest. This was child's play in view of the Blackbird's ability to saturate 100,000 miles photographically in a single flight.

"Don't tell me anything yet," said Geinz, fanning out the photographs. "I'll look at your little arrows and try to figure for myself. A sort of, pardon the expression, intelligence test for an amateur."

"As you say, sir," said Captain Dumfries, restraining his impatience with this man he would never understand.

The cameras that had done the work had been contained

in a recepod 44 by 14 inches, slung beneath the airplane. The entire unit weighed just seventy-seven pounds, and it was the only reason for the unique plane's being.

The 3,000-speed film was remarkable for its consistency and capabilities. But it was the cameras and their support that made the detailed miracles of intelligence possible.

The two cameras were separated by eighty-four degrees from one another for stereo overlap—the old stereopticon brought to space.

Clicking at 1/3,000th of a second from an aircraft traveling at Mach 0.9, they used an IMC, or Image Motor Compensator. This received electronic input of the plane's speed and altitude to obtain a height-to-velocity ratio. To avoid the faintest hint of blurring, the film had to be pulled across the frame at precisely the same rate as the image was traversing the camera aperture. Standard reciprocating shutters being far too jarring for the procedure, a special revolving shutter made the exposures.

The clarity of the photographs was beyond the belief of most people. Even the head of the Joint Chiefs of Staff.

"It's a parachute," Geinz decided. "It's a parachute caught up in some trees. And there's . . . lemme see . . . one, two . . . at least four canisters on the ground around it. Maybe there are more that the tree is hiding. Of course, it could be some sort of farmer's protection from birds or something. And some lengths of irrigation pipe. But then I figure you put it through people who knew something about all that. And that's why the arrows."

Dumfries picked out a couple of other photos from the pile. "Here's the same area. We shot this in the morning."

"You're figuring that if it's going to be set up as an inside job, it's going to come soon."

"Aye, sir. But I have to tell you that we weren't as sharp as it might sound. These were taken back on June first on a routine sweep. We missed what was in them until we went back in the files for a harder peek. Look here. There's a truck out of the barn. We can spot eleven men working at that thing in the tree."

"Doesn't sound like an awful lot of men for a job on a farm. It could be something legitimate."

"Maybe. But nobody's doing anything else. Our agriculture people tell me there might be thirty people on a farm like that. And at this time of year they'd be out in the field and in the orchard there, too, doing a lot of basic things at that time of the day."

"What else, Captain?"

"It's been raining around there for the past few days. If they were using the regular farm equipment that we see parked around there, you'd see tracks all over those fields."

"I do see tracks."

"They don't follow a pattern for working crops. The tractors, the cultivators, the stuff they'd be using now . . . those things have been sitting there. No fresh tracks anywhere. All the tracks come out of that big barn, where most of the stuff sitting outside should be stored. The marks come out to specific spots over the acreage and then go straight back into the barn, Admiral."

"As though there might be trucks picking up air-dropped equipment. Excuse my slowness. Do we have any record of air traffic that was picked up by our regular electronic snoops?"

"They've been dusting crops from the air. A regular thing at this time of year. We don't keep track of little stuff buzzing around between the hills. On the other hand, I'm sure the Albanians don't either. They don't have the resources for a sophisticated air-surveillance system."

"Okay, Dumfries. Let's get some look-down radar working there right now. Everything going from Romania and Bulgaria. And the Soviet Union, of course."

"Already done, sir. We'll have a list of every nighthawk and firefly that goes over that farm."

"If it confirms, what are you recommending?"

The intelligence man looked uneasy. "Well, it'd call for a meeting of Chiefs, naturally, sir."

"Do I have to wait for you to make the Joint Chiefs to get your opinion?"

"No. No, sir. What I'd do . . . I'd recommend . . . Sir, I don't think there's any doubt. We get onto Thunder Station with whatever speed the *King*'s busted power plant can make. She can get off in seven or eight hours from where she stands now. She can make it through the Strait of Messina and be on station off Albania in, what . . . twenty hours' sailing, once she clears Naples."

"Okay, Dumfries. Suppose we do that. The news gets back to our Congress—a Congress in love with this amazing Soviet boss—that we are hightailing on Condition Three to a potential military showdown on the strength of a couple of Kodaks. At worst it's provoking our new best friend, the Soviet Union, without consultation of any kind. At best it's interfering in the internal affairs of a small, militarily weak nation in a very volatile part of the world. What's worse, we're unilaterally abrogating Washington's favorite new initiative for peace—their getting their fleet out of the Med in exchange for our eighty-sixing the Sixth. Our emergency repairs become a heinous deceit, a provocation, and maybe treachery."

"That's possible, Admiral, but—"

"If shooting starts up, it looks like we kicked it all off. Everybody was afraid we were making a move on poor little Albania to replace bases the Greeks might take away. So their people had to rout out the traitors or provocateurs or imperialists. But it's almost worse looking if they just sit back blinking and looking startled. Then we're fools as well as warmongers."

Dumfries was showing some signs of impatience with this politician-admiral. "That's stuff for the Secretary of State, I think, sir. And nothing will be as bad in the long run as a Soviet naval base opening on the Med. If we move too late—or not at all—that's what happens."

"Not necessarily, Captain. Try this one on. We ship what's here on this table to the right people in Albania. Send estimates of what we think it means. Hint that we might be available for other help if they ask real nice."

"We could never promise anything like that, sir."

"Maybe not, but it might put some extra steel in their spine. My guess is that they'll snuff what's going on. Do the whole job for us in a day or two, before Soviet units outside the country are ready to move. Then all we'll have to do is sail home and fix our gears."

"They might move, ready or not. And you can never depend on the Albanians to do anything you expect them to do."

"Well, you might say the same thing about me. Go get some sleep, gentlemen. We'll meet the Joint Chiefs tomorrow. Track those air drops, if that's what they are. Let's find out exactly what sort of seed those men are sowing."

The Stratosphere—July 4

A different sort of plane was now needed in the service of Admiral Geinz. From the RAF base at Alconbury in the United Kingdom, a Lockheed TR-1 flown by a U.S. Air Force captain rose into the afternoon sky. The officer was disappointed at having to miss the Independence Day celebration that was being given that evening by his English friends.

The TR-1 was the structural cousin of the old U-2, but much improved. Its huge 103 feet of wingspan—no sweepback here—gave the plane the speed of a freight wagon. But it also allowed its pencil-thin fuselage to hover in the sky for incredible periods. The raft could fly at 88,000 feet, but its equipment preferred 65,000.

Although the TR-1 was more vulnerable to attack than the SR-71, it was far less likely to get into trouble on its missions. The graceful plane had been designed not to cross hostile borders like the bold Blackbird, but to linger just outside like a boy peeping over a fence at the forbidden. For this, it was extraordinarily well equipped. Its package of snooping hardware weighed in at almost two tons. With its astroinertial navigation system, synthetic-aperture radar, UHF relay, and data-link system, the aircraft could look 310 miles into Albania with terrifying clarity and report back what it saw in seconds. In this case, where it was looking for something specific, it would have taken a thousand perfectly placed and invisible ground agents to replace its brilliant eyes.

Somewhere after midnight the blip it sought appeared. Moving very slowly, as a propeller-driven plane of no great size and power might, the blip moved out of central Bulgaria. It rose from no recorded field because those fields would be watched more carefully. Near the Albanian border it went down near the deck, its circuitous passage showing that it was dipping low between mountains to evade most radar short of that orbiting in the stratosphere. The blip crossed the watched target precisely, and a second plane that rose one hour later from the same location made the same flight. The action took place at nowhere near the maximum range of the TR-1's equipment. By focusing and watching very precisely, the pilot was able to pick up in infrared the exhaust and engine imprint of three fairly heavy vehicles on the ground, probably medium trucks.

As instructed, the pilot bounced his coded report to a satellite that was orbiting not all that far above his head.

Washington, D.C.—July 5

The call came to Admiral Geinz in his bedroom during an act of early morning love. Mrs. Geinz groaned and rolled off her position astride her husband. He grimaced apologetically and grabbed the bedside phone.

"It must be war," the still-handsome Mrs. Geinz muttered, as her husband held the receiver to his ear. "I can hear the son of a bitch from here."

The admiral gathered her into his free arm and pulled her

to him. "Okay, Dumfries, then it's pretty much the way we had it supposed."

"Not a damned sign that the Albanians have paid us any attention, sir. The dropping planes flew in and out without a challenge. No sign of any government action on the ground that we could read. They're not going to accommodate us. You've got to get the *King* hammering for Thunder Station."

"Negative on that, Captain."

"But sir, there's not a second—"

"Have Admiral Irons on the *King* put through to me right here. On the scrambler. No taping."

"I'll get the Chiefs called—"

"No need to convene the Joint Chiefs to bring a busted carrier back home, is there, Dumfries?" Before Dumfries could get out a response the Admiral hung up the phone.

"What did you say to get him to make that noise?" Mrs. Geinz asked, preparing to rise.

Geinz held her back by tightening his arm around her. "Do you suppose you could finish your duty to the Navy before that phone rings again?"

She gently freed herself and slid away from him. "Go poop in your gold-braided hat, Teddy. I know when you're feeding someone a line of bull, and I don't find starting the next war very romantic."

Naples, Italy—July 6

Getting a huge ship under way is as complicated as the countdown to a space shot. From the moment of the decision to sail to actually getting under way, it can be a matter of eight hours. And so the *King* became a throbbing Mideast bazaar of bells, whistles, shouts, and pressing, hurrying humanity.

The starting of the gyros and the energizing of the radar repeaters began in the night. Manning rose to the sailing orders and the need to do a thousand things, beginning with the cancellation of services from the pier and including shore power and crane service. He became so busy that he almost didn't have time to contemplate what was happening in terms of his own situation.

There was no specific sailing destination announced. But it was, of course, impossible to keep that from the huge, prying crew. The pace at which sailing was being readied was the most reassuring thing. It had all the customary dispatch of Navy make-ready operations, but none of the desperate overdrive that would have gone with going out on Condition Three.

Most delightful were the distillations of many leaks from the Navigation Department. The positive gouge was that a course was being laid out straight to good old Norfolk, Virginia. And the radio traffic building between Norfolk and Naples was delicious verification for hearts eager to believe.

The Rumor Division issued a new bulletin with the true situation promptly on the half hour. One had the General Secretary rising furiously from his sickbed and demanding that the *King* be taken out of the Med before dark or the Black Sea Fleet was going to be sent to kick some ass. Another had the engines so badly damaged that not only could nothing be done at Naples, but the ship was going to be sitting happily in CONUS—in New York or San Francisco—for all of a year.

It was true that the air group was still aboard, but there was plenty of time to get them off on the way to Gibraltar. There was enough radio traffic to various bases around Europe to make that the likelihood. And if they stayed aboard, so what? The birds had been on a long and stressful deployment. Who knew what rebuilding and modification could only be done stateside?

Manning calculated that the coming nuclear event would happen in an even safer at-sea environment than the one planned originally. It would come 680 miles to the west on the axis between Barcelona and Algiers. Only Mallorca would be seriously involved. He was stupendously relieved that he would not have to make any moves of his own to avoid a dockside cataclysm in Naples. That was the good news.

The bad news was that getting off the ship before the event was hugely compromised for the moment. His scheme depended on an emergency he had contrived in conjunction with the ship steaming into potential battle.

He reminded himself that he was the god of supply, and what went on and off the *King* was pretty much his to say. He determined to stick with what had now become a rather thin pretext. He went on to a potential question.

Would he be willing to die for the destruction of this ship? No, things like that would have to be left to the marginally insane—like Tree.

Manning would get off.

In a building crescendo, the countdown of required operations marched forward. Boats and vehicles were hoisted ashore or aboard where they belonged. Booms and brow were rigged in. The masters-at-arms checked for stowaways. Radio checks were made. The pilothouse and after steering were manned, and steering engines tested along with controls, communications, and the emergency steering alarm. The special sea and anchor details set themselves. The OOD shifted his watch to the bridge as sound-powered phone circuits were tested everywhere. The draft of the ship fore and aft was recorded and the screws checked for clearance.

Fifteen minutes from sailing, the CO's permission to test the main engines came down. The XO was told the ship was ready to get under way.

Shore connections were broken. Quarters for leaving port sounded loudly.

At last maneuvering bells were ordered. Admiral Irons, as a flag officer, was asked for permission to get under way. He gave it. The steaming ensign snapped at the sky. Zero time, the time under way, was written into the log.

Something like a massive grunt of excitement swept through all the vast spaces.

Tree burped an unscheduled broadcast to the *Vinza* offshore. The Soviet trawler, already hull down in the distance, proceeded to the west. It made sense to get out in front of the battle group early and save wear and tear on engines. The little ship would be overtaken soon enough and have to pour on the turns.

Manning hurried below to work out some dead-reckoning positions for the ship. He was going to have to move out with uncomfortable haste. Unfortunately, to maintain securely the sham he had set up, he was going to have to take his Disbursing Division felons along. Tree, he decided without much vacillation, would stay. His extinction would be as satisfying as that of Ledges.

The towering bow of the *King* swung slowly, ponderously to point out of the glittering waters of the Bay of Naples. The four escorts were off their moorings and moving out with their looming charge.

Finally, beginning to move under the power of her own crippled engines, the *King*'s horn thundered a last mighty farewell. A farewell to more than she knew, Manning thought.

U.S.S. *Ernest J. King*, The Tyrrhenian Sea—July 6

Nobody had taken special notice that Vice Admiral Irons had not been on the bridge as the *King* cleared the bay, the smaller vessels around saluting her. Part of the reason was that he didn't want to go any farther than he had to in the cruel charade he was helping to inflict on the overstrained crew of this vessel. The other was that he had a call coming in from the President of the United States.

Given the unusual way that this operation was being handled, he had felt justified in expressing his doubts to the Chairman of the Joint Chiefs that things had been correctly cleared. In keeping with his maverick nature, Geinz had not cut him to bits and ordered him to comply without question, as was his perfect right. Instead, he had told him to stand by for a call from the Commander in Chief. By the time he had realized Geinz meant it, Irons was feeling disloyal and obstructive, but there was no way to back out.

All he could think of to begin when the call was patched in on the scrambler was, "Standing by as Admiral Geinz directed, Mr. President."

"This call is being recorded for your protection and, I suppose, my burning at the stake if things don't turn out right. I'll be talking to congressional leaders later in the day and asking them to go along quietly. Maybe they will, maybe they won't. I'm hanging out naked and so is Geinz. But everything he said added up. We just couldn't give the Russians all those extra hours to spool up an Albanian operation while we were cranking up the *King* and getting through our proper channels. I don't feel great about all of this myself. But if we've fooled them about where we're really going, we've gained eight hours to get there before any overt Soviet intervention. If we haven't fooled them, we're no worse off than we'd be if we'd let them know we were coming all the way. Does that cover you?"

"Yes, sir, it does. But may I go on record as saying that what I think we're doing is wrong?"

"I've cut the recording now, Admiral. Tell me fast. Do you want me to relieve you with Captain Ash? We could promote him and brief him before the move."

"That's not necessary, sir. And, with respect to Captain Ash, nobody can handle this group as well as I can. Besides which, sir, I have no intention of missing any dust-up."

"I appreciate that, Irons. Make us look good."

"I've got seven thousand good men working on that, Mr. President."

Exactly one half hour after the battle group had left Naples Bay heading west for Gibraltar—just time enough for the escorting frigates to fall into position and all observers to confirm that the *King* was well on its way to Norfolk—Admiral Irons called Captain Ash on the bridge.

"Arlen, signal the escort of the change in course. Use the radioteletype. Follow up with a fax with details in depth. Break the news to the ship any way you want. But going to Condition Three is about the best way to wake them up that it's important."

"Aye, aye, sir," said Ash. "They'll measure up. Should we clear up some of the mess we made with all the people who are expecting us somewhere else?"

"Negative. Every second we can keep people confused counts. And we're on EMCON as of now. All ships. All planes. Put the CAP on an Alert Five. Aggressive air patrolling where needed."

And from that moment all electromagnetic transmissions from the battle group ceased. Any electronic ears seeking information about the force would have to generate it on their own.

The ship was on a condition of wartime cruising. Not the modified general quarters of Condition Two, but a huge step-up in readiness. One of three sections was always on watch, and many key stations were manned or partially manned at all times.

With a great flurry of signaling from the yardarm blinkers, the group spread out and turned southeast to clear the boot of Italy. Then it would be through the Strait of Messina between the toe and Sicily, and straight for Thunder Station.

Manning was only somewhat taken aback by the *King*'s ruse. He completely understood its sudden implications: The carrier had sailed at 1400 hours on July 6, having lulled the Soviets through eight hours of sailing preparations. She was under way a full twenty-one hours before she had been expected to clear port—and only fifteen hours before the coup in Tirana was scheduled to begin tomorrow on the seventh. Meaning that the *King* would not be removed from the earth ten hours short of Thunder Station. The mighty warship would arrive after all, in the midst of the unsupported "rebel" attack in the city—the most vulnerable phase. If the Albanian government saw its fortunes going badly, it

could ask for immediate support. There would be more than
sufficient time for the *King*'s air group to make mincemeat
of the uncovered ground forces. And, more important, the
planes would be there to prevent uncovered Soviet airborne
from intervening before the ship's immolation.

But it made no difference whatever to the assured destruction of the *King*. To Manning, that was the only point.

And his own plans were completely back on track.

He went immediately to find the executive officer, Commander Seth Hale. Whispering Seth, they called him because he delivered every word at near-peak volume. As XO,
Hale ran the million details of routine, personnel, and
discipline on the ship. He was completely overwhelmed by
the sudden changes that had been wrought upon his schedul-
ing of everything, which suited Manning's purposes admira-
bly. For one thing, the exec's personal schedule had so
broken down that Manning was able to elbow his way in to
see him.

"Commander Hale, there's been a big foul-up and this
ship's got an awful problem. I want your permission to fix
it," Manning said in a voice heavy with worry and contrition.

"Oh, Christ, what now?" hollered Hale.

"Somebody blew something in ordering up the medical
supplies. We've got a carrier loaded with an ocean of jet
fuel and explosives sailing Condition Three without any
more burn dressings than you'd find in the odd first-aid kit.
The way my computers say it, we switched a bit over two
tons of medical supplies with enough boxes of X-ray film to
take the Navy into the next century."

"Well, that's pure shit, Commander. Somebody's ass
should fry for it."

"The kind of frying I'm worrying about is what happens
to a couple of hundred kids who maybe get tangled up with
a couple of thousand gallons of burning JP-5."

"Nothing you can do about it now, Manning. Make sure
that the medical people know the problem and gather up—"

"I've got it fixed already, Commander, if you let me go
ahead with what I arranged."

"Tell me, and make it quick." The exec's attention was beginning to wander to two ringing telephones.

Manning was glad of anything that kept him from looking too closely into what he was saying. He spoke quickly. "Before we buttoned up I'd called one of our hospitals. They're the ones that got our shipment, just the way we're the ones who got theirs. I told them I'd take a chopper over and make the swap. I could still do it."

"Like hell you could. We're not sitting in Naples anymore."

"For those kids' sake, Hale, listen to me. The hospital is maybe an hour north of the Strait. All I ask you to do is call your opposite number in Air and tell him to plug me in with one of his operations officers. He could get me a chopper over to the shore and back as easy as spitting. I give the Italians what they need, I get back with what we need. I guarantee I could do the whole drill in under three hours."

"Three hours is sixty-five miles even with two screws. We might be out in the middle of the drink. How're you going to find us coming back when we're not putting out any transmissions and we have no fixed position to give you?"

"We'll have an E-2C radar plane up there sure as hell. It'll have you painted and we'll pick up your location from the downlink. Besides which, in those narrow, crowded waters I can probably drop down and ask a fisherman which way you went. Or a Russian trawler. Come on, Hale."

"Okay, Manning. I'll call the airedales and tell 'em where things stand. It's up to them whether it can get handled or not."

Within an hour Manning was talking with an air operations officer who was as dubious as Hale and had even more on his mind. Lieutenant Commander Moses Duckworth was an almost chinless man who had to show his determination in ways other than his looks. "Begging your pardon, Commander, what happened to chain of command? This should've gone through Bedford, the air boss, and been checked through big-daddy operations upstairs. The old-boy network doesn't go so good outside the office—"

214 • Donald N. Norman

"Shit, Duckworth, I'm not asking for A-6s to attack Moscow."

"Well, sir, suppose those A-6s get called to head for Moscow and I got my deck and elevators screwed up with your helicopter? I know you guys think we make up what we do as we go along, but there's a guy up on the island with a lot of guys helping him who has a table in front of him. A big table. On it is a model of every plane we got on deck. They move them around like one of those puzzle cubes. They can't move one thing without moving ten other things."

"You mean you can't hack it. Burn dressings for a ship maybe headed into battle aren't worth a little sweat."

"Maybe 'headed into battle' are the magic words, Commander. If it hits the fan, every chopper on this ship is going to have a big job to do. You have to go upstairs without any shortcuts—"

Knowing he would not get through the maze at the top, Manning played the only card he had left. "I knew you might have a problem. I found just the bird for the job, and you'd probably push it overboard to get the damned thing out of the way if trouble started."

Duckworth bristled. "Sir, I didn't know air operations were your thing."

If the chinless man hadn't unknowingly held the whip hand, Manning would have had his scalp for that tone. He tried to walk a line between authority and sweet reason. "I had occasion to borrow one of those Sea Guards from the Coast Guard for some moving I was doing around North Island. That silly pod was just the ticket then, and it's just what I need now."

Duckworth had to show that he knew his business as thoroughly as this shopkeeper. "You mean that HH-52 orphan? Yeah, I know the bird you mean. And I know where that big plastic barge that clips on to it is. The copter was kind of useful up north going ship to ship, but here, without supply ships, it's just a weight."

"Then I can use it?"

The operations officer appeared to have made his point that he was no man to trifle with. "Okay. Get me this request, in writing, and where and when you want to go. I'll have the damned thing ready and cleared if nothing else comes up. But *you*, sir, are in charge of getting it loaded. Down in the hangar bay is best, before it goes up the elevator. We've got enough going on up on the roof."

"If I have to handle that, Duckworth, I will." Manning tried hard not to let out his exultation. This self-important little prig had done away with the need for a dozen additional hair-raising details. He could have kissed him. "I appreciate what you're doing. The whole ship does."

"If you wait too long to give me what I need, Commander, you won't have to thank anybody because you won't be going anywhere. The weather is due to turn totally to shit. And fast."

With his role now dominant, Manning took iron control of the operation.

McGregor found Manning had entered the safe with the combination he held as department head. He had taken the division keys and the present vault combinations. Manning brushed away his objections. "Since you started borrowing for your family troubles, I thought I'd look after my interests in the vault a little better."

"You'll get it back," McGregor snapped.

"Sure, McGregor. I know how honest you are. Okay, I've got things to do. You men meet me in the division office in four hours—2400. We've got a big night ahead."

"Suppose we don't like you as the boss?" Ledges said roughly.

"Suppose then we make you the boss, Chief. And you can guess how we're going to get off this tub. Now get some sleep while you can."

U.S.S. *Ernest J.King*, the Strait of Messina—July 7

And so it was that McGregor, Ledges, and Lydecker arrived later at the division office to find that Manning had single-handedly transferred the money from the vault to the outer office.

From his endless ship's inventory he had produced lead-shielded canvas bags with locking seals. They were used for the transfer of X-ray film in bulk. He had brought them aboard in Naples with a few computer strokes. They were ideal both as loading containers and as cover for his story of the supplies foul-up. There were seventeen of the bulky bags. "I was so wound up I figured I'd get it done," said the sweating and disheveled commander. "There wasn't enough room for more than one to work in that vault with all those crates anyway."

"Kind of you," said McGregor dryly.

"Is it all here?" asked a testy Ledges.

The commander talked to them as he wiped the perspiration off his face with a handkerchief. "I'm happy to say we're going to take a helluva lot of money with us. I'm unhappy to say that we can't take it all. We've got weight and space limitations, even taking some inside the fuselage. We don't have as much room in the pod as you'd think, because that's where you guys are going to be."

This was the first specific thing they'd heard about how they were going to ride off the *King*. They looked doubtfully at one another.

"Where do you travel, Commander?" asked Ledges.

"Right up in the cockpit, where all good commanders belong. People might understand the head of the Supply Department going along to correct a big mistake, but not half the Disbursing Division going along with him."

"Jeez, I know that pod you're talking about," said Lydecker. "I had a case for a portable typewriter made out of what looked like the same stuff. Know what happened when I dropped it? It busted wide open. And we're gonna be hanging out with nothing but that crappy little shell between us and the Med.''

''You'll have good company. Your pals and about twenty-six million dollars.''

''How long do we hang?''

''Maybe an hour, or a little longer. Then we're at the hospital. We send the pilots out to stretch their legs and get some coffee while we set things up. I've got a van meeting us on the grounds. That'll take us to a plane, in exchange for a nice load of the Navy's medicinal morphine. And that's all you have to know for now.''

Manning checked his watch. ''We'll be lifting off about 0730 hours.''

Lydecker looked at the bags jamming the office. ''So I guess we'd better get these things loaded.''

''See, you're learning,'' said Manning. ''But one more item.'' He produced McGregor's keys and selected the pin key for the time lock. ''We wouldn't want Bluehoffer to get curious or ambitious until we're well on our way. What's the maximum on the timer?''

''Seventy-two hours on this one,'' McGregor said.

''Sounds like plenty,'' said Manning as he slammed shut the eighteen-inch-thick door and spun the wheel. After he had moved the timer as far around as it would go and punched it home with the key, he straightened with a sigh. ''Nothing short of a nuclear strike could get into there until that lock opens three days from now.''

U.S.S. *Ernest J. King*, the Ionian Sea—July 7

The giant size of the ship and the bustle of wartime preparations worked perfectly to the advantage of the plotters. Ledges and Lydecker in work clothes and baseball hats became just two more swabbies dragooned into the efforts of the massive beehive.

In the hangar bay they found that the surly but efficient Duckworth had indeed maneuvered the outcast HH-52A from its crammed and forgotten position to a spot where it was ready to move onto an elevator to the roof. The machine had been inspected, serviced, and even cleaned. Better yet, the ungainly cargo pod had been brought out and attached to it, a task that would have broken the hearts of the uninitiated. On each side of the fuselage the hinged tops of the pod waited to receive a load.

Using what Manning had told them were weight-distribution figures given him by the air people—he had actually lifted them out of a technical manual—they carried the canvas bags four at a time on a handcart to the helicopter and loaded them.

"Use all the tie-downs in the pod," Manning warned. "If we hit bumpy air we wouldn't want that weight shifting around."

Of course, they were careful to leave sufficient room in the pod for their most important cargo—themselves.

From four o'clock in the morning onward, there were tens of millions of dollars sitting unattended in the Sea Guard. Any of the milling swabbies owning some idle curiosity, a jackknife, and an inclination to be tempted could have helped themselves. But Manning now felt himself so firmly in the hands of a benevolent fate that he ignored the possibility.

With an hour to go before takeoff, he gave his fellow conspirators a final briefing. "So far, not a hitch. Here's the way it goes down from here." He pulled a map of Italy off a shelf and opened it on his lap. His finger hit a place below the instep of the Italian boot. "From a spot here, halfway across the Gulf of Taranto, we take off. Our official destination is here, about a hundred miles northwest. It's a road junction town called Potenza. NATO went into a deal to establish the hospital there with the Italians because we needed a facility with some space, and the area needed an economic shot in the arm. The staff is in a happy haze. It's like a cargo cult. Every time they look up there's another helicopter or truck coming out of heaven with a load of goodies. They've just about stopped keeping track themselves. The NATO computers are the gods in the sky, so they swallowed everything I sent them and everything I told them. When we drift down they'll be waiting with open spaghetti pots. They'll stuff the helicopter full of the burn dressings I had sent down from Frankfurt. They won't have a clue they're supposed to get something back. What we do with what we bring will be our business. All the pilots will have to know is getting there and home. There'll be so much stuff to go back that I won't be able to get aboard. I'll have to follow later. No sweat there because nobody ever sees us again anyway.''

"Nifty," said Ledges. "Somewhere along the way we slip ourselves and the bags into the van you've got waiting, and it's a long, long time before anybody tumbles that anything is wrong. But where's that van going?"

Manning's finger went back to the map. "We drive a fast fifty miles, still going northwest, to a nice commercial airstrip outside this town—Avellino. There's a fast twin there to whisk us out of the country. People have been taken care of. We have the airspace access we need to get over the right borders—if we do it in the right places."

"What borders are those?" Ledges wanted to know.

"There you go again, wanting to know more than you need to. Keep trusting me, Ledges."

"I've got to know," said McGregor. "So I can leave word for my wife somehow."

"For family matters you have to see the chaplain, McGregor. The bird goes to the roof at 0715. You three be hanging around the hangar bay from 0700 on. I'll be waiting. The copter is set up near the elevator, with the right side to the bulkhead. That's the side where you go into the pod. I'll latch you in. Ledges, take a cordless electric drill with a good-sized bit in there with you. Drill what breathing holes you need out the bottom. When we're on the ground again, stay quiet in there until I unbutton you. Can you think of anything we're leaving out?"

"Yeah," McGregor said, his eyes on the deck. "You're leaving me out. I'm not going."

The other men stared at him, Ledges and Lydecker dismayed, Manning worried.

"*Jeez*, Wade, you *gotta* come," said Lydecker in the voice of a child who has lost his father's hand on a crowded street.

"You can't back out now, Wade," Ledges said. "There's no way to unwind what we've done." He already knew his pleas could not work. McGregor had shared with him his devastating phone call from Tess. The chief knew that his friend had lost his only plan to have his family escape with him. And once the authorities were on to them, she wouldn't be able to make a move as long as her husband lived.

"I don't want you to stay with me. Go. Do what you have to do. Sorry it took me so long to figure out there was no way I could drag my family into this."

"You know what the Navy will do to you if you stay here?" Manning said.

"Maybe I can wriggle out. Playing rock stupid and lucking into a good lawyer could mean a reasonable sentence. With a miracle I could just get a dishonorable. After all, I didn't go with you."

"That's long odds, Wade," said Ledges.

"For me it's the only odds there are. You guys will have my share of what you're taking. Rocky and Hink will find a way to take care of Tess and Kiki if things go really bad."

Ledges's face was white stone. "You know we'll do that, Wade."

Manning leaned close to McGregor. "You wouldn't be considering going to somebody with evidence before we got out of here, to make things easier for you, would you? And maybe have a greeting party of Marines for us at the hospital?"

A huge fist closed around Manning's lapel as Ledges stood up and jerked the commander to his feet.

"Look, you ring-knocking bag of shit—"

McGregor jumped up and separated them. "Don't worry,

Manning. I'll keep things going as they were right up until somebody sticks out his hand to cash a check."

"Right," said Manning. "Sorry. That was dumb of me. I'll leave you guys to say your heartbreaking good-byes now. I think you're an idiot, McGregor, but good luck. You other two, stick a toothbrush in your sock and be in the hangar bay by 0700. We won't have to worry about muster for you because we've got the whole reporting chain right here." He turned and left without offering to shake hands with McGregor.

Lydecker couldn't look up. His cheeks were wet. "I hate this. I can't leave you alone, Wade—"

"It doesn't do a damn bit of good to stay, Hink," McGregor said. "Sorry I had to wimp out and do this to you."

"You gotta do what you gotta do," Ledges said. He hugged McGregor for a moment. "With a load of money like that there are people we could reach. Hot lawyers—"

"Yeah. Sure. Who knows? Spend some for me, okay, guys? Now get the hell out of here." McGregor handed an envelope to Ledges. "Just make sure you get this to Tess. There's an address in Genoa on the envelope."

When Ledges and Lydecker had gone, McGregor sat at his desk looking around the tiny room. He tried not to worry that his next room would be nowhere near as large.

Theron Tree was drenched in fetid and clammy sweat. It was a sign of happiness. He was closing in on the solution to a technical problem that a world power had decided was unsolvable outside of great technical centers. And he had succeeded in what he estimated was just under thirty hours of actual working time,

Tree supposed that he could have chopped considerable hours from that if he had been able to spread out his work on the large communal table at the center of St. Moritz —the crowded tech-rep quarters on the *King*. But that would have invited the curiosity of dozens of people who understood a good deal about the type of electronics that challenged him here. So he had gone to the only area of privacy available to him: his berth.

Shut off from other eyes by a pulled curtain, his mattress gave him a work area perhaps seven feet by four, much of it occupied by his own body. Since he needed more illumination than could be provided by his reading light, he had found it necessary to rig his own lights from scrounged lamps. Their heat made the berth, cut off by the curtain from the feeble efforts of the ventilators, almost uninhabitable. His shadow moving endlessly behind the curtain brought many rude and curious comments from his colleagues, but they knew his temper and his fists well enough not to seriously intrude.

Like all seemingly insurmountable technical problems, the key to breaking into Manning's stopwatch and obtaining the supercilious commander's personal code had been the preliminary organization—tracing the riddle along the one and only sequence that would lead to an unraveling.

He had decided that this sequence must begin with a huge calculated leap based upon what he knew from years of dealing with the black-arts departments of the Soviet Union. In his supposition, the microchip used in the stopwatch would be one done entirely by the intelligence people, because they would fear anything that they had not conceived themselves. And this would mean that the chip would be crude. There would be nothing of the subtleties available in the best Japanese and United States products. So he would assume a comparatively clumsy architecture with a far-from-limitless programming ability when put into a device as circumscribed in purpose as the stopwatch code machine.

He was also willing to gamble that the device had been prepared for just this operation—custom-made—and that his own personal code had been put into place immediately before or after Manning's, and that the changes from one code to the other had been minimal.

With that as a working hypothesis, he constructed a simple device by which he could send, receive, and analyze his own code using a minuscule signal. With this as his laboratory, he set out to explore Manning's code, whose setting on the watch he knew from having transmitted it to the *Vinza* many times.

It had then only remained for him to free and examine the circuits of the watch's chip and determine a way to progressively vary the approach to its molecular gates, hoping that the choices inside were limited enough to enable him to stumble across the right entrance.

Too simple? He thought of all the thieves who made a living off people who left keys under doormats and used their birth dates and Social Security numbers in bank code cards.

He had freed the chip and examined it with one of the powerful jeweler's lenses he used in his own work. The circuits were even more rudimentary than he had hoped. It had not been desperately hard for him to find points where he might jump in with minute bits of current applied with tiny, finely wired needles. This would serve him as a crude tuner for the examination of the output of the chip.

Many tedious hours later something was there. Something so small he questioned whether he had seen it himself.

He switched his clamps and wires and prepared his little tape recorder. Using the watch's setting devices as Manning had, Tree put his own name through the new circuit and into the tape. He now had captured the sort of signal that he had been sending to the *Vinza* for relay, a signal that would have been decoded by the sending process that whisked it to Moscow. The problem he had presented to himself was to reverse a knotty encoding device—the stopwatch—to turn it into a decoder equal to arcane equipment a thousand times more subtle.

Tree had often thought he would have made a fine surgeon. His fingers, always rock-steady, seemed to have separate, brilliant minds of their own. Following the notes on his pad to help the electronic remapping, he readjusted his intricate system of clamps and the wires they held. Then, using watchmaker's tools, he adjusted the works of the stopwatch to enable the hand to respond to the trivial traces of current he would be feeding back into it. At times the sweat running off his brow threatened disaster to the work he huddled over.

Ready, finally. He fed the message out of the tape recorder and into the watch. The hand jumped to various settings on the dial. From here on it was as simple as a Captain Midnight decoder badge.

There were four jumps. They read out to the letters *T-R-E-E*. He had Manning's code. From here he could have every word that miserable bastard sent or received.

Even as his hands flew to reassemble the watch as it was, he reviewed his case for loathing the handsome commander.

For one thing, Tree thought with satisfaction, he was totally ineffectual in the job he had come to do. He had told Tree that the bugs he had successfully tested were in place up in the island. Tree was inclined to doubt it. And even if he had succeeded, what good had it done? Here they were on a Condition Three race to Thunder Station that had come straight out of nowhere—totally unanticipated.

He snorted out loud at all the time the commander had lost trying to get the payroll theft he had discovered swept under the rug until after the operation. It was understandable that Manning couldn't afford to get swept into a major scandal at a moment like this, but the time he had been giving it seemed ridiculous.

Well, what could you expect from nonprofessionals? Imagine letting a man whose motivation stemmed from a personal grudge—a family misfortune—assume a dominant position in a job like this.

All the dangerous years that Tree had put in—years of love and devotion, years practically unpaid when you considered present rates for this sort of work—had been forgotten in an instant. It cut him to the bone.

God knew that agents couldn't be publicized like movie stars, but men like Philby had finished their lives full of honors. With showier accomplishments he could have made the Kremlin wall. The history books—*that* was a goal.

Even as he had these thoughts, guilt nibbled at Tree. His work with this watch—all those hours—were the indulgence of a petty vendetta. He had made the mistake of believing that nothing more would be needed from him, that the ship would be sitting with partially disassembled engines in the Bay of Naples when the Albanian operation began. Now he had to get back to the business of stopping this gray juggernaut under him. And he wasn't entirely without ideas.

At almost the moment he finished his work and began to sweep his equipment back into a toolbag, the great, smothering weight of depression began to come down on him as it had so many times before in his life. Now that he no longer had the work to fill his soul, the curse of his life was returning. Perhaps another quick fix would be enough.

He found an opaque plastic vial in his bag, with his white powder hidden beneath a topping of tiny screws. It was the last of four vials that he had brought onto the ship. The last one had gone more quickly than expected. He dropped a small heap of the cocaine at the base of his thumb and snorted it in. He put the vial next to a bottle marked "Penetrating Oil," but which was actually drug-free urine stored against possible need.

His shaving mirror soon showed a new wildness in his mismatched eyes, but he felt only vaguely better.

Avellino, Italy—July 7

Grave digging has never been popular work. For two men who were not only skilled pilots of multiengine aircraft but officers of the KGB, the work was not just hard but denigrating.

The ground was hard and filled with stones, and the planners had found at the last moment that they didn't have the proper tools to send along. They could have provided flamethrowers and grenade launchers on a whim. But picks

and shovels were not to be had. So Jegum and Rabnik—
they had been together for two weeks without bothering to
learn one another's first names—were working with the
short entrenching tools used by Soviet infantrymen. They
had not figured out for themselves that they were best used
from a kneeling position, so their backs felt broken.

"We're down three feet. Shouldn't that be enough?"
asked Rabnik.

"Four feet keeps the dogs away, one of the specialists
told me," said Jegum. He was markedly more handsome
than Rabnik, but lost his advantage in a sea of virulent
facial pimples.

"Full of tips, those boys. And we end up doing the jobs
of not just aerial chauffeurs, but morticians and assassins. I
still don't understand why the driver can't do the wet work.
He's trained for it."

"The sailors will be watching the driver. Remember,
they're holding all that money, and the man is supposed to
be an Italian thief."

Rabnik tied a handkerchief around his forehead to keep
the sweat out of his eyes. "Maybe you could do for the
three of them yourself. I was terrible with guns. I hated that
part of the training. I almost miss requalifying every year.
Flyers should fly and shooters should shoot."

It was cool enough in the grove of trees in which they
were digging the graves. But just beyond the foliage the
heat danced up off the crumbling blacktop of the abandoned
runway. The remaining nondescript hangar and the ram-
shackle operations shack were two thousand feet away at the
opposite end of the paving.

The strip was old, built twenty years before in high hopes
that the industries around Naples might spill out this far. It
had never happened.

Rabnik and Jegum had kept their plane with them at this
far end of the runway. It was an old propeller-driven de
Havilland Twin Otter, unostentatious and well suited to high
loads and short, rough strips. It had crossed from Bulgaria
easily. Its forged papers, written to a state oil company out

of Ploesti in Romania, seemed in perfect order. It was unlikely that any Italian would care to walk a half mile in the heat to look at the aircraft. In any case, they had pulled it off the runway with a tow bar and dragged it into the shade of the tall trees. Having arrived a day early for their job, they were going to spend the night sleeping in the plane. They didn't want heat to build up in the upholstery.

"You still look shaky," Jegum said. "Let me take you through again." He pointed to a dirt road coming through the woods from behind them. "The van will come down that road. That will give them about two hundred feet to walk before they're out of the trees. We walk down to greet them. Just the few Italian words we've been taught and a lot of nods. We're not supposed to be Russians. They see the plane, and under the wing the two handcarts for loading the money. They see everything's in order and they relax. That's important."

"How will we know the American who's in with us?"

"The driver will introduce everybody. The one called Manning is ours. It doesn't make any difference if he sees what we're up to, of course. It's the others who get the first surprise."

"As I have it," said Rabnik, "we let the driver take the lead. We come up behind. When they're in a good position and still hidden in the woods, the driver will say, 'The weather will be good for the flight.' That's the signal to fire."

"That's it. One shot each should be enough for the first ones. And we've both got seven more in the clip for the rest of the job."

"In any case, it will be easiest to take Manning last."

"The driver will ask him to help pull the bodies into the holes. I'll get him from behind while his hands are full. One shot guaranteed. The driver can dig *that* hole."

U.S.S. *Ernest J. King*, the Ionian Sea—July 7

Anger is, in its way, such a delicious emotion that even strong and intelligent people like Manning give way to its delights against their better judgment.

Tree's insolence had gotten to him. Despite Manning's urgent need to make a final report to the outside controllers before he left the ship for good, the arrogant tech rep had twice failed to show up at their meeting place at the arranged times. And when he had finally appeared, there was no pretense of apology. He had handed over the coding watch as though its return had simply slipped his mind. Fat chance.

It was not that there had been any significant delay in reporting the change in fleet heading. The *Vinza* had been fast enough to pick up the nonappearance of the *King*. The little AGI trawler had charged back from over the horizon where she had been gulled, and picked up the successful ruse on her radar. Tree reported having caught sight of her less than two hours after the southeast turn. But even though the word would have been flashed back to Moscow on the satellite link and the charge to Thunder Station fully assumed, nothing could replace confirmation from the carrier.

And certainly nothing could substitute for the assurance that the elements for the great event were in place and irredeemably destined to function.

It was here that Manning's delicious anger served him poorly. He was so furious at Tree that he took bitter satisfaction in being able to hand him, for transmission, the ciphered message that reaffirmed his immolation.

Somehow, just handing over the terse, bare facts of the matter didn't seem enough mockery against the ugly man. Manning allowed himself whole extra sentences, even detailing the placement in the vault and the detail of the time lock. He didn't even mind all the tedious extra minutes it took him to code the business into the watch before handing it back to Tree. "This should have been gone already."

"Is it important enough to tell me about, Commander?" Tree asked, his expression unreadable.

"You'll know soon enough. If there's anything else, tell me about it now. I'm going to chopper off the ship for a while in the morning. A supply foul-up I have to fix."

Tree took the watch from Manning. "Those foul-ups just won't stop happening, will they?"

Washington, D.C.—July 7

The tall, austere President of the United States had the reputation of a man who, in the spirit of his stern Boston forebears, would in no way ever be tempted to strong drink. His detractors said his abstinence was in pure fear that such indulgence would cause him to smile and crack his rigid face to bits.

The man he faced in the Oval Office, the majority leader of the United States Senate, was, on the other hand, a laugher. And one known to have brushed so close to uncontrolled alcoholism that he feared to touch a drop of the amber fire. So it gave some gravity to the moment when the President filled a tumbler bearing his seal three-quarters full from a bottle of malt Scotch and responded to a signal from the majority leader to have the same.

They were not friends. During the President's stint in the House of Representatives and during several elections the two had said unforgivable things of one another.

The little midwestern senator, silver of hair, tie, eyeglass frame, and cowboy buckle, knew the best uses of both a grudge and an advantage. The only reason the President had bothered to call this meeting at all was that he knew that the American flag the man always wore in his buttonhole was no idle symbol. He owned a couple of Bronze Stars and a dead arm from the big war. He would, if convinced, put the interests of his country above anything. There was only the matter of agreeing on those interests.

"I thought that no President would ever again try to go around the Congress, Mr. President."

"I thought somebody might, Paul. I just didn't think it would be me."

"There's simply not enough to go on, sir. For every photo interpretation expert you got, I could find ten retired guys to look at them another way. The maneuvers near the border? Even you don't sound sold on how dangerous that is."

"It all comes down to the General Secretary, doesn't it? Under Brezhnev we'd have the Med so stuffed with warships you could walk across it. And everybody'd be applauding and buying flags."

"A lot of folks think that guy can save the world. I think I'm one of 'em. Hell, even if there are some over there who don't like him and they're huffing and puffing to do something nasty, you've got to give him a chance to win out, or his enemies will mark him as either our stooge or afraid of us. He's beaten them before. His best weapon with his own people is the goodwill he's sold to our people. It shows them peace can work. We show up ready to start a brawl in a demilitarized ocean and all that's in the dumper."

"So what'll you do?" asked the President.

"You can only take my word that it's nothing political. It's what I and most of my guys believe in. We're going to settle this war-powers area once and forever."

"You'll turn back the *King* and tie her up, then?"

"No, *you'll* turn her back. That's the way it works in this system, Mr. President."

"Suppose I don't do it, no matter what the Congress says? The thing over there will have time to play itself out."

"If you feel that this thing is important enough to risk your political life and that of your party on, that's one thing. But it's never going to be important enough to take a chance on the first real shot at peace in fifty years."

"Paul, tell me if there's anything on earth that will let

that ship go on station with a weapons release and your blessing.''

The senator drained what was left in the glass. He placed his hand over the top when the President tried to pour him another. ''I can't change where I stand, sir. But I went outside protocol and talked to Geinz. He's not Attila. I know that. For him to be worried does mean something. The piece that's still missing for him would go a long way to selling me.''

''Positive word that their General Secretary is dead?''

''Yes.''

U.S.S. *Ernest J. King*, the Gulf of Taranto—July 7

Like all born landsmen, Manning was astounded by the huge and capricious powers of weather systems at sea. From where he leaned into the rapidly building northeast gale that had begun to sweep across the acres of flight deck, he could see that the ordinarily placid Mediterranean had begun to churn itself into an ugly gray soup of chopping and rolling cliffs. What should have been the cheerful light of a summer morning seemed the most miserable of winter dusks.

The plane handlers around the Sea Guard were beginning to watch the effect of the gusts as they slapped against the helicopter's side and sent the drooping blades into spastic flutters. Manning knew that the CAP was up, but the V Division was looking carefully to the tying down of the other birds on deck.

''What the hell's going on with this weather?'' Manning shouted to one of the fuelers, who was just finishing up his work with the HH52-A. ''I didn't expect anything like this.''

''Neither did the weather boys, sir,'' said the grape, his bare arms showing goose bumps under the unexpected chill in the wind. Patches of cold rain had begun to sweep through as well. "I guess that North Sea front that's been beating up Normandy decided to take an express train for a vacation in the Med. Looks like it's going to hang around awhile and get a lot nastier, too. Lucky you're going now, sir. It could be nasty getting off after a while. And don't depend on getting back too soon."

The two pilots were both in the helicopter, well out of hearing. "I'm not on any tight schedules," Manning said. "We almost ready to go?"

"Just checking the fastenings on the pod, Commander. Wouldn't want it falling off and giving somebody a headache."

Manning hoped that Ledges had not forgotten to drill his holes in the pod while they were still in the recesses of the hangar bay. Somebody catching sight of a drill poking through out here would never do. "Okay, then. Crank up the voodoo that gets us going. I'm getting aboard."

The commander was starting for the copter when the grape called to him. "Is that somebody looking for you, sir?"

The Sea Guard was sitting on the port side of the ship toward the stern, just aft of the spot where an elevator had raised the helicopter to the roof. There was no other aircraft in the vicinity, so it was obvious that Theron Tree, brightly visible in his yellow rain gear, was heading for them and nobody else as he hurried across the deck in the increasing rain.

"Let me see what he wants," Manning muttered and walked quickly to meet Tree near a tied-down Tomcat.

Tree motioned the officer to where the plane's wing glove offered some shelter. Beneath a sou'wester hat his face seemed uglier than ever, seething with tics. The pupils of his eyes were huge pools of black. He handed Manning a folded sheet of paper. It was almost completely filled with single-spaced typing. "Before you go, I want you to look this over to see if I made any mistakes."

A claw scratched inside Manning's breast. He opened the sheet and scanned it.

He needed only a moment to see that it was each and every word of the message he had coded into the watch.

The *King* and everything on it froze and hung in space. "So you know it all."

"Oh, come on, Manning. Is that pukey little croak the best you can do? Why don't you try to wrestle me over the edge? It's not so clean or so useful as leaving me here to become radioactive steam, but what the hell."

Tree looked wound up enough to pounce at the first rapid movement. Manning moved slowly, refolding the paper and slipping it into an inside pocket. "You wouldn't be the first man sacrificed in the best interests of a big operation. It's one of the things you knew when you signed on."

"How nice it is for you. Here I sit keeping an inside eye on the battle group. I sit here with my radio burper telling our good people about any changes they might like to know about, right up until the mushroom goes up. Handier than ever now, too, because the timing's gotten all screwed up, hasn't it? Things might have to be done aboard here after all."

"I wish you were capable of understanding—"

"One of the things I understand, Commander, is that maybe I'm getting left here because you don't want me to see those millions going into your kick."

"That money goes to the Soviet state."

"Are you sure? It could buy those good, upstanding United States Navy pilots and their helicopter."

One of the pilots appeared in the open door of the Sea Guard. He looked impatient, and the weather was clamping down harder. Manning was glad that the blowing rain had wet his face. Tree wouldn't be able to read his sweating agony so easily.

The tech rep was obviously going to keep up his cat-and-mouse until he was ready for a final bite into the neck. "If it's money you're thinking about, I'm sure there are wonderful things that can be worked out. Apologies? Compensation? Those can be gotten if you like. I can get you into the helicopter right now. Those pilots just want to be out of here before they blow overboard. Come with me. Disagreements between professionals can always be handled."

Tree clamped a steely hand behind Manning's neck and pulled the officer's face to within inches of his own. "*Professional!* You, with nothing driving you but some adolescent family gripe, have the nerve to use that word to *me*. I, my father, my *grandfather*, for chrissakes—we've been hanging our balls down into the nutcracker all these years because we believed in something. Something that a pusillanimous prettyface like you couldn't understand if a million starving kids came and screamed under your window. I've been tripping over phonies like you all my life."

As close as he was to Tree, Manning was able to see the traces of white powder around his flared nostrils.

"I'm going to show you—and *them*, safe in Moscow—what *professional* really means."

With difficulty, Manning twisted away from the imprisoning hand. "We're both after the same thing. Now let's get in that machine." There was no way, of course, that he could discuss his near-total disinterest in the operation beyond the humiliation of the United States Navy and the disintegration of the *King*.

A parody of a grin congealed on the tech rep's face. "No, thank you, Commander. I'll be staying."

So there it was, Manning thought. Tree was pulling the plug on the whole thing. "Listen, you've got to let it happen. If you really believe in what you've been doing, you'll climb aboard that—"

"It's *going* to happen, Manning. I'm staying here to make sure it does."

Manning was dumbstruck. "What the hell have you been taking?"

"You can't believe there are still men like me, can you? Those new people in Moscow wouldn't have believed it, either. So I added a few things to that self-serving diatribe of yours."

"You *sent* my message?"

"*Our* message, Commander. Now they know who's really served them. When this story goes into the history books, the big name isn't going to be yours. They'll know who ran out. They'll know who made the sacrifice."

Whatever Tree had been ingesting, he had dosed himself with it heavily before he had come to the flight deck. The drug was still increasing its hold.

"What can you do here?" asked Manning. "Why—"

Tree affected an elaborate sarcasm. "Oh, yes. What possible need for someone aboard the ship? How nicely you forget what a big hole there is in our plan now. The plan you never cared about except in settling your stupid grudge. We left Naples eleven hours earlier than we were supposed to. This ship is going to be sitting off Albania for a lot of hours before the big cherry bomb goes off. That's an awful lot of time for planes to fly if somebody decides they should. Who's going to try to keep that from happening? You, eating anchovies in Moscow, or ugly old Theron Tree staying right here?" His hands closed on Manning's elbows with an unbreakable grip. "Or maybe I'll just hold you here with me. I'm sure you'd be willing to help me out. Become part of the fleecy white clouds glowing their way across Italy."

Manning was thinking of driving his head into Tree's face with all his strength and running for the helicopter, when the terrible grip on his arms released. *Play to him*, Manning thought. He let himself tremble. "I . . . couldn't stay here with that thing—"

"Exactly, you shit-livered slob. You'd blow it. You'd have them hacking at that vault in five minutes."

"I can't help—"

"Get the hell off this ship. You're as yellow as the braid on your hat."

Without another word, Manning turned and ran for the helicopter. As he was strapping in, the pilots were rushing through their checklists and release procedures.

Straining to see the light changing from yellow to green on the island, Manning caught a glimpse of Tree beginning to enter a ladder well. He turned and waved what might have been thought a Godspeed to the copter whose blades had begun to spool up.

Minutes later the Sea Guard, tilting sharply against the stiff and erratic wind, lifted into the filthy skies that were beginning to press down into the building waves.

Manning felt no pity for the buffeted men hidden in the suffocating blackness of the underslung pod. It was better than a submarine filling with cold seawater.

From McGregor's position on the opposite side of the flight deck, something over two hundred feet from where the Sea Guard lifted off, the helicopter was almost instantly lost in the muck of the weather. Its navigation lights had hardly disappeared when the full weight of his many failures came down upon him.

Had he not let down a second family by pulling out on Ledges and Lydecker so abruptly? He had worked hard at making himself believe that the sacrifice was his—that he was forsaking the wealth and freedom to which they were flying. But the dangers and difficulties into which they headed were in fact vast, and in all likelihood insurmountable. Even if Manning could be trusted, which he doubted, there were many people—even governments—who might butcher them for the wealth they carried.

For all their incomparable physical courage and quickness of mind, they were essentially trusting innocents outside the world of the Navy. What they lacked more than anything in this audacious flight was a more reasoning, more cynical mind. The mind of a bookkeeper, in fact.

McGregor had remained distant from the lift-off only partially to avoid calling more attention to the helicopter and what it carried. There was something in him afraid that he might suddenly leap aboard in his agonizing indecision, screaming to be taken along and ruining what remote chance at success still remained to the others.

Sopping and shivering, crushed by his thoughts, he had hardly tried to contemplate what Tree might be doing with Manning in the moments before departure. Indeed, he hadn't been sure it was Tree until the frightening-looking tech rep brushed past him on his way below.

A startled "McGregor" was the only word that escaped Tree. There had been more than casual surprise in the ugly eyes. It almost appeared he would stop to say something.

McGregor felt so lonely that he thought he might have welcomed that.

Tirana, Albania—July 7

Considering that he had been fighting for his life for all of the six hours since he had been ambushed at three in the morning, and that an Albanian Army Shilka self-propelled gun was intermittently firing its quad-mounted 23-millimeter cannon at him from behind a pile of rubble, Ali Mahmoud was reasonably happy.

He moved some fallen concrete around on the high-up windowsill to give better cover to the bipod-mounted PK machine gun he had been cradling against his cheek. If the Albanian Army continued to be as brave and stupid as they had been until now, another infantry squad would move down the street toward him, and he would add their bodies to those already scattered on the pavement.

The government had moved as he had suspected they might. They had waited for the discovered coup to go forward so they could wipe away the traitorous Albanians along with the Soviets. They had apparently pinpointed Bartsev's fifty-five men on the farm and had observed them moving out to their rendezvous. But then it had all started to go wrong for the inept ambushers.

They had let the *Spetsnaz* pass into the capital riding in their five farm trucks. The chance to blow these formidable fighters to bits with mines, tanks, or rocket launchers had gone glimmering on the hope of wiping them out with the local subversives.

Unfortunately for the ambushers, the *Spetsnaz* had split up as soon as they were into the maze of city streets. Some had gone on foot, others riding to their various join-up and attack points. If the stalkers had split efficiently to stay with them, or just concentrated their forces with some armor at the likely points of attack, their trap might have succeeded, however messily. But they had blundered early.

Going around some dark turns, a unit of *Spetsnaz* had come upon a large group of drunken young farmers on their way home from a wedding party. The drunks' effusive greeting to the surprised Soviet special forces convinced the nervous security forces that this was the link-up of the imperialists with the renegades. Their firing was wildly premature and alerted the Russians, who stalked and shot down the disorganized security men with admirable dispatch.

The other Soviet groups heard the shooting and quickly contacted Bartsev on their hand radios. It took only seconds for Bartsev to see that things had gone very wrong, but he had been trained for seven years to fix such things.

The *Spetsnaz* colonel went to one of his contingency plans. Within the remaining hours of darkness, his troops eluded all pursuers, regrouped, and stormed the city's largest police barracks without the loss of a man.

The thickly walled compound had been constructed more as a fort against a counterrevolution than as a barracks. It could accommodate a formidable military garrison and keep it supplied with food and ammunition against a severe siege. Moreover, it was in the heart of several closely spaced and massive buildings, with no good field of fire for artillery or tanks. Only with difficulty could it be hit from the air without devastating the surrounding areas, and it had a Shilka of its own against low-level attacks.

The further success of the compromised mission could be attributed chiefly to Ali Mahmoud. With a handful of trusted countrymen shooting past anything that opposed him, he'd broken through to the people who were to have been with them for the surprise capture of the government. The locals had been ready to vanish into the mountains before Mahmoud convinced them to rally to the barracks with the *Spetsnaz* and fight to hold until the Soviet airborne was called in.

Mahmoud had held up his wristwatch to them. "It's five in the morning. Hold out until nine o'clock tonight, just long enough for the world to believe that perhaps this might be a genuine revolution of the oppressed. You'll see how pretty the last sun looks on drifting parachutes."

With those who had fought their way inside later on, there were now 450 of Bartsev and Mahmoud's men in the barracks redoubt. Many of them were from the toughest units of the army. Most fought from inside the walls, but many others prowled the surrounding buildings and streets, sniping and firing grenade launchers to slow up the besieging government troops.

Mahmoud heard two roars from the adjacent streets. Colonel Bartsev's thoughtfully placed antitank mines were keeping any significant tank-mounted artillery away from them. They might well hold for twenty hours before they were overwhelmed by their outmatched but determined attackers. As though to bolster this thought, the approaching Shilka quad 23-millimeter blew up in a great shower of white sparks as two RPG rounds pounded through its thin armor.

Someone shouted a command, and a platoon of soldiers ran down the center of the street, bravely and stupidly oblivious to the fact that their automatic-weapons support had vanished. They were firing as they came, an old Soviet military tactic for a different sort of battle.

Having the luxury of a belt-fed weapon in this age of clip feeds, Mahmoud shot a dozen of them down so easily that his mind had time to wander to his million waiting yen. And even to the white beach on the Algarve.

The Cruiser *Kirov*, the Black Sea—July 7

Admiral Sarkissian had moved his base of operations to sea in the *Kirov* to discourage visits from politicians. Unfortunately, there was no way to sever the phone lines. From what had been the wardroom, he responded to Gavenko's call. "I assure you I had no part in delaying the relay of the last message from the *King*. You have to understand the military priorities."

Gavenko quieted down somewhat. "I had Zyshnikov read the transmission. He was disturbed. He found the tone of it dismaying and amateurish. And there were parts of the wording, down toward the end, talking about the man Tree, that bordered on the unhinged."

"Our own intelligence people didn't miss that, I promise you. But I'll remind you that these men performed brilliantly. People who have been to war could tell you that the greatest heroism often comes out of pressures that induce something like madness."

"But will they unravel? Will they give away what we're trying to do?"

"Be calm, Gavenko. Their part will succeed."

"Fine. What about our part?"

"There we continue to have troubles. They were laying for us, trying to get all of our people and theirs in one bag. But they may have outsmarted themselves. Bartsev's boys were more than they bargained for. He's got a good position consolidated and a lot of Albanians helping him."

"But we never got the leaders or the radio station. We're not rallying the people."

"That's only effective when the people want to be rallied. We're jamming, and we have our own radio working hard to keep this a people's rebellion."

"Bartsev can't succeed on his own anymore."

"That might be a reason why Albania won't ask the *King* for help before she . . . leaves."

"Then you won't call in the airborne early?"

"No, Comrade Gavenko. Bartsev must hold until the *event*. But I need your agreement on a tactic."

"Name it."

"If the Americans guess that we've frozen our air forces out of Albania, it will make them reckless, more ready to gamble. I'd like to send a significant air probe toward their battle group. Challenge them sharply to make them more cautious."

"Suppose it just wakes them up and makes them ready to eat red meat?"

"Which way it turns out will depend on the young men they send to meet us. I can guarantee you, Gavenko, that we will send the very best. Permission, then?"

"All right, Sarkissian. Granted. I didn't expect this to become so difficult."

"All books on war could begin with those words. I have to be about your business now, comrade," Sarkissian said, replacing the receiver before the next leader of the Soviet Union could say another word. He was happy to have the politician's permission, though. The admiral had put through the order to fly a half hour before.

Moscow, U.S.S.R.—July 7

Basil Lurakin felt the bittersweet triumph of having one's most pessimistic predictions realized. His had been an absolutely classic KGB abduction. The men who had seized him knew his habits and schedule better than he did. He had occasionally thought that his habit of using the backstairs of his apartment on Prospect Kalinina made him vulnerable to a quiet disappearance. He had also meant to schedule enough false appointments onto the calendar on his secretary's desk to make his movements more unpredictable. But the rise of the present General Secretary had suddenly made all that seem less urgent.

Anyway, they had him now, after taking him off the second landing and hustling him into a Zil that had arrived at the rear door. They departed with him without having come to a full stop. The meeting he had been scheduled to attend was daylong and far out of town. He would not be missed for a long time. Not that it made any difference, now that the grim old days were returning.

The men who had grabbed him were slow to get back into the old habits. They had actually seemed polite, almost apologetic. And they had neglected to give him one of those smashing blows to the ribs or kidneys to insure quiet compliance. But the extra-dark tint on the Zil's glass was entirely familiar from the old days, and Lurakin didn't expect a long freedom from discomfort.

As they drove down the wide Moscow streets, in the center lane where officials were privileged to speed, he guessed that Rhonev had been taken, too. The rift he had faked at the Glorious October Chess Club would have saved the more conservative of the two liberals—himself—if it had been going to work.

He imagined that the state of his freedom depended entirely upon the future health of the General Secretary.

When the automobile stopped and he was hurried out of it, he was depressed to see that he had been taken to an unfamiliar public building. This little incident was not even slated to make the back pages of a carefully controlled press, for all his resounding title. Side alleys and darkened doors like the ones he was led through boded ill. It was the kind of place where interrogators appeared not in uniforms and suits, but in soiled undershirts.

They went upstairs and around several turns before he was prodded into a dim, cinder-blocked room that appeared to be used for furniture storage. Piled against the walls of the space, lighted by a single dirty window, were stacks of wooden chairs and tables. At the center was a jumble of couches, the imitation-leather type found in middle-level bureaus. On one of these sat an oddly old-fashioned figure who motioned for Lurakin to take a seat beside him.

"Lubachevsky," said Lurakin, unable to conceal his surprise. "Are you and Gavenko so short of supporters that you're doing your own wet work? Are all your bullies in Albania?"

"I won't waste any time being arch with you, Lurakin. If it makes you feel any better, I'm in more danger at this moment than you are. When you get to your meeting in an hour or so, apologizing for your lateness, your life won't change a bit if you don't want it to. But I will have put myself entirely into your hands."

Lurakin sat down cautiously. "I must say I have trouble with that word 'myself.' I never think of you as separate from Comrade Gavenko."

"But that's just what I'm asking you to do. Everything that happens here is separate from him."

"Suppose he knew we were here, Comrade Lubachevsky."

"Then I would die as soon as you after he becomes General Secretary."

"I take it that our leader is not recovering."

Lubachevsky lifted a newspaper off his lap to reveal some large, glossy photographs. They all covered the same subject.

The most interesting ones showed Lubachevsky himself, looking oddly wide-eyed and frightened, beside a refrigerated tray of the kind used in morgues. Upon the tray, his head turned partially to the camera to show dulled eyes not quite closed, lay an unclothed man.

The hands were partially raised off the tray, so even the one on the far side could be seen. The fingers and wrists were frozen in an animated configuration—a pianist caught in the midst of a moderately difficult passage. Or perhaps those fingers were poised to claw at the crude black stitches that closed the terrible, crossed incisions that ran down his breastbone to his abdomen and beneath his ribs.

The face, complete with its world-famous scar, was without question that of the man still known as the General Secretary of the Communist Party of the Union of Soviet Socialist Republics. The ravaged torso was clearly the work of a thorough autopsy.

Lurakin couldn't hide his shock. "My God. My God. What an awful thing. What a tragedy. Did . . . Was it—?"

Lubachevsky patted the stricken man's shoulder. "As natural as the stupidity that made him let that ulcer go. We've got drawers full of proof. I can't say that I feel as badly as you do, in honesty, but there were things I admired about the man. Things that I envied."

"I'm sure his job was one of them."

The older man almost smiled. "You're getting to my point faster than I am. Bluntly, Cyprien Gavenko is not the man to lead the Soviet Union into the future."

"And you are?"

"Exactly so."

"Strange, Lubachevsky. I couldn't have told your politics apart from his under a microscope."

"Perhaps not, but I offer Russia something he won't—a government with the likes of Basil Lurakin in it."

"In return for my wholehearted support for you for the top leadership? And for my lining up Rhonev and the rest of our faction for you?"

"You have it. Nobody else is placed so well as you. Your break with Rhonev reassures the conservatives, but the liberals still trust you."

"You think Gavenko will be so easy to brush aside, Lubachevsky?"

"I think the people of Russia will not be easy to brush aside anymore. The Broom's changes have seen to that. The new man will have to go through with his reforms."

"Nobody who has the support of the military has to go through anything at all."

"True. But I'm not as much a friend of the military as Gavenko. And there might be something happening that will make it comfortable for them to be rid of the man who led them to great embarrassment."

Lurakin could see that the tension was tiring Lubachevsky. "You've done a lot of thinking about this."

"When you've waited as long as I have, Lurakin, and you're my age, you have to move on your opportunities."

A floorboard creaked outside the door. It reminded Lurakin that, if his answer was wrong, the only meeting he would be leaving for was likely to be with a bag of quicklime. He couldn't go wrong pretending to bargain. "You guarantee a place for me and my friends near the top?"

"Not too many of your friends. And not Rhonev later on. But you'll be heard. I can do no better."

"Neither can I. I'll go along with you."

The way Lubachevsky fell back into the cushions showed, for the first time, how much he had invested in this meeting. His eyes closed. "This will be important to you, my friend. Unlike Gavenko, I'm one who knows how to show gratitude. In more ways than you now understand."

"Fine," said Lurakin dryly. "Let me know when you're starting."

With his glasses off, Lubachevsky was rubbing his closed eyes slowly. "Does your daughter—the one who married the Italian—still go to that nice place on the Adriatic? Near Bari, I think it was."

"She does, for most of every summer. She's there now with my grandsons."

Now Lubachevsky found a small plastic bottle in his pocket. Tilting his head back, he began to squirt drops into each eye. "Here's some advice. Have them come north. Quickly. Claim a heart attack, if you must. I'll help with the communications if it's necessary."

Something ice cold ran through Lurakin's blood. He didn't lack for hints at what was brewing off Albania. He thought of the *King*. He thought of Plesetsk. And of the many seemingly safe miles that separated the east coast of Italy from the carrier.

The drops were stinging the old man's eyes. He squeezed them more tightly shut. Lurakin thought of what his grandfather had told him of the perilous early days of the Great Revolution. "Every day we were walking blindfolded on a tightrope over a wolf pit in a high wind. One misstep and you didn't even get the chance to scream. But there was no turning back. The next step had to be taken."

In the slow motion of a nightmare, Lurakin reached into Lubachevsky's lap directly beneath the thrown-back chin and gently lifted away one of the dozen pictures. He had it inside his vest a split second before the other man forced open his lids and squinted at him.

"I'm sure you have business you want to be about, Lurakin. Good day."

The Sky—July 7

Lydecker's foresight in taking a flashlight into the dark pod had not extended to making sure that the batteries were fresh. There was barely enough reserve to illuminate the sweating Ledges lying alongside as he tried to drill more holes through the bottom of the suffocating plastic shell.

The erratic jolting of the Sea Guard in the rough air kept bouncing the tip of the drill bit out of the holes the chief was trying to get started. The comparatively thin plastic had proven almost impervious to drilling, and not more than ten ⅜-inch holes had been completed. Even with their faces thrust close to the vents, they were on the brink of asphyxiation. Already, working less than half an hour, the heavy-duty battery of the portable hand drill showed signs of weakening.

The worst lurching of the helicopter sent the heavy money bags sliding against their legs or heads. Inexpert work with the tie-down straps hadn't secured their cargo nearly as well as they had thought.

"Rock," Lydecker moaned, "how would you feel about me throwing up?"

"Nothing you could do could fail to improve this situation." The chief got one more hole punched through, the drill dying as he finished. He threw it aside.

Lydecker pressed an eye down to one of the holes. "I can't see shit down there. It's like looking down into a box of used cotton balls."

"Yeah. This is the kind of stuff you usually get around Iceland in November. The weather gets flukier every year. My grandmother always said that it must be the bomb."

The flashlight died. A huge aerial upheaval caused the two to bump heads hard. Ledges swore and Lydecker groaned.

"Let me tell you, Chief, I'm ready for the bomb. Ohhhh. Do you think puke hurts the value of money?"

"No worse than piss," Ledges said.

The angle of the floor changed abruptly and the sailors slid a full yard backward.

Six feet above their heads—a world away—Manning was facing the baleful stare of the helicopter's wispily mustached co-pilot, Ensign Harkness. The pale young man had eased back from his seat to check the lashings on the bags stacked in around the commander. "Sir, whoever stowed that stuff in the pod seems to have done a shit job. We're liable to have some real trouble."

Although his seat-belt harness was as tight as he could get it, Manning found himself holding hard to both sides of the frame of his seat. "Maybe we'll fly out of it."

"Not likely, Commander," the pilot called back, against the thrumming of the laboring rotors and the lashing of the storm against the hull. Lieutenant McHenry was a black ex-footballer from Michigan who respected force, whether in linebackers or weather. "It's coming down on a broadening front and building up worse than ever in the north."

"Could you go above?"

McHenry guffawed. "These things like to go at under three thousand feet. Hell, we don't even wear parachutes. The top of this stuff is around forty thousand feet and going higher."

Manning could only be glad that they had come this far before trouble began. It would have been disastrous to turn back. They were no more than a half hour from the hospital now, and with its NATO affiliation and helicopter pad it had a TACAN unit right on the grounds. On the instrument panel he could pick out the quivering yellow needle and the digital readouts of bearing and distance.

"Hey, Lieutenant," Harkness called as he tightened a strap. "You think it trims better with me back here?"

"For now maybe. Every time that shit shifts, something different comes up. I'm going to have a few things to write about that humping pod. It's got the aerodynamics of an anvil. But I should've checked the loading like the book says. Well, screw me."

They throbbed along more or less in equilibrium with the aerial element for more than ten minutes. Then they came upon a great, slab-sided mountain of boiling cloud.

"Sweet dingleberries, this is going to be fun. Better get up here, Harky. I might need some extra hands."

Harkness was almost to his seat when the Sea Guard lurched wildly. The young ensign found himself glued first to the overhead and then to each bulkhead in turn. Only his helmet kept him from being knocked cold.

Whiter than his scarf, he snatched at a few seconds' lull in the gyrations to pull himself painfully into his seat. He barely had his harness in place when the grayness pressing against the windows turned a nasty, squirming black. The cold, uncaring hand of the sky closed around the Sea Guard and twisted.

The nose of the helicopter pitched sharply down. From beneath there came a sliding, shuddering *thunk*. McHenry fought the controls, but the expected rise of the nose became a sideways slide.

Manning was no pilot, but he had heard enough tales about "coning"—the stress phenomenon that causes a helicopter's main rotor blades to fold upward like the spokes of a blown-out umbrella—to understand the ghastly look that the pilots exchanged.

The altimeter was one gauge whose location he knew. He watched it unwinding sharply from three thousand feet. He had no idea about the height of any mountains below, but knew that Italy had high ones in abundance.

An eternity passed in seconds. The bird came drunkenly erect.

"She's out of trim real bad now," McHenry said between clenched teeth as he fought the collective. "That motherless pod."

In that instant Manning saw the thing to do. He leaned forward and clamped McHenry's shoulder. "Dump it," he said. "Dump the damned thing now, while you've still got some control."

The pilot answered without diverting any attention from his controls and instruments. "I thought the stuff was critical to the ship, sir."

"What we're picking up, not what we're bringing."

"But losing the pod—"

"If we're not splattered all over Italy like tomato sauce, we can at least bring back what we can cram inside here. Now *drop* the bloody thing."

"Sir, I command this bird, and the decisions—"

"Then make the decision to save it," Manning exploded.

The Sea Guard bucked and started to slide sideways again.

"Right, sir," McHenry finally said. "Harky, it's pretty sparse country under here. Blow it off now."

"I wish to hell I knew how to do that, Lieutenant," said Harkness. "That's one piece of the manual I'm not up on."

McHenry arrested the slide again. "Well, you bet your ass *I* read it before we lifted. You've got to lean out that side door. You'll see a red stirrup handle flat against the pod near the back. Flip up the safety catch and give it a pull. It's fixed to a cable system that will flip up the clips on that side. As soon as you get release you yell 'clear' as loud as you can. I give us a fast tilt to the right, the other side slides off the holding lip, and the son of a bitch is gone."

"I can't wait," said Harkness, beginning to release himself from his seat.

The biggest jolt yet hit the Sea Guard. The chunky helicopter began a great downward sweep. Both pilots sweated, worked, and swore until the movement was arrested.

Manning saw that the altimeter had unwound to beneath two thousand feet. "Stay in your seat," he said unsteadily. "I'll do it."

"We'd sure appreciate that, sir," grunted McHenry. "There's a safety harness on a winder next to the door. Get it on. And don't wrap your thumb around the handle or you'll follow the pod down."

"Got you," Manning said. He made his way across to the wide sliding door at the right side of the Sea Guard. His mouth went dry as he slipped himself into the safety harness.

If their death wasn't as clean and swift as he would have liked, it would be fast enough. And it would make the work on the ground so much cleaner.

He easily shut out of his mind all thoughts of the long, blind, terrifying tumble in the blackness of the falling pod, and jerked back the door latch.

The door leaped aside as though on a spring, responding to a tilt of the copter. Another latch caught it and held it open. Out the door Manning faced a billowing Hades of black clouds. A sea of blowing rain lashed in at him and drove him back on his heels. A second later a gyration brought him back the other way, and he found his feet swung out the door into the void. The harness jerked him up short so that he found himself dangling outside, hips level with the door frame, his legs forced outward by the rounded sides of the pod curling up from below. His cap disappeared into the slipstream.

Breathless with terror, he grabbed the bottom of the door frame and pulled himself in against the battering wind until he could sit inside the frame. His desperate eyes found a grab bar on the bulkhead just above his head and he clamped a hand around it. Now he could force himself to look downward at the job he had to do.

The red release handle had been positioned perfectly by the designer. It lay flat against the pod at a level just below his knees, the grip facing him. He took a deep breath and leaned into the rushing air to take the handle.

He closed his eyes, cleared his mind, and jerked back with all the strength in his biceps and shoulder.

There was a knifing pain below his collarbone, and the handle tore from his grip. *"Clear,"* he bawled back to McHenry and felt the Sea Guard tilt to clear the other side of the pod off the retaining lip.

The expected upward leap caused by the falling away of the weight and drag did not come.

Manning looked down. The pod and its red handle were still there, firmly in place under the sheets of water.

He heard McHenry's dim bellow. "What the hell happened?"

"It didn't release," croaked Manning, barely able to unstick his tongue in his arid mouth. "I'll try it again."

He waited until the Sea Guard's attitude held upright for a moment and then took hold of the handle again. This time he kept both eyes wide open as he pulled. Nothing. He tried changing the angle at which he tugged. Then he varied the way he brought on the pressure, alternating between jerking and long, continuous applications of strength. The handle remained immobile, the pod tenaciously attached.

Furiously he kicked his dangling heels at the handle, a childish punishing of the malfunctioning mechanism. Then he thought there might be a way to jolt the release loose with some sort of tool.

With his model-maker's feel for the way things went together, he estimated the sort of force that had to be applied. Simple. Blows had to be directed backward against the handle in the same direction he had been tugging. Now . . . what tool?

If it had been possible for any human being to laugh with relief in this situation, it would have been Manning. His first despairing glance around the helicopter's interior swept his eyes just above where his hand clawed onto the grab bar. And there, neatly set into a perfectly designed Navy clamp, was a crash ax. He reached across and took it in his free hand, first winding his wrist into the attached lanyard so the tool wouldn't be lost out the door. "I think I can get it now," he shouted back into the helicopter.

The crash ax was not the ideal tool for the job. Made for cutting through aluminum, it featured a variety of smooth and toothed edges made to slash rather than hammer. However, the release handle lying flat against the pod made it hard to get a clean shot at the bottom of the stirrup handle. He would have to fix that.

He selected an edge that was pointed and took aim into the center of the stirrup. At the third blow the point went through the plastic pod. Soon he had enough holes to switch to the blunter side of the tool. As he had hoped, the weakened segment cracked and then fell through into the pod. With the area inside the stirrup now a ragged hole, he was able to take a swing where he could catch the center of the handle with a rising blow.

Concentrating every nerve in his body, he leaned out the door of the veering craft as far as he dared and began to hammer at the handle with great grunting swings. Blinded by the rain and half strangled by the wind, he missed many times. Parts of the pod away from the handle began to crack and cave in. His wrist and shoulder screamed their distress, but he smashed doggedly past the pain.

Below Manning, inside the pod, a new light was making its way into the blackness.

Ledges and Lydecker, sliding in vomit, choking in the foul air, looked toward the growing hole in wondering horror.

"My God, Rock. Something's breaking loose. It's tearing this thing off its moorings."

Ledges's bulk kept him from moving toward the crumbling area. "I can't even get over there to get a look at what's killing us."

The slim and agile Lydecker had no such problem. He slithered past the sliding bags of money to where the hole was growing. But before he could get close enough to see all he wanted, the pod's streamlining squeezed the area down to where it was impassable even to him.

And then the banging stopped. The roaring sounds that remained seemed like a hush compared to what had stopped. The hole grew no bigger. Rain ran down inside and started a trickle down the sweep of the pod that would soon form a miserable puddle under the agonized sailors.

"You know something?" said Ledges. "Sometimes ignorance *ain't* bliss."

Above, Ensign Harkness had appeared at the door behind Manning. "Sir, you're going to slip and cut your leg off doing that. Let me get in alongside here. I'll get me a hold on this other grab bar, and then we can each get a hand on the release. When I say yank, we both give it all we've got. That should work."

Manning looked like an old man when he glanced up. "Okay, Harkness. Slide in and get ready."

The ensign squeezed in beside Manning and braced himself. They both reached down and took strong grips on the handle.

"On three," Manning said through gritted teeth. "One . . . two . . . *thre-e-e-e!*"

The two strong men jerked up. The handle came back a full inch.

"Once more and we've got it," Harkness cried. "Let's go. One . . . two . . . *thre-e-e-e-e—*"

Their all-out effort pulled the release out another inch before the handle broke where the ax had bitten into it too often.

The men fell backward. Harkness quickly rose and scrambled for the cockpit. "Close up the door, Commander. That pod is with us for better or for worse, in sickness and in health."

"Can you keep her in the air?" Manning called as he wrestled shut the sliding panel.

"The country flattens out some between here and Potenza," called McHenry. "That might take some of the bumps out of the sky. I'm reducing speed, too. We're close enough to luck it through, I think."

Manning raged inside. He supposed he was the only man

in history who ever lamented not being able to dump something like 26 million dollars overboard.

Washington, D.C.—July 7

Any cabdriver in Washington could have told you that there was going to be red meat on the table around the capital today. Something had hummed out into the ultrasensitive antennae of the government and media, and the anthill was in turmoil.

From the liberal strongholds the word "impeachment" was muttered under some breaths.

It was a uniformed aide of the Director of Central Intelligence who went into the angry swarm of political hornets that had clustered around the Senate majority leader and asked him to please come along with him on a matter of the greatest urgency. He was taken straight to the Oval Office, leaving the disgruntled press corps behind him.

The President greeted him outside the door and led him in himself. Waiting were Admiral Geinz, the CIA director, the top figures of Naval Intelligence, and the Secretary of State. The looks on their faces gave the majority leader the sort of feeling he hadn't gotten since he was a teenager listening to an old cathedral radio on a December Sunday in 1941.

"Paul," the President said, "excuse the melodrama. I know we're crossing in front of your steamroller, but it will save a helluva mess if you get in on this before you turn us around in the Med."

The senator couldn't help being a bit disappointed at this interruption in what was obviously to have been a rousing day of victory for him. "I'm glad to see you know we've got a lock on stopping you. And that you're not going to go ahead and do something disastrous on your own hook. May I say, too, that I shouldn't have been brought here alone."

"I ask that you keep the number of people in on this as

small as you can. I'm doing the same. A leak here can turn the world inside out."

"Sir, I find myself hoping you're not here with all this brass to blow some smoke up my butt to back me off for Old Glory's sake."

Admiral Geinz came forward with a large sheet in his hand. The senator could see it was a blowup of some sort of photograph. "This came over a secure wire right out of the center of Russia. The quality was good to begin with, but we've enlarged it, reprinted it, and put it through computer enhancement. It's not a composite, as far as our experts can tell. See if you recognize anybody."

The majority leader carried the picture to a lamp and turned the light up to its highest intensity. *"My sainted mother,"* he said when he had caught his breath. "That's Lubachevsky himself off to the side there. I've been close enough to him to be sure. He and Gavenko are joined at the forehead. Hold on. No agent could get hold of a picture like this—"

"Of course not," said CIA. "It was leaked to us."

The senator held a hand to his temple as though his head might explode. "Did they kill him?"

"Those are autopsy cuts. Probably not."

"So the conservatives have been covering up and trying to run an operation before we catch on there's somebody new running the store."

"That checks out, sir."

"And lucky for us somebody's out to torpedo the Gavenkos and Lubachevskys. How do we break it?"

The Secretary of State had been waiting for the question. "We don't," he said. "If we blow this open, the cold war goes right back to deep freeze. No American will ever trust a Russian again. The papers will howl for their blood and a thousand more MXs. The Gavenkos will try to blame it on the General Secretary and his people and blow them out of there for good."

After some thought, the senator nodded. "What do you want us to do?"

"Call off the wolves in the Senate," Geinz said. "Tell 'em that we've got a hush-hush situation here that you've been briefed on. That the President had an emergency call from people close to the General Secretary. Tell 'em that the conservatives are trying to depose him. They're the ones who are doing Albania. The liberals think they can stay in control, but the military adventure must fail. They'd appreciate it if we stood by off Albania, ready to be asked in. They're sure that'll back the power grabbers off without any wars inside or out of the Soviet Union."

"So you expect me to get that howling mob of mine to let the *King* go into the middle of somebody else's shooting, and without telling anybody but the top people why? And you're asking me to ask them to *sit* on it. You're not asking much, are you?"

"Paul," the President said, "if you're half as good at beating up your own people as you are beating up mine, you won't have any trouble."

The senator stuck out his hand. "Okay, Mr. President. I'll deliver. The *King* stays on Thunder Station, with our blessing."

The Sky—July 7

Mudcat Walker was afraid his surging F-14 would explode with his own joy. The thundering twin Pratt and Whitney F-30s and their 20,000 roaring wild horses shot him up out of the overcast at 38,000 feet. A mile to his right the Tomcat carrying Mickey Maussman broke out at exactly the same angle as his own, and they shot together for the sun in the icy-blue air eight miles above the stormy Med.

Both his RIO in the backseat and his wingman knew enough to stay out of Walker's ears as much as possible. He had reverted to another form of being—a hunter with instincts brought intact from the age of prowling man-apes. But now his stone ax was a multimillion-dollar gray shark

bearing the scarlet-dripping tub holding a grinning Satan—
the emblem of the VF-36 Bloodbaths.

One of the thousand things that Walker loved about the
F-14 was that the "paperwork"—the electronic blizzard
that had to do with navigation, vectoring, intercept, and all
the rest of it—was in the hands of the brilliant clerk in the
backseat. Back there the RIO, Bad Apple Burns, watching
two crowded display screens and more instruments than
most people knew existed, left the pilot comparatively free
to just fly the airplane.

"Two targets two-ten miles out, bearing eight-niner. Making six hundred knots straight for Big Ernie territory," said
Burns from the back.

Walker grudgingly looked at the horizontal situational
display screen set into his panel. This HSD duplicated the
tactical information display on one of Burns's screens.
Threat display, they called it. He'd show those bungholes
who the real threat was. He swung the big fighter to bear on
the distant target.

If he had not been his own God, Walker might have
thanked Him. To be up fresh in the CAP with 16,000
beautiful gallons of JP-5 cramming the Tom's six internal
tanks while a hot contact was coming in was more good
luck than anybody ever deserved. And the electrons weren't
describing any lumbering old prop-driven Bears, but some
beautifully nasty fighters.

The Tom was as electromagnetically silent as the ship. It
sent forth no signals for the Russian bogeys to read. All his
information on the target was coming to him out of a
high-flying E-2C Hawkeye higher up and hundreds of miles
away. The King kept one of the ungainly little twin-prop
radar planes on station twenty-four hours a day now. The
radar downlink told Walker and the ship all they had to
know.

A lot of the information he already had. His electronic
countermeasures equipment picked up signals of the Russian
planes' searching radar beautifully. It was able to accom-

plish that feat long before the Red aircraft could pick up anything on his own flight.

One of the fascinating things that Mudcat Walker knew as he hurtled ecstatically toward interception was that these bogeys had come straight out of the Soviet Union and refueled in the air. It was no reconnaissance mission or they'd have used the Bears. Walker was guessing that they wanted those fuel tanks topped because the Soviets were on the prod.

They weren't going to have their snoopers shoved around the sky anymore. They were going to see what the United States Navy fliers were like when they faced men and equipment that could stand up to them. And most of all, they were going to try to throw a little scare into Uncle Sam. Show him that he had plenty to worry about from the aerial matadors of the Soviet Union. In short—it made Walker quiver with rage to think about it—they were going to see if they could make Mudcat Walker back up. He found himself pushing more on the throttle. The fighter passed Mach 1.2 and automatic controls completed the full sweep-back of the swing wings to their all-back angle of twenty-two degrees.

He didn't expect war, because this wasn't the way you committed planes for that. But the CAG had it straight from the top that the President officially felt there was no longer any need to be especially sensitive to Soviet feelings.

This would be no standard encounter of their high-tech age. His opposition was clearly counting on that. If it were for real, he would be carrying AIM-54 Phoenix missiles. These weapons, half-ton monsters thirteen feet long, could kill planes en masse at beyond 50 miles. They were keyed into the onboard AGW-9 coordinated weapons system that turned the Tomcat into a murder machine linked to electronic brains on the ground, elsewhere in the air and on its own hurtling platform. The AGW-9 system could track twenty-four targets simultaneously, and select six of them for death in priority order. The Phoenix could fly at Mach 3 and had its own radar. The Russians would be having none of that if they were intent on real shooting.

As it happened, Mudcat Walker was not carrying the Phoenix, or its smaller less expensive cousin, the Sparrow. Walker's missile load was eight Sidewinders. For an F-14 these modest old heat-seekers, under two hundred pounds each and with a range under ten miles, were the equivalent of thrown rocks. But even those were not to figure in Walker's plans.

What he had not mentioned, even to Burns, his closest friend on earth, was that he intended to close with the Russians using the most primordial of the sky warrior's weapons—the snarly old mother-loving machine gun.

True, the electrically driven General Electric six-barrel Gatling cannon cased on the left side of his fuselage was a good distance removed from the old Spandau or Vickers. Its 675 rounds of 20-millimeter shells spitting at the rate of 6,000 rounds per minute gave him seven seconds of fire-power that might leave a destroyer in shambles, much less an opposing airplane. But at bore-sight ranges his Vulcan was the type of power-driven weapon that required pilots to live and die by stick and rudder, not microchip and diode. Brilliant electronic devices might dupe a million-dollar missile. Nothing could confuse 20-millimeter shells fired so close that you could smell the other pilot's fear.

There was the matter of prestige, too. No matter how accomplished the sniper, he was never held in the same high regard as the duelist.

"Closing fast, Mud," said Burns. "Lemme turn on our toys. Maussman ain't the kind of farthead you are, and he's gonna wanna light up."

"Yeah, yeah, okay, do it." Walker felt awful for RIOs like Burns—people who couldn't hack it as pilots or, worse, people who didn't want to. They were condemned to ride like conductors on a commuter train. Burns would be moving his fingers like the organist at the Radio City Music Hall, reading the massive capabilities of the Tom's radar. Both pulse and pulse-Doppler, it could search the air and ground in so many ways that he should have had a staff back there to evaluate the information. As far as Walker was concerned, he felt warmest about Burns's job when they were in an aerial knife fight at close quarters and the RIO pulled his head off the gauges and became, in effect, a wingman flying five feet behind. Having somebody to watch your six o'clock at times like that was worth ten million bucks in black boxes.

He almost laughed when he saw that the bogeys were trying to get electronic jamming going for them. The Tom's astonishing radar could burn through ECM with high-pulse repetition frequencies in six figures.

As his mind galloped ahead, Walker had to keep reminding himself that this was certain—virtually—to be bloodless combat. He must not glide into such concentration that he forgot that and triggered something lethal.

He also trusted Ivan would bear in mind the same thing.

CAG—the air wing commander—had warned his pilots that the Russians' bogeys would likely be flown by military test pilots with thousands of hours in top-of-the-line aircraft. These men were calculated to be far superior to the pass-through flyers of the United States Navy, most with only several hundred hours in their kites and anxious to be gone to the airlines after a hitch or two.

Mudcat Walker hoped with all his heart that they had sent him the shit-hottest pilot in all the huge Soviet Union.

And there was something else—almost *too* much to hope for. He wanted their very latest fighters, not some tired MiG-25 Foxbats, but their superbly upgraded descendants, with powers unknown.

"Almost on 'em, Mud," Burns twanged.

"In sight," Walker said, almost giggling. His astounding eyesight had picked them up at a range he correctly estimated at fourteen miles. That means the humpers are big, he thought. Rare birds. Not Foxbats, made small to follow the standard Soviet doctrine of not designing planes they could not manufacture in huge numbers. Something made husky enough to match the B-1 and the Tom.

Mickey Maussman came up to line abreast a thousand feet off Walker's right wing.

As Walker watched them, the bogeys, who had been flying a close formation at the same altitude, executed what was plainly a rehearsed spacing maneuver.

Both planes were below them, apparently spoiling to accept combat maneuvering by the carrier's defense cap. They were obviously initiating at a lower altitude for a reason, since a B-1 killer would have a higher service ceiling than the F-14.

The most impressive computer on the F-14, the brain of Mudcat Walker, raced through the likelihoods in the split seconds available to him before he was eyeballed.

As though he were tied into one of his plane's fabulous radar boxes, he felt he could read the mind of the man leading the Soviet flight. He would be a military pilot first class, probably a full colonel. Probably flew in Afghanistan. He would not only be the finest airplane driver they had, but a man as familiar with United States equipment and tactics as the Navy pilots were themselves.

It flashed on him that a Russian as good as that would start with the limitations of his own equipment and the advantages of what the Toms carried.

One of the bogeys had smoothly dropped back, giving up altitude and falling back from the leader. Why?

"Nothing else in the air, Bad?"

"Negatory, Mud."

The way a single synapse firing in the brain of a concert pianist can trigger a hundred explosive movements of a trained hand, Walker saw the setup: simple and very smart. The lightning reflexes of the radar in the United States flight would lock furiously on to the first target they acquired, the one uppermost and farthest in. Superbly trained in priority target-acquisition tactics as they were, the Navy pilots would initiate a headlong coordinated move on that target, meaning to hound it out of the skies. The second bogey, overlooked in the heat of a high-tech prosecution, would sweep around the rear unseen and take up an unshakable kill position on Maussman as he covered Walker. With Maussman lit up by the Russian's missile lock on him, he would be out of the fight on the point of honor. The second Russian could then wait for the leader to maneuver Walker into a box where the two-on-one odds would be reversed.

The chance to go two against one almost won out, but Walker couldn't let the Mouse be humiliated. He called Maussman. "Bloodbath-Two, start down with me, then break fast for a low bird who's laying back for you. Keep him tied up while I go in the furball with his boss."

Walker heard a keyed mike acknowledge him and went to full military power. He stayed away from what he might do in a shooting war. This tussle was about something else. He wanted to see what he had here and give the Russian leader a chance at some good old-fashioned close-in knife fighting.

The Russian on top spotted him coming down and broke left. The maneuver slowed Walker a bit, and he saw that the Russian did not execute the expected roll and dive to force Walker into a negative parabola. Rather, he went straight up, corkscrewing.

Good move three ways, Walker saw. It gave the splitting ruse a chance to work on Maussman, it put Walker's plane below him, and put the fight immediately into the high-angle-of-attack tactics at which Russian pilots liked to think they were invincible.

Walker was more than good enough to have had some chance at a shot here in a death fight. But for the moment he just wanted to size up his foe.

He brought his dive so quickly shallow and his turn so tight that his G-suit punched him like a good middleweight. But he got the glimpse he wanted. And his heart soared.

The Russian's long lerxes—leading edge root extensions—sweeping back from the nose to the forward ring root told him he was fighting nothing less than a MiG-29 Fulcrum. *Hot goddamn.* He couldn't have picked a worthier opponent by hand. It was the plane the U.S. superplanes had forced them to build. Except for that it had no swing wing and its unknown ceiling was expected to be hugely higher than what Walker flew, it was as close to a Tom as the Russians could build a plane.

It was going to be a matter of the men flying.

As he began to relax Gs and follow the Russian up, he took stock of the Soviet's armament. He had spotted an array of Aphid AA-10s beneath the wing, the rough equivalent of Sidewinders. And his infallible memory called up the fact that the Fulcrum had two big-mother 30-millimeter single-barrel cannons up front. It didn't take many hits from those to give you a bad day.

"How's the Mouse doing, Bad?"

"Breaking even. Just. That other guy's good. Hey! What the hell—"

Walker shot straight up the center of the Russian's climbing turns until he had the bogey behind him. Then he eased the throttle back. "Let's make this interesting for everybody."

Burns screeched in frustration and fear. "You put him right up our tail pipe. Get that throttle up or we've got a compressor stall coming. I can't believe this."

The Russian couldn't believe it either. He tightened his corkscrews and fought to bring his Aphid system to bear. Walker knew where the Fulcrum was, the way an expert tractor-trailer driver knows the precise location of his unseen tailgate, and used the remarkable power of his fighter to stay just out of the Aphid missiles' sight envelope. At no moment did he expect to hear the sound of a missile lock-on and defeat. That just couldn't happen to Mudcat Walker.

When he was certain he was in close-up plain sight of the Russian, he sent him the message he wanted him to see. He first waggled his folded-back wings to indicate communications. Then he selected his Gatling and hosed off a two-second burst into the empty air ahead. The Fulcrum couldn't miss the puffing smoke or the backing off of airspeed of the plane ahead. The Fulcrum might have been sprayed by the empties coming back.

It also couldn't miss the announcement: This was a man-to-man knife fight. Guns only.

"Hey, that Roosky's waggling us. What's he—"

"We've got an understanding now, Bad. Shut up and let me handle it." With the Fulcrum having no backseat help, that seemed only fair.

From that moment on, Mudcat Walker became part of his weapon, part of his adversary, part of the universe. He flew as an organism never before seen. The brilliance of his foe only served to show better that the twin-burnered gray killer, the perfectly melded, man-and-machine-stalking ghost, could not be bettered.

The Soviet pilot never made a mistake. He initiated the high-angle-of-attack, turning, scissoring duel of which the Fulcrum and his training should have given him full command. But some unearthly genius was flying the Tomcat.

The Tom had no ailerons. A system of spoilers on the stubby wings and taileron controls gave it its guidance. And the American pilot manipulated these as though he had a direct wire that kept him one-ten-thousandth of a second ahead of whatever his enemy would do.

As soon as he sensed the first nibble of frustration in the Russian's otherwise flawless flying, Walker made his own spectacular break to the right and upward. The Soviet's reaction was infinitesimally behind, and he lost his position. But he followed the book on supersonic dogfighting to the letter.

Battles in the sky had always been to some degree decided on who could turn inside the other, who could outspeed the other, and who could outclimb the other. These fights had not changed very much in close, with the pilots suiting a plane's strong points to the situation. One great difference was that the turning and climbing battles that had been fought inside hundreds of yards now spilled out over tens of miles.

High angle of attack, the degree to which a plane's nose could be held more steeply into the air under controllable power than its adversary, was a key to these duels. It put terrible demands on engines, men, and airframes. Because it wasn't just power, it was maneuver. The battles were scissoring duels, the planes being the blades. These blades passed through one another and attempted to shorten themselves to gain the favored rearward killing position.

Walker judged that the Fulcrum had a basic advantage in rate of climb, but he was making use of something in the design of his aircraft that the Russian might not have recognized. The space beneath the fuselage and between the Tom's wide-spaced engines was nicknamed "the pancake." And it was more than just a filler. In the F-14's design it served as an extra wing surface. It had been shown able to keep the plane in the air when the folded-back wings were stalled out. It was by this slender technological margin that Walker now went steeper and closed the scissors inexorably despite the sensational climbing characteristics of the Fulcrum.

Whenever the Russian passed through his Sidewinder envelope, Walker let him hear the hum of the locked-on sensors that told him he could be dead. But this was not that kind of fight. The Russian still had his chances, and he tried them all.

The tactics turned to dives, breaks, afterburners, spoilers, and corkscrews. But always they went back to the high-angle duels that the Fulcrum seemed determined to win. Walker never faltered.

Endurance became the game. Even though these combats were measured in minutes, the toll on nerves and muscles exceeded what could be poured out in a hundred-yard dash.

The plane's endurance came into play, too. Not just the pressures on electronically swiveling controls and on air-frames, but on fuel. They were burning hundreds of pounds a minute, and these planes were not gentle gliders that could be coasted down on a short strip when they ran dry. They glided like bricks.

With skills that he had only suspected he owned, Mudcat Walker closed on the Russian to where his shadow must have crossed the man's instrument panel. There was no longer any question that his Tomcat's Gatling could have taken the Fulcrum out of the sky. There remained only the question of getting the other pilot to admit it.

"Going on guns, Bad Apple."

"Don't do it, Mudcat. *Don't do it*."

"Ain't gonna hurt him." Walker slid off to the Russian's beam, where a great pilot's vision could pick him up peripherally. He selected guns on bore sight and squeezed off on the stick. Perhaps twenty pounds of steel, emphasized by tracers, flashed just yards in front of the Fulcrum's nose.

Perhaps out of reflex, perhaps out of stubbornness, the Russian ran again through a beautiful repertoire of tactics. In vain.

Walker, growing furious, closed again, and straight up they went. Running me out of altitude, Walker guessed. He had the stuff to do it, unless Walker could run him out of fuel first.

The Tom's maneuvers now took the Russian wide, slewed him around the sky, and forced him on burners.

"Watch them pounds," Burns warned, referring to the rapidly diminishing fuel weight.

"Let him watch his," said Walker, beginning to contemplate dissolving his obstinate opponent.

Abruptly there was a series of smoky flashes from the full-out Fulcrum. Its airspeed fell back for a moment.

"What in the sweet name of shit was *that*," yelped Burns, whose position in the Tom's high-mounted bubble gave him a perfect view of the target.

Burns heard awe in Mudcat Walker's voice for the first time since he had known him. The awe, to be sure, was of his own prowess. "That, Mr. Bad Apple Burns, was a shit-hot pilot firing off into the sky his whole load of air-to-air and 30 mike-mike. The aerial equivalent of laying down your arms, I'd say."

He then broke off and put the Tomcat through a series of victory maneuvers that even its designers might have deemed impossible.

Mudcat Walker, king of the air, was the number-one fighter jock in all explored space. He was completely above the minor problems of finding his wingman and his carrier and setting down his fuel-starved fighter in a rotten blow.

When the real blood was ready to drip, he knew he could

use his full complement of astonishing weapons to defeat anything anyone could put up against the *King*. No matter how fast, how well flown, how surprisingly weaponed, if you came up against Mudcat Walker, he would kill you.

What a feeling.

Potenza, Italy—July 7

The thump of the Sea Guard onto the ground near Potenza was the best moment of the year for Ledges and Lydecker. But with the airstream no longer helping to push air into the few holes in the pod, the stench and suffocation closed in on them quickly.

The flashlight had died long ago and the blackness was almost total. The rain that had blown in through the opening, which had appeared so terrifyingly, had grown into a formidable puddle inside. It lay icy under the sailors. They had to keep telling themselves and each other that they were supposed to stay inside quietly.

Lydecker groaned and Ledges punched him gently. "Manning'll spring us as soon as it's clear. Let's not blow it with a lot of noise."

Their freedom didn't come as quickly as they would have liked. The pilots seemed to want to stay around forever, probably talking about their recent trials. Their unintelligible words droned on, Manning apparently having difficulty in getting them to go get themselves something to eat and drink.

Then some Italians came. From what muffled voices Ledges could make out, Manning was convincing them that there were many papers to fill out inside before any moving of supplies could be done.

A half hour of silence followed, broken only by the continuing sounds of rain and wind against the plastic.

Desperation had almost begun to set in when they dimly

heard hurrying footsteps and the coded knock on the pod. Some latches clicked and the top went up like the lid of a coffin. They blinked in relief, the thick gray light almost blinding them. The cascading rain was so sweet and cool that they were almost tempted to remain lying there to let it cleanse them. Then Manning was grabbing their hands and pulling them over the side.

A blue Fiat van was cutting across the parklike grounds from a distant road. Behind the helicopter, half hidden by trees and mist, graceful hospital buildings could be seen. Nobody else was in sight.

"Where were you when all the fun was going on?" asked Lydecker groggily.

"Smile, Lydecker. I'm the only reason you guys and our money are not permanent and colorful parts of beautiful Italy. Those whacked-out pilots got leaky when the pod got the bird out of trim. First they tried to jerk the release. Then they tried to hammer the damned thing loose. I almost had to break that guy's arm to get him to stop swinging that crash ax."

"Where are those sons of bitches?" growled Ledges. "I'd like to show 'em a little hammering of my own."

"I told them to come back here in an hour. And to head back alone if I got held up. I left the Italians with enough paperwork to last the afternoon. We'll be mighty long gone before they're out here wondering where I am and why this chopper is empty."

The van pulled up, spraying mud. A short dark man, quick and muscular, jumped out of the driver's seat. *"Buon giorno,"* he said. "I am Orlando."

He looked Italian enough to Ledges, although his accent wasn't right, even for those short words. As for the suit he wore, no Italian he knew would consent to have it in his family. A Slavic ethnic from the northeast frontier, Ledges supposed.

"Let's get the bags moved," Manning said as Orlando raced around to open the rear of the big van. There would be barely room for all of them and the money.

Quickly the van was loaded.

Manning said, "Ledges, Lydecker, slide yourselves into the back. There's just room up on top between the bags and the roof. Maybe you can catch some winks before we get to Avellino."

"It's too damned much like where we just came out of," Ledges said, but he jammed his body into place as suggested. Something bit into his lower back. He had to adjust the .45 automatic that he had shoved down into his waistband there. He had figured that all those greenbacks might invite unwelcome company, and he wasn't going to roll over easily after all this trouble, sure as hell.

Manning and Orlando took their places in the front seats, and the van fell into gear and moved out briskly.

Lydecker was able to whisper to Ledges over the roar of the winding engine. "Hey, Rock," he breathed. "Would one of those pilots have been a commander?"

"Not goddamn likely."

"Would they be wearing uniforms or flight suits?"

"Flight suits, numb-o. You know that."

"Now, understand I couldn't get all that far back to that hole somebody was chopping in the pod. I could hardly see anything. But the arm that was swinging that crash ax . . . it had gold stripes on the sleeve."

Stiffened by his torturous morning, Ledges could hardly unbend his body to crawl out of the van. His feet sank almost to the ankles in the leaf-covered mud of the rain-soaked forest floor. He shielded his eyes against the torrents pouring down through the trees, squinting up the narrow, unpaved road to the edge of the airstrip. "Can't we pull closer?"

"Nope," said Manning, turning up his collar against the wetness. "Big tree's down across the road."

Since Lydecker had told him what he thought he had seen from the pod, Ledges's mind had not been still. Now determined to miss nothing, he let his eyes wander into the woods.

He spotted a fresh stump perhaps seventy feet back into the woods. The branches that been dragged up to hide it didn't quite cover the whiteness of the newly chopped wood. They had done a better, though not perfect, job of hiding where they had dragged the tree to the road.

Ledges thrust his hands inside his jacket as though protecting them from the chill. One of them closed around the grip of the cocked .45 that he had transferred to the front of his waistband. "It's going to be some job manhandling all those bags with that gunk underfoot."

"How're you doing, Rock?" asked Lydecker sleepily as he eased out past the van's front seats. Ledges envied the young man's ability to drop off under any circumstance.

"Ah, here come our pilots," Manning said.

Two shapeless figures covered from their heads to their knees in dripping ponchos were hurrying down the trail from the airplane. Orlando hurried up to meet them, and they exchanged some *paisano* embraces and spoke a few unheard words. Then Orlando led them back and introduced them and his passengers.

The pilots were called Salvatore and Melo, and were distinguishable under their poncho hoods only because one had a great many pimples.

In shaking their hands, Ledges saw mud on the fingers and felt broken blisters. These were pilots who had been doing heavy and unaccustomed work.

Orlando pointed toward the plane. "There are carts there to help us bring the bags." He waved them all up the road.

"No use going empty-handed," said Ledges. He tapped Lydecker and went to the back of the van, where he took a bag over a giant shoulder. Lydecker did the same with much more difficulty.

They began the trudge to the plane, Orlando leading and Manning directly behind him. Ledges and Lydecker walked abreast, the weight on their shoulders causing their feet to slide in the mud. The pilots fell in behind them.

As Ledges had put it together for himself during the ride to Avellino, Manning would be the leader of any move

against them. The commander had ramrodded the whole
escape operation, and these men all answered to him somehow. It was unclear whether they knew what was in the
bags, but if they were well enough paid, that would make
no difference.

After a lifetime of sizing up men, he thought he could
spot the dangerous ones. Orlando was one of these. His
eyes were either vacant or burning a hole in you. His hands
never stopped sliding out of sight. The pilots? Not dangerous by nature, he thought. But they had the programmed
movements of followers. People without imagination were
people to watch, because imagination and conscience went
together.

The carried money bags were more than an afterthought
for Ledges. Lying across the shoulders, they blocked easy
access from behind to the head, neck, and the portion of the
upper back behind which lay the heart and lungs.

The yards went by. Orlando looked back frequently, first
smiling, then concerned. By the time they had come to the
edge of the trees and he was standing beneath the wing of
the Twin Otter, he was clearly annoyed.

Manning never looked back at all.

Even against the sounds of the storm, Ledges was aware
of whispers between the trailing pilots. The chief continued
to shelter his free hand inside his jacket.

Orlando spoke, the sharpness of his voice not a match for
the smile he tried to maintain. "The weather will be good
for the flight," he said.

Ledges might have smiled himself at the words made so
ludicrous by the drenching gale. He reacted to the signal a
heartbeat more quickly than the pilots. Digging his front
heel into the mud for purchase, he propelled himself backward, swinging the money bag 270 degrees around his body
as he moved.

By the time he snapped himself around, the pimply-faced
pilot was flat on his back in the leaves, the sodden bag
across his midriff and the automatic pistol jarred askew in
the hand that had broken his fall.

The other man held the same sort of weapon, but he had it under control. Holding it in two hands, he had taken some fast steps ahead on the outside margin of the road to try to get a shot at Lydecker's head, around the money bag. There was a short, powerful crack from the pistol, but the bullet meant for the young sailor's brain lodged itself in several hundred thousand dollars of packed currency. The shooter kept moving forward to clear his target.

Ledges had no doubt about his priorities. He slid out the cocked .45 and began blasting at Lydecker's attacker. Colt .45's were built for this urgent short-range work. The heavy automatic's echoing reports came three times. The chief never got anything like a center shot, but one of his bullets appeared to break a shoulder. The arm holding the slender pistol fell out straight and the weapon slid down into the soaking leaves. The man howled and ran in the direction of the Twin Otter.

Attempting to track him for a finishing shot, Ledges caught sight of Orlando, holding a big automatic of his own. Unexpectedly, he snapped it toward Manning's head and fired. The commander went down with a startled look, the side of his head glistening scarlet.

The shocked Ledges had gained a split second. He dropped to a sitting position, both to present a smaller target and to be able to steady his elbows against his knees.

Orlando's automatic roared out twice and Ledges felt something hot brush past his ear.

"*Rock, watch it—*" Lydecker yelled.

The chief heard a series of short cracks and felt a searing jolt in the thick muscle beneath his left arm. The pilot under the money bag had come up firing, he knew, but he could not turn. He was vaguely aware of Lydecker sailing over his head as he began firing at Orlando.

The first shot went low and wild, and the .45's considerable recoil caused the second to miss by a still wider margin.

Ledges took a breath, squinting down his wavering gun barrel. As he brought the trigger back, there was one more report behind him and something slammed the edge of his right elbow.

Before the flying shell case had cleared his vision, Ledges saw Orlando fold forward as though punched in the stomach by a sledgehammer. He sat down with his legs out straight and his face nodding down toward his knees. An intense red fell over his lap.

"I got this other bastard, Rock. I got 'im now—" Lydecker was snarling. There was a series of sodden thuds that cut short a man crying out foreign words.

The numbness that had spread down Ledges's arm kept his fingers from properly engaging his gun's grip and trigger. He managed to shift it into his left hand, but by then all the reasons for shooting seemed to be over.

Ahead, Orlando had now fallen over sideways with frozen, staring eyes. Manning had never held a weapon. Sprawled on his belly, the officer raised his head out of a reddened heap of leaves. No sound came out of his working mouth. The fleeing pilot was not in sight.

Spinning himself around, Ledges found Lydecker. The young man was just throwing aside the large, smooth stone he had used to change the shape of the head of the man alongside the dripping money bag. The wrist of the hand that held the pistol was bent back at an angle unseen in life.

Lydecker scrambled to Ledges, still panting. "Oh, Jesus, Rock. Did he get you?"

"Yeah. But in good places. I can mostly move okay."

"Get your jacket and shirt off. There might be a first-aid kit in the plane."

They rose shakily. "We've gotta check Manning first," Ledges said.

"Was he in with them?"

"Well, he wasn't shooting. But he sure wasn't hanging on Orlando's gun arm, either. Anyway, they crossed him just like they crossed us."

"God, there was so much for everybody," Lydecker said as they wobbled down the road.

"Know something, Hink? That guy you put down yelped out in Russian, I think."

"You don't have to be Mafia to love crime. Look at us."

They knelt by Manning. Ledges stripped off his jacket and folded it under the fallen man's head.

Orlando's hurried shot had caught the back corner of the skull. There was a four-inch cap of bone missing. The brain was visible in the carnage of torn red tissue and hair.

One of Manning's eyes had grown fixed and the iris had dilated wide. The other rested on the sailors. His lips were trying to form words. Ledges leaned closer.

"I . . . I'm . . . sorry."

"Sure, Commander, sure."

Manning seemed not to have heard. "I'm sorry . . . I'm sorry . . . Daddy . . ." The functioning eye fell closed and Manning stopped breathing.

"Jeez," said Lydecker. "He thought you were his father." Not knowing what else to do, he took out a handkerchief, opened it, and laid it over the dead man's bloody face. "Let's get after that first-aid kit."

They were almost under the wing of the Twin Otter when the ground in front of them erupted into explosive geysers and a hammering chatter filled the air. They dived instinctively to the ground and caught sight of the remaining pilot. He was at the cockpit window. The muzzle of an AK-47 had been thrust out the vent, and the clip had hung itself up on the lip of the fuselage. It was preventing the man, who appeared to be working with one arm, from adjusting his angle of fire to the spot where they were lying.

Ledges knew that in another moment the wounded pilot would make the adjustment that would kill them. He lurched to his feet and ran forward as fast as his limp would let him.

The face in the plane's window craned up frantically to keep Ledges in view. The AK's barrel clattered against the window frame as the pilot fought to bring it to bear.

The target in the window was impossibly small to Ledges. As he ran to within four feet of the high cockpit, he could only estimate where the man's body would be and fire through the thin aluminum of the fuselage.

He pointed the automatic and began to pull the trigger. The gun blasted only twice before the slide jumped open on empty.

The Kalashnikov's barrel was jerking in the window. It tilted upward convulsively and hosed out a burst that ripped deafeningly through the high wing of the Twin Otter. A cascade of reeking aviation gasoline poured down from the ruptured fuel tanks. Ledges hardly had time to react before the gun spat out one more stream.

Again the burst from the wavering AK-47 screeched into the wing, but this time there was a puffing white flash. For a moment the flames were mostly wisps peeking through the torn holes, dripping down in thin streams, running along the wing's lower edge.

Ledges sensed as much as saw what was to happen. He whirled, stumbling back the way he had come, waving to Lydecker to back off.

The gasoline puddling on the ground shot flames upward at the same moment that the fire from the wing tank exploded downward. The fireball expanded to engulf the cockpit, aided by the gusting wind. The rain was powerless against the gasoline.

The flames, turned by the gale into a blowtorch directed against the fuselage, bit quickly through the aluminum, crinkling it away and exposing the aircraft's frame.

When the flames shifted for a moment, the gun barrel could be seen hanging limply out the vent, a curling, blazing shadow behind it.

Soon there was another sharp white explosion from the cockpit area.

"Oxygen bottles," Ledges shouted above the uproar.

Seconds later the tanks in the other wing went up and the Twin Otter was one vast windblown flame. Only the drenching rain saved the overhanging trees from going up with it.

The sailors looked numbly at one another, shivering. They felt as lonely and terrified as the last men on earth.

"Rock . . . Rock, we just killed people. It wasn't supposed to be this way. And it's my fault. All of it."

"You were trying to help Wade, Hink."

"And now I've wrecked what was left of his life."

"What the hell ever made us think a big enough heist would make us happy to be thieves?"

"The only thing I'd like to do with that money, Rock, is buy those lives back."

"Amen, friend. Amen."

"You think anybody saw or heard, Rock? Will anybody come?"

Ledges squinted at the wild, dark sky. "Not likely. Not in this stuff. We've got time to do whatever we decide."

"And what the hell would that be?"

Ledges's thinking remained clear. Once he got Hink to understand that all the things they would be doing from here on in would be difficult and unpleasant, they were able to order their tasks.

The van had reasonably clean curtains across the back windows to serve for bandages. And they found Orlando's flask of brandy in the glove compartment for use as an antiseptic.

While they worked on his wounds, Ledges told Lydecker how he expected to proceed.

"There were a couple of shovels lying near that plane, with a lot of fresh mud on 'em. From the shape of those hands on Salvatore and Melo, I'd say we won't have to look far in these woods for some fresh new holes in the ground. They were meant for us; we'll just change the intended tenants. And we'll strip the papers off the bodies to delay ID if they find them too fast. It might help slow up any chase."

"But how do we get out of here with no more plane and no more pilots?"

"We've *got* a plane and a pilot."

"My God, yes. The *Cub*. Vincenzo's farm's not more than a couple of hours from here. We could get there in the van. Money and all."

"We're a lot less conspicuous in the air than on the roads. Flying low and slow, we could sneak over a border somewhere. We can't take all the cash with us right away, but we can handle more than enough to get us under cover."

"We stash the rest with Vincenzo."

"Right. He's an old pirate, but he'll go along with anything that he thinks is screwing the authorities."

"Funny how perfect an idea can look when there's nothing else you can do."

It wasn't until they were halfway to Vincenzo's in the speeding van when Ledges, gathering the papers of the buried men for disposal, found Tree's copy of Manning's message.

The Road to Avellino, Italy—July 7

They sat staring as though turned to wood, looking past the thumping windshield wipers, not at the rainswept road passing under their wheels but at a deadly sunburst.

"Wade's out there with that thing," Lydecker managed to whisper.

Ledges separated the rest of the papers and wadded them into tight balls. Then he threw them out the window one at a time. "We've got a little breathing room. It's what . . . 1600 now. That's five hours until that thing . . ."

"It's locked in the vault. On the time lock. We saw Manning do that."

"Yeah. No way in except through the steel."

"Hey, they can just cut into it. They cut through titanium on the planes."

"Not eighteen inches of it. And not without any time."

"Where do we stop? What's the best way to get the word through?"

Ledges didn't speak for several minutes, and Lydecker knew enough to let him keep on thinking.

When the chief finally spoke, it was with a despair that Lydecker had never heard from him before. "Look at what we're up against. Everybody on that carrier and those four frigates is looking out for only one thing: people trying to stop the *King* from doing what it's there to do. Now supposing we achieve the never-before-seen miracle of getting through on a rural Italian telephone to somebody in authority in the Navy. Suppose further that they've lost their minds enough not to hang up on a couple of voices claiming to be us and claiming that there's the end of the world locked in a vault in the Payroll Division. Even if they risked their careers putting such claptrap through, and even if they could buck it around channels in under three weeks, what do you think the skipper would say?"

"He'd say I thought those nuts only called airline terminals. Jesus. What are we gonna do?"

Ledges folded Tree's translation carefully into his wallet. "The only thing we can. We'll deliver the message ourselves."

Avellino, Italy—July 7

Vincenzo had lived long enough to know that anything can happen. He also knew that it often was not a good idea to know all the things that had. He took the van in exchange for storing the bags that were in it in his wine cellar. They knew he suspected everybody of wanting to steal his wine and allowed no one through the locked door that led from his kitchen.

During the early years of Vincenzo's life in Sicily, he had seen enough wounded people appear out of nowhere to understand that this was a time for fewer questions, not more. Who could guess what great thefts or blood feuds had caught up these Yankees.

The old man had a fifty-five-gallon drum of gasoline for his farm equipment and a hand pump to transfer the fuel.

The side of the barn creaked with the wind and leaked rain generously as he topped off the tiny fuel tank and made sure that the old engine could not accommodate another drop of oil.

"This old canary will blow away in that terrible wind, my captains."

"It's blowing the way we're going, Vincenzo," Lydecker said, as he fastened some road maps he had found in the van to his thigh with some twine.

"You will not see the ground," Vincenzo cautioned.

"We will if we're low enough."

The ancient Italian moved slowly to the door and rolled it back. The stormy scene outside set two old horses shying and whinnying in their stalls.

Ledges stuffed himself into the front seat and strapped in. Lydecker took the pilot's position at the rear, making sure his seat belt didn't interfere with his road map, which was, other than an old magnetic compass, his only means of navigation in the barely instrumented Cub.

"You got it all straight?" Ledges asked him.

"Yep," Lydecker replied.

"Let's go."

Lydecker bawled at Vincenzo, "Switches on, you old *scungile*. Let's have some *contacto*."

Vincenzo spun the wooden prop, and the engine caught perfectly after two short coughs. Smoke billowed, the spluttering settled down to a smooth clatter, and they were ready.

"Conquer, my captains. Conquer," bayed Vincenzo, pulling at the chock ropes.

The antique Cub moved its fragile, graceful little form forward and gunned out into the open. The mud in the fields slowed it some, but the fat tires, buoyed by an on-the-nose wind, rode over the slop lightly. The tail came up before the downslope of the hill ahead was reached, and the tiny bird lifted off into the brutal sky.

Vincenzo lost sight of the Cub even before the howl of

the storm ate up the feeble noise of its splintery, laboring propeller.

U.S.S. *Ernest J. King*, The Adriatic—July 7

Like so many sailors, Admiral Irons hated to be wet. On the other hand, he found he couldn't properly get the feel of a situation at sea unless he was out in the elements. So he and Captain Ash, muffled in foul-weather gear, stood dripping on a bridge wing atop the five-story island of the *King*.

The sea below—what they could make out of it in the blowing rain and darkly plunging ceiling—was a ferocious caldron of high-leaping waves. They could scarcely tell where the wash of the towering carrier left off and the gnashing of the Adriatic began. The speed of the ship had now been greatly reduced as the battle group steamed on a figure-eight course off the Albanian coast.

"Thunder Station," sighed Irons. "That'll sound glamorous in the history books. Nobody'll realize it was only seven thousand scared sailors steaming around in circles off a hostile shore in a blow. And that we didn't really know what was happening inland or what we were expected to do out here. Hell, something could come out of this soup around us and make the bottom of the Adriatic look like the Truk lagoon—a museum of sunken ships."

"Admiral," Captain Ash said, "we've got tens of millions of dollars worth of radar, guns, air cover, and missiles to keep that from happening."

Irons gave Ash a hard sidelong stare. "So did the British at the Falklands. And do you know what warning system picked up the Exocet headed for H.M.S. *Sheffield*? The eyes of a lookout, when it was too late. They were no better off at early warning than Lord Nelson. Everything's so slaved together and automatic and brilliant that civilian airliners get shot down and frigates get creamed in broad daylight on calm seas."

Red Bedford came toward them. The air boss had thrown a tarp over his head like a shawl. "Nothing from the hummer, sir," he said to Ash, referring to the E-2C Hawkeye radar plane flying high above the weather. "That brush with Walker seems to have diminished their appetite for off-the-cuff tangles. No significant air action anywhere. They're being real careful to show that they're cooling it in the air."

"When's this stuff going to keep us on the deck, Red?" asked Irons.

"Damned soon, I'd guess."

"Push the envelope then. It's time to take some chances. Use your best men more. Find a way to make it all right."

"Aye, aye, sir. I was figuring it that way anyhow."

"I want Toms on those catapults and men in those cockpits. And I know that some of them have their headsets wired to hear rock tapes. That's a general court from here on."

"Already taken care of, sir." He hesitated, then plunged in. "Sir, may I ask what we're looking for?"

Ash glowered at the impertinence, but Irons seemed ready to talk. "Theoretically, the hummer tells us that a bunch of troop-carrying helicopters and air-drop transports are heading out of Apache country toward the fighting in Tirana. We get a release from Washington and in a couple of minutes we're offering our services to the government. They either accept or they don't. If they don't, we either go home or go in anyway, depending on what side of the rotunda the Congress got up on. If we go in, we try to pinpoint ground support in a crowded city, with shaky target programming and horrendous weather to make it even more fun. We also establish what is clearly a fighter picket line that it would be unwise for Soviet airborne to cross. They either cross it or they don't.

"Let me know if anything in that reassures you, Bedford. I would certainly like a full explanation."

The Sky—July 7

Chief Ledges had reason to wish that the passenger in a Piper Cub had seating to the rear of the pilot instead of ahead. As it was, he watched an endless, gut-wrenching series of mountaintops, cliffsides, poplar trees, and TV towers swim out of the streaming windshield. Then they would tilt madly as Lydecker, in the rear, wrenched *Carlotta*'s creaking old ribs and fabric into a frantic evasion tactic.

Flying higher was out of the question because that would have put them out of touch with the roads and topography included in their road map.

"Where we at now, navigator?" asked Lydecker, trying to peer around Ledges's mass for a better view of the spinning magnetic compass.

Ledges had finally taken control of the road map, and he referred to it. "That river under the wing should be the Ofanto. The town coming up had better be Melfi. If we're lucky, we'll turn up between Minervino and Murge in another twenty minutes."

"Arrival times are out the window. This wind keeps moving around."

"We're lucky the place we're trying to hit is on the coast and the biggest town in these parts. If we hit the Adriatic and don't see Bari, we can fly up or down to hit it and get a course correction—*watch it!*"

Lydecker stood the Cub on a wingtip to slip past a tall crane that had risen unexpectedly into view. "Then out to sea we go?" asked the unshaken boy.

Ledges found himself trying to reswallow the previous evening's meal. "We set down outside town and top off the gasoline."

"How come? We should have half a tank left."

"Hey, fogbrain, we're crossing a hundred miles of open ocean to find five ships. Also we've only got an educated guess where they were headed, all based on gouge. That means when we get over to where they might be, we've got about an hour's flying time to find 'em, even with the tank topped.''

"And these seat cushions don't float," said Lydecker.

U.S.S. *Ernest J. King*, the Adriatic—July 7

The cocaine had Tree moving along nicely. Nothing seemed beyond him now. Behind the closed curtains of his berth the evening before, he had speed-read through a copy of *Principles of Naval Architecture*, making notations on his blueprints of the *King*.

What had seemed like an insurmountable task only a few hours ago now seemed almost simple. To his drug-speeded mind a ship this complicated presented more opportunities for telling disablement than he could deal with. He had even begun to suppose he might slip away in a life raft to be picked up by the *Vinza* before the inferno.

And now, as he made his way down into the bowels of the ship, he had not yet fully decided on what vulnerability he would approach.

Like a spelunker going deeper into a cave, he was able to calculate his progress into the depths by well-known signs.

His destination was those compartments adjacent to Main One, the slang designation of the number-one machinery room. As he approached it, the air became thicker and hotter. And noisier. Hurrying pit snipes—boiler technicians—wore ear plugs to protect their hearing.

The catapults were what he was ultimately after. With them in casualty the *King* could only become a spectator in the hours before her evaporation.

The launch-valve mechanisms were no longer available to him after his successful work with Hatten, and the physical mechanisms, the gigantic pistons, trollies, and jiggers, were beyond his ability to damage. Besides which they were duplicated in four catapults. So it was the propelling substance, the steam, that he had decided to go after.

Despite all the awed deference to nuclear propulsion, the reactor was still nothing more than the flame under a teakettle. And the propulsive force it generated—steam—was not anywhere near as effective a turbine driver as the gas turbines in the escort frigates. It was the same force used by James Watt two centuries before.

His ultimate goal was to trigger a mechanical marvel called the Engineering Control and Surveillance System. In the sprawling world of close-tolerance machinery on the *King*, certain failures might go undetected by humans until the whirling and reciprocating steel had turned itself into scrap. So computer-tied sensors in the system shut the system down without a human touch. As Tree saw it, it only remained for him to determine the best way to trigger a shutdown that would deny steam to the great accumulators at a critical moment.

He was aware of provisions for battle override in the system. But his experience with the Navy told him that things seldom used seldom functioned the way they were designed to. All he wanted to do was create an initial shambles in the first moments of an all-out launch.

As he paused at an intersection of passageways and overflying catwalks, he let his attention wander for a moment as he referred to a folded sheet of notes. He was contemplating the arcana of trip alarms, overspeed alarms, contaminated boiler-feed water, and boiler overloads when he heard above the din the last sound on earth anyone would expect here, the throaty, threatening growl of a large animal.

The dog was behind him. Wisely, he did not turn. He knew the dog. It was the Doberman known unaffectionately as Denny the Dope Dog. And he would be in the company of an armed Marine as he made his unannounced rounds of the ship, sniffing for stored narcotics—the sort that was in the vial in Tree's breast pocket.

The tech rep pretended to decide his destination and

hurried off down the passageway most likely to take him away from traffic. A ventilating fan cut in with a roar that could have drowned out the request to stop, although Tree in fact heard it plainly.

Fury built in him as Tree hustled along faster, heading for the building sound of a circulator pump. Again he pretended not to hear the call from behind.

He hurried around a turn and found himself in a maze of piping and valves. The equipment was chest high, with narrow spaces between. The noise level was as high as he could have wanted, and there was nobody else in sight. This would be the right place.

The call that now reached him was close enough so that no one could suppose it had gone unheard. The exasperation in the voice was evident.

The man Tree turned to face was a squat Marine in his early twenties. He was in jungle fatigues and held the surging Denny on a short leash as they came down between the piping. There was an M-16 hanging muzzle down off his shoulder, but that was just part of the general arming of the Marine contingent on guard duty. The man saw nothing more than another doper to be nailed.

"Just drop them bags right down there and stand fast, buddy," he said.

"Sure, pal. What's up?" said Tree. As a component of his thoroughness, Tree had made himself familiar with the use of all light weapons. For general use on the ship he had decided to carry nothing more than a large screwdriver with a sharpened and tapered blade. It was longer and stronger than any knife he cared to carry and could have passed as a tool had he been braced. It hung in a tool belt that he wore.

"Get that stuff open," the Marine said, indicating the bags Tree had set down.

"You got it." Tree stopped quickly, opened up the bags' drawstrings, and pushed the necks open. Denny had the right idea, going for the breast pocket, but his thick handler was focused on the pouches. "Hey, can you snub that leash? I'm afraid of dogs."

The Marine, on one knee by now, grunted and tied the leash to a gauge. When he leaned over the first bag, he presented his back.

Tree struck downward with the screwdriver, going for the nape of the neck. But the Marine shifted so the blade missed its mark. It plunged downward through the trapezius muscle, missing the spine and windpipe, and plunging completely through to emerge beneath the collarbone.

The kneeling man grunted in rage and surprise. Then, with surprising agility and reflex, he struck upward with clasped fists. The blow caught Tree in the groin and broke his hold on the weapon.

The protruding screwdriver had penetrated outside the Marine's rifle sling, so the webbing caught on the tool for a moment as he struggled to unsling it. If it had not been for that delay, he would have been able to slay Tree on the spot. As it was, he dropped down on his side and squeezed off two shots on semiautomatic before the tech rep's lunge and heavy downward kick caught him at the temple and bounced his skull off the deck plates.

Tree pulled the gun out of the jerking hands and used the butt against the man's forehead until he was still. One more hard swing caught Denny alongside the ear as he came to the end of his snubbed leash and started to bark. The Doberman dropped in a heap and never moved.

Thoughts of what to do with these bodies had begun to run through Tree's mind before he realized that he had been shot. The two .223 steel-jackets had angled up under his ribs, nicking the diaphragm, collapsing a lung, and skidding up to exit his back. There had been no thick viscera to compress with shock between the point of entry and exit. No major blood vessels had been cut. He estimated that he could function for as long as the ship had to live.

The shots had not brought any investigators. Tree dragged the Marine and the dog to an open area before a gauge board and checked the floor plates. There was one with a grip cut into it and he tugged it up. In the access space beneath he found room for both bodies.

There was a pile of wipers' rags in a corner, and he used these to blot up the worst blood from the deck. He stuck a second handful down inside his shirt and jacket to stop the bleeding.

The bad pain hadn't begun yet. He didn't feel any special weakness. Another sniff of the cocaine when he had a moment would brace him.

The bloodied condition of his clothing told him he was done moving about unobserved until he could get something to cover himself. That would be his next move.

He would keep the M-16 and the extra ammunition clips he had stripped off the fallen Marine.

His thoughts suddenly refused to collect themselves. The complications of his most recent plans seemed too much for him. He needed to get hold of himself.

He remembered the void space that Manning had showed him, where the payroll thieves had found the practice bombs. It was almost directly above him. He could climb there and hide until he was in command again.

Bari, Italy—July 7

The expected towns somehow turned up at the expected time, Ledges's moving thumb following the serpentine roads unwinding dimly below.

Forty minutes later the roads began to widen and converge. "Looks like we're coming to a bigger burg," said Ledges. "We need someplace to get gas. Something small. Not on one of the main roads. Wait'll I see something that's a little more than a goat path and—hey, here's one—to the right. Go *right*."

Lydecker picked out the ribbon and swung the Cub along it, gaining a little altitude to avoid the occasional towering tree.

Almost to the point where Ledges would have asked

Lydecker to turn back to their flight path, they spotted what they wanted. It was a small cluster of low buildings where three unpaved roads crossed near the edge of a copse of tall trees. The single gasoline pump might have passed unnoticed except for an outsized petroleum company sign, undoubtedly scrounged from a dump.

Lydecker picked out something else along the edge of the trees. Like a pathway to the buildings lay a long stripe where grass had been eroded off earth that was otherwise thickly green. "Rock . . . Rock, that could be a nice mothering little airstrip down there."

"What the hell for?"

"Who gives a turd. Here we go."

In the short time it took him to make the necessary turns to line up the wind and make his approach, remarkable changes appeared on the ground: The drenched emptiness of the tiny crossroads cluster had become a miniature beehive. Men had apparently sprung out of the ground. A half-dozen automobiles were coasting out of the trees. It would have been a lot more ominous if most of the men were not happily waving their hats and arms in welcome.

"What the hell is this?" said Ledges between oaths. "I don't like the Lindbergh routine."

"Should I pull away?"

"No. If it was a trap they'd have laid back for us."

The Cub had to hold a vicious crab on its approach into the pouring crosswind. When Lydecker kicked it straight, he almost had to dig the downwind wing into the mud to keep his plane from drifting off into the scrub. The ground population was not without appreciation of a neat piece of flying, and they were applauding as *Carlotta* rolled out near the gas pump.

Both Ledges and Lydecker jumped out to stretch their legs. The crowd that surrounded them was a mixed bag of rough rurals and low-order urbans. One man stood out. He was casually elegant, handsome in a hatchet-faced way, and magnificently mustached. He protected a white straw hat and a cream-colored suit with an enormous umbrella. His expression was friendly, and he used a wonderful hand gesture to denote his confusion.

"Anybody speak English here?" blurted Lydecker, the way he started most conversations in Italy.

"Oh, yes," said the elegant man. "I am Gerardo Della Brovino. I am the schoolmaster of our town down the road." His bright eyes picked out the edge of the bloodied bandages under Ledges's partially open shirt. He also did not miss the elements of United States Navy clothing. "You are from *Signor* Zito?"

"No," said Lydecker, pointing to the pump. "We're just here to buy some gas and get the hell on our way."

Some people in the surrounding group, which had grown to twenty or so, seemed to speak some English. They translated to the others and there was an agitated stirring.

Della Brovino cast an anxious eye first across the surrounding countryside and then the lowering sky. "Even if you do not come from *Signor* Zito, do you bring us anything?"

"No," said the puzzled Ledges. "We don't bring anything at all."

"Yes. Your airplane is so small." He waved away some people who were crowding forward to peer into the Cub. Then he gestured to a man at the gas pump and spoke rapid Italian. The pump man called out in turn, and many hands moved the Cub to where the nozzle could reach the tank opening indicated by Lydecker.

"What are you looking for?" Lydecker asked.

Della Brovino smiled his refusal to discuss that. "I can see that you are Americans, and I can see that you are in trouble. Perhaps with police. We understand that well and we sympathize. But you create trouble for us, too."

"Hey, we just want to gas up and vamoose," said Lydecker.

Ledges was trying to sort out the terrible Italian dialect of the increasingly voluble crowd.

"You see, *signore*," said Della Brovino, "for many years we were left out of the prosperity that came to many in

Naples and a certain family we have in Marseille. And now at last we have a small share. This poor airstrip makes our living and sends our children to fine schools. This can only be done with the understanding of certain police in Bari and across the water," he said, waving in the direction of the Adriatic. "*Signor* Zito pays for discretion. But only for his people. You arrive close to visitors from *Signor* Zito. They do not like sneaking in deliveries of the powder. Although you have nothing for us, they will not understand that perhaps. People in our town are paid to inform on unexpected visitors. But now you can see."

Ledges and Lydecker followed his gaze across the distant fields. On the dim, rain-lashed horizon they could see the silhouettes of two small automobiles on the paralleling road. The braying of police hooters could be heard.

"How fast can they get here?" snapped Ledges.

"Four minutes, I think. Maybe a bit more because of the mud. But maybe they will send the helicopter, too. They have prospered along with us."

The man that was pumping the gasoline into the Cub withdrew the nozzle and entered into an argument with people clustered around him.

"What are they saying, Rock?"

Della Brovino answered, "Some of the young ones are saying that since you are not with Zito, there would be an advantage in holding you here."

"But why?"

"To show good faith. . . . Perhaps for a reward . . . perhaps for a bribe."

"Can you talk to them, *Signor* Della Brovino?" asked Ledges.

The elegant shoulders shrugged. "I am a spokesman, not a leader."

The approaching cars took a turn that brought them more on a direct heading to where the plane stood. The hooters grew louder. The chief's empty .45 had been buried with Manning. He hopelessly began to estimate the strength of his exhausted and wounded body against the crowd.

Suddenly Lydecker was shouldering in. He had two inch-thick packets of hundred-dollar bills in each hand. "Would this handle it, pal?"

Della Brovino deftly interposed his body between Lydecker and the crowd. "I believe it might. These people are good at heart and have no love for authority." His hand made the packets disappear so quickly that he might have been a conjurer.

Mustaches bristling with indignation, he turned and sailed into the heart of the crowd around *Carlotta*. He scattered the men with his elbows and his wrath. His Italian flew so quickly and furiously that Ledges did not have the slightest hope of keeping up.

At the end of a full minute there was a break in the crowd. The younger men slouched away sullenly, their hands making the gestures of dissension and resignation. The elders sent up a happy jabbering and urged the gas pumper to greater efforts. The headlights of the approaching police cars were blinking for attention. Only the unseen appearance of long curves in the old road kept them from being upon the crossroads in moments. They were no longer than a minute away.

The gas pumper bawled out the completion of refueling and screwed the cap back onto the tank. The sailors were still climbing inside when eager hands swiveled the plane and positioned it on the runway.

One of the speeding police cars broke off the road and began to bounce over the fields. Its occupants knew all there was to know about the strip and were intent on blocking it.

Lydecker pointed to the cars and yelled out of the lowered side flap to Della Brovino. "Couldn't you give them something to get lost?"

Della Brovino's manicured hand clutched at a handsome cravat. "*Signor*, these are sworn officers of the law. And they should make their own way in life. The best of luck to you."

Ledges's Italian served to get the propeller pulled through and turning. Lydecker pushed the throttle forward, but the thick mud allowed little progress. "Shit," yelled Lydecker. "We're gonna stick."

Then there were a dozen hands on the wing struts, pushing as fast as the clumsy footing would allow. The speed increased a bit. There was a short rocky patch and the pushing hands were at last outdistanced. The wind veered a bit to the nose and the fat tires got their bit of lift against the sucking ooze.

One of the police cars was sliding around the turn behind the gas station. The other was bumping across the field to a point substantially in front of any possibility of takeoff.

Carlotta gained momentum now. Ledges stuck his head out the open flap and looked back. The old men, in mock confusion, were milling about to impede the progress of the car near the gas pump. The one in the fields was having mire problems, but, deftly driven, was making presentable progress.

After an interminable dozen seconds, the tail of the Cub came up. With the air moving properly over the control surfaces, *Carlotta* battled toward flying speed.

The rapid closing of the hooter from behind told them that the impeding crowd had been bypassed. There was every chance, given the antique plane's modest takeoff speed, that they would be rammed from behind. The intercepting car ahead got its wheels onto some hardpan and gave a good surge. It was going to be on the road before they could get by.

Lydecker kept the throttle grimly to the firewall. The engine could not wind any higher. The police were not shooting. They didn't have to.

Ledges watched the white and green side of the police car move directly into the Cub's path and stop. He thought of the twelve gallons of fresh gasoline positioned literally right in his lap. He almost wanted to yell out to the two policeman, who he could see plainly, to jump out and save themselves from the inferno. He braced his hands against the instrument panel.

"Hold your socks, Rock," Lydecker hollered. Although

they were below flying speed, he put a pilgrim's faith into the fabulous high-lift wing and jerked back on the stick. The ungainly bird jerked free of the ground and made a great, nose-high, ungainly lurch that bumped both the front wheels and the tail wheel against the roof of the car, leaving substantial dents. The yells of the terrified policemen were audible.

Stalled out now, the Cub fell flatly back onto the road, its airspeed bled almost back to zero but still turning full throttle and headed down the rainswept runway.

Above the roar of the groaning engine, they heard a resounding thwack of metal meeting metal in quantity. Ledges swung his head out the flap again and strained to look backward past the fishtailing fuselage.

It only took one glimpse to tell it all. The pursuing car had met the blocking car squarely. The policemen were just starting to scream at one another.

The strip was long enough to accommodate planes much heavier and more powerful than theirs. It looked as though they had plenty of room to get off. Not until they had broken into the air did Ledges notice that they were skimming between high-tension towers and were brushing below the crackling droops of wire by perhaps four feet.

"Rip for the coast, Hink," Ledges said, trying to get his throat completely open. "The signs at the crossroads said that the big town was Bari. We're on target."

"Give me a compass heading. Not that it'll be worth much of a shit in this wind."

"Try eighty-five degrees. We might have to hit the Albanian coast and fly out from there."

"Roger."

"Now would you mind telling me where you got that money?"

"If we make it to the ship, we're going to have to have something to make them believe some of this stuff. I figured a petty officer third class with a quarter of a million might do it."

"I think the fishes are going to be the only ones to hear that story."

The weather closed tighter and Lydecker had to skim the terrain again.

They were almost to the coast when Lydecker looked up through the skylight between the wings and saw, through a break in the blowing scud, the navigation lights of a helicopter. It was moving in the angry, tilting swoops of a search. He thought he could make out police colors before the gap in the blowing clouds closed down.

Then they were crossing a highway and a rocky beach. They were barely above the mast tops of boats at a quay as they moved out into the Adriatic.

If they had owned a radio, they would have heard the police helicopter broadcasting word of a drug-smuggling aircraft believed to be heading out to sea.

The message was one of thousand collected and processed by the overwhelmed ears of the fleet on Thunder Station.

The Sky—July 7

This time Bad Apple Burns was in charge. No matter what thunderbolts were running through the veins of Mudcat Walker in the front seat, he was just the driver in the long two hours of flying combat air patrol.

The Tomcat was fresh in the air, far above the boiling storm that enveloped the battle group. Burns had inherited a picture of local traffic in the air and on the sea from the previous CAP and the hummer hovering above, and he was getting his own handle on it.

Burns's cockpit was terrifyingly more complicated than Walker's. To accommodate the sea of instruments, switches, and knobs, the RIO was faced with a center panel, a center console, a left vertical console, a left knee panel, a right instrument panel, a right vertical panel, and a right knee panel.

"Shit," Burns had wailed during his training, "I can't find all the consoles and panels, never mind what's on 'em."

Burns had a stick in his cockpit, too. But it had no connection to the maneuvering controls of the F-14. It was called the Hand Control Unit, HCI in shorthand, and it provided the awesome link to the formidable skills of Bad Apple Burns and his awesome arsenal of sensors and weapons.

As he moved the short stick with a neurosurgeon's precision, manipulating a thumbwheel in precise conjunction, he moved the beams of search radar restlessly and relentlessly around the sky above and below. If he found what he sought, a sweep of his free hand around the other panels would tie in the killing systems. Let Walker play all the Red Baron games he wanted. This was the office that would decide the issue when they were playing for keeps.

Bad Apple Burns shared an unspoken sentiment with Walker. Between them they could defend the whole hulking motherless United States Navy all by themselves.

Walker's Tomcat, with Mickey Maussman a mile away on the wing, soared in the clear sunlight at 32,000 feet. He began the first of many fifteen-mile legs of the CAP's racetrack-shaped course.

"I rode the E Train once in New York," Walker said sullenly into his mike. "It was more exciting than this. And more dangerous."

"Cheer up, Mud," Burns said without looking up from the screens on his panel. "Maybe something thrilling will happen. Like flying into the ramp, trying to land in this shit."

"Well, at least *somebody* would be getting killed."

Burns killed his mike and said aloud to himself, "Mud, I sometimes wish I could find a button that would shove this stick right up your big-mouthed ass."

* * *

Ledges felt bleakly ridiculous seated far out over a hostile sea with an Italian road map in his hands.

They were flying so low that the sea spray blew repeatedly onto the windshield and built up opaque films of salt. It only washed away when they chugged into a Niagara of rain that washed things clear for a short while.

The bobber outside was almost halfway down, indicating that they had one more hour of fuel. The old compass gyrated crazily, its ancient correction card outmoded and in any case unreadable. Still, the same unknowable right-brained instincts that made Lydecker such an incredible creature on a surfboard had made him a master of the old instrument and the plane around it. He had brought them through weather as unspeakable as this before in their drunken and foolish quests for rural romance.

But they had known where the likes of Rosalia and Concetta were located. And they had not been protected by a United States Navy battle group.

A wheel caught the top of a swiftly rolling wave, and the plane mushed perilously.

"Should I take it higher?" Lydecker asked.

"Not if you don't want a Standard flying into your jock," said Ledges with the certainty of a man who spent a lifetime around the fleet's weaponry. "Stay loose. We might be getting close. We can start flying a pattern then."

"You really think we'll find them?"

"Probably not before they find us."

"I'm leaving you my Hobie, Rock."

U.S.S. *Ernest J. King*, the Adriatic—July 7

McGregor was working with Lieutenant Bluehoffer on the phantom payroll for July 15 when news of the murder swept in from the passageways.

A yeoman called Stuffy, who had it straight from an

ordie, who had it straight from a pit snipe, sketched in the details. "Somebody took that jarhead off, Commander McGregor. No doubt about that. Y'see, Denny's other handler, a gunny name Pflug, got worried about feeding the mutt when he didn't get back on time." As a dope dog, Denny got little of the affection customarily accorded to animals. "So Pflug goes down and combs over the the area the other jar—his name was Oliver—was sniffing over."

"Where was that?" asked McGregor, trying to keep on with the job.

"Just outside Main One. Anyway, Pflug sees a piece of Denny's leash tied to a wheel down in a pump room. The chain is busted right in the middle like somebody strong and in a hurry gave it a helluva jerk—"

"Ease up, Stuffy. That's the second time you almost knocked my coffee over four hours work."

"Sorry, sir. Anyhow, he spots some blood on the deck plates. And it looks smeared, like sombody'd been trying to wipe it up. There was some more on one of the lifting grips in the plates. Pflug heaved it up, and there was Oliver and Denny stuffed in side by each. They both had their heads stove in."

McGregor gave a soft whistle. "Denny must've come up with a big stash. It made somebody nervous enough to save his butt no matter what."

"That's the way they got it plotted, sir," said Stuffy. "Thing is, though, that the jarhead's M-16 is gone, and so's his ammo pouch. The guy might be tough to take. But they're sure going to be turning this whole ninety-one thousand tons upside down, Commander McGregor."

"Not right away, they aren't, Stuffy," said McGregor. "They've got to keep the ship together as a fighting unit until we're off station."

Bluehoffer, white-blond and looking like a refugee from junior high school, ventured a rare opinion. "It would be a needle-and-haystack job anyway. Nobody saw the guy, and he could hide a gun in a thousand different places."

"Maybe it's not so tough as you think, Lieutenant

Bluehoffer,'' Stuffy said. ''They did a fast breakdown on the blood off the plates, and it doesn't belong just to Oliver. They found a couple of .223 cases kicked under a pump. Looks like the jar got a couple off and maybe hit somebody. They've got the sick bay staked, and they'll be checking people out at muster.''

''Okay, Stuffy,'' said McGregor. ''Thanks for the bulletin. Now get the hell out of here if you expect to get paid this month.''

When the yeoman had gone, McGregor tried to return to work with Bluehoffer and several clerks. But Stuffy proved to have a dozen successors, and they leaked into the office under pretense of doing some division-related chores, offering all their pet theories and suspects.

After an hour spent vainly trying to stem the tide, McGregor left Bluehoffer and returned to his compartment with some correspondence he could handle at his own desk.

Knowing that any prolonged introspection of his situation would drive him mad, he was, however irrationally, trying to concentrate on his work through every moment.

He had been working an hour when the phone on the bulkhead rang.

At first there was only breathing. Not the ordinary out-of-breath laboring of a man who had just come up several levels of ladders, but a bubbling that was almost one with a long, insistent cough.

''Hello . . . hello—'' Like all veteran Navy people, McGregor became impatient when the crisp shipboard phone-identification protocol was not followed.

''Is that you, McGregor?'' asked a rasping voice, trying hard to hold volume.

''Yes—''

''Are you alone?''

Something in the tone made McGregor turn to check, even though he was sure that he was. ''Yeah. Who is this?''

''I'm a friend of Commander Manning's. My name is Tree.''

McGregor went on full alert now. "I know about you. Where are you?"

"Where nobody will find me. I need help."

He gambled that Tree knew everything. "I'm out of the deal. That's why I'm still here."

"I figured you chickened when I saw you waving bye-bye to your pals. I know you don't want me to make a lot of trouble for them beginning right now, so you're going to do me a bit of a favor. It's simple and safe, and I won't ask any more of you."

McGregor knew he was nailed. "Okay, Tree. What is it?"

"Get a pencil and write this down." Tree gave him a location by compartment-designation code. "All you have to do is get hold of a first-aid kit. Just pull one out of a life raft somewhere. Put it in some kind of bag to hide it and leave it up on the overhead pipes outside that compartment. I'll give you an hour."

"You're hurt?"

"Fell down a ladder." He fell into a rumbling cough.

"I'll have the kit there," said McGregor, the danger to his friends the only thing he clearly understood.

"Any chance of getting that vault open?"

"Huh? No," said McGregor, jolted by the question.

There was a grunt and the phone went dead.

McGregor pushed aside his work and tried to think this thing through.

In contemplation it didn't surprise him that Tree might be a doper. He had been watching the tech rep since the shadowy connection with Manning had become known. He sometimes had the look of a man with something racing inside him. And dopers might do anything. Even murder.

But he must be hit seriously to have chanced such a call. And no matter how impaired his wits, he must know that even a healthy man couldn't long avoid the search so sure to follow.

And the vault question. If Tree knew what they had been doing in the vault, he might have been cut in. But then why had he remained behind? He had seen Manning leave, so he hadn't been deserted.

Perhaps he was to be paid later. Maybe he somehow expected something from what had been left behind in the vault—the case whose money had not fit into the pod.

Plainly, though, he couldn't spend any money if he bled to death or was sent to prison for fifty years.

Wounded as badly as he was, he couldn't hope to get off the ship. Even if he did, the only potential rescue ship likely to be of use to him would be the Soviet AGI trawler behind them.

McGregor turned to stare at the vault, its glistening door wrapping its charged time lock impregnably.

Something awful seemed suddenly to be seeping straight through the foot and a half of chrome steel.

The Sky—July 7

"I'm eyeballing ahead and to the left, Hink. You handle the right. Just don't forget to keep *Carlotta* in the air."

"You call this being in the air?" said Lydecker, trying to search a universe that could expand to a half mile and then instantly contract down to the wingtips. "What's the gas look like up there?"

The length of the bobber had much diminished in fighting the rough air. "Maybe twenty minutes left, I'd guess."

"Want to give it another ten and head for the coast?"

"Did we suddenly decide that we're out here to save our asses?" snapped Ledges.

"Just making sure that you're as big an asshole as I am, Rock."

The vast technological meat grinder that was the *King*'s battle group was the product of incalculable expense, politics, confusion, and fear—of attempts to close every tiny door of vulnerability. But some remained open:

If all the lofty engineering intellects in the United States had sought the ideal machine and the ideal jamming facilities for an approach to the hotly defended *King*, they might have come up with something like this: a small target, capable of skimming the sea at an altitude not greatly exceeding ten feet. That target should be made of materials of the lowest possible radar reflection. Its power plant should radiate only the smallest amount of heat. Its own electromagnetic emanations should be nonexistent. Its ability to fly an erratic approach at slow and variable speed amid a widespread jamming grid would greatly enhance survivability.

This was a fair description of a fabric-covered Piper Cub flying a wavetop search course in winds that sometimes reduced its over-the-water speed to 35 miles per hour. The ungainly missile owned no electronic or navigation equipment to offer a signal for detection, and its 65-horsepower engine created not much more detectable heat than the fast-beating heart of a seabird. The widespread jamming medium through which it flew was a storm filled with fast-moving rain cells and a sea studded with high-tossed waves.

Carlotta had in fact been spotted not once, but several times. Unfortunately for the United States Navy's radar watchers aloft and at sea, she seemed to be one of an endless series of false returns picked up by the finely tuned machines.

On the frigate *Randall*, one operator had picked up the blip for long enough to consider a warning. But then it had faded in the sea return—the reflection of radar off the ocean surface—and he became less certain. There was also a traffic report that an Italian police helicopter had pursued a drug-smuggling plane out over the Adriatic on that heading. He muttered to himself, "I ain't gonna risk lives running after some Beech Bonanza carrying a hundred pounds of hash that I'd like to be smoking myself sometime."

The E-2C high above was looking down on a 250-mile

circle. The three men at its consoles in the rear strained to find the supersonic intruder that might be breaking into the edge of their screens, or an airborne armada coming out of the east. The large glowing blot that was the *King* and the smaller beetles that were the four escorting frigates held center stage, thus far unthreatened. One or two of the careful men may have caught a glimpse of *Carlotta*, but nothing that held up. And, of course, the Toms and the ships would be handling any close-in flashes that bothered them. One airborne operator said, "If they chased every false alarm in this mess, they'd need two more carriers to handle all the fighters down in the gumbo."

One of the Toms might have had the Cub on its down-looking pulse-Doppler radar. But the fighter was flying almost perpendicular to the little plane's course at that moment, and inability to see that approach well was one of the few weaknesses of the system.

The F-14s also had their much more powerful high-PRF radar going. But the very strength of the huge number of pulses that allowed it to see so many miles and burn through jamming worked against it in this case. The time interval between the pulses was so short that some were transmitted before the echo returned. So the RIOs couldn't really tell if the echoes were from a small target at relatively close range in the ground clutter or distant commercial airline traffic they were intermittently monitoring. They decided on the latter, and *Carlotta* flew on as one more occasional sprinkle of brightness in the sea return.

Ten minutes after they had last spoken, Lydecker was aware of the lightness in the plane that signaled the seventy pounds of fuel they had burned. There might be six or seven pounds left. He wondered whether the empty tank and hollow framework would provide enough buoyancy to overcome the weight of the engine if he could flop her down in one piece in a trough. Not that the waves wouldn't break her to matches in short order.

The young petty officer was wondering about sea temperatures and scanning out his right-hand windows when the Cub slowly began to overtake a small, ungainly looking ship. Dimly seen in the sheets of rain, it was making heavy going at a speed that even Lydecker knew to be excessive in such a sea. His heart bounded and he swung over toward the craft. "Chief Ledges, my man, would you please get a look at the flag on that tub I'm heading for."

Ledges whooped. He didn't have to look. He had watched that squat outline trailing behind them from the middle of the Atlantic. "Dip me in whale shit if it ain't my favorite AGI trawler in the whole world—the good old darling mother-humping *Vinza* herself. Get her heading, goddammit. *Get her heading!*"

Lydecker flew right up over the stern, having to gain altitude to do so. "Fleet course is two-seven-niner on this leg if that bastard is doing his job." He jammed the throttle on full. No more fuel economy needed now. The next ten minutes would find them either in heaven or on the roof aboard the *King*.

The four frigates escorting the *King* moved about her in a wheel four miles across. At the moment they were roughly off the quarters of their huge charge, two having dropped back off the stern. This pair, the *Blackston* and the *Randall*, were positioning to back up the plane guard helicopter that had risen for the changing of the CAP fighters. Pilots who went into the sea in this sort of weather and visibility would need all the help they could get.

One of the radarmen in the Combat Information Center of the *Blackston* was the first to realize that a new shape had risen out of the familiar blip that he knew to be the *Vinza*. He paused just long enough to be certain and to get some sense of the speed. "Jeez, the friggin' trawler's got a cruise comin' at us," he blurted before he got to the proper business of reporting. "Contact astern bearing two-eight-zero . . . range three miles . . . speed seventy knots." Even as he spoke, he knew that something wasn't right. A Soviet cruise missile like the AS-6 would be closing at five hundred miles an hour, with impact in seconds. But it was no time for quibbling.

Instantly the clamorous gonging of general alarms swept through all the ships in the group. The impossibly intricate electronic net made a single entity of the ships and the planes overhead. Zebra—full wartime conditions—came into full force.

As though he sensed the peril in what was happening ahead of them, Ledges called to Lydecker, "Get those wheels back in the water or we're dogmeat." He rose up against his seat belt as Lydecker made the rapid dip and left the *Vinza* dropping astern.

The Cub's approach had caught the battle group at a moment that was propitious for its defense.

A new CAP had been catapulted off the roof ten minutes earlier. The Tomcats of the previous CAP were coming down. The trap of the Tom carrying Mickey Maussman meant that there was only one plane still up. It was even now turning at "the break," the imaginary spot downwind where a carrier plane turns to commit for its landing.

Its wings were at full extension, its wheels and spoiling devices deployed, its nose high to show a belly heavy with two big AIM-54 Phoenix missiles and four AIM-9L Sidewinders.

At its controls was Lieutenant Commander Mudcat Walker.

The unfortunate affairs of the *Stark* and the *Vincennes* had wrought emotional havoc on the shipboard officers of the United States Navy. Whether you reacted too slow or too fast, you were apt to end up with dead people and a dead career. Each commander kept to himself what he thought the mistakes were, and each had his own way of responding to a future crisis.

Rough, pragmatic Admiral Irons had correctly assessed the potential for chaos in the electronic jungle of defenses. He had perceived that he might survive any shortcomings in his own systems if he could completely baffle the enemy's.

Considering electronic jamming a necessary but complicated and chancy thing, he saw a fleet's salvation in a system of beautiful simplicity.

The Royal Navy in the Falklands campaign had proved the huge effectiveness of chaff launchers in the hard laboratory of battle. Again and again they had fired clouds of aluminum chaff into the sky to confuse and neutralize determined Argentinian missile attacks. And the Navy's ordnance people had taken the art far forward. Captain Ash had been given to know exactly how the admiral felt.

In the short minutes before expected impact, Combat Information Centers had to deal with some bafflements. Trained incredibly well to deal with each thing that could appear, they were much more at a loss when something did not appear.

The incoming contact was emitting none of the hallmark signals of an active homing system. They had nothing to home in on but the contact itself. And that had now ducked down into the sea clutter, where it proved difficult to hold.

The two frigates wheeled on the target at flank speed. Weapons were freed on all units. Word went up to the one aircraft close enough to help—Mudcat Walker in the returning CAP. "Bloodbath One, we've got an incoming target flying on the deck bearing two-eight zero, three miles out. Break off . . . break off."

While the IFF system built into the Tomcat could differentiate friend from foe, it was not made for split-second reading in close-in combat. If the aircraft came down into the defensive melee it invited destruction from friendly weapons.

Irons's prebattle decision to go heavily to the chaff in the event of close penetration overrode all the rest of the decision making.

On the converging frigates and on the carrier there erupted a series of dull booms as the mortar tubes of the launchers began to fire in a carefully programmed sequence. On the *King* the six tubes of each of the four Mark 36 high-velocity launchers loosed cartridges containing packets of foil. The cartridges flew upward at angles of fifty-five, sixty-five, and seventy-five degrees to blanket the most possible angles of approach. Every charge dispersed radially before the packets exploded 3.4 seconds after launch.

In several of the launch tubes were Hycor Infra-Red Anti-Missile decoys—HIRAMS. They deployed a sophisticated flare by parachute to confuse infrared sensors that might attempt to cut through the radar jamming of the strips.

The idea was to keep aloft a continuous screen of these confusions, causing incoming barrages of antiship missiles to home in on the decoys, veer hopelessly off course, and fly on harmlessly. It would have worked beautifully against an electronically guided missile. On a chugging Piper Cub it had no effect whatever, other than an unintended one— Admiral Irons's well-reasoned last-ditch defense served sensationally well to blind the massive inventory of radar-guided defensive weapons in his own fleet.

The thirty seconds after firing caused wildly ambiguous emotions across the four-mile diameter about the *King*. Some of the men watching the radarscopes were elated at the speed and thoroughness of the defensive cloud. Others, the ones trying to lay fire against the suddenly invisible target, were horrified.

Mudcat Walker took Bad Apple Burns's backseat report of what was happening and nearly burned off the RIO's ears. "Those assholes are blinding us. How're we supposed to find anything in this shit?"

The racing frigates would occasionally get a momentary radar cut when the tiny, skimming target blinked above the sea clutter or appeared around the blizzard of blowing, blinding, ever-renewing chaff. The poor quality of the locks meant that the accuracy of any loosed missiles would be highly compromised. But weapons, however inaccurately, were meant to be loosed.

Across the *King*'s five-ship force, two dozen launchers of destruction swiveled eagerly, cycling, sniffing electromagnetically. On each of the frigates the foredeck Standard-missile launcher, the Vulcan-Phalanx Gatling, and the OTO Melara fast-firing 76-millimeter cannon swung toward the cloud of bewilderment astern of the carrier. On the *King* itself the Basic Points Defense System primed itself. The egg-shaped turrets of the Vulcans, manned by unseen operators below, readied their 3,000-round-per-minute firestorm. The firing circuits of three eight-celled Sea Sparrow plane-killer missiles hummed alive.

"Nothing we can do about this, Mud," soothed Bad Apple Burns. "Let's get clear before some stray skyrocket locks on our tailpipe and spoils the evening."

"Bullshit," bellowed Walker so loudly that Burns's head rang. "We're going down there and smoke that humper."

Burns's long, hopeless wail of dismay came over the mike as he went about the business of cleaning up the landing-ready Tomcat for war.

Two miles behind the carrier, at an altitude varying between six and ten feet, Ledges and Lydecker were mercifully unthinking of the deadly stir forming ahead of them. They had problems of their own.

"Tell me that I didn't hear that engine stuttering, Hink," said Ledges, the bandages around his chest and arms now as drenched with sweat as they were with blood.

"Maybe it's only the sludge at the bottom of the tank mucking up the carburetor. But we're pretty close to dry."

"That means we're pretty close to wet."

There was nothing to guarantee that the projected track of the trawler would lead them to the group. Or that the *Vinza* hadn't been laying back twenty miles instead of the usual two-to-five. Besides which, even if they missed by only two hundred yards, a blowing rain cell could render even the looming *King* invisible.

The chief was dividing his attention between searching and listening to the uncertain engine when he became aware that they were flying through something more substantial than rain. The churning wooden propeller was bringing back a blur of something else. Some particles of it stuck and smeared across the windshield for a moment before they blew off and back.

He finally recognized the material. *Chaff*, he gasped. "They're blowing off chaff at us. We're *close*, Hink. Give us some S-turns. Wide ones. And pop us up once in a while so we can grab a wider look. We're okay while we're in the aluminum."

"Roger. Coming up to fifty feet for five seconds."

The move took the element of sea clutter out of the Cub's advantages for some moments. The radar gained momentary views and some useful cuts. The target was moving with such puzzling slowness that it was hardly closing on the forward-charging *King*.

Standards and Sea Sparrows flashed out over the sea, their snaking gray smoke trails quickly lost and scattered in the storm, their onboard and shipboard illumination systems stuttering and frustrated by the thick rain and blowing chaff.

Ledges watched a blazing telephone pole flash across an opening over the nose of the Cub. The blood surged against his temples as he realized how close they must have been to setting off the proximity fuse in the missile. Through the same opening something sleek and terrible shot from another direction, passing below their height. From dead ahead something shot distantly past the right wing. The plane gave a burble that might have been more than the weather.

With that, he realized that *Carlotta* was the prize in an electronic duel between the chaff and the group's defensive thunderbolts. They were flying through a sea of death more devastating than the one that surged beneath them. *"Down. Now! Down—"*

Five miles away, at the outer rim of a flown circle calculated to bring him back to the unseen hostile contact below, Mudcat Walker fought the seconds. The throttle moved to afterburner. The variable-geometry wings of the F-14 swept back electronically to give the best possible configuration for the speed.

"Mud, you keep them burners on and we're going to run

dry before the next time we blink,'' said Burns, knowing the reception of the warning as he spoke it.

"Screw it."

"They'll smoke us as quick as the bogey—"

"Screw it. The chaff'll bugger them just like us. Now fiddle them knobs while I'm finding him the old-fashioned way."

Burns made sure for the thousandth time that the weapons control system's knob was in the STBY position and the liquid cooling switch was at AWG-9 and not OFF. Walker was in pulse single-target tracking. This was compatible with all weapons including the Vulcan cannon. The enormously long-ranged Phoenix could now be used in short-range mode utilizing its own onboard homing, nothing being wasteful when the mother ship was about to die.

The RIO saw that Walker, his head locked on the heads-up display in his windshield, had selected the bore-sight mode off the air combat maneuvering panel. The pilot was distrustful of the ability of his radar to function in the confused environment and wanted to waste not a microsecond in even a moderately narrow scan. His projected radar cone was now a tiny 2.3 degrees and straight along the axis of the Tom—knife-fighting mode, dependent unreasonably in these circumstances on the reflexes of a mere human being.

At least the bulk of the huge carrier was not hidden from their scopes. They hardly noticed the crushing pull of the G's as they went screaming for the ship's stern, off which the closing prey must be hidden.

On the surface, lack of coordination in the battle group had reached a peak. True to the military dictum that no fighting plan could survive the opening contact, the men trying to blind the enemy fought the men trying to destroy him. The superb sensors of the missile layers met the superb functioning of the chaff blowers head on, the situation becoming worse as the pursuer closed and the decoy blooms squeezed inward.

What visibility there was fell rapidly as the hour of the

day and the thickness of the weather caused a dense, premature dusk to fall upon the sea.

And now there was the high-speed contact curving into the fur ball that the swearing carrier controllers said was one of their own.

The ships would fire on everything.

Mudcat Walker decided to go booming in low and head on to the target. The F-14 went screaming down out of its wide turn, approaching the carrier from the bow quarter.

It was at this moment that *Carlotta*, having begun to pass the unseen carrier to the port, almost ran sidelong into the converging *Blackston*. Lydecker stood the Cub on its right wing to swing wide of the frigate's oncoming superstructure. The Standard launcher on the bow being empty and the rear-mounted Vulcan Gatling and OTO Melara dual-purpose gun being blocked off by the radar masts forward, the swinging ship could not for an instant bring her blinded weapons to bear.

Lydecker's first hint that the darkening gray cloud toward which his turn had taken him was the towering side of a huge ship came when the plates bloomed with flashing sparks.

The hailstorm of 20-millimeter from the *Blackston* was flashing past to contact the hull. The OTO Melara rapid-fired three 76-millimeter shells out of the seventy-shot circular magazine beneath its turret before the crew realized how they menaced the carrier and stemmed the barrage. The gun's depressed barrel put the proximity fuses into the wavetops, and the shells detonated before the Cub was in their killing field.

As Lydecker put *Carlotta* into a banking turn to the left that almost dug its wing into the sea, the maelstrom of fragments and flying debris off the ship buffeted the little plane. She hopped, thumped, and pinged against the stick. Pieces of plexiglass danced out of the frame and ugly holes appeared in the wing fabric. Impacts from behind told that she was hit back there, too. But she rolled out nicely, indicating that the control surfaces had remained untouched.

"Stay along the hull, kid," croaked Ledges. "You'll stay under the carrier's fire."

As they flew along toward the bow, the chief tried to figure their best maneuver to the flight deck. These thoughts were terrifyingly interrupted.

Few fighter pilots on earth could have commanded the reflexes to attempt the shot that lay before Mudcat Walker. With only the idea of placing his hurtling Tomcat outbound from the carrier's stern where his quarry must be, he had not looked to meet any target until he had passed the radar image of the carrier as it moved on his display. He had tried the gimbal-mounted infrared sensor mounted beneath his fuselage, but a HIRAM had exploded inconveniently for that. Burns worked like a concert pianist at his equipment trying to defeat the chaff, but his efforts came to nothing.

Walker's incredible eyes found the Cub.

A moving hole in the blowing weather showed him a flash of yellow just above the sea, just beginning to move off the *King*'s building-high bow. *"Got 'im—"*

In three beats of his pounding heart, his genius and his million dollars of training took over. A hairbreadth twitch of the stick jinked the big fighter to bring it down and swing its nose. By the time he swept above the Cub's wavering yellow wing, he had somehow triggered off two mighty Phoenixes and a burst of the Gatling.

For once the nervous system of a man moved more effectively than the electrons of modern war. Even the minuscule scan of the boresighted Gatling and the hair-trigger guiding system of the AIM-54s wavered behind.

The men in the ancient yellow kite got a glimpse of war that was not meant to be survived. Before they could get their mouths open to scream, a series of hurtling flashes lit up a hole in the storm. Two blazing candles, each trailing a smoking white billow, thundered down upon them. Set on impact fuses, they roared by like thirteen-foot avenging angels, their tugging sensors trying too late for the fatal maneuver. At the same instant a hundred pounds of depleted-uranium bullets from the Gatling hit the waves beneath the nose and threw up an awesome, geysering wall of seawater. The Cub shuddered and almost fell out of the sky.

One blink later, the thundering tons of Walker's Tomcat boomed by just off the wingtip, its wash rolling *Carlotta* to the limits of Lydecker's power to recover.

Ledges was aware that the Gatlings beneath the flight deck were swinging out after the fighter. More chaff clouds arrived from an inbound frigate.

They had by now flown past the carrier's bow. Lydecker started a desperate, climbing circle back toward the stern. "We're coming aboard like the big boys, Rock. Right over the ramp."

"Yeah, if we can catch this big mother." The *King* was running into the stiff wind. Between the Cub's feeble speed against the gale and the carrier's accelerating twenty knots, they would be making torturously slow progress toward their hopeless goal.

Meanwhile the frigates were pinching in from astern somewhere, and above, in the soup, the brilliant ghost flying that F-14 would be wheeling on burners to try again.

"Did you catch what that son of a bitch was, Mud?" hollered Burns into his mike.

"It's nothing but a little ol' yellow airplane, son," snarled Walker. "And he wasn't flying into the hull, because he knew that load of boom-boom he's carrying will work best right in the middle of the roof where the deck park is thickest."

"Get us around, Mud. Pour it on."

"Not this time, baby." They were in a booming six-mile turn, going almost straight up. Burns felt power coming off. He had been trying to ignore the fuel warnings. "God, I thought we had a little left."

"That's me, Bad," muttered Walker through clenched teeth as he poured on the G's. "Let's get the speed bled off and we'll dirty ourselves up. Wheels, speed brakes, flaps, spoilers, the works."

"Hey, we gotta burn down there *fast*."

"What we gotta do is not miss. He's getting us with his lard-ass slowness. No guns, no radar, no speed. I'm gonna play it his way. Just find the bird farm and call off the shooters for me. He's deader'n a buzzard's dinner."

The wind proved an invaluable ally for *Carlotta*. It swung and swept the worst of the chaff right along with the charging fleet. The *Randall* helped, too. In the unending volley of overburdened communications, she missed the signal to stop firing her radar-blinding RBOC launchers. Boring in astern of the *King*, she loosed one more obfuscating spread, including an infrared-garbling HIRAM.

The hunters would be groping in an electronic dusk as dense as the one induced by the worsening blow.

Ledges noticed that he was able to see the filthy gray sky through some of the holes in the wing fabric. A strut on the left side had been shot through, and that wing appeared to twist and flap in a new and ominous way. He wondered whether *Carlotta* was going to withstand the hard turn and climb into which Lydecker would soon jerk her.

When the stern of the carrier had glided dimly past, Lydecker allowed himself two hundred yards before turning left onto the base leg of his approach. He estimated that his laboring engine and holed wings would need that space to climb from among the waves to the ramp of the speeding carrier.

The wing warped but held. Twenty seconds later they began a climbing turn onto final.

"Pray, Rocky—"

Ledges had time to think that he wouldn't stick God with this mess. The aged engine was beginning to scream its agony. The fuel-tank bobber had just about disappeared.

Rising from the sea and laboring toward the ship, Lydecker could only think of the bane of all carrier pilots—a ramp strike. Their pieces would fall into the whipping caldron of the wake.

Radar aimers caught glimpses of them as *Carlotta* moved higher. The *Blackston* and the *Randall* again had reason to curse the rearward placement of their nonmissile batteries. They swung as slowly as all ships and their guns, still not getting their information properly—swung, nodded, and coughed rounds into the mist.

The sky had become full of iron and flame around them. A wingtip disappeared. Lydecker saw a wheel sail away and curve behind as a jackhammer stroked them from below. He could see one of the frigates, and in a moment they would be eyeballed themselves.

A 76-millimeter shell brushed close enough to the looming *King* to set off the fuse. Metallic hail hit the rear of the plane. Control of the elevators fell off sharply under Lydecker's hand.

The Vulcan-Phalanx under the carrier's stern saw them clearly at last. It jerked around and spat, its radar direction taking the fractional second to correct for the close-in target.

Suddenly the gun was gone, vanished in a fiery, sparking ball.

The flurry of Sidewinder heat-seekers launched by Mudcat Walker hadn't all been seduced away by the errant HIRAM. The white heat of the spitting Gatling had drawn one. The gun's stunned operators below the deck could only assume that the intended target had fired first. The rest of the AIM-9s blazed past *Carlotta*'s petrified crew.

Now the ceiling lifted just enough for the horrified watchers on the *King* to perceive their situation.

A tiny, wavering yellow target had lifted its nose above the flight deck. It was closing no faster than an automobile on a city street, but it was clearly headed for the angled deck. The pilot had only the smallest correction to make to put his explosive load into the plane park.

But off the starboard quarter help was charging in. A Tomcat, wings fully extended and all its slow-flight gear deployed, was coming in under full, beautiful control, this time undefeated by its blinding speed.

Walker had the Cub bore-sighted perfectly.

"So long, you ass—" Mudcat Walker was saying when

the *Randall* flashed across his head-up display, neatly obscuring his target. *"Shit!"*

He was already caressing the firing button. The electric
winder brought the Gatling to its full 3,000-round rate.

An exploding scythe moved across the frigate. The radar
masts and fire-control director above the bridge vanished in
turn. Crewmen survived only because they worked from
below.

The gun, its seven seconds of full-rate firing exhausted by
this second pass, went empty just as Walker swept over the
cleared superstructure of the frigate. And just as the ship's
leaping metallic debris was sucked into the two big square
intakes of the jet and ripped disastrously into its spinning,
white-hot blades.

It was something like being hit by flak. Mudcat Walker
felt the plane that was the beloved extension of his own
fine-tuned body buck in agony and gasp away its power.
Only his momentum was driving him now. But the straining
yellow target was in plain view just ahead and below, and he
had his ultimate weapon under his hand.

"We're flying through him, Bad," Walker hissed, skillfully
maniuplating his throttles to nurse the last pound of thrust
out of his mighty, dying TF-30s.

Ledges, as though already dead and watching from another world, saw the lethal F-14 clearly against the black
plume rising from the ravaged frigate. The fighter was now
suddenly pouring its own ugly smoke rearward.

Looking ahead, he saw *Carlotta*'s coughing engine, barely above the level of the ramp and fading downward,
struggling to close the final forty yards. To his right, the
obliterating bulk of the huge Tomcat sailed toward them
surreally, an airborne locomotive.

Mudcat Walker did not fail. His every estimation was
perfect. He simply ran out of time and space. Because his
wings were now fully extended for slow flight—their thirty-
eight-foot span having become sixty-two feet—he caught
a wingtip on the corner of the *King*'s flight deck.

Another fighter might have disintegrated, but this one was

built by the fabled "Grumman Ironworks." The wing folded backward halfway to the fuselage and threw the Tom into a pancaking spin about its own axis.

Even Mudcat Walker knew that he was not to get his kill, and that he and Burns had only until the cockpit came off upright to get out alive. "*Punch out, Bad.*" Walker hollered and jerked at the black-and-yellow ejection loop under his knees.

The F-14 was at the ragged beginning of a flip. If the charge blew them out while the top of the cockpit was facing the ship, they would be splattered over the plates.

The explosive bolts blew the canopy away. Then a rocket charge shot out Burns and—a preset instant later—Walker. Strapped into their seatpans, they narrowly missed the mushing approach of the tattered Cub as they soared into the sky.

The empty Tomcat went over onto its back, shedding the crumpled wing and bouncing across the sea before being caught and tumbled in the carrier's thrashing wake.

The drogue chutes popped and then the mains. The *Blackston* was close enough to see both descending aviators.

The sailors near the ramp at the *King*'s stern witnessed an astounding sight.

A ghost plane floated in above the deck. Its antique lines, its faded yellow skin hanging in tatters, its shattered landing gear and flapping wing hinted that it was from another world.

Carlotta mushed and floated. There were no light weapons on deck to deter her. She made no move to veer toward the millions of dollars of parked warplanes, but headed down the angled deck, wobbling, performing a comic imitation of a carrier aircraft recovery.

"*Here we go, chief.*"

Ledges felt the Cub come down tailwheel first and flop onto its belly, as what remained of the the ravaged landing gear collapsed. The wooden propeller broke itself off short after beating the deck. The arresting cable that had been ready to meet the hurtling tons of Walker's Tomcat rushed up and intercepted the skidding *Carlotta* like a steel bar. The little bird slammed to a stop against it with such force that its riddled fuselage cracked in two right behind Lydecker, joined quickly by the drooping wing.

The chief punched the side flap down. "Let's get the hell out of here and get our hands up."

They rolled quickly out onto the deck, aware that they were the target of a running, converging mob.

Ledges was very glad to see that Wade McGregor would be the first to reach them.

The Disbursing Division office was packed, by the seven men crammed into it.

Admiral Irons, Captain Ash, and the ship's quiet executive officer, Commander Ruhlbach, were grouped about a metal desk. Working at the desk was the overweight head of the Engineering Department, Commander Ramsay.

McGregor was seated between Ledges and Lydecker on the deck along a bulkhead. Although he had experienced none of the horrendous hours shared by his friends, he looked every bit as spent and damaged as they did. He whispered beneath the striving voices of the other officers, "It's looking like you might just as well have kept going."

Lydecker shook his head wearily. "We couldn't do that, no matter what, Wade. It got too ugly."

"Yeah," breathed Ledges, "we had to do some things back there. . . ." He dropped his head down onto his huge forearms, either asleep or listening to the urgent exchange above him.

"I can't *believe* there's no way to get into that vault inside an hour," snapped the unbelieving admiral.

Irons had lost almost an hour in deciding his reaction to the story brought by the yellow calamity that had fallen upon him out of the sky.

This was not unlike the West German youth's penetration to Red Square in a light Cessna, passing through hundreds of miles of the world's most sophisticated air defenses. But the Soviets didn't have a forty-million-dollar fighter plane in the water and a frigate whittled down to look like a flattop. That the fleet had experienced no human casualties other than some splinter cuts was God's own mercy.

"It's eighteen inches of chrome steel, sir," said Ramsay. "We can't punch into there nearly fast enough."

The bristly Irons was too good a flag officer and too good a man to put any thought of his professional salvation before that of his fleet or its assignment in the battle being played out ashore. So he kept the most careful inner eye upon himself as he considered what an enormous amelioration of his plight it could be if the thing inside that vault was there as these thieves and deserters said, and he could dispose of it crisply.

"You don't mean to say, Commander Ramsay, that we can only wait here until 2100 hours to find out whether we have a national embarrassment or a national disaster?"

Ramsay had managed to find a blueprint of the vault in his voluminous archives covering every nut and bolt on the ship. He studied the specifications and shook his head. "Even ashore, where we could get special burning rods, it would go two or three hours. Aboard, it would be more like ten."

Ledges wondered how much deeper into the nightmare they could sink. Every moment brought new calamities, and the faces of the men they had killed grew ever more distinct.

In the frantic explanations of the returnees, the theft had been the easiest to verify. The fresh currency that Lydecker had brought along, the validation by McGregor, and some cross-examination of the bewildered Bluehoffer had sufficed in that matter. Ash would have had the plotters in restraints already if it hadn't been for the investigation into the more pressing matter.

The hot argument among the *King*'s highest officers was whether this was a benighted attempt to distract from a failed theft or some desperate scheme to draw the ship off its station.

If the battle group steamed to open water at best speed to spare civilian populations, dispersing its escorts and possibly even beginning an abandonment of the ship, the Soviets would have accomplished what they couldn't have attempted with squadrons of warplanes. Albania would lie open to them.

The most terrible specter—the equivalent of atomic annihilation—did not have to be mentioned: What if they fled, deserted their station, failed their mission, and then opened the vault to find . . . *nothing*.

Irons had quickly made his major decisions.

He would resist the temptation to share the crisis with Washington. That included laying it off on Geinz, as much as he trusted and respected the man. Such notification would have the effect of destroying the head of the Joint Chiefs if all went wrong, and of inviting total paralysis of decision making when everybody inside the Beltway tried to get into the action long distance. The admiral knew it was he alone who could guarantee the presence of a ready *King* in the Albanian support mission. All would be subordinate to that.

So the *King* would move perhaps ten miles farther to sea in her figure-eight steaming, but she would remain effectively on Thunder Station.

He would loosen the patrol area of the escort, but keep it close enough to continue its screening role, however tarnished that now seemed. Even the damaged *Randall* would remain, her radar and sonar image on enemy equipment potentially important to the diversion of incoming ordnance.

There remained only the question of the impenetrable vault and the ticking nuclear weapon it might hold. And the hour and eight minutes remaining until 2100 hours, when they would know for certain.

Ruhlbach, the XO, asked, "Should we ready for a nuclear event, sir?" The question was not quite out of his mouth before he realized how silly it had been.

Irons answered anyway. "If that thing pops, it won't make any difference if we've got the ship sealed or the prewetters going. We're cinders. We can at least continue to function as an air weapon until . . . whatever it is.''

Ledges struggled to his feet. He had hidden the extent of the wounds beneath his shirt, but now there was blood dripping from his palm. Irons spotted it.

''Get a master-at-arms in from the passageway and have him take this man for medical attention.''

''I'm okay, sir,'' the chief rasped. A fever had started to dance in his eyes. ''I think I know a way to break into that tin box real fast.''

''Then share it real fast.''

''Remember we had those Army pilots and technicians aboard while we were doing the Norwegian exercises? Part of Admiral Geinz's interservice coordinating. They were showing our chopper pilots how they could rig those TOW antitank missiles onto their birds and use them to kill armored assault boats.''

''It was a botch. A shambles,'' recalled Captain Ash.

''Yes, sir,'' said Ledges. ''But we still have a load of TOWs in the magazines, I believe. And the way I heard it from the Army, they can penetrate any armor known, including the front plates of the new Soviet tanks.''

The admiral drummed his fingers on the vault's blueprint and then turned to Ash. ''Get me the head of the Weapons Department here right away.''

That was a squat, conscientious mustang named Jolling. Ordnance was his religion. He made it his business to know the working and capabilities of every firecracker on the ship. That included the TOW, until this deployment a stranger to his magazines.

Jolling did not say a word until he had heard the entire problem and Ledges's proposal all the way through. Then he spoke briskly.

''Admiral, the chief has a helluva notion there. But when a weapon is used in a nonstandard way with no time to do the charts and calculations, you've got to make a lot of educated guesses. I would like to present mine.''

''Shoot, Commander.''

"To the question of whether the TOW can punch through that much special steel, I estimate yes. There's an eight-pound shaped-charge warhead that can melt and penetrate a two-foot hole in the front of a Red Army T-62. And they have the best armor there is."

"Tell me all the problems."

"Well, the speed of these missiles is a component of their penetrating power. That's about three hundred seventy miles an hour for a TOW. So we can expect less than optimum performance in this space from what is essentially a standing start."

"Hold it, Jolling," said Ash. "What do you mean 'essentially'? You're not thinking of *firing* that thing at the vault door down here, are you? Surely you should be using just the shaped charge, to get away from all that fuel going off."

"I can't, Captain," Jolling said. "We don't have time to begin any complicated planning and tinkering. And if we did we'd be liable to screw up the punching power. I'd say let's clear the space we need and adapt the firing rig right out of the chopper installation. Hell, sir, I don't even know if we have time to do *that*."

The admiral leaped back in. "Commander, the captain is thinking of what happens when you set off all that rocket fuel in this little area and add the warhead's blast to it."

Ash nodded emphatically. "In the Falklands the Exocet's fuel did almost as much to destroy the British ships as the explosives. It would be something like taking a direct missile hit."

"I haven't forgotten the point, sir," replied Jolling. "The TOW is a midget compared to an Exocet—under four feet long. But it does have two rocket motors packed with Hercules K-41—that's a solid propellant that whips out an awful lot of energy. The first motor just gets it out of the tube and puts it out front to get the crew away from the heat of the second burn. We're going to have to deal with that heat without any help from the open sky."

"But we have some advantages," said Ramsay.

"I'm dying to know them," said the white-faced captain.

"The shaped charge means all that force will be projected at the vault. It shouldn't do much ancillary damage other than buckled decks and bulkheads. Here on the two level we've got the splinter deck over our heads to keep anything from burning through or blowing out onto the roof. We can get rid of all the ignitable equipment. We're all steel down here—none of the light metals that ended up burning on the British."

Irons nodded. "And we've got the best fire-fighting teams and equipment in the world. We can have them ready by the time you're ready to blow in. But first the big question. Will the heat or the shock of what you're going to squirt into that vault set the thing off itself?"

The slowing of Jolling's response showed he had become less certain. "Beyond the fact that we have no other choice, sir, I'm depending on something."

"Other than prayer, I hope."

"I'm betting that whoever put that trigger together was the best man that they had. And that he's protected the detonating explosives as well as he has the device itself. Even plastic explosives are only stable to something above four hundred degrees. It'll be a lot hotter than that in there. But if I was putting a special nuclear device together, I'd make damn sure it could live through the equivalent of a plane crash."

The admiral's fingers drummed steadily on the blueprint. Then he turned to the captain. "Right, then. We'll put all our chips on their triggerman. Gentlemen, get it done." He tapped his watch. "In fifty-seven minutes."

The high officers surged out the door, leaving the plotters sitting where they were. It took them awhile to realize that those waiting outside had followed Irons's group and that the felons had been forgotten for the moment.

"Let's go be useful," McGregor said. "It might be the last exercise we get this side of the rock pile."

With its ocean of jet fuel and truckloads of high-performance ordnance, an aircraft carrier is a thousand foot firebomb.

Commander Ramsay deployed his fire fighters and their equipment as carefully as an island commandant preparing against an invasion. He had the important advantage of knowing where his fiery enemy would strike, but a vigorous enough attack could overwhelm any defenses.

The first line of resistance against fire on a warship is the attempt to deprive the flames of oxygen and solid fuel. But in this case he also had to make sure that the weapon could breathe well enough to do its job.

With the Disbursing Division office on the ship's centerline and directly below the flight deck, Ramsay was reasonably sure that the rocket burn that was his chief worry would not create pressures sufficient to blow through into the open air. The bulk of the ship horizontally and downward and the bomb-resistant splinter deck above should see to that. But the complications of naval architecture made him uneasy.

He expected that the fuel burns of the missile's two solid-fueled motors would melt through whatever was behind it for the space of several compartments. He had no wish to baffle this backward blast with sheets of steel because he preferred to deal with damages in a predictable direction. What worried him most was the maze of ventilators, pipes, and electrical conduits that ran through the ship in almost unknowable profusion. Although the procedures for closure included securing the ventilators, heat and flame under pressure were infallible at finding escape. Ramsay had heard about ships where supposedly flameproof bundles of wires had served as reluctant fuses into fuel lines far removed from the blaze.

All he could do was get ever deeper into his blueprints, marking any vulnerable points with a red pen until the paper seemed to be running blood.

Then he set his troops and weapons—fire boundaries, nozzle men, hose men, plug men, access men, foam supply men, CO_2 supply men, electrical-kit men, and closure details. The firemain system was checked and rechecked.

Proximity suits would be issued to special volunteers. If anybody was alive after the TOW did successful work, these men were to squirm into whatever opening there was and confront the inferno of the vault. Then the real job would begin.

Their familiarity with the vault and its area made it possible for Ledges and Lydecker to plead their way into the proximity suits for the entry. Each had been previously trained on a fire-fighting team, and they were easy in the equipment—a one-piece coverall of glass fiber and asbestos, the surface aluminized. They waited at the expected boundaries of the blast, already encased in hoods, boots, and gloves. They had begun breathing with the A-4 apparatus—a chemical-charged breather.

Lydecker fidgeted. "Suppose the hole isn't big enough to get into? Suppose all that chalk talk about how to get the door opened from the inside gets aced out by the damage? Suppose—"

"Suppose we get all those kilotons in the face and get to have lunch with Marilyn Monroe?" said Ledges. "Hey, they're counting."

Ramsay, at a safe distance, prepared to detonate the armor-piercing missile using an adaptation of the same controls that would have launched it in the field.

Ledges and Lydecker tensed. A giant swung a sledgehammer. The deck seemed to jump away as the bulkhead before them bulged outward and blackened, shooting paint like needles. They feared that their hearing would not return.

Even in their suits they felt the crush of heat around them. The blackening raced everywhere along the metal. An overlooked aerosol can exploded in flame.

Then the hose and nozzle men, also dressed against the fire, surged in behind them. Access men pried open a door, jumping aside as the water shot inside from expertly handled all-purpose nozzles set on high-velocity fog. While there might be fire, priority was given to cooling the area for entry.

Ledges and Lydecker did not enter the hose stream. Wet

suits made for unwanted weight and held the danger of scalding when the water could no longer be applied. They took up powerful hand lamps.

"*Going in,*" one of the hooded nozzle men shouted through his mask after a while.

The two ducked through the buckled door behind the others and found vision reduced to inches by smoke. They went forward by feel and familiarity, hearing shouts through the bulkheads around them and the sound of high-pressure water hitting steel.

They groped on until they found what had been the bulkhead fronting the Disbursing Division office. It sent up clouds of steam as the water hit it, changing the world in front of the faceplates from black to gray. The steel beneath their feet had the contours of a plastic knife dropped onto a barbecue grill.

"Move slow," the leader of the hose team said. "We've got a lot of cooling to do."

The steam intensified for a time and then seemed to clear a bit along with much of the smoke.

The hole became visible. It was pouring thick billows outward. The edges glowed until the hoses hit them.

Ledges's mask misted over as some backspray hit it. "Is it through? Can we get in?"

The answer didn't come as quickly as he would have liked. "We blew through it. I got my arm inside to the shoulder. It's not all that big, though. You can forget it, Chief. The other guy . . . I dunno—"

The chief edged close and estimated the penetration. It was at hip height at a precise spot where Ramsay estimated it would not interfere with drawing the locking pins from inside. The hole would never accommodate his massive shoulders. "Hink, my friend, here's where you grow up. I think you've got the only boyish figure here that can have any chance of getting in with this crap on. Thank God we're dealing with canisters and not air bottles."

"Jeez, Rock, I was kinda depending—"

"Good luck, pal." Ledges gave him an awkward one-armed hug and guided him toward the hole. "We'll try to feed you in there like a torpedo into a tube."

"Thanks for not saying like a hot dog into a microwave. How're we fixed for time?"

"You've got eighteen minutes."

On the bridge, Admiral Irons received Commander Ramsay's progress report.

He looked anxiously over the port quarter. Directly in line behind the Tomcat sitting in the number-four catapult in the Alert Five sat a Sea King. The helicopter was positioned there because it was only steps from the giant elevator that they hoped would soon bring the ugly package from below.

"I waited too goddamn long," Irons said to Ash. "If that thing is really in there and timed as they say, I'd want to chopper it four hundred miles south before it blew. Now we're going to be lucky to get ten minutes flying—maybe thirty miles."

"One thing is certain, sir," said Ash. "We sure as hell don't want it going off in the air. Maybe we should just get it into the sea and steam off at flank speed. We could get clear—just. Even though we're so close to shore, we can bet that the depth will smother the worst. The wind is pretty much south now. The contamination will be heading out to open water."

"We'll see how much time the guys below can give us. If any, Arlen. If any."

The Trawler *Vinza*, the Adriatic—July 7

Captain Lieutenant Tiomkin, out in the storm and the darkness descending upon the AGI trawler *Vinza*, had all sorts of problems. His lookouts had made contact with a light airplane flying into the heart of the *King*'s battle group. After that, his radar had identified nothing but confusion.

The escorting frigates had reacted to an all-out attack. Missiles of every sort had been launched, some of them flying in directions that made him believe he might be under direct attack himself. He had hastily given orders to drop his ship back and eliminate the chance of mistakes.

The captain lieutenant's radar had been further baffled by a man-made storm of chaff fired by all the warships. There had been runs on what must have been the light plane by a high-performance fighter identified as coming down from the *King*'s combat air patrol. But when the chaff had cleared, both the fighter and its target had vanished.

His frantic attempts at communication with his own people had produced no verification of an unannounced attack on the Americans or any change in his orders.

Those orders had been quite simple. He was to stay at a discreet distance and keep his cameras clicking on the *King* at 2100 hours. There was no hint why, only an indication that it was important.

Of course, those instructions had been given before the extent of the weather problems were known.

He was a man who understood the importance of carrying out commands. Tiomkin gave the engine orders that would bring the *Vinza* close enough to have the *King* in camera surveillance.

U.S.S. *Ernest J. King*, the Adriatic—July 7

Tree was glad of the cold rain lashing the flight deck. It revived his spirit from where it had sunk in the time he had spent in the dark, stifling void compartment trying to bind his wounds. Also it gave him cover. A blowing downpour separated people into their own compartments of discomfort. And it permitted the voluminous rain gear that concealed rank, purpose, and identity. In his case, it also permitted the hiding of a significant weapon.

He had the M-16 slipped down inside a pants leg, held in place by a hand at his side.

The other hand manipulated the controls of the electric tractor. He knew just enough of deck routines to move the squat, yellow machine about the vast deck area with enough apparent purpose to keep from being challenged. Not that there was anybody keeping an eye on things like wandering deck tractors. The word that something big was going on in the Disbursing Division office was all over the passageways below as he had made his way above.

It hadn't taken him long to deduce what it was about, and why the Sea King was waiting near that elevator.

Faking his work carefully among the parked aircraft, he made his way slowly astern. The pain and bleeding of his wound had begun to lighten his head beyond the effect of the drugs he had absorbed. But he imagined he had enough left to make him sufficiently effective over the next several minutes. After that it wouldn't matter.

The electrical-kit team reenergized the ventilator to the vault whose distant fan had survived the holocaust inside. By the time Ledges had fed Lydecker—with hideous difficulty—into the vault feet first, the worst of the smoke had been sucked away.

Lydecker turned the light on inside and found what remained of the crate.

All else in the blackened, steaming space had been incinerated and melted. The wooden outer shell no longer existed except for fragments of wood still glowing beneath the thick metal casing that it had hidden.

"It's here and it's in one piece," Lydecker shouted.

"Get that door open fast or it's not going to make any difference."

Working from the vault blueprints, Ramsay had placed the missile in a position meant to breach the wall area of the vault, leaving the lock mechanisms as intact as possible. The last thing on earth he had wanted was to weld shut the six locking pins that radiated from the round door. Like many vault locks, this one could be opened with the spin of an unlocking wheel from inside.

"You see the wheel, Hink?" Ledges shouted inside.

"Hold it . . . I'm looking. . . . Jeez, Rock. It's gone. There's some metal goo run down the side. Melted, I guess."

"Is there anything at all left? A stump from the shaft?"

"Lemme see. . . . Well, there's some kind of blob."

"Does it look like it's fused to the door?"

"Can't tell."

"You think you could get some kind of big pipe wrench on it? To get it turning and draw back the locking pins."

"Can't tell that either."

"All we can do is try." The chief bawled for a selection of wrenches, and they quickly arrived at his feet with a clatter. He selected the biggest one and passed it inside. "Here's number one. Hurry up."

Lydecker had souped up enough automobiles to have a good feel for tools and metal. The melted wheel had run down to make a rough lump around the shaft. He guessed that the shaft had been made of the much harder steel used in the locking mechanisms. He thought he could find a grip, but the massive serrations of the jaws of the first wrench could not maintain a purchase. "Send in a size smaller, Rock."

The second wrench came in. He screwed down the jaws on the lumpy shaft and tugged down, first gently, then harder. The grip held. "Got it. Going for the turn."

Lydecker set his slender frame and bore downward on the wrench. Nothing turned. "It's frozen."

Ledges cursed. "Can you shift it so you can lie on the deck and push up—like a bench press?"

"Nope. It's too high off the floor."

The chief shouted to men behind him. "Get him a pipe to slip over the handle of that wrench. He needs more leverage."

Two agonizing minutes later the pipe went in through the opening. Lydecker slipped it over the handle of the huge wrench and bore down on the extension. "Still no dice. What now, Chief?"

330 • Donald N. Norman

"Nobody else as slim as you to get in there to help, kid. Hey, can I get an arm on that extension to bear down with you?"

"It's in the right spot, but I don't know how much of you can get in through that hole. You've got me by a hundred pounds."

"Going for it, Hink. Give it all you've got when I do."

Ledges gulped a deep breath and tore off his breather. He quickly thrust an arm into the opening and as much of his shoulder and head as he could. He felt Lydecker place his hand on the pipe at the right spot. Before he would be forced to take a breath of still-fouled air, he braced against the top of the opening and pressed downward with all his strength. He heard Lydecker grunting as the boy did the same.

Something moved downward. Just the wrench handle bending or beginning to break? No. The movement was steady.

"*It's turning, Rock.* Lemme reset the wrench." He nudged the chief's hand away and took a new bite with the wrench jaws, bringing the handle high again. "Go again."

Ledges set his hand again and shoved down mightily, beginning to want air desperately.

The handle moved.

"I got it now, Chief. Back off and get that forklift ready for the package if this son of a bitch opens."

Lydecker grunted heavily, resetting the wrench twice more. The locking shaft had been bent enough in the blast to make the going rough.

At last the wrench met solid resistance. Either the pins were drawn back completely, or the damaged mechanism was simply frozen with the locking steel only partially removed.

"That's all I can get," said Lydecker in a voice weaker than he had meant. "Open that latch and yank."

The outside latch was a turning handle set flush with the vault door. He had noticed that it had survived the inferno.

THUNDER STATION • 331

"We're on it, Hink." Some moments passed. "Something's still frozen. Maybe we can get something to pry—"

Lydecker frantically, hopelessly threw his shoulder against the hundreds of pounds of hardened steel, and he was rewarded only with agony.

On his third frantic, painful thump the door lurched, then swung slowly outward on its own weight. His light met those of the men standing outside in the smoke.

Before the insane cheering had died, the men were crowding inside to get at the encased horror.

Ledges kissed Lydecker on his faceplate before he slipped back into his breather.

They had fourteen minutes left to get the inaudibly ticking shell off the *King*.

The pilot and RIO of the Alert Five Tomcat on catapult four leaned out of their bubble to watch the drama unfolding behind their plane. The huge plane elevator that had dipped down below the flight deck to the hangar-bay level was again rising, and now it bore a mob of blackened men in fire-fighting suits. They surrounded a forklift bearing a scorched metal box.

The Sea King helicopter that had begun to wind up just behind the elevator minutes ago tilted free of the deck and rose a short distance into the air. A heavy cargo sling trailed beneath it, spread on the deck for rapid delivery of its expected load.

The F-14 crew was so riveted that they never noticed the yellow tractor gliding silently around the nose on the ocean side of the plane until the man at the controls spoke to them. "I want you to climb down out of that cockpit as fast as you can. Throw down the guns first. Stay away from the mikes. Be quiet. I'm not fooling."

The driver the flabbergasted flyers looked at was grotesquely ugly beneath his soaking rain gear. His disarranged eyes stared wildly, and he appeared to waver slightly in his perch. But the M-16 he leveled up at them was held without a tremor.

"Do it, Eddie," the pilot whispered breathlessly to the hesitating RIO. The man below was wound to an insane pitch.

They pitched their .38s onto the deck before they went frantically about undoing the tangle of safety harnesses, leg restraints, lip microphones, and hoses from G-suits and oxygen. They scrambled down the ladder and ran off toward the island in response to a menacing wave of the M-16's barrel.

Of the men waiting for the elevator to fully rise, only Wade McGregor took his eyes off the terrible box long enough to see Tree coasting toward them from the other side of the lift. He was making no attempt to hide the M-16, and McGregor saw his intention instantly.

The warning he shouted was torn away in the uproar of shouted orders and the thunder of the hovering Sea King. He couldn't get to Ledges or Lydecker on the ascending elevator.

If he was to be of any help, it wouldn't be from here. He raced to the closest edge of the flight deck and rolled over to drop down into the gallery beneath.

Above, the elevator bumped to a stop and the man on the forklift bearing the box maneuvered to run his cargo to the helicopter sling.

Racing forward on the tractor, Tree swept the M-16 in a low arc, shooting for the legs of the crowding crewmen.

What men weren't cut down saw what was happening and flung themselves flat against the deck. The man on the forklift caught a bullet squarely in the side of the pelvis, and it knocked him out of the seat. The forklift glided to a quick stop as his foot came off the accelerator.

Ledges felt his right thigh break. Lydecker, trying to support him in his fall, was borne to the deck and pinned by the huge chief.

They watched Tree load another magazine and glide the tractor through the sprawling men. There was not so much as a slingshot in the hands of anyone in a position to stop him.

He glided alongside the forklift and switched vehicles. Waving the gun to intimidate, he moved quickly out of the circle of bleeding and cowed crewmen.

The tech rep didn't go far. He guided the forklift to the only shelter available to him—beneath the vacated Tomcat. Its bulk and armor would protect him from any Marine marksmen firing from above on the island.

He ran the forklift under the fuselage until it ran a wheel into the catapult slot and stuck itself. The box almost slid half off the toe plate. Tree didn't care. He was right where he wanted to be. He dismounted and crouched behind the heavy metal of the tilting vehicle, the M-16 laid out over the top with two extra clips, ready if they rushed him.

It was a position he couldn't hold indefinitely. But then he only had to defend his package for another seven minutes.

He wondered if there would ever be a patriotic Soviet father naming his son Theron.

McGregor eased himself up a ladder from the gallery. By poking up his head, he had a distant but perfect view of Tree. His invulnerability beneath the empty Tomcat was painfully clear.

In the startling mental processes of such desperate moments, McGregor found himself marveling that all the mighty firepower of the astonishing multimillion-dollar warplane standing above Tree was of absolutely no value against the deadly enemy standing just inches away. A club in the hand of a determined caveman would have been more useful.

And just like that, he saw the one chance. "A phone! Find me a goddamn phone—now, now, now—" McGregor half climbed, half fell down the ladder, howling so loud he could be heard on the flight deck.

"Lemme go, Rock, damn it," yelled Lydecker, struggling in the crushing arms of the big chief pinning him to the deck. "What the hell is the difference if we get it five minutes sooner." He raised his voice over the roar of the Sea King still hovering helplessly. "Everybody who can run! Anybody who can limp! Move on your bellies and spread yourselves out. Then wait for my go. And we rush the bastard.''

"Hold it," said Ledges, not loosening his grip on the boy. "Suppose the fire killed the thing."

"Suppose it didn't, and we're lying here on our asses when the thing goes up. C'mon, Rock, you're not my father—leggo!"

Ledges finally turned him loose. "I think I can hop at least."

Lydecker raised his voice to the men huddled against the deck. "Start moving. Slow at first. Don't let 'im see what we're getting ready for."

The men who had not been hit moved apart cautiously. Another precious minute ticked by.

Finally they were as ready as they were ever going to be.

"Everybody set?" Lydecker called, hoping the chopper would continue to drown him out to Tree.

A nervous but determined ripple of assent came from the extended ring of sailors.

"*Now!*"

Ledges, Lydecker, and a dozen men sprang or staggered to their feet and hurled themselves forward at the tech rep's impregnable position.

Tree, the last of his cocaine rushing sweetly through his veins, moved coolly. To give himself his best shot at the unarmed rushers, he stood up and propped a knee on the seat of the forklift. On his knee he placed a steadying elbow and sighted carefully, readying a burst from left to right across the running, limping line. He let his breath out carefully and began to stroke down on the trigger.

The steel beneath his feet thrummed and slammed, blasting up blinding white billows.

McGregor's call had reached the launch officer.

Below, the tons of steam in the twin pistons of the C-13 catapult mounted in the number-four slot fired its trolley toward the bow, whipping the shuttle with it. Fixed to that shuttle by its launch bar was twenty-eight tons of Grumman Tomcat.

The bottom edge of a huge engine intake caught Tree somewhere below the shoulders. The top of him disappeared into that intake before the blood could fly. The rest bounced fifty feet along the deck, briefly pacing the accelerating F-14.

Unpowered and unmanned, the outflung Tomcat hit the end of the catapult shuttle travel without enough power to cleanly break the hold-back bolt. The fighter, brought up short, flipped onto its back with an earsplitting crash.

The sturdy package of the bomb had been spilled onto the deck as the driven fighter brushed aside the tractor.

"No time for the chopper," shouted the running McGregor. *"Get it over the side."*

Everyone who could hobble struggled toward the annihilator. In breathless, incredibly silent urgency they carried, slid, tumbled, and otherwise bore the box toward the edge of the elevator, where no galleries beneath would impede a clear fall to the sea.

Ledges found that he dared not look at his watch.

To Lydecker, the final five yards appeared to marshal all of nature's forces against the sailors. Gravity was doubled, every raindrop weighed ten pounds, and every gust was a typhoon. Their muscles seemed to turn to slush inside their limbs.

When the box went over the edge, McGregor thought for a moment that it would hang there in the air eternally. Its fall was to him the slow downward wafting of an autumn leaf. The splash by which it entered the sea opened as gradually as a flower on a summer morning.

Irons and Ash watched it all from a bridge wing. They had given all the orders they could. The ship, already making all the speed available out of its struggling power plant, was putting all the distance it could between itself and what was sinking to the bottom of the Adriatic.

Below, the *King* was being rapidly transformed into a gas-tight envelope, and its crew was being ordered down inside it. Even now the hovering Sea King came down to perch and its crew boiled out, joining the men in the disposal crew in running for cover.

Damage-control parties were preparing for a sort of damage no manned ship had ever had to encounter before.

"Think she'll blow, Admiral?" asked Ash.

"No . . . the heat . . . . the shock . . . the water. It can't. It just can't."

"Think we'd better get off inside?"

"Yeah, maybe we'd better, Captain. Hey, what's that?"

A dim, low shape had become visible perhaps a half mile astern.

"That's the AGI. Radar's been tracking him in. He wants a better look."

"Uh, oh. Let's move."

The Trawler VINZA, the Adriatic—July 7

The forward deck, pilothouse roof, and bridge wings of the *Vinza* held tripods bearing sophisticated long-lensed cameras.

Captain Lieutenant Tiomkin's worries about the visibility conditions were somewhat alleviated by the diversity of the imaging equipment. The stills, the motion picture film, the videotape—some of it would be successful in recording whatever it was that his leaders wanted to capture.

He had given the orders to start all cameras operating at 2059 hours. You never knew when some little hitch was going to upset the timing and cause you to miss what you were charged to get.

The *King* was now making almost twenty-three knots, obviously pushing what was left of her engines to uncomfortable limits. An unaccustomed smile brushed Tiomkin's lips as he wondered whether they were fleeing his little bathtub of a ship.

"Bring her up a little closer," he ordered from the lofty

perch of his swiveling command chair alongside the helmsman. He watched the engine revolutions come up.

Beneath the sea, in the minutes following going overboard,
the box had drifted rapidly downward. As the *King* had
moved away from the descending shell, the trailing *Vinza* had
moved up, over, and then past it. In the final minute of its
life, the little trawler would seem to have moved a sufficient
way past the nemesis lying 320 feet below on the seabed. But
when Major Leshko's flawless trigger tripped itself, there was
a deadly fact of physics involved.

The fatal grapefruit of uranium releasing its energy in a
microsecond brought incredible overpressure into the rapidly
expanding bubble of superheated gas formed by the fission.
In open air that overpressure, in a relatively low-yield
weapon such as this one, would have peaked and dissipated
itself rapidly, losing force quickly over distance. Confined
by the sea, the peak value of the gigantic shock wave
maintained itself long beyond an event in the sky. Worse
than that, the wave reflected itself off the bottom, so the
crushing slam was not to be in any way glancing or lessened
by a lucky angling of the ship's hull.

The nuclear fist rebounding from the seabed headed for
the broad bottom of the *Vinza* at an angle as perpendicular
as that of a sledgehammer headed for the head of a nail.

As a last consolation, many dying men are privileged to
experience unimaginable glories of sight and sensation.
Captain Lieutenant Tiomkin was one of these.

Seated in his command chair as he was, the *Vinza*'s
captain did not have his hip joints broken by the deck
slamming upward from beneath him as many of those
standing did. He survived upright to see and feel his ship
punched high into the air on the back of a blue-black bubble
the size of a small island. When that bubble blew out, it was
replaced by a thrashing white world of foam that rose about
the ship and gradually tilted its bow to the sky.

For one terrifying, exhilarating moment Tiomkin was

looking out the pilothouse windows into the black and stormy sky above, a beautiful tunnel of dazzling white water and steam framing it all.

He had only time to experience all the tons of the split-open *Vinza* hanging weightless at the apex of her fatal flight before the arriving heat, pressure, and shock killed him painlessly.

U.S.S. *Ernest J. King*, the Adriatic—July 7

At a porthole off the *King*'s stern gallery, Ledges, Lydecker, and McGregor reeled against the shock and brain-melting roar. They watched an upwardly vomiting quarter mile of sea become billowing steam whose climb to the heavens was obliterated by the weather and encroaching night.

What might have been a flash of the *Vinza* vanished in the tumble of an outflowing twenty-five foot wave that rushed toward the carrier.

"Poor sons of bitches," Ledges said shakily.

The jolt that they had felt through all the vast mass of the *King* told them there would be dished and ruptured plates, and maybe even some broken frames. But she would easily survive on station.

"Hang on," said McGregor. "Here comes the wave."

It seemed to represent what was bearing down on the rest of their lives. They tightened their handholds as it broke thunderously against the stern.

The truth of events over the following three days would only be dimly known to the future.

What was recorded was for the most part managed from above. What was not recorded was, of course, more interesting.

Tirana, Albania—July 8

With the tail of the lingering storm still clouding the morning light, Ali Mahmoud and Colonel Bartsev looked upward from the last strong point in the police barracks and listened to the beating rotors of a large, powerful helicopter that they could not see.

The fact that the besiegers' firing had stopped told them that the invisible machine was not there to help them. Their few shoulder-fired SAMs had long since been expended. The two dozen surviving defenders had perhaps a day's ammunition left.

The ceiling had lifted a bit. Soon they saw a great, dark shape floating down from above them. It hung from two rectangular parachutes.

"What the devil is that?" asked Mahmoud.

The knowledgeable colonel had been a young advisor in Vietnam and knew it right away. "It's what the Americans called a daisy cutter. Not designed as a bomb, actually. Supposed to clear a wide landing zone for helicopters in thick jungle or dense urban areas. But those ten thousand pounds of explosives became useful against hardened positions."

Mahmoud fired an AK-47 upward hopelessly until it clicked empty. "So they asked the Americans for a hand, after all."

"Because we were embarrassing them holding out this long. And because the Americans knew there would be no air action to help us. In this soup nobody will ever know who did it."

Bartsev took up a hand radio and barked out some call signs. There had been no answer for hours, but they knew they were being monitored. "Care to join me in a good-bye to our leaders, Mahmoud?"

The Albanian grinned mirthlessly and leaned close to the mouthpiece with the colonel. "For that chance I'll give you my million Japanese yen."

They were screaming unspeakable obscenities into the phone when the daisy cutter went off and flattened everything inside their strong point into bloody dust.

Tyuratam, U.S.S.R—July 8

Major Leshko was passing the time at a work table in his trigger room. He had no illusions that he would finish. When he had heard about the failure of his handiwork, he knew that he and his staff could not be left around as a potential future embarrassment. There would have to be assurances to an entire world that the malefactors had been dealt with. Well, he thought, he had always been most comfortable underground.

He had ignored the phone as it rang several times during the morning. He preferred to have them come to him.

When they did, he was glad to see that Zyshnikov had arrived to oversee things personally.

"I'm sorry, Major Leshko. There's going to be an investigation. We're going to need you."

Leshko noticed that the holster flaps of the two officers who accompanied Zyshnikov were unbuttoned. "For how long will you need me?" he teased.

"Less than twenty minutes, I imagine." The KGB man saw he did not need to be devious. "It will be fast, I promise."

"All right then." Leshko stood up and pointed to the corner of the table nearest the intruders. A badly soiled tablecloth had been thrown over something shapeless. "But will you please tell the others down here that they are under no circumstances to touch that material without full contamination protection. And certainly not until they've reconnected the radiation alarms."

Zyshnikov's eyes flashed up along the raceway that ran

where the roof met the wall. A section had been taken out. The multicolored wires had been cut and stood splayed out.

One of the officers lifted the sheet aside. On the table stood several metal containers, square and gleaming. They were grossly thick in comparison to the tiny cylindrical openings drilled into them. Alongside the containers sat what were obviously the screw tops meant to seal them.

"You can see what I mean," Leshko said with some degree of satisfaction. "There's enough plutonium exposed there to give a lethal jolt to anybody who so much as walks into this room."

Zyshnikov, looking at Leshko's smile, imagined that he could already feel the tiny nuclear knives beginning to dissect the contents of his cells.

Moscow, U.S.S.R.—July 9

There is something about a prison that instantly diminishes even the mightiest man. Gavenko, Lubachevsky, and Sarkissian, seated about a bare table in a bare room with a single high window, looked shabby, smaller, weaker to one another.

"A good gamble," Gavenko said. "The odds were more than reasonable."

"Yes," said Lubachevsky. "We agreed on that, however it turned out."

"I'm worried about my family. Do you think they'll make them pay for me?"

"Comrade Lurakin isn't that type of man. He's building a new Soviet Union. Remember?"

"I suppose there's no doubt it will be execution."

"None whatever," Sarkissian said. He mocked the tones of an official spokesman: "Those who attempted to exploit the death of the General Secretary and plunge the nation into military adventures must be dealt with in the harshest way.''

''What about the fabled kindness of our next General Secretary?''

''He in fact would spare everyone,'' ventured Sarkissian. ''But the military has so much to hide and so little to hide behind, they insist somebody pay their bills for them.''

Gavenko could only shake his head sadly. ''The end of a great nation, comrades. When that thing went off so uselessly and all the political howling began all around the Mediterranean, nuclear weapons in Europe began to die. As dead as our seaport and our national destiny.''

''Yes, you'd think that the fallout from that little burp of a shell had poisoned every baby in Italy and Yugoslavia instead of blowing out to sea,'' said Sarkissian. ''They didn't monitor over two hundred rads anywhere important.''

Lubachevsky rubbed his unshaven cheeks. ''Anyway, everybody seems to be in love with being in love. The Americans and Europeans are mourning The Broom as though he were George Washington and Mother Teresa rolled into one. And Lurakin is going to have the English grandmother and this oilman President to Moscow for a political ménage à trois.''

''Maybe they'll get to see the execution,'' Gavenko said.

The steel door opened and a guard stepped inside and waited at attention.

''We must be away,'' Lubachevsky said. He stood and held out his hand to Gavenko.

''The best of luck, comrade,'' said Sarkissian, doing the same.

Gavenko contemplated the hands for a moment before shaking them both. ''Perhaps you will need the luck more than I will.''

''Yes,'' Lubachevsky said. ''Maybe when he no longer needs a bridge to the conservatives.''

''Or the support of the military against the KGB,'' said Sarkissian.

Gavenko checked to be sure the guard had gone outside.

"He's not the trusting marshmallow you might have believed. I hear that his friend Rhonev will be implicated in our . . . excuse me . . . in my manipulations. How did I ever miss him?"

"Or we," said Sarkissian. "Well, Comrade Lurakin has already learned that you can't have too few competitors."

They marched out, leaving a package of sweet cakes on the table for Gavenko.

He unwrapped one and contemplated it wryly. "Not exactly the prize I had in mind," he said to the stone walls.

Avellino, Italy—July 10

The hard men in civilian clothes carrying United States Navy credentials who swept out of the sky onto Vincenzo's farm did not dissemble. They marched straight into the house, found the correct door, requested the key, and went to the wine cellar.

They moved the bags out and into the waiting Sea Stallion helicopter with dispatch, leaving the old Italian with a strong admonition to discretion and five thousand dollars.

They also unknowingly left him with one of the bags he had hidden on the off chance it might one day be to his advantage.

Monaco—September 30

The outdoor cafe had a good view of both the Old Casino and the yacht basin. The wine was sublime and the golden autumn afternoon sunshine warmed and dried without sting. It was a place where nothing could be wrong.

Except that Ledges had one leg still in a brace, the group

might have been a prosperous, vacationing family fresh off the tennis courts. Out of uniform as they were, the chief might have been a loving uncle to Lydecker and Kiki. McGregor might have passed for a tanned executive and Tess the beauty that all successful men marry.

"You have to be kidding," said the wondering McGregor. "Back in the deck force? Not only with that foot, but now with that pinned-up leg. You got a hundred-percent disability going there."

"I'm saving the taxpayers the hundred-percenter they're paying to you for not getting shot at all," countered Ledges.

"Jeez, Rock," said Lydecker, "am I going to have to stay in to shove you around the roof in a wheelchair?"

"Entirely up to you, sonny. I'd enjoy the company, though."

"I still think the next Secretary of the Navy is going to ship us to Portsmouth after all," said Lydecker.

"If they were just showing their gratitude, you might have had a point," McGregor said. "But they do have an interest in us staying very quiet about what could make faces red and international affairs chilly. As long as they want to play along with that story about a Russian boomer losing a live nuclear torpedo, they've got an awful lot of swabbies to keep quiet and happy."

"They're doing a swell job so far," said Ledges, signaling for more wine. "I think you're going to like that job looking after contractor payments for Hydralectric, too."

"As long as they do what they say they will for Kiki, they've got my loyalty and affection. In fact, they've got it anyway." He raised a glass. "The United States Navy, gentlemen. Even with its head up its butt, the best ever made."

"Here, here," Ledges said with feeling.

Tess looked so worried that Kiki took her hand.

"I'll admire it from a distance," McGregor assured her.

A stocky young man with two expensive cameras hanging from his neck stopped in passing, then approached them. His short hair was impossibly black and thick, spiking like the fur on the neck of an aroused attack dog. The way his lips drew back over huge white teeth in a powerful jaw and his pale blue eyes glared hot and unblinking, the loungers feared for a moment they would be attacked by an overwrought local agitator. "Hi," he said in a clear, mild voice. "Good to see ya."

The men at the table looked at him with the desperate air of all people trying to place a vaguely familiar person. They shook his hand in turn as they stumbled out their greetings.

"I want to tell you guys that some of us know more about what happened than anybody thinks. And we appreciate what you did."

"Hey," mumbled Ledges, "that's nice . . . thanks."

McGregor took a gamble that he was someone off the *King*. "You . . . out now?"

"Aw, hell, no. Just a little vertebrae problem when I came down wrong. The hospital pushed it where it belonged in a few weeks. I'm back on board next week."

"You look great," Lydecker mumbled.

The young man turned to him. "Man, it must feel great," he said.

"What?"

The glare seemed to cut to afterburner. "To be the only mother in the whole history of man from now to eternity to splash Sebastian Walker man-to-man, air-to-air."

"Aw, hell," blurted Lydecker in the flash of recognition. "I owe it all to my plane."

The man made a magnificent effort to smile before nodding his good-bye.

They watched him hurrying away across the sunlit expanse, pointing and shooting his cameras with customary Mudcat Walker speed and precision.